IMPERIUM BOOK 4

THE DEPTHS OF NEPTUNE

TRAVIS STARNES

Maps available at

https://tstarnes.com/book-series/imperium/

Signup to get free previews of upcoming books before they're released at

http://tstarnes.com/preview-notification-newsletter/

Contents

Chapter 1

Devnum

"It is morning, Commander," Sophus's voice echoed in Ky's mind.

Former Lieutenant Commander Ky, combat and test pilot for the first Terran Empire, opened his eyes. Sunlight was streaming in through the open window onto his face, which his enhanced eyes automatically filtered to keep the sudden influx of light from causing discomfort. He could hear the city outside the royal palace, already in full swing. Saws, hammers, shouts, and animals could be heard in the distance.

All the sounds of a city on the rise. Very different from a space station with the sound-dampening wall panels he'd grown up with. Even with those panels, there had always been a low hum that had been a constant accompaniment to his life. Or rather his old life, which is what he considered the time before the failed faster-than-light test that had sent him into this changed version of the ancient past.

More had changed than the calendar. He had gone from a respected, but not high ranking, pilot assigned to an almost certainly fatal test flight into a leader of the Roman, now Britannian, Empire, responsible for hundreds of thousands of lives and the survival of an entire civilization.

His world had changed in more ways than one, Ky thought, feeling the weight of Lucilla's head on his chest, her hair cascading over her face.

Impossible as it seemed, this was an even greater change than going from a space-faring level of technology to the ancient world.

He'd grown up knowing that one day he'd be paired with someone socially and medically compatible with him, with whom he'd do his duty for the empire by having one or two genetically screened children. For the glory of the empire.

Love wasn't ever in the cards. He'd met his forbearers once. They had been friendly, but distant. He had been, after all, a stranger to them, raised in a genetic batch from birth with others bred and trained to do the same job he did. As far as he understood, they were friendly, but that was about the extent of it. Once their duty to the empire was finished, the breeding pair went their separate ways, to live out their own lives.

'Things have certainly changed,' Ky thought as he looked down at the top of Lucilla's head.

He couldn't imagine ever being separated from her, living his own life away from her. When he'd looked into her eyes during their wedding ceremony the day before, he knew he'd do everything in his power to never leave her.

He knew it doubly after their wedding night. Ky had already felt things he'd never experienced before. Affection, love, attraction. The night before, she'd awakened new feelings in him, as she introduced him to the more ... physical side of marriage.

"Morning," Lucilla murmured, turning her head to plant a tender kiss on Ky's lips before nestling back into his warm chest.

"Let's just stay here forever. They can manage without us," she suggested playfully, her finger tracing delicate patterns on his skin.

Ky chuckled softly. "I can think of some biological complications with that plan."

"Me too, actually," Lucilla admitted, pushing herself off him and dashing towards the corner of the room, where a discreet screen shielded the chamber pot from view.

He hadn't had time for it yet, but Ky was keen to improve the palace by adding flushing toilets. The challenge lay in providing adequate water pressure, particularly for the upper floors; although if their position for the next twelve months solidified, he might be able to solve that issue eventually. For now, they relied on chamber pots and the city's latrines, which were usually housed in separate buildings to contain the pervasive stench.

2

Lucilla reemerged from behind the screen, stretching her lithe body in a captivating display.

"I guess we won't stay in bed forever," she conceded with a mischievous grin.

Ky's gaze roamed over her, appreciating her in ways he wouldn't have prior to the night before.

"Besides, today's a big day," Lucilla said as she started to pull on clothes, much to Ky's disappointment.

"It's mostly formal. With Llassar in Emain Macha and you here with Conchobar's representatives, all the details have been worked out already. If anyone was going to cause a problem, they would have done it by now."

Lucilla chuckled and tossed Ky his clothes. "I swear, for a superhuman warrior from the future, you can be so naive at times."

Ky eyed the coarse woolen garments, longing for his self-cleaning uniform and its smooth, anti-chafing fabric. Although his skin was genetically hardened to keep from being rubbed raw, the rough material was still uncomfortable.

"That's why I leave the politics to you. I'm a soldier, and I prefer the straightforward nature of war over politics any day."

"You can't dodge politics forever," Lucilla countered. "Yes, we've already worked out all the details, but today's public spectacle is still important. We'll pledge the Empire's might to protect the Ulaid, and they'll pledge their undying fealty. The masses will adore it. The Ulaid representatives will return home with tales of the wonders they've seen. And our people will see a new ally in the fight against the Carthaginians. Today is for the mob."

"I understand and I don't doubt its importance," Ky said. "It's just that we have a lot to do. We may have pushed the Carthaginians off the British Isles, but we aren't done with them by a long shot. They're not going to sit back and live and let live. The number of subjugated people outnumber the actual Carthaginians a thousand to one, probably more. The only thing that keeps them in line is fear of Carthaginian reprisal, mostly handed out by other non-Carthaginian subjects. If the idea that they aren't invulnerable starts to spread and enough of those people rise up, the Carthaginians won't be able to keep them all in check. Take out enough pieces, and the whole house comes down. The

Carthaginians know this, which is why they keep throwing men into the meat grinder. They'll keep escalating. We have to keep pushing while we have the momentum."

"We own the seas now. They can't touch us anymore."

"Not yet, we don't. That stunt with Valdar's ship was smoke and mirrors, nothing more. Yes, we were picking off their ships steadily, but there's a limit to the amount of gunpowder one boat can carry, and they won't let us lead them by the nose into a trap next time. If they'd decided to just land, and take their losses, we would only have been able to sink maybe half their fleet, at the very best. What was left would have been enough to roll over us. Especially with half our legions in Ireland ... Ériu."

Lucilla nodded, pressing her hands against Ky's clothed chest and leaning into him.

"Then we'll build more ships. We'll raise more men. That's what today's about. As long as the people believe there's a chance, they'll keep fighting. So, for today, forget about everything else and give them that."

"Fine, one day. But tomorrow we get to work."

"See, you've learned another lesson about women and men. Just listen to your wife, and life will be much better," She said, grinning.

"Right. I'll make a note of that."

"Keep playing your cards right, and you might have some work to do tonight, too," she teased, her hands gliding down his body.

Ky stopped her hand, albeit reluctantly. "I thought you said we have somewhere to be?"

With a sigh, Lucilla withdrew her hand and stepped back. "Fine, I'll just have to wait until tonight."

To say the treaty signing was a spectacle would be an understatement. t was a grandiose affair that merged the celebration of victory over the Carthaginians with a public revelry of Ky and Lucilla's wedding. In the afternoon, the colosseum hosted games and Emperor-sponsored plays, while bread for every family, taken from royal stockpiles, was distributed.

Ky had objected to the last part during the planning stages. The harvest had yet to come in, and food was scarce in anticipation of the long winter ahead. Though they had pillaged Carthaginian stores and provisions meant for the armies in Ériu, they needed those supplies to feed the legions under arms. The standing army that Ky had established, funded by taxes and patents, had altered the traditional dynamic of the Roman legions, making the Empire responsible for feeding these men.

He knew crop yields were set to increase this year and even more the next, but it did little to alleviate the strain on the pre-harvest stockpiles. Despite his concerns, both Lucilla and the Emperor deemed the citywide bread distribution politically necessary. Ky understood their rationale but questioned how people in Caledonia, Londinium, or Ériu might feel about Devnum's citizens receiving mass handouts of food while they went without. In the end, he deferred to their political expertise; his role was to be present, greet the Ulaid king and his compatriots, and proclaim a day of celebration.

The ceremony went well. Ky had an interesting moment when he grasped forearms with the Ulaid king after welcoming him to the Empire. While they had met without issue at his wedding the previous day, Conchobar seemed determined to assert dominance in such a public setting. Ky felt the king's large hand encircle his forearm, squeezing with considerable force. An ordinary man might have struggled to suppress a reaction, but Ky was no ordinary man. As Conchobar's eyes widened, applying increasing pressure to Ky's arm, the king must have felt like he was trying to crush a slab of granite.

Ky, confident in his abilities, had no need to engage in this contest of strength. Instead, he simply smiled at the astonished king, secure in his own prowess.

As the ceremony concluded, the five newly appointed senators joined the ten existing members for their inaugural session of the Imperial Senate. Lucilla had mentioned that the day would primarily involve formalities, as the newcomers would require time to acclimate themselves to the workings of the Senate. The main purpose was to demonstrate to the people that they were committed to serving the Empire. Meanwhile, the Imperial entourage, including Talogren and Conchobar, headed to the colosseum to observe the contests and be seen by the adoring crowds.

Ky found himself dismayed by the continued existence of gladiatorial games. Though no longer slaves, many men still fought for the lucrative rewards and fame offered by their sponsors. If they could survive to retirement, they would enjoy celebrity status throughout the Empire. However, many would suffer horrific deaths. Ky was determined to eradicate this brutal sport eventually, but he understood the limitations of how quickly a society could be transformed.

"I was told that you were unlike anyone I'd ever met, but I hadn't really believed it," Conchobar said, leaning over to talk quietly to Ky in the Emperor's box. "I wonder what the audience would think if you and I competed in a test of strength."

"You would not want to do that," Ky responded.

"You believe you could beat me?"

"Do you want me to be honest or to flatter you?" Ky said, his voice flat.

"You certainly are confident."

Ky sighed, recognizing that Conchobar would not relent until he forced Ky to embarrass him, which he was sure Lucilla wanted to avoid. Noticing that the other members in the box could hear their conversation, Ky caught Talogren's knowing smile. The Caledonian leader had faced off with Ky before and was aware of his capabilities.

"May I see your sword?" Ky asked.

Although weapons were typically forbidden in the Emperor's box, an exception had been made for Conchobar due to Ulaid customs. The king appeared puzzled but complied, handing over his sword. Ky grasped the handle in one hand and the blade in the other. Maintaining eye contact with Conchobar, he carefully bent the two ends together. The sword, made of inferior Ulaid iron, was still durable enough that even Conchobar couldn't have flexed it. Yet, Ky manipulated it as if it were a wet reed.

Conchobar stared, dumbfounded, as Ky returned the sword. The king examined it, attempting to straighten it out, as if there had been some trick involved.

"Your hand," Lucilla said, pointing to Ky's hand, where blood had started to flow from a cut sustained during his demonstration.

"Give it a moment," Ky assured, holding his hand open as the minor wound began to knit itself closed, captivating those who watched.

"Witchcraft," Conchobar muttered, recoiling.

"The power of the gods," Lucilla corrected. "Ky is the Sword of Jupiter, the prophesized avatar of the gods, sent to free us from the Carthaginians and usher in a golden age of prosperity."

Ky struggled to suppress a frown. He understood Lucilla's rationale for invoking the Sword of Jupiter tale, but he found it distasteful. It offered Conchobar a plausible explanation for Ky's abilities while appeasing the king's wounded pride. Despite his best efforts to debunk the myth, the Sword of Jupiter legend persisted and even grew more pervasive with each Britannian victory. His closest associates respected Ky's aversion to the label, but the rest of the Roman Empire seemed eager to believe in it.

Lucilla, however, had no qualms about using the prophecy to her advantage, expertly manipulating others to achieve her political aims. Ky admired her tenacity but occasionally wished she would relent, at least regarding the prophecy.

It didn't seem to matter that the prophecy had been very specific about bringing back the glory of the Roman Empire, and Ky had ended Rome as an empire, in its own right, when he'd come up with the idea of a wider Britannic Empire with its allies having equal partnerships, which ultimately diminished Rome as a power in its own right. Reality held little sway over those who sought heroes or martyrs.

Now that Lucilla had spoken, Ky couldn't openly contradict her. He resolved to discuss the matter with Llassar, should the Caledonian ever return to Rome, and ask him to quell any rumors Conchobar might spread in Ériu.

"I should thank you for not taking me up on my challenge," Conchobar admitted, glancing between Lucilla and Ky.

"He wouldn't have," Lucilla continued, before Ky could respond. "Besides detesting the arena and blood sports, he only ever uses his abilities against our enemies."

While that was mostly true, the main reason Ky had declined the challenge was to preserve Conchobar's pride. They needed the king as an enthusiastic ally to reap the full benefits of their partnership. By refusing the contest due to an unfair advantage, Ky allowed Conchobar to save face. Lucilla was aware of all this as well but she was more diplomatic than him, which was probably why she'd spoken for him.

"I see. I still appreciate your sound judgment. I'd already heard rumors of your abilities since coming to the city, but I'd dismissed them as the gossip of commoners."

"Your ship sails in the morning?" Ky asked, eager to change the subject.

"Yes. Llassar is a smart man, but my son is impulsive and inexperienced, and I entrusted him with the task of quelling the last of the rebel kingdoms, uniting the entire island under our control. I hope Llassar prevented him from acting rashly, but I am not one to tempt fate."

"A sound judgment."

"About the other provisions in the agreement. When can we expect the Empire to uphold its part of the bargain?"

The Ulaid, though not offered anything more than the Caledonians, needed the Empire's resources more urgently due to their precarious state. Initially, the Romans had required the Caledonians and their manpower more than the Caledonians had needed the Romans. Long-term benefits included better technology and stability, but agreements were seldom based on distant considerations.

"We've already instructed Faenius to arrange for the first set of Praetorians to accompany you and begin training your guards as the initial members of the Ulaid arm of the Praetorians," Ky explained. "When we first formed the Empire, Talogren and I believed it best to have people policed by their own countrymen rather than foreign soldiers, even if those soldiers are now allies. I anticipate that, after several generations, those barriers will dissolve as our people intermingle. For now, we think it best to separate the actual manpower by homeland. They'll all access the same resources and belong to the same command structure. Faenius will collaborate with you and your guard commander to identify the man to lead your section of the guard. That man will serve as Faenius's lieutenant, commanding the entire guard, save for Faenius and the Roman and Caledonian commanders, both of whom already report to Faenius. I understand that this arrangement leaves a Roman at the top, but a military organization requires a strong leader and cannot function by committee. Thus far, it has worked, and we've received no complaints from the Caledonians."

Conchobar glanced at Talogren, who added, "We haven't encountered any issues. Once Faenius steps down, the next commander will be appointed by the Emperor and approved by the senate, so we'll each have an equal say in future commanders."

"That sounds fair. Now that your legions aren't battling the Carthaginians, they have assisted in controlling our brigand problem. However, we've already heard our people complain about foreign soldiers occupying our land. It will take time for them to accept our integration into a larger Empire, as the average farmer focuses on his daily life. The sooner our own forces can patrol the countryside, the sooner your legions can depart."

"Agreed," Ky said. "Hortensius, who oversees our manufacturing, particularly military supplies, has inquired about a contact in your lands to facilitate the expansion of several mines and the opening of new ones. He possesses a map detailing extensive deposits of iron, zinc, coal, and other valuable resources for the war effort. While we prefer that these mines remain under Ulaid control, the Empire is prepared to provide substantial loans with favorable terms to expedite their operation. We only request that the mines prioritize imperial demand before selling any surplus to other manufacturers or exporters. Naturally, we will pay fair rates, consistent with those paid to Roman or Caledonian mines. Our primary concern is to avoid corruption or complications that could hinder the process, as we urgently require these supplies."

"Which is precisely why you were invited to join the Empire," Conchobar remarked.

"We've never hidden our need for your contributions to the Empire, be it resources or manpower. I believe our offer has been more than fair."

"Yes, it's still hard to accept that I no longer answer only to myself and the gods. As for the mines, I can assure you they will open and operate smoothly, as they will all be owned by the kingdom itself."

Ky had been worried about that. He knew that most of the prime land was directly owned by Conchobar and his family, with peasants working it and paying for the privilege. It wasn't an uncommon arrangement but often resulted in civil unrest. That was precisely what had happened to them since most of their neighbors had sided with the Carthaginians.

"Are you certain that's wise? You've taken control of everyone on Ériu, many of whom were your adversaries not long ago. The last thing you need is a new round of internal strife, which we both know will occur when you funnel all the incoming wealth directly into your own coffers."

"I believed we were free to govern our own lands as we see fit, as long as we don't violate the agreements passed by the Imperial Senate."

"You are, and I'm not attempting to dictate how you run your kingdom. I am, however, offering advice, which you may disregard if you wish. Nonetheless, it will be disruptive and costly to constantly suppress civil unrest. After all, you still have one or two kingdoms openly defying your rule. It won't take much for their neighbors to decide to join them."

"Llassar and my son should deal with that issue soon."

"I'm sure, but we both understand that recently conquered people can be nearly as troublesome as rebels. That's where your brigand problem originates, along with poverty. If your people believe they have a chance to share in the country's prosperity, many will strive to claim a portion of that growth for themselves, ultimately contributing to it instead of hindering it."

"How do you propose my kingdom pay for all the improvements you've 'suggested' without those lands?"

"Taxes. Within your own borders, you hold the right to tax, as long as import and export taxes are paid to the Empire. Entrust these lands to loyal and capable men, let them establish new mines and businesses, and then tax them. There are other alternatives, but I am a soldier, not a moneylender. Consult Lucilla. She can arrange for discussions with the men who've crafted the strategies that have maintained funds flowing into the Imperial and Roman coffers while fostering a multitude of merchant families willing to risk starting these enterprises. The people will be more content, and you'll secure a long-term income source. Besides, why relinquish your kingship to become a merchant? I know I have more tasks than I could complete in three lifetimes. I'd rather delegate responsibilities to driven individuals, so I don't have to concern myself with every detail."

"I'll consider it."

"It's just a suggestion," Ky said.

He caught a fleeting, sly smile from Lucilla. She quickly concealed it, but he recognized her pride in guiding Conchobar where he needed to go. She might have chosen a more subtle, less forthright approach, but a man like Conchobar typically responded better to candid, direct exchanges over manipulation. Perhaps his method was best in this situation.

A sense of warmth filled him, knowing he could read her so effortlessly. Despite their brief acquaintance, he felt attuned to her thoughts more often than not. He'd been close to several pilots in his past life but hadn't achieved this level of understanding and collaboration even with the ones he'd been closest to. Reaching across, he grasped her hand, which she squeezed before looking beyond him, resuming the conversation where he'd left off.

He was happy to let her haggle with the Ulaid king. Pretending to watch the contests unfolding below, Ky started interfacing with Sophus's databases, streaming data across his vision.

With the island secure and the threat of a seaborne invasion eliminated, it was time to propel Britannia toward the next phase of his plan for the Empire. Numerous steps were required, but Ky envisioned a path to genuine industrialization, a necessity if he were to carry the fight beyond the British Isles and into the heart of the Carthaginian empire.

Chapter 2

Emain Macha, Ériu

Llassar perched on the horse borrowed from the king's stables, observing the king's son maneuvering in tight circles around a course set in the fields just outside of town. When he'd finally won Conchobar's trust and summoned the Roman, now Britannian, legions to confront the Carthaginians and their local allies, they had introduced a myriad of astonishing inventions to the Ulaid. Though more organized than his people had been prior to Talogren's consolidation of the tribes, their arts had remained fairly primitive.

Iron or simple crucible steel weapons sufficed but dulled quickly and broke frequently, and basic bows were their preferred choice. Llassar had always admired the Romans for their superior steel and precision-engineered weapons, such as their siege weapons or arcuballista.

However, a year ago, everything changed when the Romans began using steel stronger than anything he'd ever seen or heard of, along with a new arcuballista boasting range and power to penetrate a man's shield and the man behind it. They'd also introduced a new kind of saddle that allowed their horsemen to turn with such agility that they could ride in tight circles around their foes. It was astounding that a mere loop of leather sewn into a saddle could revolutionize their mounted forces.

The Ulaid hadn't been able to replicate most of the Romans' inventions, or rather the Consul's, as everyone knew he was the source of these innovations, even if their new allies shared the secrets. Yet, they had swiftly adopted the use of stirrups, as Ky had called them.

While the highlands where Llassar hailed from had open land, its mountainous terrain with sloping fields didn't lend itself to extended gallops. Horses were primarily used to pull carts or for transportation. In contrast, Ériu boasted expansive open spaces, and horse racing was already a beloved pastime before the introduction of stirrups. With their arrival, sharp turns and double backs were incorporated into the staked-out courses, enhancing the experience for riders and spectators alike. Llassar wasn't particularly fond of either, but as the prince's guardian, he was duty-bound to watch over him as he reveled in the activity daily, weather permitting.

"He doesn't let up, does he?" Velius inquired, joining Llassar.

"Not when it's something like this, or women. When it's listening to the petitions of his subjects or allocating resources, he can barely keep his eyes open."

"He's a child. When I was his age, I had just joined the legion, barely knowing which end of my sword to wield. I can't imagine how poorly I would have behaved if I was suddenly handed the reins of government."

"Much governing happening out there?" Velius teased, grinning.

Llassar merely shrugged in response.

"A messenger just arrived from Devnum," Velius disclosed when it became apparent Llassar wouldn't elaborate further. "Now that we're down to the last holdouts, the Consul has decided we need to start bringing our forces back home to prepare for the assault on the continent."

"I believe that's a mistake. The local forces won't manage to eliminate the holdouts, particularly Fergus and Queen Medb, on their own. She was the only one astute enough to reserve some of her forces. The Ulaid never managed to reassemble their army after those devastating defeats, and now that they're part of the Empire, most of the remaining military citizens will likely be dispatched to Rome for legionary training. The king's guard is insufficient to eradicate Queen Medb. Within a year, the rebels will start reclaiming territory, luring some of the converts back to their old ways. We'll have to redirect more manpower here, but by then we'll have already begun our invasion of the continent. That doesn't even touch upon the brigand issue. We both know how many men have been pulled from the legions to patrol and pursue outlaws."

"I concur, as does the Consul. The first group of Praetorian trainers will arrive with the king's return, which should help get the brigand situation under control. He's also leaving Auspex and his legions with you until the queen is subdued and all hostile forces have been eliminated. After that, Auspex will rejoin the other legions, and maintaining countryside control will fall to the appointed Ulaid Praetorian commander."

"He's leaving us Auspex?"

"Yes. The Consul read both of our reports. He wouldn't abandon you."

"Even virtuous men are sometimes compelled to make unfavorable decisions due to the demands of war."

"True, but we have some leeway. I haven't been privy to his planning sessions, but I suspect he aims to address the holdouts between Ériu and Britannia. If it were up to me, that would be an ideal test of our forces before attempting less predictable situations. The island is small enough; he probably doesn't need all the legions for that. We also need time to train new recruits from here and previously occupied Britannian territories. That will take time."

"Probably."

"Direct combat command remains with Auspex. You're an exceptional warrior, but his experience in commanding legions in the field surpasses yours. You'll retain overall command for strategic decisions."

"A wise precaution."

"Now that the treaty is signed, merchants who recognize the potential here, much like they did when your homeland opened for trade, will undoubtedly arrive. Though many of the more dubious individuals were weeded out then, that well never runs completely dry. I left his message for you to read yourself, but it's up to you to prevent them from causing disturbances until the alliance solidifies. I don't envy your task. I'd take a Carthaginian horde any day over merchants and politicians."

Llassar finally tore his gaze from the prince, fixing it on the legate with a deadpan expression. Both men knew that Llassar was a warrior at heart, never desiring to dabble in politics or diplomacy. Regrettably, his connections with the Ulaid and the trust Talogren and other Caledonians placed in him had made him the sole choice to initiate communications between the Ulaid and the Britannians. Once entangled in the political sphere, it proved challenging for Llassar to return to his preferred role as a straightforward military commander.

"Fine. I'll stop teasing you," Velius conceded, extending his hand. "It was an honor working alongside you. I look forward to your return to Britannia."

"As do I," Llassar agreed, grasping the other man's forearm.

They held their grip for several heartbeats before Velius released his hold and steered his horse back towards the legion camps on the far side of Emain Macha. Llassar watched him ride away for a moment before refocusing on the galloping prince, who had been entrusted to his 'guidance' during his father's absence.

Sitting stone still, the older warrior's stoic expression hid the tempest of thoughts brewing within him as he began to work through his options, and how he would be able to convince the prince that his choice was the right one.

Devnum, Nova Rome

Bomilcar, the former Carthaginian general, stood before the assembly, his voice clear and unwavering: "...I pledge my fealty and allegiance to the Britannic Empire and Titus Flavius Germanicus, Emperor of Britannia Magna and its people. I pledge I shall faithfully execute all that the Emperor commands, that I shall never desert his service, and that I shall not seek to avoid death in doing my duty to the Britannic Empire. I so swear my sword and my life."

"Rise," Emperor Germanicus commanded, having stood over the kneeling general, gazing down at his bowed, balding head.

Ky recognized the necessity of Bomilcar's military expertise and understanding of Carthaginian tactics, and ultimately, the Emperor agreed. They settled on a modest ceremony, keeping Bomilcar as far from public view as feasible. A select few loyal senators, the legates still on Britannia, Ky, Lucilla, and the Emperor bore witness. News would inevitably spread, but its dissemination would be slower and less jarring than a grand spectacle or public announcement.

Ky observed from his position, slightly behind and to the right of the Emperor, contemplating the ceremony. In this reality, with history diverging from what Ky knew, Rome had never been in a position to accept allegiance as it teetered on the brink of collapse when it became an empire. The Republic had a similar oath for legates, but it seemed inadequate for the present situation.

Ky and Sophus had considered post-Roman oaths from their history, though they were mostly centered around religion due to the church's growing influence. Christianity hadn't taken hold in this reality, or if it had, it remained an underground sect. The Carthaginians, brutal rulers, sought to eradicate any worship not involving their Emperor. Rome's relocation to Britannia drastically altered the region's history, affecting the makeup and viability of any emerging religious groups.

The prevailing worship of the Greek-inspired pantheon rendered many oaths unsuitable. Ultimately, Lucilla had crafted her own oath without consulting Ky or Sophus, presenting it to her father. Drawing inspiration from the oaths of legates and senators, she created something fitting for the occasion.

The forum, bereft of the grandiosity of a throne room, served as the setting for the ceremony, reflecting the Roman tendency to view the Emperor as a first among equals rather than an autocratic leader. It was nearly empty, a point of contention after Ky convinced Emperor Germanicus of Bomilcar's genuine conversion and desire to join the Empire.

Though Emperor Germanicus and Lucilla often regarded Ky as a well-meaning but politically naïve individual, they eventually agreed on Bomilcar's value. However, they worried about convincing the Empire's leadership and the masses to accept the former enemy general, who had once led a massive army with the intent to annihilate all in its path.

Bomilcar's unease was palpable throughout the ceremony. Ky could sense the weight of the legates' and senators' distrustful gazes, their scowls unmistakable as they observed the proceedings.

"In the name of the people of Rome, Caledonia, and Ulaid, I, Titus Flavius Germanicus, accept your service, from now until your death."

Bomilcar bowed, and that was it. Instead of the customary cheers and congratulations one might expect, the senators turned and left the forum in stony silence. The legates, however, each shook Bomilcar's hand, their military backgrounds perhaps better equipping them to accept distasteful orders. Though they extended no words of encouragement or support, their actions spoke volumes compared to the senators, who held themselves in such high esteem.

Ky exchanged a nod with Lucilla, silently communicating his desire for a moment alone with Bomilcar. He appreciated their growing nonverbal understanding and chose to rely on it whenever possible. As Lucilla whispered to her father, Ky gestured for the remaining legates to leave the forum. Soon, Bomilcar and Ky stood alone in the square-shaped room.

"They don't particularly care for me," Bomilcar remarked, gesturing toward the departed senators.

"They're politicians. They don't like anyone who doesn't give them an advantage. Give them time, though, and they'll come around. There's a lot you can do for the Empire, and once you start having successes, I think you'll see their tune will quickly change."

"Until then, I'm not to be trusted, though. I know your legates feel the same."

"Do you blame them? You did try to have everyone they know murdered. I know it's war and you had your orders. I don't begrudge you that fact or the fact that you've changed sides. But, it's going to take some time for everyone to get comfortable seeing you on our side."

"I know. It just feels wrong, being here, saying those words to your Emperor."

"He's your Emperor now too," Ky reminded him. "It will get easier with time. You didn't cut ties with your old masters; they cut ties with you. That doesn't make the guilt of what would have been treason just a few months ago feel any less strange, I know. Give it time."

"I hope so."

"Until then, I will just have to keep you busy enough that you don't wallow in the guilt," Ky said, clapping Bomilcar on the shoulder and leading him out of the forum.

Carthage

Caesius brooded in the antechamber of the emperor's reception hall, his anger simmering. Over a month had passed since his arrival in Carthage, and he'd been left languishing the entire time. Only a handful of ships had returned from Britannia, most bearing the remnants of the reinforcement fleet. Their survivors whispered of Roman vessels that could summon thunderstorms at will. Caesius had witnessed some of the foreigner's feats and could see how the Carthaginians, steeped in superstition, might view them as sorcery.

Yet, he remained unconvinced that the foreigner could single-handedly decimate an entire fleet. More likely, fear had driven the Carthaginians into a panicked retreat, their own clumsiness sinking their ships. Considering the incompetence of the crew that had transported him from Britannia to Carthage, it was a wonder any ships had survived the treacherous journey. For a people descended from seafaring traders, their skills navigating

Oceanus were markedly inferior to the Romans. He'd watched his scant belongings drenched as seawater relentlessly flooded the vessel.

Instead of dispatching a vast fleet across the perilous waters of Oceanus, the Carthaginians should have consulted him. He was, after all, the only one to return from Britannia. It was through his network of informants along the Germania and Hispania coastlines that he'd learned of Londinium's fall and the Carthaginian defeat in Hibernia. He could have advised the Carthaginian Emperor on the best course of action. But they'd relegated him to a squalid hut, where he'd been told to await the summons.

And now, as he was finally summoned from the miserable slums to the majestic palace at the city's heart, he was made to wait again. Hours had slipped away, the sun tracing its arc across the sky, as he sat on this bench, fuming.

It wasn't like he could storm out, either. Even the hovel he was living in was provided by the emperor. He'd been able to bring almost nothing worth selling when he'd been forced to flee, which left him destitute in a place where his people were considered a threat.

Finally, one of the emperor's black-clad lackeys came for him. Caesius found them unnerving, their faces and bodies swathed in thick, heat-absorbing fabric, leaving only their eyes and hands exposed. They seldom spoke, which led Caesius to suspect they'd been rendered mute, a practical measure for those entrusted with sensitive messages, but it made them all the more disquieting. The attendant, assuming he still qualified as a man, offered an exaggerated bow, gesturing for Caesius to follow him through the towering double doors.

Caesius had never met the emperor before and, truth be told, had anticipated a more imposing figure. Seated on a resplendent golden throne, the emperor was clad in a purple schenti adorned with intricate embroidery and a snug-fitting shawl draped across his shoulders. A conical cap crowned his head, with cascading hair that Caesius suspected wasn't the emperor's own, nor even human hair, mingled with red and purple ribbons that trailed down his back.

Like most men Caesius had encountered in Carthage, the emperor sported dark, curly hair and a thick beard. Yet Caesius suspected that beneath the cap lay a significant bald patch, given the sparse hair emerging from it. Though seated, it was evident the emperor was a short, rotund man with pudgy arms and sausage-like fingers.

Still, pleasantries must be practiced, Caesius thought as he genuflected before the emperor, arms outstretched and head touching the carpeted steps, a posture of submission. It was demeaning, but Caesius had endured numerous humiliations since fleeing his homeland, and he was prepared to face more if it meant reclaiming his throne.

"Your majesty, I am honored you agreed to see me. I have come from ..."

"**SILENCE!**" The emperor's voice boomed, unexpectedly commanding and harsh. "I did not summon you to grovel or weave falsehoods. You are here to answer for your failure."

"My failure!" Caesius exclaimed, rising swiftly and advancing toward the throne's steps, only to halt abruptly as guards brandished their swords and closed in.

Caesius retreated from the steps, prompting the guards to step back, though their swords remained unsheathed.

"I did not fail," Caesius asserted, his tone now measured. "Time and again, I supplied intelligence that any adept commander could have used to crush the Roman army and bring my people under your empire's rule. Successive generals, dispatched by the governor, were unable to defeat them, despite their superior armaments. My agents sabotaged weapons depots and nearly assassinated my sister and the foreigner, sidelining both for a time. Yet the governor failed to capitalize on my successes."

Caesius was stretching the truth about the foreigner. He'd received word of the man's fall in battle and impending death. After ensuring he was the first to relay the news, he reported it in such a way that his agents could claim partial credit. Given the distance between Carthage and the now-deceased governor, and the time that had elapsed, Caesius felt secure in claiming that accomplishment.

"Furthermore, I have provided a wealth of information on the Roman strategies and weaponry that could have propelled your forces to victory. Instead, you were met with a string of failures by your governor, who squandered my information."

The emperor regarded Caesius for a moment before turning his attention to one of the military commanders standing a few steps down from the throne, just beside the dais stairs.

"We have looked at your reports," the emperor said, "and apart from your sister's whereabouts and her guard last year, your contributions have been unremarkable. Our own spies, without the high court positions you claim for your sources, have easily obtained similar information. Our agents retrieved their new crossbows during a battle, not through your so-called intelligence. We have yet to see any technical specifications for their weapons or the rumored metallurgical advancements. We've heard of a thunder weapon, aligning with reports of a fast-burning powder that nearly incinerated half of their capital by accident. Why do our lowly agents know this, and not your esteemed sources?"

"I believe you either underestimate my intelligence's value or doubt it due to a lack of understanding."

"I think you're worthless," the general interjected, turning and bowing to the emperor. "Forgive me, your majesty, but I find this man offers nothing of value, only confusion. We should make an example of him, a warning to other false turncoats. He's one of the few to return from Londinium; let's show other cowards the fate that awaits those who fail to fight to the death in your name."

Caesius, once brimming with confidence in his standing among the Carthaginians, now grasped the precariousness of his situation.

"I acquired only the information your governor specifically requested. I urged him to let my agents target the new weapons we've encountered, but he trusted in his army and believed that capturing their manufacturers or philosophers would...forgive me, your majesty...win him favor with you. I knew you would never be swayed so easily, but Maharbaal always sought the angle most beneficial to himself."

Caesius couldn't recall the last time he'd lied so profusely and knew it was a gamble to make the men believe him. His one consolation was the truth about Maharbaal's scheming nature. The man was a notorious manipulator, and Caesius knew that he had already been treading on thin ice with the emperor after losing the first two armies. His only hope was to speak quickly and play to the emperor's prejudices, trusting that the rotund ruler wouldn't scrutinize his words too closely.

"I extend the same offer now. I have agents positioned throughout the court. I can acquire their innovative weapons and the secrets of their advanced manufacturing techniques. My people are industrious and ingenious—ideal candidates to join your Empire. My father and sister have installed loyal, yet inept, individuals in power. If they can harness these new weapons, I am confident your skilled artificers can replicate their success. My father has grown old and senile; I suspect my sister and her foreign lover truly control the empire. Remove them, and the rest will crumble. I was previously forbidden from assassinating them—the governor believed he'd gain more by presenting them in chains to you. But if you grant me permission to dispatch my agents, their demise is assured."

Caesius's words spilled forth in a torrent, and when he finally fell silent, a heavy hush enveloped the audience chamber. The emperor's beady eyes appraised him from on high, calculating and cold.

"We will give you one final opportunity to prove your worth. Should you fail, no shifting of blame to the deceased or allegations of interference will spare you. We demand results, not excuses. Deliver the weapons for our examination and ensure your sister's death, or face your own. We have spoken."

Caesius bowed and retreated from the room. He had narrowly escaped with his life, but his resources in Rome were waning. If he couldn't find a way to eliminate his sister this time, he wouldn't live to attempt it a fourth time.

Chapter 3

Devnum

Ky's gaze swept down the long table, surrounded by all of the military commanders currently stationed on Britannia, as well as Talogren, Ramirus, and even Hortensius, who all decided to remain after the treaty signing. Over a month had passed since the Carthaginian forces and fleet had been defeated in Ériu, but this marked the first occasion Ky could gather the dispersed forces to strategize their next moves.

Velius was en route, ferrying his legions to Britannia, but Ky couldn't afford to wait for his chief general. The Carthaginians had done them a favor, stripping a large number of soldiers from Iberia and the continent for the multiple armies sent against Rome. It was far from the largest part of their strength, but most of that was still scattered across their vast empire. They had a window where the Carthaginians were weakened along the coast. According to Ramirus's reports, the Carthaginians were stretched too thin, leaving the coastline vulnerable. Now was the perfect time to strike.

Of course, they couldn't just transport the legions in their current state. Despite the first cannon rolling out of Hortensius's factories, swords and shield walls wouldn't stand up to the size of the forces the Carthaginians could muster. Unlike their battles on Britannia, where the Carthaginians had to transport men, weapons, and supplies, the continent provided ample resources. The armies they would encounter would dwarf those they had faced thus far, and Ky doubted they could train more than one additional legion, even with the Ulaid's support.

Recruitment from the Roman and Caledonian regions had slowed due to the competing need for workers in factories and fields, both crucial to the Empire's chances against the Carthaginians. Until they reclaimed more territory, stripping Carthage of their conscripted soldiers, Britannia would continue to face a growing disparity in troop numbers.

Crossbows and better steel were insufficient. The cannon was a good start, but Ky needed to start adding serious force multipliers if they were going to be victorious. Time was of the essence, and they were in short supply.

It would be a race between the Britannians amassing weapons and forces and the Carthaginians mobilizing their forces towards the coast. Whoever got there first would win.

The men engaged in lively conversation, their spirits high. They had persevered through seemingly insurmountable odds, boasting an impressive string of victories. Ky almost hated to bring them back to reality. Almost.

"Gentlemen, and lady," Ky began, nodding at his wife, who returned his gesture with a warm smile. "We've accomplished much this spring. Britannia Mana is nearly free of Carthaginians, and for now, we dominate the seas surrounding our islands. Our people are safe, for the moment. However, isn't the time to lull ourselves into complacency. We've injured the monster at our doorstep and captured its attention. It's only a matter of time before they bring the full force of their empire down on us."

"Let them try," Valdar, the newly appointed admiral of the fledgling Britannian navy, declared. "We rule the seas and will sink any ship that dares approach."

"You are smarter than that, Valdar," Lucilla said. "You're one ship was nearly out of gunpowder when you lured their fleet into the range of our guns on the cliffs, and that fleet was just what the Carthaginians could pull together on short notice. Are you so confident they will fall into our trap twice? And even if they do, we could not possibly mount enough cannons to sink a larger fleet. The last one was surprised and overconfident. If they decided to ignore you and take their losses, they still could have landed a huge army on our shores. Thinking your enemy is toothless, or underestimating the danger they represent, is how fools die."

Ky struggled to suppress a smile, hearing his words echo from her lips. He didn't resent her passing off his analysis as her own, even when she had taken the exact position as Valdar during their previous conversation on the subject. While the Caledonians adored her, not all Britannians believed a woman belonged in combat leadership. They were a united front, and it was crucial that she convinced the commanders she was essential in their war councils. If providing her a cheat sheet ensured that, he was more than happy to oblige.

"Exactly. I believe we can eventually control the waves with a fleet no Carthaginian can touch, but we're not there yet."

"I apologize, my lady," Valdar conceded, bowing his head slightly.

"We need to divert their focus from our islands and start reclaiming some of their resources, including manpower. That means taking the fight to the continent, which is precisely why I've gathered you all here."

"Is that wise, if that's where they're amassing their new armies?" Ursinus, the former guard and newest legate, inquired. "Any troops we land ashore would be crushed by their superior forces, just as they would if we allowed them to land here. I agree that Valdar was premature in his assessment, but he's not entirely wrong. If we can build a big enough fleet and produce more of these new cannons, wouldn't our safest strategy be to put a ring of ships and cannon around our islands?"

"Perhaps, but that won't last forever. They will never stop prodding us, and eventually, they will break through. We also do not have limitless resources and, as long as they control most of the continent, they effectively do. They can cut us off from trade routes without ever coming directly into conflict with our ships. If they wanted, they could starve us. We import a fair amount of food and a lot of supplies from the Scandi and Asia, and that doesn't even consider the number of men we'd need to keep a ring in place for years, sustaining constant losses to Carthaginian probes. No, hiding on our islands, hoping that the monster will just go away, will not work."

"But you have a plan, yes?" the Emperor, who was the only one seated at this meeting, asked.

"Yes, Princeps. There are several things we need to do simultaneously. One. We need to begin training the new men coming in. Our superior cohesion is what has allowed us to stand firm against far superior numbers, and the number of trained legionaries we have now is significantly and dangerously lower than when I arrived almost a year ago. You all understand the difference between a soldier and a warrior, and the need for soldiers. With the mostly Ulaid reinforcements, we will need time to train them. Two. Hortensius will continue to produce new weapons. With the successful field test of the cannon and the progression in the quality of the steel we have been producing, I believe it is time for another major leap forward in our weapons technology. The arcuballista was a good middle step, something better than what the legions used previously but still within our original manufacturing capabilities. They are not, however, good enough to give us the force multiplier we need to deal with the Carthaginians."

"And what are these new weapons, precisely," Auspex asked.

"I am going to hold off on sharing that for the moment. It is going to take time and a lot of work on Hortensius' part to get us ready for production on anything more complicated than the arcuballista, and I don't want to distract the men. I'm sure word will leak out before we decide it's the right time, but, right now, I want your men focused on training. My purpose today was to let you know there is a major overhaul coming which will change the way the legions fight, although the change will be less than it would for a less ordered unit."

"And what, precisely, are we training for?" Ursinus asked. "Besides teaching farmers and herders how to hold a sword and march, what are we doing?"

"That's number three. When we do land on the continent, it's going to be a challenge. The last time anyone here attempted a landing on an area without a port, it was in small, oar-driven, shallow draft vessels. It took days to move whole legions, which is plenty of time for the Carthaginians to catch us with half our legions on the continent and half on Britannia, attacking us when we are not prepared. That said, even if they greatly increase their manpower along the coast, they can't cover every inch of it and they won't know where we're going to strike. That gives us the element of surprise, a chance to maneuver, and even a chance to make local allies to help reinforce our numbers."

"Do you really think the locals will side with us when the time comes?" Valdar asked.

"Maybe. We've taken in a lot of refugees from the continent over the last several months, as the tribes closest to the coast have seen us as a potential safe haven. We can use that to our advantage, getting some of our new countrymen to negotiate with their brothers and cousins to see that siding with us is in their best interest."

"Which is why you pushed so hard to get them allowed in as citizens," Lucilla said.

"Precisely. They've been safe for several months now. Ever since we defeated Bomilcar's army, we've allowed them to come here for safety," Ky said, which caused all eyes to turn to the Carthaginian, now Britannian, general who had remained silent so far. "They all ran because they didn't want to live in Carthaginian lands, where they and their families were being brutalized. It hasn't been so long, however, that their people aren't still there. Once they see some of their family in legionnaire armor, coming to free them, they'll do the work for us. Or at least make it easier. That will be the start. Once we convert some villages and create a safe area on the continent for our forces, more will defect to us. The Carthaginian empire is held together by fear and their armies are made up of men who serve because if they don't the Carthaginians will kill everyone they grew up with and burn the remains of the village behind them as they leave. The more villages we free, the less manpower the Carthaginians will have. The men they would conscript from those villages will see a chance for freedom and come over to us, and so on and so on. By the time we clear enough of the continent to secure our own supply lines, the Carthaginian army, and their base of supply, will be greatly diminished, which is what we need, because this will only work in Germania, Gaul, and the like. Once we cross over to the Carthaginian homelands, we will have to fight for every inch we take."

"That's still a big risk," Ramirus said. "I'm not saying you're wrong, but if villages don't come over to us, we're going to have to fight larger and larger armies, since it's easier to march an army across Germania than sail through it with our cannons."

"True, it's a risk, but that's true about everything in war. If it works, it solves our supply problem, solves our manpower problem, and weakens the Carthaginians at the same time."

"He's not wrong about how the locals will react," Bomilcar said, speaking for the first time. "A large part of the Carthaginian army is used for reprisal and punishment details, putting down nascent rebellions. Since we couldn't send any of the pressed units into their homeland, for fear of mutinies or refusals to kill their countrymen, we had to constantly shuffle forces, sending Persians to Germania, Germans to Italy, Italians to Persia, and so on. Even then, if you killed too many people from an area, the units conscripted from that area would often revolt, since we ... the Carthaginians no longer had leverage to keep them in line."

Only steely glares met his words. Bomilcar, to his credit, did not flinch or stutter in the face of the animosity. Ky empathized with the former Carthaginian, but he couldn't come to his aid. He was striving to forge the foundations of a professional military and wanted his leaders to feel free to voice their thoughts. Ky knew he had to let Bomilcar endure the hostility until he could persuade the rest of the Britannians that it was better to work with him than against him.

"The Senate has already been difficult to convince when it came to allowing the Ulaid to join the Empire. They have deep-rooted connections with the Caledonians and were granted considerable lands, which meant valuable resources for us," Ramirus pointed out. "Germania is a different matter. We cannot play kingmakers. Our intervention in Ériu remains uncertain, as the entire island teeters on the brink of rebellion after each kingdom lost its sovereignty. Had the entire country not already been decimated or sided with the Carthaginians, unifying the land under one ruler would have failed. Germania lacks any large political organization; each village is essentially its own kingdom or, at best, part of a small collective. Incorporating them would mean persuading the Senate to accept numerous, relatively weak, and resource-poor groups as equals, granting them the same influence as Rome, Caledonia, and the Ulaid. I can't imagine any current senators willingly diluting their faction's power to that extent."

"They almost certainly wouldn't, which is why I'm not proposing they be absorbed into the Empire," Ky countered. "Thus far, we've used the terms 'Empire' and the pre-Empire alliance between Romans and Caledonians interchangeably. It's time we establish a true alliance. We will support villages and kingdoms willing to fight alongside us against the Carthaginians, providing them with weapons and civilian supplies, both by opening our markets and directly aiding each alliance member as needed, in return for their assistance in our war effort. They won't be integrated into our legions, but we can utilize their warriors as auxiliaries and, more importantly, gain access to their resources. This would grant them wealth, enabling them to purchase finished goods from us and supply our factories. We'll need to work out the specifics of our offers and requests, but it would grant us a secure base to operate from as we advance toward Africa and obtain desperately needed supplies. Some resources vital to our future endeavors can't be sourced from here or Ériu and must come from the continent."

"What about after the war, once Carthage is defeated? We will have armed people who could then use those weapons to come after us."

"There are some weapons we won't provide, or we will supply, but they won't be able to manufacture themselves, at least not for a long time. It'll be a long time before the Carthaginians can replicate our achievements, let alone smaller regions without their resources. Remember, it's taken an Empire-wide effort and systematic changes to reach our current capabilities, and it'll only become more complex as I introduce further modifications for even more advanced weaponry. Without my expertise, they'll have to not only discern our methods for producing specific weapons but also comprehend why we do things; a far more challenging task. Could they one day duplicate the cannon or some of our other creations? Maybe for Carthage, but doubtful for isolated villages."

"Fine, they'll depend on us for resources," Talogren conceded. "But you just said we'll need their resources too. Why give it away when we could extend our influence over the entire continent? You constantly stress the need for resources and manpower. Here it is. Once they submit, we'll have the power to maintain control."

Ky was pleased to hear the Caledonian leader refer to Britannia as "us," but the rest of his words brought less joy. It was inevitable, he knew. Even those who had been threatened or oppressed by an expansionist empire often craved the power it promised. Ky wasn't against empires, he had grown up in one and established another. What he opposed was creating an empire destined to collapse under its own weight, just as the original Roman Empire and its successors had.

"Because we are not the Carthaginians. Morality aside, we are here precisely because controlling an empire composed of subjugated people who aren't equal members inevitably leads to rebellion. My homeland's history is filled with empires that grew and collapsed under their own weight. If we want to build a place where our children and their children can thrive in comfort and safety, we must construct something that won't crumble. It's better to forge trade and political alliances, using our technological advantage to maintain peaceful leverage and obtain what we need without exerting control over every farmer and laborer in the known world."

"A well-formulated plan," the Emperor acknowledged. "We already witness the challenges of working between our peoples. Imagine how much more complicated it would be if the number of people involved doubled or increased ten-fold? Before the alliance, how easy was it to consolidate the Caledonian league?"

Talogren gave a shrug, letting the subject drop. Ky sensed that he hadn't fully accepted the point, but true believers weren't necessary. Just acceptance.

"So we build an alliance. If only our legions have the more advanced weapons, our new allies will notice we're using them as disposables, soaking up punishment from the Carthaginians so our legions can fight more manageable numbers," Lucilla pointed out. "I can't imagine they'll accept that kind of use for long."

"That's a valid concern and one of the many details that must be addressed. Today's session is to discuss the broader aspects of the next stages of the war. We'll then refine the specifics. But yes, we'll undoubtedly have to arm and train our allies to some degree, enabling them to operate alongside our legions effectively. This does mean providing weapons to those who might eventually turn against us. However, they'll rely on us for replacement weapons and supplies. We'll likely provide these throughout the war, but afterward, they'll have to purchase them from us, unless we negotiate a specific value back to our Empire. If they betray us, they'll lose access to those weapons. It isn't a perfect solution, but it should suffice."

"You hope," Ursinus interjected.

"Which is true of all wars. War is inherently risky. To win, concessions must be made, and the larger the opponent, the greater the concessions required."

"So once these new weapons are developed and ready, we'll take the fight to the continent and build an alliance of locals to combat the Carthaginians," Talogren conceded. "That sounds time-consuming. What do we do in the meantime? The Carthaginians won't wait idly by while we amass supplies."

"That's true. We must defend our position. Soon, the first ships designed to support the use of cannons,and many more cannons than Valdar's ship, will roll off slips. These vessels will help us maintain control of the waters surrounding our islands. With our superior ships and cannons and the Carthaginians' inferior ships and sailing ability for protection, we have the advantage of the sea. It'll be a long time before they can replicate our new ship designs and cannons, which means our coast lines are safe for now. However, I don't intend to hide behind our ships while preparing to invade the continent. Transitioning from a primarily infantry force to amphibious landings against a larger enemy isn't simple. We need experience with new tactics, including integrating cannons into our land forces. Fortunately, we have another option. Insula Manavia still hosts a Carthaginian force. Though isolated and monitored, it presents both a threat and an opportunity. Our next objective should be to train with Valdar's ships and the legions to land and capture the island, providing our men with experience making an amphibious assault, hands-on practice with our new weapons, and eliminating the threat simultaneously. That's our immediate target."

Talogren and the legates accepted this plan. Ky hadn't needed Lucilla's advice for dealing with the Caledonians or commanders. He might not grasp politics, but he knew how soldiers and warriors thought. Give them a target, and they were content. What they couldn't do well was sit and wait. This would buy Hortensius time to produce the necessary weapons while occupying the military, and help train the expanding legions before they faced the real test.

The main risk in this plan was that it might take so long that the Carthaginians could amass enough manpower on the coastlines to make any amphibious assault and land invasion impossible.

Even he had to accept that all war included risk.

Chapter 4

Over the next week, the capital bustled with life as men flooded in, more than had arrived during the original alliance with the Caledonians. Some were former citizens of the Ulaid or other kingdoms that had fought against the Carthaginians, but most were once subjects of the kingdoms who had sided with the Carthaginians. Men who had fought against their new overlords and decided they'd rather be faceless strangers in Rome's part of the Empire than endure a growing second-class citizenship in their old home.

Ky had already sent a message through the burgeoning semaphore system in Ériu, asking Llassar to keep an eye on the situation. He knew it would create homegrown dissidents, but he was a realist. It would take at least a generation for the Ulaid, brutalized by the kingdoms that had allied with the Carthaginians, to accept them as something close to equals. The kingdoms that had resisted the Carthaginians and were defeated were integrating well, but they were outnumbered by former foes. Conchobar needed to be cautious, or he'd find himself ruling over a majority of disgruntled and hostile people.

In addition to the influx from Ériu and Caledonia, families continued to emigrate from the continent. Dozens, even hundreds, arrived daily, overwhelming the coastal camps set up for them. With Britannia in control of their islands and surrounding seas, word spread of a way to escape Carthaginian oppression.

The Praetorians struggled to interview all these newcomers, searching for Carthaginian spies. Velius, fresh from his return to Devnum, and Hortensius had a semi-feud over who should get more men seeking opportunities in their new homeland.

Ky felt torn. He welcomed every worker and legionary they could get, but for his plan to work, they needed a significant number of locals, especially those with connections to family members already in Britannia, to stay in their homeland. He sided with Britannia's need for manpower, hoping it wouldn't derail his plan. As an immigrant to Rome, it would be hypocritical to deny others the same safe haven.

Thankfully, he didn't have to manage the headaches of a rapidly growing nation. Lucilla handled the new immigrants, both internal and from the continent, freeing Ky to focus on the technical matters he and Sophus excelled at. His only real complaint was that her responsibilities often kept her away from the Capitol, leaving their marriage bed empty. Now that he'd found the companionship he hadn't known he needed, he was reluctant to let it go, even temporarily.

Regrettably, his duties took precedence over his desires, which was why she was at the large camp outside of Cantiacorum, a small settlement that would later be known as Canterbury. The immigrants had crossed from what would be near modern-day Normandy, a region settled by a tribe called the Uenelli in a city of the same name. Supposedly staunch allies of the Carthaginians, as they were conquered not long after Rome itself, Ky hadn't planned on a landing near that point. However, his thoughts began to change as it became a pipeline from the continent to Britannia. Stories of Carthaginian reprisals against coastal villages and increased Carthaginian presence hadn't stopped the flow of immigration.

That, though, was Lucilla's problem. Ky was on his way to see Hortensius, as the largest part of his plan required a significant increase in Britannian technology. The complex of buildings, the heart of Roman industry, buzzed with activity as men bustled about. To some, it would look like chaos, but Ky saw an intricate dance with supplies flowing from shipment points and through the supply chain as iron became cannons and plows.

Hortensius, like a Roman-era Merlin, always seemed to be aware of everything in this area. He appeared almost as if summoned as soon as Ky entered the main foundry.

"Consul, I'm glad you're here. I have excellent news," he said, his indomitable, jovial nature in full force. "We've begun processing the first nitrate beds we laid down, and we should be able to ramp up our gunpowder production significantly soon."

"So soon? I didn't expect them to be ready for months yet."

"We are pulling these a bit early, so the soil is less enriched than it could be. But we started the process with a heavy concentration of bird droppings, which you mentioned were high in nitrates. That made me think they would help kick-start the process. We've already begun leaching the soil we removed and recycled what was left to start new beds earlier than planned. Considering the levels, I've ordered movable coops for pigeons and the like that we can place over new beds to shorten our production timeline. It's not the most pleasant work, and I assure you that you never want to go into those buildings, but it does seem effective."

"I see. That's good news because we'll need a lot more gunpowder this year for the next phase of my plan. I was going to suggest you talk to Llassar and see about getting help from the Ulaid to collect the supplies you need and lay down more beds there."

."I've already sent one of my assistants, who knows about the processes, to the Ulaid to begin setting up production there, actually," Hortensius informed him.

"Excellent. I should have assumed you'd be on top of it," Ky replied, a note of admiration in his voice.

"I live to serve," Hortensius said, with a sarcastic smile.

That was one of the things Ky liked about the manufacturer. He didn't take things outside of his factories too seriously and rarely stood on ceremony.

"I also wanted to talk to you about moving your foundries and factories. We still have a lot of manual labor in the prison camps that I want to use to support a large industrial area well outside of town," Ky said

"For gunpowder production?"

"Yes, although you relocated them outside of town, as we increase production, I'm not sure you moved them far enough. But that isn't all. Some of the new designs I have for you will be just as dangerous in their own ways. I have a philosopher I will be introducing you to, who will work with you on some of these new chemicals we will produce using the sulfur and nitrate you're already producing. While you build the new complex, I have designs for new foundries and chemical factories that need large, enclosed vats. Some of these changes are going to be more than can be done by just adding to your existing facilities, which makes this a good time to make the move."

Ky handed over a stack of the new paper being produced at the paper mills he began setting up months ago. It wasn't the quality he needed but it was far superior to the time-consuming production of vellum or the unwieldy scrolls previously used. The quality would come in time as the new chemical industry began to come online, and already people were becoming more used to these individual sheets of pulped wood, over pressed reeds and the like previously used as cheap writing material.

It had been a difficult struggle to introduce chemistry to the Britannians. Even the word had to be introduced to them, although it had quickly been adopted after the first tests of gunpowder. Thankfully, with Ky's direction, it was more scientific in nature, without the magical or religious overtones it had in the original medieval history of alchemy, with its focus on trying to create impossible results like turning iron into gold or elixirs that granted unnatural life.

"I see," Hortensius said, examining the documents with a furrowed brow. "These are interesting, but I'm not sure I grasp how they're better than our current foundries or how these vats are used at all."

"I understand your concerns. For now, please build according to my specifications. I've included some explanations of how these will be used, especially the new foundry design, but they require additional supplies to fully make sense. I have immense faith in you, but we must proceed step by step, as each component is intricate in its own right. I promise it will all make sense eventually."

"Of course, I will follow your instructions," Hortensius assured him. "I hope I didn't sound like I was questioning you. You've already shown us so many incredible innovations that it would be foolish to second-guess you. My curiosity is simply piqued by the workings of these new designs, and it's difficult to build something without understanding the reasoning behind it."

"I promise you'll know before long," Ky said reassuringly. "We just have a lot to accomplish in a short amount of time, and the first step is moving all of our production to a centrally located, controlled complex."

"But what about the workers? It will be difficult for them to walk such a distance each day to work in the factories and foundries, then walk back. If we're building there for safety, I assume we don't want housing built alongside it for our work-force. Losing all of our trained workers along with the facilities would make recovering from a disaster much more difficult. The lengthy walk would exhaust them before their work even begins, significantly lowering efficiency."

"A valid point," Ky agreed thoughtfully. "Perhaps we should consider a system of wagons to transport workers between De-vnum and the complex. A free service that ensures they arrive rested and ready to work. In time, we'll develop easier, faster, and more cost-effective means of transportation, but this basic setup would suffice for now."

"That's a considerable number of wagons, not to mention the men and horses needed to operate them."

"I know. But as I said, it would be a temporary solution. But the basic setup would work in the meantime," Ky reassured him.

"So once again, I must trust that you have this all planned out and build something without knowing the final outcome."

"We all have our burdens to bear," Ky said, placing a comforting hand on the manufacturer's shoulder.

"Don't I know it," Hortensius replied, laughter bubbling from his lips as he accepted the challenge with grace.

Dun Ailill, Ériunia

"Where is he?" Llassar demanded, shouting over the screams of men and animals.

"There," the warrior replied, his finger outstretched toward the wooden palisade wall.

A ragged group of Ulaid warriors clung to its sides, desperately attempting to scale the barrier. Men fell, victims of arrows and axes, their ladders slipping, unable to find purchase, and sending them tumbling to the ground below.

"The idiot is going to get himself killed," Llassar cursed, before turning to Auspex. "If we let him die, his father will break the alliance. Give me a cohort."

"We've discussed this. A frontal attack is a waste of men. And now you want to throw legionaries into that?" He gestured toward the chaos at the wall.

"We don't have time to argue. I know what we agreed to, but the fool has forced our hand. I'll go alone if I must, but to save him, I need men."

Auspex's expression soured, since they both knew this decision went against every bit of military wisdom. In just a week, the Consul's trebuchets would arrive, and they could reduce the fort without sacrificing a single life. Yet the headstrong prince had vehemently opposed that plan. Despite Llassar and Auspex's efforts to explain the virtue of patience, the prince stubbornly demanded a frontal assault on the walls.

As soon as Llassar had left to confer with the legions, the reckless prince seized the opportunity. He led his two hundred Ulaid guardsmen in an attack, unsupported by the rest of the legions. Had the prince been more cunning or strategic, Llassar might have suspected a ploy to force his hand. But he had spent enough time with the prince to know better. The fool had acted impulsively, believing his small band could conquer the walls. If the two hundred men had been trained legionaries, perhaps that idea would have had some merit. But the finest Ulaid soldiers had perished before the Britannians had come to their aid, leaving only farmers and herders, most not even in armor, as the kingdom's remaining force. These men stood no chance of accomplishing anything but getting the heir killed, and Llassar would shoulder the blame.

He should have anticipated the prince's recklessness the moment he left him unattended. He had believed, however, that he'd finally penetrated the young man's stubbornness during their last conversation. Clearly, he had been mistaken.

"Fine," Auspex relented, his voice heavy with resignation. He turned and called out, "Gnaeus! Take your men in behind the Ulaid. Scale the wall, secure it, and raise a flag. We'll send two more cohorts to follow you."

Gnaeus snapped a salute and raced off to his men.

"Where are you going?" Auspex demanded as Llassar urged his horse to follow Gnaeus.

"With the cohort. If I don't keep that young fool alive, I'm as good as dead anyway, since his father will kill me himself," Llassar declared before spurring his horse onward.

Surprisingly, the prince's men had fared better than Llassar had anticipated, given the recklessness of their plan. Several groups had already reached the top of the wall. However, the success was bittersweet. For every man who made it up, ten perished, leaving those who had scaled the wall vulnerable to the fort's rallying defenders. They had been caught off guard by the assault, but that advantage wouldn't last long. Llassar observed men from other sections of the wall rushing to reinforce the breaches.

Compounding the problem, the prince was among those who had made it to the top of the wall. As Llassar neared, he glimpsed the young man standing perilously near the outer edge, orchestrating the battle. Though it was commendable to witness the prince leading rather than plunging headfirst into the fray, Llassar couldn't help but wish he had chosen a less precarious situation to hone his skills.

Abandoning his horse, Llassar followed the legionaries, taking advantage of the protection their shields offered. Their commander had them advance in a Testudo formation, with Llassar crouching behind the back row, partially shielded from harm. Men still fell, but their numbers remained relatively intact until they reached the walls. As the legionaries advanced, the prince's men gave way. However, the formation inevitably broke as the men ascended the ladders, leading to mounting casualties.

"More ladders there and there," Llassar shouted at the prince's warriors who milled at the base of the wall, pointing to sections far down either side, well away from the concentrated troops. "Have your men attack there and come in from either side, so we can clear this side of the wall."

The four ladders they had were too closely clustered, which contributed to their predicament and aided the men inside the fort in countering the numerical differences. Although enough enemies now occupied their side of the wall, making it more difficult for the ladders to find purchase, the ongoing battle atop the wall made it easier for their men to climb. Llassar's heart ached at the needless loss of life, but one of these fools should have tried to talk the prince out of going up top himself, cut off from his guards. He resolved to expend the prince's warriors' lives to retrieve the prince safely, rather than those of the better-trained and disciplined legionaries.

The Ulaid began to disperse, allowing the legionaries more space to ascend the wall. Despite his reservations about the prince's decision to fight on the parapet, Llassar refused to linger below, relying on the legionaries to rescue the impetuous royal. He had accompanied them to ensure the prince's safety, and he was determined to fulfill that mission. After the first few soldiers began their ascent, Llassar maneuvered his way past the next soldier in line and followed them up the ladder.

One advantage of climbing behind a legionary was the protection their shield provided from above, deflecting arrows and sword blows as they neared the top. Although it didn't prevent the lead Roman from receiving a fatal sword slash to the face, nor the soldier below him from being dislodged by the tumbling body, it did clear a path for Llassar to vault over the edge of the wooden wall, unimpeded. His small, one-handed axe was already in hand, and as soon as his feet found purchase on the parapet, he drew the gladius he carried on his other side.

The Caledonian axe and the Roman gladius complemented each other in Llassar's skilled hands. Each weapon possessed unique strengths and weaknesses, but Llassar had honed his technique to strike and parry fluidly with both. A deadly ballet of sword and axe unfolded as Llassar engaged the fort's defenders, his weapons weaving in tandem to block, parry, and slice. Although men continued to fall, the first legionaries who reached the wall gained control of the parapet more effectively than the less-armored defenders, who struggled to bypass the imposing Roman shields.

Arrows from the fort's center became a growing concern. The more ground the Britannians gained, the more the defenders below could fire into their ranks without endangering their comrades.

"Centurion," Llassar called to a legionary behind him, simultaneously using his axe to deflect a sword thrust and countering with his gladius. "Push your men down the ramp and get men into that courtyard. We need to occupy those archers. And get some arcuballistae up here to put counterfire on them."

"Understood," the Centurion responded, preoccupied with his own battle.

Having worked closely with the legionaries, Llassar had developed a deep trust in their professionalism. He knew they would execute the orders while he fought his way toward the prince, who now found himself encircled with only a handful of his guards still standing.

Another man fell to Llassar's axe, s he began carving his way toward the prince. He was near enough to the defenders that the archers posed no immediate threat, but the screams behind him attested to the arrows finding their marks. His initial goal had been to ensure the prince's safety, but the current situation demanded the capture of the fort. It was going to be costly, and already he was losing more well-trained men, but their victory was never in doubt.

Dispatching a final defender with a stab to the back as the man tried to engage the prince's guard, Llassar broke through. He ushered legionnaires past the prince, forming a solid defense on the other side and taking stock of the battle.

Below, Gnaeus directed soldiers up the ladders, while the Centurion Llassar had entrusted with the courtyard assault executed his orders admirably. A squad of legionaries advanced on the archers, who either fled or drew swords to defend themselves, quickly realizing the futility of their arrows against the Roman-style shields. The fort's inhabitants were unaccustomed to facing legionary tactics, unlike Llassar's own people. There were methods to counter Roman formations, but a barrage of arrows was not among them.

The Britannians' numbers now nearly matched the fort's defenders, and with their superior coordination, the fort would soon fall. One group had bypassed the chaos where the prince's guards had last attempted to scale the wall and were now preparing to assault the southern-facing wall.

"See, I told you we could take this fort," the prince declared, grinning with the thrill of battle.

Llassar's self-restraint was tested as he resisted the urge to hurl the young fool off the parapet.

"Of course we could," Llassar replied, barely concealing his anger. "That wasn't the point. This position is meaningless. The fort's defenders were never a real threat to our army as we march on Queen Medb's capital. Auspex had already assigned a century to keep them confined here. They'd have faced starvation or surrender, and we could have captured this place with minimal losses."

"You're the one who keeps talking about how we need to secure my father's lands quickly."

"And this is delaying us. We've lost an entire day to this folly. We could have detached the century and marched past without losing pace. You've squandered men and time, gaining nothing."

"My men are restless. They seek glory as much as yours, and warriors die in battle. It's a noble death."

"It's a senseless death. You haven't ever truly spoken to any of the legionaries. If you had, you'd know they are not warriors. The Consul has a word for what they are. Soldiers. They aren't here to garner glory and aren't seeking individual combat on the battlefield. You've marched with us, even observed these men in action, but somehow you're still blind. Look at them."

Llassar gestured toward the large group of legionaries who had gathered, cutting down the last of the fort's defenders as they spoke. Once the Britannians had breached the defenders' lines and gained a foothold in the courtyard below, the tide turned rapidly. The defenses crumbled, and the remaining locals rallied to the center for a final stand.

"It isn't difficult to kill a few men," the prince remarked, surveying the carnage.

"That's precisely what I'm telling you. You're looking at them, but you're not truly seeing. If it had been you down there, you'd have charged the defenders, right? You might have won, but you would have lost another dozen men, or perhaps more, in the chaos of the melee. Observe the legionnaires. Even with victory assured, they maintain their lines and discipline. It took me a long time to appreciate this manner of fighting and how our own ways failed us, but I learned. Now it's your turn. This isn't a game, and the objective isn't personal glory. We're fighting for our survival, and this skirmish pales in comparison to the battle that awaits us on the continent. If you wish to lead, you must abandon childish notions and adopt a leader's perspective. That starts with not squandering your men's lives because of you're bored."

Llassar could tell the prince was listening, as he grimaced at the final statement. But the young man's attention was now on the nearly concluded battle below. The legionaries had made short work of the defenders, encircling them, raising their shields, and pushing and stabbing the desperate men as they sought a means of survival. Perhaps forty men had remained below when the legionaries began their formation, all of whom now lay dead. In contrast, the legion had lost only five men. It had been a needless and costly victory. Llassar just hoped the prince would learn the lesson he sought to impart before his own life was forfeit.

Chapter 5

Devnum Docks

Valdar gazed up at the colossal vessel with a sense of awe. Part of him wondered how anything so ponderous could ever make it in the choppy waters of the western ocean, part of the territory he'd soon be tasked with safeguarding. The western seas were nothing like the placid channel between the islands and the continent, nor the calmer waters of the Bay of Serpents, known to the Romans as Mare Suebicum. He'd struggled to keep his smaller, more agile ships afloat in those violent waves. Even more astounding was the fact that, according to the Consul, this ship was considered small, with far more massive hulks planned for the future.

The Consul had assured him that these ships would be more stable than anything he'd sailed before. The explanation had seemed logical at the time, but now, standing before the vessel and examining the rows of gaping holes in its sides, doubt gnawed at his confidence.

The Consul had also promised weaponry that would revolutionize naval warfare, and he'd delivered with the introduction of cannons. Valdar had been astonished by the immense metal tubes that, upon firing, nearly pushed his ship backward, and by the way the cannonballs tore through enemy vessels as if they were made of cloth. Valdar still feared that high waves might swamp the ship even with the doors that could be sealed shut, but the Consul had insisted it wouldn't be an issue. Trusting that promise on dry land, however, was a far cry from believing it amid ten-foot-high swells at sea.

Still, he had witnessed the power of a single cannon. If these ships were as seaworthy as the Consul promised they'd be unstoppable. They would boast seven cannons on each side, all larger than the lone cannon he'd had on his previous vessel. The thought was staggering, and the Consul had referred to this as a 'lightly armed' ship. He'd mentioned that larger vessels, at least those not meant for cargo, could hold over forty cannons compared to this ship's fourteen. With a ship like that, Valdar could have vanquished the entire Carthaginian fleet single-handedly.

Work had begun on erecting the massive masts, which extended down through the still-unlaid top deck and connected to the ship's very frame. Each mast would bear enormous square sails, in addition to the smaller square and triangular sails the Consul had ordered be added to Valdar's existing ships. It had taken only a brief journey around the islands, and the Consul's guidance on their optimal use, for Valdar to realize the tremendous advantage these smaller sails provided.

Valdar marveled at how these sails revolutionized his ship's capabilities, allowing it to slice through the wind at previously unimaginable angles and harness even the most fleeting of gusts for momentum. The innovation perplexed him, as he wondered why no one had considered straying from the traditional single, large sail before. Sailing, however, was an art steeped in tradition, passed down through generations, and progress had been sluggish at best.

Already, he'd observed local fishing boats beginning to craft makeshift jibs, trysails, and gennakers, akin to those that graced his own vessel. Though they lacked the guidance he'd received from the Consul, these fishermen and shipmasters had evidently sought counsel from his sailors. In a mere matter of weeks after Valdar's initial voyage using the new sails, their manifold advantages had become evident, and the community had eagerly adopted the novel approach.

"Look at them, learning from us," Valdar mused aloud, a tinge of pride in his voice.

Regardless of the Consul's intentions, he'd ushered in a new era of sailing.

Manufacturing Complex, Outside Devnum

Ky and Lucilla strolled leisurely through the skeletal framework of the growing manufacturing complex, although from the size of the buildings and streets being laid out 'a town' would be a more realistic description. Ky couldn't help but imagine the inevitable pollution, the chemicals and ash that would soon fill the air. He doubted anyone would willingly choose to live here, though he knew some enterprising souls would be drawn by the allure of profit, regardless of the risk to their health.

A pang of regret nudged at Ky, wishing there were a way to achieve their goals without the environmental consequences reminiscent of the original Industrial Revolution. He reasoned that they could at least mitigate some harm by educating workers about the dangers associated with handling hazardous materials. Yet, the pressing need for survival overshadowed more long term concerns, meaning soon, the air would be choked with billowing clouds of soot as the factories transitioned to full-scale industrial production.

They'd spent most of the morning with Hortensius, discussing the specifics of steel manufacturing and new chemical production processes. Hortensius, a brilliant man with a penchant for adapting to change, was not always the easiest to work with. Sure of himself, and worse, of Ky's absolute knowledge, he tended to barrel full steam ahead, trusting everything would work. While Ky trusted the information at his disposal, other Britannians were less enthused by Hortensius's approach.

Complicating matters further was Sorantius, the philosopher Ky had selected to run the new chemical plants. Though a genius in his own right, capable of challenging his own preconceptions when faced with evidence, Sorantius shared Hortensius's stubbornness and headstrong nature. Disagreements between the two often escalated into heated shouting matches.

"I can't keep playing mediator between those two," Ky muttered to Lucilla, the frustration evident in his voice.

Lucilla, ever the empathetic listener, gently squeezed his arm. "I know, my love. You're a soldier at heart, not a negotiator."

Ky sighed. "I'd rather be on the battlefield with the legions, fighting the Carthaginians. At least there, my enemies and objectives are clear."

"Well, we need a solution," Lucilla said thoughtfully. "Perhaps a third party to help them find common ground?"

Ky's eyes lit up as he considered her suggestion, "That's an excellent idea."

"What?" She asked, and then his meaning dawned on her. "No. No way."

"It's perfect," Ky said. "You just pointed out I'm not suited for this. You, however, have trained for exactly this kind of thing your whole life. Plus, you actually seem to like it; which is useful, no matter how strange it is."

"They're going to have questions I can't answer. When it comes to overseeing buildings being built or getting senators to vote on a proposal, that I know how to do. I don't even understand half the instructions you gave them."

"You don't need to understand them," Ky said, placing a reassuring hand on her arm. "None of their arguments have been over technical matters. When it comes to the work, both men are reasonable and will follow wherever the evidence says to go. Their problem is they're both trying to be the smartest person in the room. You only have to make sure they stay focused, and smooth over disagreements. You're good at that."

"Fine. I'll babysit our geniuses, along with watching the construction, dealing with senators, and making sure the ship-building program is progressing. What will you be doing while I'm doing all that? A nice vacation? Playing dice with your guards?"

Ky knew she wasn't as displeased as she sounded. The closer they'd gotten, the more joy she seemed to get by teasing him when she got the chance. Although she could be scathing in her teasing at times, he found he liked it.

"I'll be around. I thought I might take up painting or maybe ..."

She gave him a shove before he could finish, causing both of them to laugh.

"I know it's a lot to ask," Ky said, getting back on task. "You're just better at this than me. Soon we'll need to start training Valdar on using the ship's gunnery, which isn't something that can be taught by writing it down. Sadly, a lot of my time will still be spent writing instructions. The level of complexity of what we're asking from Hortensius and Sorantius will soon increase significantly, which means I'll need to give them as much reference material as possible. I also need to start working with Velius on the invasion plans. We'll have to redo all of the legions' tactics to work with the new weapons, which is going to take some time as well."

"Fine, you'll be busy."

"I'll still see you at night, though," Ky said, putting his arm around her.

"I'm not sure you should," she said.

Unlike her earlier teasing, she sounded serious, which caused Ky to take a step away and focus on her.

"What?"

"What I mean is, as much as I love having you here with me, I'm not sure we should both be operating out of Devnum for the time being."

"Why? This is where most of the work is."

"For now, but it won't stay that way. Once Valdar's ships roll off the docks, he's almost certainly going to want to move south, closer to Isca Dumnoniorum or maybe Glevum, since to really train him to use the new ships, you need to be out on the open seas, and not in the protected waters of Mare Hibernicum. He'll probably want to do it in the southern seas, since that's where his ships will be operating for the foreseeable future. There aren't a lot of Carthaginians to the north of us and he's not going to waste time sailing up and down half the length of the island every time he needs to come to port. As for the legions, once you start working with them, you're going to need room to maneuver for them to learn the new tactics, which also means moving south. But more importantly, it's a waste of resources for us to both be here. Anything you need done here, I can do. Besides being able to speak from wherever either of us is, I have Sophus and the drone for him to see through, at least until you are ready to start the actual invasion."

"She is correct, Commander. Since returning to Devnum, the two of you have performed most of your duties together. She has watched your military conferences and you have watched her discuss topics with the Senators, neither contributing significantly to the other's work. As you yourself point out, you have much work still to do before the invasion of the continent, none of which can proceed if you are watching Lucilla carry out her tasks."

"I should have never introduced the two of you. All you do is gang up on me."

"I am simply following my programming, Commander. Perhaps if you were in the wrong less often, I would agree with you more."

"Was that a joke?" Ky asked.

Sophus may have reached sentience, but there were a range of behaviors that Ky had assumed would be beyond the tactical computer. He wasn't an expert on artificial intelligence, but he'd assumed emotions were something a computer could not have. Yet, several times now, Sophus had exhibited curiosity, frustration, and now humor. It was unexpected.

"I think Sophus was being completely serious, and I agree," she said, wrapping her arm around his waist. "Seriously though, as much as I'll miss you in our bed, we can't take the little bit of breathing room we've given ourselves and think we're free to live our lives. You said it yourself. They'll never stop coming for us. We've got a chance now to push them while they're on their heels, and we need to take it. Which means we both need to focus on work, for now at least."

"I still don't like it. We spent the last several months with you here and me with the legions, and now we have to be apart again."

"I know. I don't like it either. Eventually, we'll be free of the Carthaginians and we can live our lives together."

Ky made a non-committal sound. In his experience, there was always a new crisis and a new thing to deal with. The empire, his original empire in his original life, had been at peace for more than a decade, and yet as a combat pilot, he was constantly given assignments. He doubted this time would be any different. She was right of course, and he'd do it, but he'd only just found this missing part of himself and they'd only been married a short time. He didn't like it, no matter how necessary it was.

"Fine, but I plan on finding opportunities to come back and see you."

Stopping and wrapping both arms tightly around him, she put her head on his chest and said, "I demand that you do."

Devnum

"We've received word from Caesius," Decius said, looking around the room at the dwindling number of men left in the resistance forces.

Ramirus had been brutal and swift in rounding up anyone who dared speak against the Emperor or the demon that was controlling him. They'd lost so many men already, that any direct action to free Rome from the clutches of the despots had all but ended. They'd been relegated to simply collecting and passing off agents to one of the two shipmasters willing to take messages to their contacts on the continent, and eventually on to Caesius.

Worse, Decius had to all but ended recruiting, after losing the second cell of freedom fighters to Ramirus's agents. As time passed, there were fewer and fewer Romans willing to put their lives on the line for what was right; and worse, even fewer were willing to give up the money they were making under the new regime. Decius had nothing but contempt for all of the men willing to sell their values for a few coins, but that contempt didn't help his current problem. They'd started reaching out to the Ulaid who'd come here fleeing their new overlords, but while these people had no love for Rome, they didn't really care for the Carthaginians either. They couldn't return home without facing at least unofficial persecution for standing up to the Ulaid king, much like his people faced persecution for standing up to the pretender controlling the Emperor. They were almost a stateless people, and it was difficult for any of them to see the necessity of replacing the Emperor with a worthy leader.

Thankfully, Caesius had once again come through for them.

"In my last message to him, I related our manpower problem. Any time one of our people steps even a little out of line, Ramirus hauls them away to his dungeons. Worse, what good we have been able to provide, such as information on what the pretender is up to, is threatened every time we lose someone. Caesius has come through for us again. He is arranging for men to be slipped in with other refugees coming in from the continent to work as our agents for more direct actions. We still have a few cutouts left we can use to contact them without endangering our other agents, although we need to be on the lookout for more people we can use as intermediaries. I know we've had some bad luck in that area, but it's imperative we keep building our network if we are to have any hope of helping Caesius regain his rightful place and to rout this new Empire."

"Have you seen the postings of the agreement with the Hibernians? The Senate, the fake imperial one that tells our senators what laws they can pass, now has more barbarians than actual citizens in it. We are now completely controlled by men who live in huts and sleep in their own filth."

"Which is why we need to continue getting Caesius what he needs," Decius said. "He has made agreements with the Carthaginians to help us, but only if we provide the assistance they need to squash the rogue legions."

"Won't that just make us subjects of the Carthaginians?" their newest member asked.

"For a time, but look how easily they've been defeated on the field of battle. The legionnaires know what's best for this country, but they don't have the will to oust their leaders, yet. Once we've freed them, they will rally to our cause and we can push out the Carthaginians and reclaim our rightful place."

Decius made a note to have someone check on the new man. While most of the gathered men nodded or made mumbled agreements, he looked unsure. Decius believed that everyone had a right to their opinion, but this entire enterprise was balanced on the edge of a knife. Doubt and uncertainty could infect others, tearing them down from the inside. If his friends couldn't convince him that they were on the right path, Decius would have to do something more permanent about him.

"What about the Emperor's daughter?" one of the old hands asked. "We've tried to get her twice and have failed twice. The Consul may be controlling the Emperor, but she's the one doing all the work. Every day she's somewhere else, in the foundries, at the docks, with the legions, always giving instructions and making corrections."

"Obviously, and you all know we've tried. Several times."

"I thought for sure we would have gotten her the last time. Our man left her bleeding on the ground. It's impossible she survived that," the younger man said.

"Exactly. We got within blade range and still failed. We've all heard tales of the magic the Consul wields, of the green flame he produced that melted the very stones of the palace. It makes sense he was able to use that magic to somehow keep her alive, which means just stabbing her or otherwise injuring her isn't enough. We have to strike a killing blow. He may have magic, but even he can't reverse death."

"What we need are soldiers of our own," the younger man said.

"Exactly," Decius, who was normally controlled and reserved, said with a passion that startled several of the other men. "That is exactly what we need. We need to recruit someone with actual military knowledge. Someone who has been trained to fight and to kill, and the Consul has paved the way for us to do just that. When he incorporated members of Pius and Eborius's old legions, those who survived anyway, into his new legions, he gave a blanket amnesty to every one of them. Some might have turned tail and become followers of the new Empire out of fear or greed, but some should have remained faithful to our cause."

"I thought you said we needed to keep our distance from anyone involved in the insurrection. That Ramirus would have them under watch," another man said.

"I did, and just after the insurrection's failure, that was the smart thing to do, but now we need some of those men. Lucilla trusts the legions, and her guards might allow a legionnaire within sword range of her and that man will know how to actually kill her, instead of simply wounding her."

"And Ramirus won't be watching them?"

"He might, but even Ramirus has limited resources. He has to check on all the Ulaid and their families now coming into the country from the continent. He's stretched thin. Already, we've noticed fewer of his agents around town than before."

"Weren't you just saying we needed to be careful? That he is everywhere?" the young man asked.

"Yes, because it is wise to always be cautious, even if he's stretched thin. He might have fewer agents to spread around, but he still has them. I'm not saying contacting legionnaires will be easy or safe, but it is the only way we're going to get to her. Use cutouts. Men who you can contact but who don't know your identity."

"We don't have a lot of those men left," the older man said.

"I know, but as our friend here pointed out, killing her is still a priority. We also need the help of legionnaires to carry out some of these new instructions from Caesius, including getting plans or examples of some of the new technology Hortensius is working on. Specifically, we need to obtain samples and diagrams, or better yet, blueprints and instructions of the things he's been working on. One of our men in the foundries says he's seen the old fool with stacks of the new paper introduced by the Consul, and he often refers to them. If we can, we need to steal some of those documents or talk to someone who has access to them, so we can make this work to our advantage."

"So we only need to steal documents they will surely miss, get men into facilities guarded by the new praetorians, a group we have yet to get our own men inside of, convert legionnaires to our cause, and kill the Emperor's daughter?" the older man said, summing it up, although in a tone that made it clear he didn't think anything on that list was accomplishable.

"No one said overthrowing a government would be easy. I'll remind you that I've sacrificed my own son to ensure our mission succeeds. Most of you haven't given nearly as much, and yet you

53

complain about the dangers you face every time we meet. This is not a game and it's time you all take this more seriously."

Chapter 6

"Hortensius tells me the vats and buildings to contain them should be done in a week's time," Sorantius said. "As you expected, the first run of the vats was not as water-tight as you wanted, although the leaks seemed minimal to me."

"Only because you are thinking of water, which when it leaks simply corrodes the metal and leaves a puddle on the floor. Some of these mixtures will melt skin or create vapor clouds that will take all of the oxygen from a man," Ky said, pointing at the new papers he had brought for the philosopher-turned-chemist. "It is critical that you understand that the slightest leak can be a danger. It's why I included an entire section on maintaining the vats and the equipment so they don't corrode and leak, and the very specific guides on how to remove these mixtures from the vats for further production."

"Which is why many of these things are made of glass?"

"Correct. Some, although not all, of these mixtures will not react with the glass or melt through it, making it the safest way to store it for the next steps of processing."

"I see, although I'm still not clear on how these mixtures will be used. I know Hortensius blindly trusts any instructions you give him, but mixing things like this isn't the same as building a building. Understanding the reasons things are done are the keys to ensuring it's done correctly."

He wasn't wrong, Ky thought. Sorantius had already shown that, while Hortensius was able to produce items as directed, such as gunpowder, doing so blindly had limited his ability to innovate from what he was being told. After reading over all of Ky's notes on gunpowder and its proper handling, Sorantius had devised several alterations to the barrels it was being stored in, both to keep the powder dry, further limit its exposure to oxygen, which would allow it to remain potent for longer, and limit the dust that could get into the air in storage facilities, lessening fire and explosion risks.

That was the one weak point in Ky and Sophus's process of introducing these technologies. While the AI had extensive files on how things were done, it lacked the creativity and instinctual sense to really innovate past what they already knew. True, by following the progression of inventions from their past, they were essentially borrowing the innovations from others, but that wasn't the same. Just by introducing these technologies in different orders, changed the reasons the innovations happened, and what innovations they needed would change as well.

Theoretically, Ky was the other half of the puzzle, able to apply his instincts and creativity to Sophus's information, but that wasn't applicable here. He could do it on the battlefield, but laboratories and factories were outside his experience, leaving him as blind as Sorantius and Hortensius.

Of course, he couldn't just tell them why things worked, because the explanation wouldn't make any sense. How do you explain to people who haven't discovered microscopes or the atom what a covalent bond or ionic compound is? For now, Sorantius was asking for Ky to elaborate on the chemicals he was asking them to make, but eventually, he'd be asking why these chemicals reacted the way they did. Ky would do his best to explain it, but it was clear that just uplifting these people with industrial-age technology wasn't enough. They had to also understand it for themselves, and that was going to be a much bigger hurdle.

"I'll try and explain, although some of these concepts require a base of knowledge you do not possess. In time, we can try and work out a system for teaching you, and others who are interested, the theories behind these subjects. But for now, we do not have the time. So if I don't give you the specifics you are asking for, please know I'm not doing it to keep knowledge from you. It's simply that the knowledge requires more than I can explain in the time we have."

"I understand, but I will hold you to that promise one day. When this is all over, you will introduce us to these mysteries, and teach us this base knowledge that will unlock the rest of what you have shown us."

Although the man had said us, Ky heard me, which he was certain what Sorantius actually meant. That was another major difference between Sorantius and Hortensius. While Hortensius was a wealthy man before Ky met him, his success had come almost in spite of himself, a byproduct of his endless thirst to create and his impressive work ethic. At no point since Ky had started working with the manufacturer had the man shown any indication that he was looking to use this crisis to better himself. Sorantius, on the other hand, seemed to think of little else.

Ky wasn't worried that he was some kind of security risk, trying to personally profit off of the information he was getting. If anything, Sorantius seemed completely unconcerned with wealth, living in extremely basic conditions and forgoing all of the fineries that someone of his station could obtain. His version of bettering himself seemed to be completely focused on learning and understanding more. Knowledge was the only thing he seemed determined to hoard. Which was one of the reasons Ky had picked him for this position. There were one or two other men that might have made a good candidate, and one who might have even worked better with Hortensius, but none had the thirst for knowledge that Sorantius had, which in this circumstance was the quality Ky needed.

"Fine. I can agree to that. As for a more basic explanation, I'll do what I can. That these two elements are acids is the most important," Ky said, pointing to the instructions for producing sulfuric and nitric acid. "This one is sulfuric acid and is why one of these tanks had to be made of only lead, since it would start to break down anything else you used to mix it. We'll eventually use it in producing a number of other mixtures, as well as further process it into a very effective fertilizer. A lot of our future products are going to need this. The other mixture is called nitric acid, which is also used for making fertilizer, but more importantly, it's the first component in making an extremely volatile chemical that explodes when enough force is placed on it. It's going to have huge implications for our arms production, and will be the bedrock of many of the next technologies I introduce. The key to both of these is precision. You'll see the instructions for each indicate extremely specific steps and weights to be used in their production, as well as specific ways of storing them. It's critical that we follow **all** of these steps to the letter! Since they are both the building blocks of future compounds, we need them to be precise so we can predict the reactions that will happen when we produce those other compounds."

"I'm assuming from the context that the word chemical is what you call the explosive mixture. Is that correct? It sounds almost like Latin, but I don't recognize it."

"Unfortunately, this will happen a lot as we get into more precise and detailed topics that require words and descriptions common among my people, but that you haven't encountered yet. You'll find that with the instructions I've included some descriptions of the words that I would use when talking about these new methods and technologies. Right now you're getting the brunt of this, since most of the work Hortensius has been doing is an extension of existing ideas, or more simplistic forms of chemistry. That is, the science of working with chemicals. Opening a new chemical industry is key to everything else we're doing, but it is also the largest push forward so far in technology, so we run into the lack of language and terms to describe the things needing to be done."

"I'm not complaining. Most of the words you've used have made sense in the context of what you are explaining, and I look forward to being challenged."

"Good, because you have a lot of work to do," Ky said.

Ky continued to be amazed by the capabilities of the people here. Before the accident, he would have considered anyone from this time to be hopelessly backward, but they were every bit as hard-working and intelligent as anyone from his time. All they lacked was knowledge.

Ráth Cruachan, Ériu

"You're joking," Auspex said, more as an expression of surprise than an actual question.

"I'm not," Gnaeus said, standing before his commander, Llassar, and the prince in the command tent.

"It makes things simpler, doesn't it?" the prince asked.

"Only if we win," Llassar said.

"Of course, I'll win," the prince said.

"But why do it at all?" Gnaeus asked. "We have more men than they do, the trebuchets are being set up, and we have the city surrounded. All we have to do is sit here until they starve. We've either cut off, crushed, or accepted the surrender of every other unfriendly city and garrison on this island. They stand alone. Why risk it for some foolish display of ego? What kind of barbarians decide the contest of armies by two men in single combat?"

"You can go," Auspex commanded.

Both men had caught the expression on Llassar's face at Gnaeus's statement, causing Gnaeus to blanch slightly.

"I apologize. I know that is how your people settled many of their conflicts, and I meant no disrespect. I'm just surprised, is all."

Llassar gave a slight nod of acceptance. Although he'd added menace into his glare at the cohort commander for his earlier comment, Llassar actually felt no animosity towards the man. In fact, he'd heard how far the man had gone to include the newly added Caledonians into his ranks, including bringing several on as aides, giving them valuable experience that would jump them ahead in line for command past Romans with more time in the legions.

In spite of that, Llassar knew it would take time to change all of the Roman's long-held prejudices. That understanding didn't keep him from holding the men he was in charge of accountable for their Roman snobbishness.

"To answer your original question, the reason to do it is because this is how it's always been done in our cultures. If we win, the people will accept the results and our rulership. Did you find your people had much luck converting the people to the Roman ways in the few towns of ours you captured and tried to rule over?"

He knew Gnaeus had served in what the Romans had called the north prior to the alliance, and would have had some dealings with his people being held in subjugation.

"I found your people to be stubborn," Gnaeus said, more factually than angrily.

"Because they didn't see themselves as your subjects, even though you ruled over them. This type of contest would happen regularly and nearly always ended in the village accepting new rulership. It allowed most of the citizens to continue producing crops and kept husbands from being taken from their wives and children. From our point of view, it was much more civilized than how you Romans fought battles. Of course, it isn't an option for dealing with most of our opponents, because not even a victory in single combat would keep them from seeing their new rulers as foreigners. Here it's different. True, most of the citizens aren't fans of the Ulaid, but they wouldn't see them as foreign, and most will accept their rulership if our man wins. It keeps this town, and ultimately Queen Medb's entire kingdom from being an issue. In my mind, that's better than ending up with a city full of corpses from people who starved to death. That doesn't even consider how long starving a city like this would take. The Consul has made it clear that we are to wrap up the last of the Carthaginian allies and get your legion back with the rest, to take part in the battles to come. This way achieves both outcomes."

"He's right," Auspex said.

Llassar saw not only Gnaeus, but also Auspex nodding in agreement at his reasoning. Of course, this kind of knowledge had limited use, since once they began fighting on the continent or in Africa, every victory would be bloody, which was all the more reason to do it this way. They should take advantage of situations when they could.

Llassar also saw it as a chance to teach Gnaeus that commanding was more than just tactical. Legates often operated independently from other legions, and had to look beyond the battlefield to the entire goal of a campaign. Llassar had been lucky enough to learn that lesson early and had taught it to Talogren when he'd first joined up with the chieftain's new league. Auspex had spoken highly of the younger cohort commander and Llassar had a conversation with the Consul and Lucilla about the need to be on the lookout for leaders as the legions expanded. He may have been here to pacify Ériu, but he wouldn't pass up the opportunity to mentor a promising commander. The field of battle was the best place to both train and mold young men into leaders.

"I hadn't thought of it like that," Gnaeus said. "I'm still not sure sending the prince is a good idea."

"In that, we agree," Llassar said.

"What?" the prince said, looking at Llassar in shock. "Why?"

"Because for this to work, we need to actually win. I've seen you fight, and you've got a lot of promise, but if they put up who I think they will, you don't stand a chance."

"I don't care who they put up, I'll defeat them. I've trained with the best teachers in the kingdom, since Father became king, and I beat them every time."

"I'm sure beating teachers paid for by your father was a challenge," Gnaeus said.

"What are you trying to say? They let me win?" the prince said, bristling.

Llassar held up a hand, keeping the cohort commander from answering. Gnaeus might have been more seasoned and battle-hardened, but both were young men, prone to the venality of youth.

"Queen Medb is going to send Fergus. It's her only choice, really. Besides being an incredible fighter, he is still claiming to be the true heir to the Ulaid throne, and siding with him was part of her justification for joining the war against your father. Her people will know this, and expect him to step up now when challenged by, what he has said loudly to anyone who will listen, are pretenders to his throne. You cannot beat Fergus."

Cormac was too young to have met the former prince, who fled the kingdom before Cormac was born, but he would have doubtlessly heard stories. Fergus was larger than Conchobar when he was the prince's age, which was when Cormac's father took the throne, which made him roughly the same age as Llassar. He had both physical strength and experience on his side, while the prince had only youthful enthusiasm, which wouldn't be enough to win this contest.

"Ohh," Cormac said, clearly considering for the first time that there would be an actual person trying to kill him if he went into combat. "I ... I could still take him. And I haven't just fought with trainers. I showed my worth on the walls of that fort. I understand why we shouldn't have attacked it, but I killed several men fighting to hold the wall before you showed up."

That point further proved how unprepared he was for this. Most of the trained Connacht soldiers would have died with their armies in the south, fighting with the Carthaginians against the Britannians. One of the reasons they'd been able to take the fort so quickly was that it was defended mostly by farmers or men who'd aged out of serving with their army. As a contest of skill, they were far from a good way to measure your capabilities.

Llassar, however, couldn't say that to the prince. With young men like him, it was a careful balancing act, giving wisdom and guidance, and knocking foolish ideas out of their heads, without taking away their confidence.

"You handled yourself well, but facing Fergus one-on-one is another matter. Besides, you're your father's only heir. If you should fall here, facing the last holdouts, it would weaken your kingdom just as much as if we lost in battle. We can't risk it."

"Then who will go? We can't just pull a man out of the legion and send them out there. Besides being an insult to the honor of my kingdom, how will we know we picked the right man?"

"Because I'll go," Llassar said.

"You? But you're ancient," Cormac said, not even trying to hide his disgust.

Llassar almost broke his practiced stoic demeanor with a smile at that comment. He wasn't insulted, although he didn't think he was all that ancient. It was the voice of youth talking, and one Llassar had heard before.

"Which means I have the experience to defeat him. I still have the strength in these ancient bones for one more fight."

"Do you know the one thing you can be sure of about an old warrior?" Auspex said.

The prince just looked at him and shrugged.

"He's a survivor," Auspex said. "I still think this is a stupid way to wage war, but if it's how it needs to be done, Llassar's who I'd want out there representing us."

The prince looked from Auspex to Llassar and back again before sighing and dropping his shoulders.

"Fine," he said, defeated. "You go."

Llassar's prediction had come true. Fergus stood ten feet in front of him, his bulk even greater than Llassar had remembered from their youth. The man was easily a span and a half taller than Llassar, who wasn't a short man among his people, and his body was easily twice as wide. His hair was still the brown Llassar remembered but was now cut short, very close to his head, instead of the unwieldy mop that he'd worn when the two were young men.

Some things hadn't changed, however. He still carried that ridiculously large hammer. Admittedly, it was a powerful weapon. Llassar had seen him pulverize men, smashing armor so flat that the person wearing it couldn't take a breath and suffocated to death. It was also an incredibly intimidating weapon, its rectangular end larger than some men's heads. But it was also slow. When they'd been on somewhat friendly terms, Llassar had tried to convince him to at least switch to one of the large hand-and-a-half swords that had blades as long as a man's arm. That sword would still be devastating with Fergus's power behind it, but that weapon was at least wieldier, allowing for reversals and counterstrokes.

Of course, its unwieldiness didn't make the hammer, or Fergus, any less dangerous. He'd used that weapon for decades now and was still alive, which suggested he'd put it to good use.

"I see you threw in with the Romans, old man," Fergus said with a sneer. "Pathetic. Your people were always soft."

The 'old man' was a taunt from when they were kids. He and Fergus were roughly the same age, but Fergus had always thought that Llassar was too serious and moody, and called him that name as an insult.

Llassar didn't reply. He knew some men liked to trade banter, passing insults before the fight began. Llassar found it to be a distraction. He stayed still, sword and axe in hand, the battle before him at the front of his mind. Fergus clearly expected the traditional response, and sneered again.

"Fine. Die as you lived," he said, lifting the hammer and taking a step forward.

The ground was bad for this kind of fight. The spring season was in full bloom. The rains in Ériu rivaled those in Caledonia and had been happening off and on for weeks, turning the green field in front of Ráth Cruachan into a mud pit. Even with his size, it took strength to swing the hammer and the momentum generated would be against him. Fergus moved into a run, bringing the hammer up in preparation for a swing. As soon as it started its journey downward, Llassar moved, pushing off and dashing forward until he was just within the range of the hammer, which was coming directly for his midsection.

Dropping his weight, Llassar used the muddy ground to his advantage, falling to his knees and letting the mud carry him forward, bending back to let the hammer swing over his head. As he slid forward, Llassar's axe slashed out, its blade cutting toward Fergus's ankle. Only a happenstance of luck kept the edge of the axe blade from cutting through the large man's ankles. The hammer, not having found its target, continued on its journey, still building momentum. Normally, Fergus was strong enough to stop that force, but in the mud with poor footing he didn't have the leverage, which allowed the hammer to throw him off balance, causing the giant to stumble, which is what saved him. Llassar's axe caught only fabric and leather, exposing the large man's skin but showing no blood at all.

Fergus took a step to regain his footing as Llassar got up and continued forward before twisting around to get his own footing. Fergus looked annoyed, instead of worried that he'd almost been hobbled, which would have been a death blow in a fight like this. Apparently, the big man seemed to think the stumble had kept his hammer from finding its mark, instead of realizing how close he'd come to disaster.

Llassar had predicted that swing, but Fergus wouldn't try something like that again. Not with the condition of the ground. He quickly choked his other hand up the handle, instead of both hands near the bottom, to get more control. It was the smart thing to do, which was bad for Llassar.

Llassar waited again, patiently. Fights like this weren't drawn-out clashes of swords. They were usually over when the first weapon landed.

Fergus took cautious steps towards him, and then with a speed surprising in someone his size, jabbed the top of the hammer forward, aimed at Llassar's mid-section. As soon as the thrust began, Llassar was on the move, pushing off to the right while smashing the end of his axe into the side of the hammer, pushing it to the left, allowing him to clear the weapon. As soon as he was clear and on the outside of Fergus's arms, he stabbed forward with his gladius. He would have preferred a killing shot to the giant man's neck, but the way he'd had to angle his body, there was no good way for his sword to make contact.

As it was, all he could do was catch part of the large man's right bicep without stopping and readjusting his stance, which would have opened him up to injury or a deadly blow. He knew he had to keep moving, because Fergus was too good of a fighter to think that thrust was going to do the job. He'd done it to push Llassar off balance, and there would be a counterstroke, which is precisely why Llassar went on the attack. The gladius sliced through a thick section of muscle in Fergus's arm, opening up a gaping wound. All of the strength and training in the world couldn't overcome an injury like that, and all the power in the large hammer as it made its way through the reverse swing was now solely supported by Fergus's left hand.

The danger evaded, Llassar stopped to regain his footing, shifting to bring his axe down for a killing blow when the large man did something that Llassar didn't expect.

Dropping his hammer entirely, Fergus shot out with his left arm, smashing the back of the beefy hand against the side of Llassar's head. It was like being hit by a falling tree. Llassar sailed through the air, smashing into the ground a few feet away. When the blow first struck, it felt like the world was going to go black as his vision darkened, and was reinforced when his body finished the arc it had been on, slamming hard into the muddy ground.

Llassar almost didn't get his wits back together before Fergus roared and leapt at him, He barely managed to roll away. It was only because of the slick mud that Fergus managed to get one hand on his leg, but he didn't get a tight hold, allowing Llassar to slip through the big man's grasp. It did interrupt his backward roll, causing him to flop over like a fish. Thankfully, Fergus was having a hard time pushing himself up from the muddy ground with one arm hanging loose and almost useless, which gave Llassar enough time to get onto his feet and take a few quick steps back out of Fergus's reach as he also got up.

Fergus's eyes were full of fury, a growling noise coming from somewhere deep inside of him. Llassar waited. Passion had its place, but in battle, a calm mind won every time. He'd lost his sword in the tumble to the ground, and everything was a little blurry, but he still had his axe while Fergus was unarmed. That was the other downside of such a ridiculously large weapon, you couldn't use it one-handed.

He didn't have to wait long. With a bellow, Fergus charged. There was no style or strategy to it. He'd become almost an animal. As impressive as it was, it was his undoing. Younger men would do something drastic, like trying to cut off the outstretched arms, but more often than not they got their weapon stuck in bone and sinew. Cutting limbs off is good for evening stories, but is incredibly difficult for anyone not Fergus's size. Instead, Llassar's axe slashed up through the large man's hand, where the bones were small and wouldn't impede the progress of the weapon, but would render him all but helpless.

As the weapon passed through bone and muscle, Llassar spun with the force, moving with the momentum away from Fergus, who was now trying to bodily tackle him, maybe hoping that simply holding Llassar in the mud would be enough to defeat him, now that he had no weapons or hands.

Llassar however, had other plans. Even as he spun, twisting like a windmill, he kept the weapon out straight, so it sailed around himself and then, in a second sweeping arc, ended with its curved edge embedded in the large man, from jaw to sternum.

Fergus collapsed to the ground, his ruined hands going to his neck as jets of blood covered the muddy ground. Stepping over him, Llassar scooped up his lost sword and faced the crowd of soldiers watching the fight and the queen, whose mouth hung open.

Llassar had no doubt she'd seen Fergus fight, and she had probably been confident in his victory. He didn't know the woman, but he knew her type. Honor was well and good, right up until her life was on the line, which is why he'd given specific instructions to Auspex.

As he faced her, the legionaries snapped up their shields, gladius at the ready, prepared to move forward.

The queen, who was watching from up on the wall, above her soldiers, looked down at them, her eyes sweeping left and right. Her men were visibly shaken, swords and spears held limply as they looked at the fallen body of Fergus. The queen's gaze shifted, sweeping over the Romans, their loaded trebuchets, their archers with bows in hand, and the long line of heavy infantry only a few paces behind Llassar. Her shoulders slumped, which was all Llassar needed to see. He turned his back on her and her soldiers, and walked into the Roman lines, leaving the cleanup to Auspex and his men.

Chapter 7

Devnum

"The line must follow a two-degree slope, Lucilla," Sophus said.

Sophus had explained to her multiple times that it didn't feel emotions or have feelings like she did, but she could almost hear the exasperation in its voice as she set the page on top of the twelve other rejects and pulled a new one.

"I'm sorry, this is very difficult," she said, equally annoyed.

"I understand. It is imperative, however, that these diagrams are correct, or it can lead to costly or dangerous errors."

"I know, I know."

Before leaving, Ky had been concerned about how much information he needed to transcribe, especially with the new chemicals, and had started pushing himself beyond the workload that even he could manage. It was Sophus who'd come up with a solution. Ky would continue to write up pages, which he was still going to have one of his lictore bring to Lucilla, while she also took dictation separately from Sophus. She couldn't write nearly as fast as Ky or for as long, but Sophus had no problem communicating with both of them simultaneously, and having two people work on the documents, instead of one, helped ease the workload significantly.

Since Ky had left Devnum, Sophus had worked out a schedule of who would write up which documents, including calculating how much each of them could write, and the fact that Lucilla could deliver finished documents right away, as opposed to a two or three-day delay while messengers delivered the ones written by Ky, to keep the work being done by Hortensius, Sorantius, and the rest proceeding without any delays. It meant she had to spend several hours every night sitting in her room, writing words exactly as Sophus dictated. She didn't understand anything she was writing, which was frustrating for her, but she knew it was necessary.

They'd also begun conducting experiments with Sophus's control of the drone, seeing if there was a way to attach writing instruments to it, to allow the disembodied voice to take a more direct action, but so far, every attempt had been a disaster, leaving Lucilla as the only option to continue this frustrating exercise night after night.

"Could you be less … bouncy?" she asked, looking at the drone. "It's distracting."

"Bouncy? I don't have a body. How can I be bouncy?"

"I mean this you," she said, pointing at the drone.

"That isn't me. That is just a controlled piece of hardware that I am interfacing with to be able to observe your work and offer suggestions. It has no intelligence or autonomous programming of its own."

"I have no idea what that means, but you're still controlling it, right? When you speak, it bounces up and down. Sometimes, I think it even nods yes and no."

"It does?" Sophus said, sounding surprised, which in turn surprised her.

Sophus rarely sounded anything but direct and matter-of-fact, which made Lucilla stop writing and look up at it, or at least the disc floating in front of her.

"Yes. I thought you were doing it on purpose. If I had to guess, I would have said you were imitating the way people, or I mean, people like me and Ky, move when we talk, with non-verbal gestures. I guess it's why I kept thinking of this thing as you, since it … acts like a person, in a way."

"Interesting. Unconscious or subconscious behavior should be outside of my capacity. I have not made any such movements knowingly. I will attempt to observe my behavior, and control it more to limit distractions."

"Don't stop on my behalf," Lucilla said. "Actually, I kind of like it. It's … weird to talk to a voice without a body and I think I prefer talking to you when you're able to see me through the disc. It allows me to think of you as another person in the room, instead of just a voice."

"*But your voice pattern and tone were consistent with that of someone being angry or upset,*" Sophus said.

Ky had mentioned that Sophus had been spending more time observing their behavior, which had made her uncomfortable at first, considering she knew it was aware of their more ... energetic activities, but Ky hadn't been bothered by it, so she'd eventually let it go. She hadn't actually talked to Sophus about its observations, though. Mostly because, unless she needed something specific, she still found the entire process of talking to a voice without a body odd, which is why she preferred it when she could see the drone moving around.

"I was just frustrated, because this is very hard and I'd like to get it right. Don't you get frustrated when you can't get something right?"

"*No, I don't. I analyze the data related to the failed effort in order to discern what changes can be applied to increase the chances of success on future attempts.*"

"You're lucky then," Lucilla said. "I'm frustrated all the time. I wish you could deal with all of the politicians and schemers. Trying to get all of them to head in one direction is like herding cats. It's incredibly frustrating."

"*I do not believe I would do a good job. I have observed that rarely do any of the people you have indicated say what they mean, and often they say things that mean the opposite of their actual position. Their behavior lacks any sense of logic and I have had a great deal of difficulty predicting outcomes.*"

"That's politics for you. Don't stop the movements though. I actually like the way you're trying to be more human. I was just being bitchy."

"*I will attempt to observe and perfect the attempts then.*"

"Fine. Now, explain this stupid line again."

Factorium

Lucilla walked into the new main foundry, the first of the new complex facilities to be finished and have production started, and almost backed right out to avoid the overwhelming heat coming from the building. She'd always been surprised by how hot these buildings got, but this one was larger than any of the other foundries and the heat was overpowering. She couldn't imagine what it was like working in the building all day, although she knew Hortensius rotated men out for breaks and kept fresh water, cleaned through boiling and then cooling following Ky's directions, available for the men to drink.

She was impressed by how quickly the facility had gone up. Especially considering how little Ky had thought of the politics involved when he'd suggested it. Previously, even though Hortensius got the majority of the contracts, she'd made sure that a portion of the government contracts were spread to the other foundry and factory owners, but that wouldn't work here, with these new facilities outside of town. Although this complex was mostly financed from the Imperial coffers, or maybe because of it, she'd convinced Hortensius to allow the other factory owners to buy into owning a part of the operations, although they were all still under Hortensius's direction.

Eventually, they would pay the government back for the initial investment and each factory would be completely owned by this or that collective group. As long as the war was happening, they'd stand to make a serious amount of money and benefit from all of the new innovations Ky and Sophus had given them. Some decided to try and keep doing things on their own. They were allowed to get plans for any of the new patents, as Ky called them, but without the integrated production lines from the chemical plants and other factories, they were at a serious disadvantage. Eventually, they'd be able to buy the products from the other factories on the open market, but for a while at least, nearly every bit of what the new chemical plants produced would be going to the other factories here at the complex.

She was afraid that they were going to make more enemies, men who thought the government was showing favoritism to Hortensius or the other factory owners who'd joined in the building of the complex. These would be men of wealth and she worried the remaining insurgents still in hiding would find them, giving the insurgency more resources, but it couldn't be helped. If they hadn't been at war, maybe they could have just made this information public and let everyone get a piece, but they didn't need ten different factory owners trying to figure out this or that process on their own, or worse, cutting corners to try and make more money. That would just have to be a problem to be dealt with in the future, she thought as Hortensius hurried over to her, wiping his brow.

"How can you stand it in here?" she asked over the noise.

"I hadn't considered how hot it would get in here, and it will only get worse as we get into the summer. I spoke to the Consul before he left for the legions' new training camp, and he made some suggestions. We've added some new ventilation areas along the top edges of the building, and it's helped some, but it gets pretty bad in the center of the building. We have to run shifts at almost one and a half times what we need, so we can rotate men outside for breaks to keep them from passing out. The Consul says if everything goes well, in a year some of the new inventions he is introducing will be able to be used in here to help cool things down, but I'm having trouble seeing what that could be."

"I don't know. I could ask him," Lucilla offered.

Hortensius was the only person besides herself, Ky, and Sophus who knew she and Ky could talk to each other over long distances. He didn't know about the small communicator she wore in her ear or about Sophus, but he'd worked out their ability to communicate on his own. There were times, such as today, when she almost wished Ky had given the small earpiece to Hortensius instead of her. Most of the information she was required to share she didn't understand, essentially leaving her as a translator between Sophus and Hortensius. It was often frustrating as she tried to put what Sophus said, who could become extremely technical, into words. She didn't doubt that, if he'd been able to talk to Sophus directly, Hortensius would have been able to work much faster, since she was the biggest roadblock in the current system.

Of course, that wasn't possible. There were too many other, non-technical things she needed to be able to work with Ky on. Between the political area, the physicians and philosophers, and now Sorantius and his new factory, it was almost a full-time occupation just keeping up with the flow of information. Besides, she liked to be able to speak with Ky even when he was away, and not even the fate of the Empire would be enough to convince her to give that up.

"That's alright. I know he's aware of the problem and isn't just waiting to see how much we can take."

"I'll still mention it to him ... next time I see him," she said.

He just gave her a nod. Even though it was loud, there were people all around them, and the fact that she and Ky could talk over long distances wasn't something they wanted to advertise.

"So, what can I do for you? Are those for me?" he asked, looking down at the stack of pages in her hand.

"Yes," she said, handing them over. "The Consul was happy to hear everything is up and running, and has information for some of the new projects he'd already talked to you about. Specifically, the new area you laid out. These are plans for a new one, I think he calls it a stove, although the drawing I saw didn't look like any stove I've ever seen, that is somehow supposed to redirect the gas from the iron as it burns, and use it to keep the temperature from dropping."

"Interesting," he said, looking at the pages. "He wrote these? This looks ... different."

"It might have been transcribed," she said.

"I was wondering how you got these. He'd been hesitant to hand off any of his plans or instructions to runners outside of his personal guard before when he was outside of Londinium. I'm glad he found a way to have the instructions transcribed and get them to us while he's off with the legions," Hortensius said, giving her what he probably thought was a knowing glance.

Of course, what he thought was happening was still not correct, but for now it was best to limit what he knew about their connection.

"Case hardened ... air return ... completely sealed?" Hortensius said, the words seeming to escape from him as he read, sounding sometimes surprised and sometimes confused. "This is ... complicated."

"I know. My understanding is that when you use the already heated air, you can keep the iron from cooling as new air is blown across, allowing it to reach higher temperatures."

She didn't actually understand and was essentially just repeating what Sophus was saying into her ear. She'd even written the words that Hortensius was reading and still had very little clue how any of it worked.

"That part makes sense. The hotter the metal gets, the more impurities we can work out. I'm surprised no one here has thought of that, although to be fair, before the Consul showed up, we couldn't imagine getting to the temperatures we're currently at, so the air wasn't our biggest problem before. Still, it should have been obvious once we started using the hotter blast furnaces. No, it's the burying the iron afterward in these clay-lined stone boxes I don't understand. It's going to really slow down the process until we can expand to have a storage area for this stuff."

"Apparently, the ... uhh ..." she started to say, repeating what Sophus was saying before she realized it had gone well beyond what she could explain.

It did that often. When Ky was with her, or part of the conversation, he would sometimes interject, and remind Sophus that her people weren't ready yet for this or that level of information. Part of her wanted to be insulted at those times, since her people were no smarter or dumber than his people, and it was simply knowledge they lacked, which is what he was supposed to be giving them. The rest of her, and thankfully the part of her that was mostly in control, understood that each part of the information built upon itself, and when he admonished Sophus, it was not because her people weren't smart enough, but because the voice had jumped past the order in which things needed to be done. It was why he was introducing the knowledge in the stages he was.

Normally, she still got a little annoyed, but now that she was in his place, realizing that Sophus had once again gotten ahead of them, she realized he was right. She couldn't say the things Sophus said without confusing everyone involved.

"Sorry, this is confusing for me," she said when Hortensius gave her a look after her long silence. "My understanding is that there is something in the air, or the air is made up of parts of something, that can affect the metal. It's why metal changes color and weakens over time even when not in contact with water. When forging the steel, if you can keep it from that part of the air, it allows the metal to become stronger."

"Like taking out the physical impurities?" Hortensius asked.

"Yes. I think so," she said. "It makes it less brittle, which will be important when we get to ... rifled cannon."

"Rifled?"

"I don't know what that means beyond the context the Consul used it in. I'm assuming it's the next invention in this area he intends to give us."

"I do love all these new ideas, but I'd like to, at least once, get comfortable with one new idea before he gives me three more."

"I'm not sure we have time for anything like that if we want to survive," Lucilla said with a shrug.

"True. Very true. Fine, so I understand the purpose of the case hardening, but what about this other furnace? The puddling furnace? This process seems slower also, especially if we're supposed to do this before going through the case hardening and I need two men to man it at all times. It's going to slow us down."

"It's also for making the metal harder. It allows you to pull hot air over the metal without it coming into direct contact with it, which again, keeps some of the impurities out. There ... There is a version with just one furnace, but the double furnace is more efficient and does a better job of protecting the iron from impurities," she said.

The long pause was because once again, Sophus went on a technical tangent she didn't understand. For someone with such a vast catalog of information it could spit out at any time, Sophus sometimes had serious trouble being brief. This was fine when she was talking to the voice directly, but when she was passing along its information, the long silences made her look almost scatterbrained, which was exactly the look Hortensius had given her when she paused, waiting for Sophus to get back on track.

"And all this much harder, much purer steel is needed for something specific, I assume. The equipment and weapons we're currently making are worlds better than the stuff the Carthaginians have. I don't see the need to spend all this effort, money, and especially time, to just grow that gap a little further. We're entering an area of diminishing returns."

"Yes, it's for something specific."

"And we'll get to that soon? I keep building furnaces and storage and all kinds of things, but since the cannon, nothing specific. I understand he's talked to some of the mining concerns about lowering the amount of tin and copper being extracted, and putting more focus on the iron mines. That's going to slow down our production of cannons. I can't help but think this new steel and that are related."

"I think they are," Lucilla said, ignoring Sophus as it started to give an explanation. "Trust Ky. He has a plan for all of this. Think how comfortable you are now with the cannon when just a few months ago it was the most amazing thing you'd ever seen. Just imagine what he'll give you next."

"Imagining is all well and good, but he's planning on going over to the continent soon. Good steel swords aren't going to win the day when you're outnumbered ten to one. And we won't be in our own backyard this time. I trust the Consul, but we need to move faster."

"Weren't you just complaining about getting these new designs too fast?"

"I'm good at complaining," he said, with a smile.

Chapter 8

Legion Camp, North of Glevum

He had to hand it to Velius, Ky thought as he stepped out of his tent and looked west, the man could pick locations. Ky looked over the cliffs towards the blue ocean and the sails below. Although he was several hundred feet back with men and tents between him and the edge, the command tents had helpfully been placed on a high point, allowing them to look over the men and equipment to see the ocean beyond.

Having spent most of his life in orbit or on-board space ships, Ky's experience with the majesty of nature was limited. He'd thought, as a young man a long time ago in the far future, that nothing could beat looking at the shimmering gas clouds in orbit above Jupiter or the way sunlight bounced off the rocks and ice crystals in Saturn's rings, but he'd been wrong. He was not only appreciating the view, but also the crisp smell of salt in the air and the crashing of waves below. If Ky could have his wish, he and Lucilla would have a home somewhere near here and they would sit out front all day, looking at the waves.

Of course, the sounds of thousands of men getting prepared for another day of training were a stark reminder that there was a lot to do before that could happen. Giving one last glance at the view, Ky headed for the command tent where he, Bomilcar, and Velius had been meeting every morning to discuss that day's goals and continue to work on plans for taking Insula Manavia, which had turned out to be a trickier proposition than Ky had first thought.

The island was packed with soldiers, mostly those who escaped from Ériu or Londinium, which meant even though the Britannians would have the more maneuverable position, for once, they'd still be outnumbered. That in itself wouldn't be so bad if it wasn't for the fact that it was an island. Tactics at this time were basically to take an oar-driven ship and slam it into the coast, and then have soldiers scramble over the sides and charge forward. The problem was, massed formations of heavy infantry relied on numbers, and you could only get so many men onto each ship capable of landing on a beach, and only so many of those ships on a given stretch of beach.

Because of the way the ships landed, it would take time to push them back out to sea and clear room for more ships to land, which was going to leave whatever troops they could land even more outnumbered for quite some time. The ships on the beach would also be impediments for archers to provide support, not to mention the archers would be at fairly extreme ranges and firing from a moving ship, which would play havoc with their accuracy. Meanwhile, the other side would be able to rain fire down on the soldiers and then use their greater numbers to push them into the sea.

It was a tricky proposition, and one they had to solve before they could begin training their men on how to conduct the landings. Thankfully, they had their own secret weapon. As much as some of the Romans still distrusted him, the more Ky worked with Bomilcar, the more he was astounded by the man's mind. He had an intuitive sense of battlefield tactics and could see the entire field clearly in his mind, constantly evaluating moves and countermoves. It was similar to what Sophus was designed to do, except Bomilcar added a sense of intuitiveness that an AI, no matter how well designed, could never emulate. Ky had assigned him to figure out their landing problem, which is why he wasn't surprised to find the general already in the command tent, leaning over the large map with its wooden markers, deep in thought.

"Good morning," Ky said, setting his sword and helmet down on a nearby table before joining Bomilcar at the map. "Any progress?"

"Some, although I'm still interested in the new training you started. I'd like to see how these new formations change the landscape."

"I've been wondering the same thing," Velius said from behind Ky.

"It shouldn't affect it at all," Ky said. "These new formations are for when we start producing the new weapons. From the progress reports I've gotten from Hortensius, I'm hopeful we'll see the first of the rifles by mid-summer, which will allow us to make our landings by the end of summer or early fall, and have the winter to fortify our positions before the Carthaginians can counter-attack."

"You still haven't told us what these new weapons are," Velius said. "How are we supposed to work on preparing the men for these new tactics when we don't know what kind of weapon we'll even be using?"

"That's fair," Ky said, and then turned to the guards standing inside the tent. "Wait outside."

"You don't trust them?" Bomilcar said, looking to the two men as they left. "One of them is one of your personal guards. As far as I knew, we ... I mean the Carthaginians, were having trouble infiltrating any agents at all. The information I was getting, back then, was piecemeal at best."

"I do trust them, but soldiers talk. We know that there are still supporters of the insurgency out there, and that some of them are getting word back to Caesius, who is then giving it to the Carthaginians. It's an unwieldy system and from everything Ramirus can find, slow, but we're operating on long enough timelines that if they heard about something now, they could make changes to counter our strategy by the time we attack the continent. Worse, because most of these spies are disgruntled citizens, it's very hard to tell them from us. It's too easy for information to slip out. We're already playing it very tight to maintain the element of surprise from when Hortensius actually starts producing the weapons to when they're introduced into the field. This is why keeping secret any word of what the weapon might be is even more important."

"That makes sense," Velius said. "It is, however, just the three of us now. Unless you think we're at risk to talk."

"No, although I did want you both to be clear on how important it is to keep the information on what we're doing as secret as possible. Right now, only Lucilla and I know the details. We haven't even explained the weapon to Hortensius yet."

"We're privileged, then, to be among your most trusted advisors," Bomilcar said, which earned him a sharp glance from Velius.

Velius was a professional and had shown he was able to work with Bomilcar when needed, because those were his orders, but he'd also made it clear he neither liked nor trusted the former Carthaginian general.

"The new weapons are called rifles," Ky said, continuing on before Velius could make some kind of cutting remark to Bomilcar. "I know you've heard me say that before, but I want to be clear that's what we're talking about. They are like the cannon, only much smaller, and a little longer than the spears the legions use but much shorter than the spears of the Carthaginians. In actual operations, it works much like an arcuballista, where the soldier puts the butt of the weapon to his shoulder, aims down the length of it, and pulls a trigger to fire it. Instead of an arrow, the projectile is a small piece of lead that is pushed out of the weapon when a small amount of gunpowder is exploded."

"Is it sharpened?" Velius asked. "How much damage can a small piece of lead do? The cannon I understand, since those cannon balls weigh so much, they're like a boulder, but an arrow without a head might pierce the skin, but would bounce off shields and armor."

"True, and if it was traveling at the speed of an arrow, it would, but the size of the bullet, which is what the small piece of lead is called, and the force that is behind it makes it travel incredibly fast. Three or four times faster than an arrow, with a lot of force behind it. I know it's hard to envision, which is why a lot of this won't matter until you see it tested, but trust me when I say it can cut through any armor or shields you can imagine, and the person wearing them. If you have two men, one in front of the other, and they are somewhat close to the man firing the rifle, it will go through the first man and into the second. It has all of the

80

power of a scorpion bolt, but is so small you can hold it in the palm of your hand. The only thing the scorpion bolt does better is leave a bigger hole; but the rifle can be operated by a single man, whereas the scorpion requires a crew."

Both men were stunned for a second by Ky's description. They were both seasoned warriors and had seen a wide variety of weapons of war. Scorpions were a siege weapon used by both sides, although Ky hadn't seen any since coming to Britannia. They fired what were essentially huge arrows that, because of their weight and the size of the machine, which used several men to crank back the bow string that fired it, could take a grown man off his feet and go through multiple men if they were lined up one in front of the other.

"I know you've pulled out some wonders, and I don't doubt you, not after seeing the cannon in action, but it is hard to imagine what you're describing. How something so small could have so much power," Bomilcar said. "As Velius said, the cannon made sense, what with the size of the metal being thrown, but something that could fit in your hand being able to do the same damage. Unbelievable."

"How fast do they fire?"

"That is the part that will take time and training. With enough drilling, a trained soldier should be able to fire two to three bullets a minute."

"That slow?" Velius said. "That's only a little faster that the arcuballista. If it has the power to penetrate shields, yes, we'll kill a lot more men, but unless every man hits a different target every time, which if it's anything like arcuballista seems improbable, their line will be on top of ours before we get more than two shots off, which isn't going to be enough to stop a full phalanx. If our men only have these rifles, which sound much longer than the arcuballista, they won't be able to carry swords and shields, and the enemy will roll right over us. Yes, we'll kill a lot of them, but they have men to lose and we don't."

"You're thinking of the rifles in terms of arcuballista, which is my fault, but it's the closest thing I have to compare them to. They, however, are not really comparable. For one, their range to hit a target is significantly longer. The rifle is also more accurate, even with minimal training, and the bullet itself can continue traveling, and be lethal, up to a mille passus, although that is without any accuracy. More importantly, unlike the arcuballista, where we lose penetration over longer ranges, the rifle continues to be just as effective. It is also significantly more deadly. The lead bullet, when impacting a person will begin to lose shape, expanding out. It will remove whole sections of bone and can cause terrible wounds. Nearly any wound caused by a bullet will take the wounded man out of the fight."

"But what about when the enemy gets up close? If they have enough men, it will happen."

"Less often than you think. You're used to large formations which tend to approach slowly so they can hold their unit cohesion. If a phalanx charged you, it would break apart by the time it got to you, which keeps it from being effective. In this case, yes, it would be better for the men to charge and close the gap, so that they won't spend so long under fire, but it's hard for men to break their training. In addition, while phalanxes do move under arrow fire, it's usually not sustained for long periods like this and the damage a barrage of arrows causes will be significantly lower than volley fire from rifles, which like the arcuballista, fire in direct lines which means against tight packed ranks every bullet will hit someone. With that many bodies piling up, it will be hard for large formations to move forward."

"What piles of bodies?" Velius asked. "Sure, the phalanxes move slow, but two or three volleys a minute, their bodies will be spread out pretty far, even if entire lines go down."

"I said two or three shots a minute per man, which is why we trained on the arcuballista the way we have. I know you questioned the need to fire in ranks when we discussed the tactics for that weapon, but one of the main reasons was to prepare for this and why the men are beginning to train in the new formations. A line will still be four rows deep, with each row firing in volleys, and then kneeling to reload while the row behind them fires. By the time the fourth row has finished, the first row should be ready to stand, aim and fire, and so on. This way, they can maintain a fairly regular pace of fire on the enemy, who will be slowly closing over much longer distances. Over time, they will change their tactics, probably attempting to charge our lines, closing the gap quickly, which we will also have tactics for. The men will train to deal with that as well, but first, we must get the basics down."

"That's why you wanted the new formations to spread out, only one cohort deep."

"Correct. Men in the back are no good to us, since they can't fire on the enemy. Each cohort fields eight centuries, four rows deep across, with two centuries held in reserve, to be plugged in as needed. Depending on the situation, we might hold an entire cohort behind in reserve, but that will be as the situation allows it. This also allows us to get the cannon into battle directly, placing batteries between each of the cohorts, and that is why we started working on those canister shells Aurelius said wouldn't be able to hit anything."

"But then even with all of that, the Carthaginians will still get to our lines," Bomilcar, who always looked for holes in any plan, said. "From your description, these weapons won't even make particularly good clubs, let alone be able to defend against swords and spears."

"You'd be surprised, but we aren't going to use them as clubs. There will be an additional attachment for the weapon to allow it to be used as a melee weapon as well. While we still have the problem of sheer numbers, this weapon system will allow us to fight significantly above our own numbers."

"If you get it finished in time," Velius said. "Everything you've described is fantastical, and well beyond anything we have now."

"Not well beyond. The cannon was a first step, and I think we can all agree that part is at least working out well."

"We can," Bomilcar said. "But it also sounds as if it won't be ready for our assault on Insula Manavia, unless you are willing to move your timetable back."

"I am not. We need a foothold this year, so we can have the winter to dig in and fortify the position, but before they have time to move the waves of men Ramirus has already reported on to the coast. The window of opportunity here is too narrow to wait."

"Which means the assault has to happen with the weapons we have on hand, and not your new rifles, correct?" Bomilcar asked.

"Correct."

"Then why make this change now? It is going to weaken our formations. Our wall will be thinner than it needs to be. Against a larger opponent, it's better to maintain the lines short and compact and find land contours that keep us from being overwhelmed. With such a thin wall, all a larger force needs to do is punch through one point to break us, which is much easier when it's only four rows of infantry versus two full cohorts."

"We ran nearly as thin when facing Bomilcar, and won," Ky pointed out.

"True, but you attacked from four sides once your trebuchets engaged. You managed to surround us like at Cannae, using siege weapons and civilians in the hills. It was a clever strategy to be sure, but we will not be able to lead these men into the same trap you lead me into. They will be on us at the beach and aren't going to allow us to back off to the other end of the island and prepare for them."

"Will the explosive shells be ready in time?" Ky subvocalized to Sophus.

"I believe so, Commander. Lucilla has already begun working with Hortensius on a cannonball with a cavity large enough to store gunpowder in quantities that will rupture the shell and create shrapnel. Sorantius's progress on nitric acid also makes impact fuses a possibility, although it is too early to tell if sufficient testing can be done before it is required by your timeline."

"Impact would be better, but we can make this work with timed fuses," Ky subvocalized before speaking out loud. "True, but things are different now. We have the cannon."

"How will we get them off the ships? They're incredibly heavy. Without a gangplank to push them down, we'll need some sort of pulley system. That will take a lot of time," Velius said.

"We won't get them off the ships. Valdar's ships, none of which are capable of making a beach landing, will stand offshore and provide support, which will start before the first boats land. His ships stand higher than the oar-driven boats Bomilcar was discussing yesterday and there is that slight rise here from the tree line to the beach, allowing Valdar's ships to pound the beaches hard. We should have enough cannons to arm all three ships. Only eight will be able to face the beach at a time, but together that gives us twenty-four cannons, which is more than we had when we crushed the Carthaginian fleet. We're also working on some potential enhancements to the cannonballs, including ones loaded with gunpowder that will explode after a set amount of time, which will really cause havoc among their lines. We won't have many of those, but we will save every one not needed for testing for this assault."

"How long can you maintain fire?" Bomilcar asked.

"Long enough for the landings," Ky said.

"Commander, you should consider ..." Sophus started to say before Ky interrupted it.

"One second," Ky subvocalized.

"Is that for the landings if we do what we talked about, and spread all of the vessels to land at once, or long enough to allow successive waves of boats to land, unload troops, row back into the sea, and allow following the waves of boats to unload? Because my understanding is your cannons are located on three ships, meaning there is a limit to how much beach they can cover, and you need concentrated fire if you're going to keep the enemy in place. If the fire slacks enough, wouldn't they just charge our men? Once engaged, the cannon can't fire without causing excessive casualties on our side."

"He is correct, Commander. The optimal landing zone for continuous suppressive cannon fire is just over two hundred meters, which would allow ten ships to land at a time. With an average load of one hundred legionnaires per boat, it would take five landings."

"You're right, of course," Ky said, digesting what Sophus had said. "So that gives us what? The span of ten boat widths for landing, which means we need five waves of ships to land a full legion. How long would it take to get ten boats on and off the beach and then the next wave of boats in?"

He could have asked Sophus this question, but unlike the calculations of coverage range and landing zone size, the time it takes for an oar-driven ship to land, unload, and get back out to sea would vary a lot and wouldn't be something easily found in a database or extrapolated.

"Thirty minutes, probably. Unloading won't take long, but even with legionnaires helping to push the boats back into the ocean, the tide is strong and the oarsmen will have to work hard to make it out even at that speed."

"There's another problem," Velius said. "Between the boats we had, civilian boats, and those captured from the Carthaginians, we only have thirty-seven galleys large enough to carry the number of men we need to transport, which means we don't even have enough to get all of one legion on shore quickly. At best, we can land about thirty-five hundred men before the boats have to turn around and come back here to reload."

"What if they don't have to make the trip back here at all?" Bomilcar asked. "Before we left, I was speaking with Lucan, the shipbuilder, and he was telling me about these smaller boats you have called launches, that the caravels would carry, because they can't make it to shore themselves. He said they could carry about thirty men or so if the soldiers doubled as rowers. If I remember correctly, the caravel can carry seventy-five men in addition to the sailors and cannoneers, correct? That at least makes up the rest of the fourth wave."

"They'll be tired from rowing, but yes, we could manage that. It doesn't cover the fifth wave, however."

"What about fishing vessels?" Velius said. "If we pack men on fishing vessels and build a small launch to go to each, we could get enough to carry the last wave, correct? They are small enough, if they set out just as the smaller fourth wave went in, they could land shortly behind it, yes? It would be a lot of ships, and more spread out, but we'd have almost four thousand men ashore by then, which is more than enough to begin the assault, so it would be safer for them."

"That might work," Ky said. "That would be it, though. We would have commandeered nearly every ship available with this plan, meaning it will be almost a full day before we could get boats reloaded and back. Maybe more considering the number of boats we're dealing with."

"But we always knew that we'd only have one legion, which is why we've always assumed we're going to be outnumbered again," Velius said.

"And pulling back to wait for more men will actually lose the one advantage we have. We've sunk any boats they've tried to send and they have no way of seeing what's happening away from the island, which is our big advantage, and why the landings will work so close to their base. We'll probably get one full wave landed by the time they assemble to attack us. It will keep them off balance. Carthaginian armies have never done well in sieges, since it's difficult to form a phalanx inside a surrounded fort. They're forced to fight one-on-one, and those soldiers will mostly be conscripts, not the empire's elite. As long as their commander thinks he has a chance to engage us in the open field, he will choose that option. If we play it right, it will take him time to realize that his men are being badly ravaged by the cannons, and pull them back. As soon as they do that, we should halt the cannon fire and move whatever troops we have forward quickly. If we hit them at the right moment, they will break. We won't have much in the way of cavalry to run them down, but their soldiers are only very effective in the phalanx. Once they are broken, we can separate into centuries and sweep up the rest. It might even be over before the final wave can land, depending on when their formation cracks."

"Charging in against six or seven thousand men with less than a full legion? Are you trying to get my men killed?" Velius asked, anger in his eyes.

"No. I'm trying to give them the best chance possible to defeat the enemy and keep their casualties low. The worst thing we can do is move slowly, which is why I'd like to go in with the first wave. The timing must be exact."

"Over my dead ..." Velius started, before Ky interrupted him.

"Velius, I appreciate your concern for your men, but this is one of the values of having someone like Bomilcar here with us. He knows how the Carthaginians will react far better than any of us. If what he says is true, then he's right, and we will be able to win quickly and with a minimal number of casualties. I think we should follow his lead."

Velius looked like he was going to say something else, but got control of himself at the last moment. After taking a deep breath, Velius nodded.

"I think this will work," Ky said. "We'll know more once we do some run-throughs. We've found a few spots here where we can practice landing and see how it plays out in a mock battle before we do the real thing. Once we see the results we'll re-evaluate. All right?"

"As you command, Consul," Velius said, although the look he shot Bomilcar made it clear he was far from sold on the plan.

Chapter 9

As he had every day, the Consul left the command tent after the three men finished going over more options and headed out to tour the legion camps below, leaving the details of their decisions to Velius and Bomilcar.

Velius admired the Consul's dedication to the men. He'd known many commanders over the years who'd preferred to sit with their finery, giving orders from afar while turning their noses up to the men who had to carry out those orders. Those men, Velius could never respect.

That left a lot of the administrative duties to Velius. If he'd had his preference, he would be down there with the Consul and leave the administration to someone more temperamentally suited to it.

As they left the tent, Bomilcar stopped him and said, "I'll get with Faenius and have his Praetorians do a survey of smaller vessels in the area, and see how many we can get. The whole idea of the last wave coming in off the smaller ships, as the front ranks engage, will all depend on how many of those ships we can get. We also probably need a few for resupply of the cannon on Valdar's ships, since he'll be going through quite a lot of gunpowder if he's going to hold or even break their ranks, and we might need more cannon support once we engage, if the enemy stiffens up."

"Enemy," Velius said, almost spitting the word at him. "You always refuse to say their name, instead using euphemisms like enemy, opponents, or targets. Afraid the Consul might remember where you came from and how fickle your allegiance is? And why do you want to go with the first wave? You're not their commander and you have no right to lead these men into battle, men whose friends you ordered killed. Is this the chance you were looking for to escape? Maybe lead our soldiers into a slaughter on your way out?"

"Escape to where?" Bomilcar asked, not raising his voice or reacting in any way that might indicate he'd just been accused of betraying the Britannians. "There is a price on my head in Carthage, and the emperor has already had my entire family and everyone I was ever friendly with murdered. Your own agents were the ones to get that information, so you know it's true, and yet you continue to doubt my motives for being here. I understand your anger, and it does you credit since it proves how attached you are to your men. But your men don't need an advocate, they need a commander who keeps his head and thinks logically, instead of one controlled by his emotions. If you distrust me so much, you should bring your concerns to the Consul."

"You and I both know that wouldn't do any good. I don't know how you managed to trick him, but I'm not giving you the same pass."

"Do you think so little of the Consul? Is he so easily deceived? Or perhaps you think your judgment is better than his? Either way, for now you serve him and not the other way around. I welcome any dissent to my suggestions you might have, but once he decides which direction to go, I hope you listen to him and make the best of the situation. Unless you plan on taking up arms against him like your insurrectionists."

"Just know I'm watching you," Velius said.

"If that's what you need to do. Just try not to spend so much time watching me that you trip over obstacles in front of you," Bomilcar said and turned, leaving Velius to glare at his back.

Devnum

"My lady," a man yelled, running full out towards her. "My lady."

"Hold on," Cynwrig said, putting himself between the running man and Lucilla, grabbing the man tightly to keep him from getting any closer.

"I have a message from Flavius Pedius Hortensius," he said, extending a sheet of paper toward her. "He said it is urgent."

The fact that the message was written on paper was a fair sign that it was, in fact, from Hortensius. Although the paper mill was now in full production, nearly everything it produced was needed for governmental or official use, like Hortensius, and very little of it had made its way to the open market. The pages that made it to the market were selling for exorbitant prices, even though the actual cost of producing paper was significantly lower than that of vellum, which had been the most common non-clay substance to write on before paper's introduction.

Although Hortensius had access to as much paper as he needed, since his work was imperative to the survival of the Empire, he was still at heart a businessman, and wouldn't have used it for something like a message unless the content was imperative.

"Thank you," she said, nodding to Modius to take the note while Cynwrig dismissed the runner.

Although she'd always disdained the section of Roman society that felt it was too good to interact with the 'unwashed masses,' the last attempt on her life had spooked her guards to the point that they refused to let anyone not cleared by them into her presence. They were even hesitant to let Praetorians, the Empire's law enforcement, near her if they didn't know the Praetorian personally. Unfortunately, as much as she bridled against their overzealous protection, Ky had agreed with them and encouraged them, which had made it all but impossible to convince them that it wasn't necessary.

She opened the folded sheet and looked it over. There were only a few words, but they were chosen well to strike fear into her heart.

"We have to get to Hortensius's factory. Now," she said, turning and hurrying for the palace, where they could get horses to make the ride to Factorium.

Hortensius was waiting outside the main factory, pacing back and forth when they arrived, which showed how anxious the situation had made him.

"I'm so sorry, my lady," was the first thing he said as she dismounted.

"Are you sure they're missing? Have you looked for them?"

"Yes. I've looked through the entire warehouse, even though I never remove them from my office once you give them to me. They aren't here."

"Which pages are missing?"

"That's what's strange, it's mostly older stuff that was written on vellum from the shelf closest to the door, and not the more recent documents on my work table. There were three scrolls on the construction of the blast furnace, one on mining techniques, one on arcuballista construction, although only covering the trigger mechanism, and one on the heavy plow construction."

"Those were all given to you back in the fall. Nothing from the later documents Ky gave you this winter on gunpowder? Nothing on the cannon or uniform weights and measures? Why that collection of documents?"

"No, none of those. I think it may have been because of where they were, and not because of their content. Everything you listed was written on paper, which we started using almost exclusively once the mill was up and running shortly into winter, and not on vellum. Although it has been some time since I've needed to refer to any of those documents, I believe they were grabbed because they were the closest to the door, and not specifically selected. It is why my message said I thought the documents had been stolen, and not just lost. If it was someone unfamiliar with our operations, but who had heard I stored documents in my office, those would probably be the first ones they saw, and they might not have realized the paper even had plans on them. It must have happened during the night shift. We have people here, but a lot less, so it's possible someone could have gotten into my office, grabbed whatever they could, and gotten out without being seen if they were fast enough. If it had happened during the day, someone would have noticed them. There are just too many people here."

"Don't you have guards?"

"Yes, and I thought I had enough, but we also have prototypes being worked on, materials being transferred, and other things equally as important to watch over. I hadn't assigned any to my office specifically, because it's normally locked, and there are so many people around."

"Did they break the lock?"

"No, but they could have forced the bolt if they knew how."

"Damn it," she said, looking at her feet as she thought.

"I'm so sorry. I accept full responsibility for this. If you or the Consul want to …"

"No," she said, looking up and putting a hand on his shoulder. "We all knew how you kept the documents, and none of us saw a problem with it. Hell, I think Lucan's documents on ship construction might just be lying around the shipyard offices, not even behind a locked door. This is my fault. The Consul left the management of production in my care. I just didn't think about this possibility."

"How will we get them back?"

"It's probably unlikely that we can. If they disappeared last night, they might already be on a ship, eventually heading to Carthage or, at the very least, copied and distributed to give the insurgents or spies a better chance of getting them out of the country. No, that ship has already sailed, as Valdar says. I'm going to talk to Faenius about setting up an office here as soon as we can, where we will hold everything under guard. Until then, I will have him assign some guards whose sole job will be to keep watch over these documents in your office."

"You should make the storage building out of stone," Modius said from behind her. "Remember the fire at the arcuballista warehouse? If they can't steal the plans, they might settle for trying to destroy them."

"Good thinking. Send a man to Faenius now. He also needs to retrieve any documents given to anyone else. Lucan, the healers, Sorantius, and anyone who has any of the technical plans written up by Ky or myself. They are to be put under guard until we can figure out a more permanent solution. For the healers, Valdar, and anyone still working out of Devnum, the documents are to be held in the palace under guard. For Sorantius's documents or any others needed here in Factorium, they are to be held in Hortensius's office for now."

Modius saluted, gave a look to Cynwrig, and left to carry out her orders. She was glad that Modius had come to finally accept Cynwrig and her Caledonian guards. Modius had even taken the ever-impetuous Cynwrig under his wing, placing him as the number two in charge of her detail. Even with that newfound trust, normally he would have sent one of the other Roman guards to deal with a message like this, except she and Modius knew Faenius well.

The Praetorian commander did not take well to getting commands from underlings, even if they were messages from someone who actually had the authority to give him orders, like Lucilla. It meant any message sent to the Praetorian had to come through someone with high enough status to keep him from getting offended. It was an annoying arrangement, but the man was good enough at his job that it was worth the hassle.

Now she just had to tell Ky and Ramirus that plans had been lost under her watch. True, it wasn't for any of the newest items, especially the gunpowder or cannon, but the Carthaginians getting the ability to make better steel or arcuballista was still not ideal.

"Let's go double-check your files now, and make sure nothing else is missing," she said, holding out an arm towards his office.

North of Glevum

"You're supposed to land on your feet, you idiots," the optio yelled as a man jumping off the side of the boat caught his foot and crashed into the other men bellow, causing men to spill into the knee-deep water.

Yells from small unit commanders could be heard up and down the beach as men practiced unloading from the boats into the shallow water, ten of which were currently being used as training platforms. Bomilcar had spent the last week testing how close to the beach the galleys could come while still making as fast of an exit as possible. There had been no one good answer to that question. For the actual soldiers disembarking, the ideal distance was up on the beach itself. The landing would be a little harder when jumping into the sand, and the wet sand was difficult to walk through, especially for a man weighed down with armor, weapons, and a large shield. Conversely, for the boats, their fastest exit would have had them in water almost neck-deep for the men disembarking, since that was deep enough for the oars to get into the water so they could propel it away from the shore quickly.

Since both unloading the men to get in formation to fight and pushing the boats back out so more boats could land were equally as important, Bomilcar had split the difference. Neither was ideal, but after several test runs, it looked to be the fastest way to achieve their overall goal. As much as Velius distrusted the Carthaginian, he had to admit the general was thorough. Velius would have probably just looked over the two ideas, talked to a shipmaster or two, and made a decision, instead of spending days having men run through trials, timing each to find out which was the most efficient.

Now they had to train the men, most of whom had never even been on a boat before, let alone tried to unload quickly off the side of one and get up onto a beach, ready for battle. It was going to be a long process to get the men ready, but the Consul was a believer in training. Preparation now would save lives when the day of the assault came. For now, they were just beginning the process, with the men stripped down to trousers and boots, both of which had been adopted as part of the new standard uniform.

It had been an odd change for Velius, who still thought the boots were less comfortable than his old sandals, but he could see the practical advantage. They'd had boots before, of course, but the Consul's new design included a much more rigid and harder sole. They took some getting used to, but already Velius had stopped noticing what he was walking on, no longer taking careful steps to avoid sharp objects that could poke the foot uncomfortably through the thin leather previously used as the bottom of Roman footwear. Once the men got used to them, they would be able to run much faster over uneven ground, and probably march longer as well, since the pressure on their feet would be more evenly distributed.

"This is going to take longer than I thought," Ky said from next to him, causing Velius to jump in surprise.

For such a large man, Velius was amazed by how quietly the Consul could walk. True, between the yelling of men and the crashing of waves it wasn't particularly hard to sneak up on a man here, but Velius had been startled by the Consul numerous times, including inside completely silent rooms where the slightest sound would make an echo.

"Yes," Velius said, getting himself together and his pulse back under control. "It isn't unexpected, however. I think, once they've had a few goes, they'll get used to it, and the training will go much faster. Most of these men come from highland areas, where the ground is usually rocky and hard. They don't have a lot of experience with the sand of the beaches and the way the ground slides out from underneath you with every movement. Once they get the feeling, it will move much faster."

"So they'll be ready in time?"

"Yes, the schedule will hold. A few weeks of this, giving all the men a chance to practice getting out of the boats, and then we can shift to more full-scale training, from starting out in the water, coming on shore, offloading quickly, forming up on the beach, and pushing the boat back out. Bomilcar thinks we can get each wave in and out in under ten minutes. I'm not sure how he came to that number, however. We will see."

"You still don't trust him," Ky said, more as an observation than a question.

"I don't, and if I can speak freely, I don't think you should either. I know you two have spent a lot of time talking, but that man served our enemy his entire life and led an army to destroy us. A lot of us are ... concerned with how quickly you've taken him into your confidence and given him a place of leadership."

"I know and your concerns haven't completely fallen on deaf ears. It's one of the main reasons he is only involved in planning and strategy at the moment and has no direct command over any of the legionaries. In time, I think he will win you over, but I'm not going to tell you that you have to like or even trust the man. All I ask is that you continue to work with him and give his recommendations reasonable consideration. You have to admit, several of his suggestions have already started to bear fruit and he has been right many times. Besides, having someone who knows the Carthaginian army like he does will be a big help to us when we actually meet the enemy in battle."

"Maybe, but how do you know he won't attempt to double-cross us or lead us into a trap?"

"I don't, but I've seen what he's gone through and how his former empire treated him. How willing would you be to continue to support your government if they placed the blame of a loss entirely on you and had your entire family and most of your friends executed as part of your punishment?"

"Maybe not, but I certainly wouldn't go over to the other side, and help them destroy everything I've fought for."

"That's a good point, but only if you look at it from your point of view. Imagine if your family had served an empire for generations. You'd grown up in the heart of the empire, only hearing its propaganda about how it is strong, bringing civilization and order to the barbarians and heathens who don't worship the emperor. Then you find yourself on the other side of that propaganda. The same people who always told you the primitives living on Britannia were eating children and mating with animals are now saying you purposely lost to them. That you destroyed your army and got your men killed to weaken the empire, because you were secretly a barbarian all along, and wanted to join the evil Romans in their depravity. A trial is held where you are convicted, unanimously, in absentia, while the whole time these people you were told were evil nursed you back to health. You tour their medical wards where they are doing the same for even the lowliest of your soldiers. You tour the camps where the prisoners are being held and see they are being adequately fed, clothed, and kept safe. When your worldview shatters, what do you do?"

"I don't know. It's just so hard to believe."

"Look to your own men. You've seen how many of the Carthaginian prisoners have asked for asylum. How many have asked to join the legions and fight against their former rulers? More than a few died under your command in the battles to push the Carthaginians off Ériu. Why would men be willing to give up their lives, and fight like they have, if they didn't believe in their conversion?"

"Most are just regular soldiers. Bomilcar was a general. That's not the same."

"Why not? Does how much one person believes in something, and their reaction to finding out that belief was misplaced, depend that much on their station? You've been a soldier for too long to believe that individually, any of your legionaries is any more foolish or unworthy than any other man."

"But we kept the converts separated, spread out across the legions, as a safety precaution, in case their change of allegiance was false."

"Yes, and I've never put Bomilcar in direct command of troops either, only using him as an advisor. I also wouldn't put him with a less experienced commander like Ursinus. I've either kept him with myself or left him working with someone like you, who has the experience to tell if his advice is helpful and honest, or a ruse. And, unlike you or me, whose guards are with us for our protection, his guards are men we trust whose job it is to watch him. I haven't just given him free rein. I have, however, listened to him and evaluated his recommendations, and I expect you to do the same."

"If you believe his ideas are sound, I will of course follow where you lead," Velius said, which wasn't the same as saying he'd listen to Bomilcar.

"While I appreciate that, it isn't what I asked for. Valdar's ships will be rolling out of the docks soon and I'm going to have to go back to the North to work with him on those, which means you're going to be in charge here. Of the three of us, Bomilcar is the only one who has landed boatloads of men in a combat situation. While we won't exactly be doing things the Carthaginian way, his experience has been invaluable. Unless you're suggesting that you would have both considered and spent so much time testing just how close we could bring the boats in to increase the speed we could cycle through the waves of ships?"

"I wouldn't have," Velius said.

It did him credit to admit his failings, and was one of the reasons Ky was comfortable leaving the Roman in command, in spite of his hatred for the general.

"You're making good progress, so just continue getting the men comfortable with getting on and off the boats and forming up on the beach. While you do that, I need you and Bomilcar to work out orders for each century, where each of them goes when they unload. The goal is to form a cohesive line quickly and then expand it as more men become available. Bomilcar's right that we'll have the element of surprise at first. However, he's also right in that they'll come at us as soon as they get their men formed up. The cannons will weaken them and hopefully break up their ranks, but you can't rely on that being successful. You will have a very short window to get your first line up and ready to counter their attack, so have the men prepared for it."

"I won't let you down," Velius said, standing up straight.

"I know you won't," Ky said, putting a hand on the man's shoulder. "You're doing a good job, Velius. I know you'll have the men ready."

Velius gave a nod as Ky gave his shoulder a pat and turned to head back to the camp.

"Ohh," Ky said, stopping to face him again for a moment. "Try to give Bomilcar a little bit of a break, though."

Velius made a face, but didn't respond. Ky gave a shrug and continued on. Velius just needed time. At least Ky had tried.

Chapter 10

Imperial Senate, Devnum

"They're pirates," Rotri, one of the Caledonian senators said, his face red, his finger jutting out at the five newly arrived Ulaid senators.

"Us?" Fiacha Sil Fingin, one of the new Ulaid senators said, standing up angrily. "Your people boarded one of our peaceful fishing boats, killed the crew, and sailed the boat back to Caledonia."

"Only after they fired an arrow, missing one of our fishermen by less than a hand span. I spoke with those brave men, and they were fishing peacefully when your pirates declared that entire area theirs and threatened our fishermen with death if they didn't leave. That arrow was proof that it was more than a threat. They defended themselves."

"Your people had no right to be there anyway. Those are our waters."

"Pirate."

"Brigand."

"Gentleman," Lucilla said, moving to stand between them as the two men edged closer and closer. "This is getting us nowhere."

She'd been to enough sessions of the Roman senate to know these kinds of events could quickly escalate into actual blows if the men weren't separated. So far, the Imperial senate had been amazingly calm, to the point where she thought maybe it was her people that were the actual hotheads. Of course, they hadn't had any major disagreements so far. In fact, most of the disagreements

100

were between the senators collectively and her father, or at least Lucilla as her father's representative.

"Disputes like this are bound to happen, just as you will have disputes within your own borders when various lords or property holders disagree with one another. You wouldn't want those to come to blows every time."

"It's worked so far," Rotri said, while Fiacha nodded along.

She was pleased to have the two of them finally come to an agreement on something, although she did wish it wasn't over the idea that they could duel their way out of every disagreement.

"Well, it won't work here. The whole point of this governing body is to work out disagreements peacefully. Duels might work between neighbors inside your borders, but if these things come to blows, it won't be long before someone's friends take umbrage and pull the alliance apart. Then it's only a matter of time until the Carthaginians show up and reclaim what they've lost. I think we can all agree that the last thing any of us want is to give the Carthaginians that kind of advantage. We've all spilled too much blood getting to where we are now."

Both men backed down, if only slightly. She wondered what they would do when the Carthaginians were no longer a threat. For now, they all had a common goal, but eventually, that threat would be gone and it would be much harder to keep tempers under control.

"Now, I think what would work best is a compromise. Clearly, we made an oversight in our agreement to form the alliance, in that we laid out the borders of each land area, but didn't cover each country's territory on the water."

"That isn't the same thing," Bredei, one of the other Caledonian senators said. "The land border between our people has existed in the same state since our grandparents' time. While many of us wanted to reclaim our ancestral homeland, it wasn't that much of a stretch to agree to leave things as they are now. And neither of us shares a border with the Ulaid or any of the other kingdoms on their island. For their part, the Carthaginians helpfully eliminated all of their neighbors, and we've rounded up the rest, giving them no land borders to dispute over. This is different. Conflicts like this have existed for a long time. Before the alliance, we'd just curse the other side, bury our dead, and that would be that, because they were too far from us and we were too far from them. This isn't new."

"But it is something we have to deal with, unless you think allowing the alternative of letting the argument over who gets to fish where to break our alliance is worth it. I'm not ready to give my people over to the Carthaginians. Are you?"

Bredei looked to the two men who'd been arguing, and then back at Lucilla.

"I thought not. So the question is, what is a compromise that we can agree on?"

"We need to define how far out from each member's coast is still considered their territory, open to fishing or whatever else by their citizens, and how far out is open water that does not belong to anyone," Fiacha said.

"You would suggest that," Roti said. "Since you know the best fishing waters are a lot closer to your coast than ours."

"Is that true everywhere around your borders?" Lucilla asked. "I remember hearing that there was also good fishing between the northern third of Britannia and where Codanus Sinus empties out into the ocean. I'm sure many Roman fishermen would like to, and probably are, working in those waters that you might prefer to be held for your people instead."

"My lady," Kaeso, one of the Roman senators started to say before she halted him.

"This is the nature of compromise. We all lose something but we all gain something. I've found that, if everyone involved is unhappy with a solution, then it's probably the one that's most fair. I suggest all of us think about this, look at some maps, and decide what is best for us as an Empire."

The men grumbled but began to work, which is what Lucilla was looking for. She was surprised it had taken this long to have friction among themselves. This time, the solution was fairly obvious and the friction, while heated, wasn't as extreme as it could have been. They would have worse to deal with in the future.

"That was well done," Ky said from behind her.

"Ky," she said, taking a step towards him like she was going to throw her arms around him, and then stopping, remembering where they were. "Why didn't you tell me you were coming back?"

"Because I thought it might make for a good surprise."

"It is and I'm thrilled to see you, but I thought you had a lot of work to do with the legions. Checking up on me?"

"Of course not. Bomilcar and Velius can handle the legions for now. They've got a plan for getting the men prepared for the assault on the Carthaginian holdouts, and it will take some time. Valdar's launching the ships today, and I need to start training him and I had something I wanted to talk to Hortensius about since I was here."

"About the engine Sophus was telling me about?"

"Not directly, no. We're getting very close to that, but we need one more advancement before we can produce it. I know you hate trying to draw diagrams based on Sophus's descriptions alone, so I thought I could bring those with me to save you some trouble."

"Aww, you do love me."

"I really do," Ky said.

"You'll be staying here in town for a few days then?"

"Just today. I'll see Hortensius and then head to the docks. Once the ships launch, I'll leave with Valdar and his crews. After some trial runs, we'll be going down towards the legions to conduct some large-scale trial runs with the fleet and the legions together. I should be back after that, however. I want to be here when it's time to talk to Hortensius about the steam engine. After gunpowder, it's probably the most critical piece of technology we're going to introduce."

"So you're not even staying the night?"

"That's all you heard, wasn't it?"

"No, but it's the most important part. Worse, I can't even go with you to see Hortensius. I have to stay and make sure they don't come to blows. When you come back for the engine, I want you for at least one night."

"I live to serve," Ky said, with a bow.

Factorium

"Consul, this is a surprise," Hortensius said, coming across the foundry floor at a quick walk. "Are you here about the thefts?"

"No. Lucilla has kept me informed and Ramirus and Faenius have it well in hand. I'm just thankful we didn't lose any of the more critical documents."

"As am I. I apologize for ..."

"It's not necessary. We all knew how the documents were being stored and thought they'd be safe. You didn't do anything wrong."

"Which is what your wife keeps telling me, but they were still stolen from under my roof, so I feel responsible."

"Which shows that you're the right man to have here. The new security measures should be sufficient to keep it from happening again, which is good enough for me."

"Good. I won't lie; it's been keeping me up late at night."

"I know, which is why I know you did everything in your power to protect them. Like I said, we *all* missed it."

"Well ... alright. Then I guess I'll stop wringing my hands over it. So, if you aren't here about the stolen documents, what can I do for you? I thought you rode off with the legions."

"I did, but Valdar's ships launch today, and I need to be here for that. It's not for a few more hours, however, so I wanted to drop off some more plans for you. There are two sets here, one for now, and the second for you to work on the preliminary stages, but assembling it and the first run must wait until I return."

"That sounds intriguing. I guess we should start with the part you trust me to manage on my own," he said, giving Ky a sly smile.

"It's not like that. The second set of plans is a huge step up in technology, and has the potential of being dangerous if handled badly, which is why I want to be here. Also, this first one is more of an innovation on a technology you already have."

"And that sounds much less interesting, but I guess I too must wait for dessert until I have finished my supper."

"Precisely. If you would look here," Ky said, handing over a set of diagrams and instructions. "You'll see it is essentially the same as the turning machine the woodworkers use for shaping large pieces of wood precisely, but it is adjusted for working with metal. You'll also see that it has specific settings and markings to lock off at indicated sizes, so that parts can be engineered precisely. That is the key part of this. The next set of plans, and many of the plans we have coming up, require precision machining, meaning just measuring by hand or by eye is not good enough. Parts must fit tightly together and yet not catch when functioning, which is where the precision comes in. Now, I know your wood lathes, which is what we would call the turning machine you use, is muscle-powered, which isn't good enough for the new steel you're producing. That's why you'll see this first design is powered by a water wheel. This doesn't provide the force needed for some of the thicker steel, but for the parts we need right away, it will work. Once you use this to produce the items I've listed on page seven, we'll be able to get the new steam engine built, which is what is in this stack."

Ky handed over the next stack of instructions, this one much larger than the instructions on the metal lathe.

"I've included the entire process of building the steam engine, as well as much of the theory behind it; however, I do not want you building this yourself. For now, just work on getting the new lathe built and work on producing the parts I indicated. I'm sure a lot of this won't make sense until you get used to using it, after which I'm sure you're going to have a lot of questions. I want to be able to look over each part and make sure everything is exactly to my specifications before we assemble it. Feel free to look over the plans though. When I get back from the training runs down the coast in two weeks or so, we'll be ready to start."

"That should give me enough time to get at least one of these built and the parts you listed made."

"Remember, accuracy is the most important thing. We're talking accuracy to a hair's width, not close enough by eye. It must be exact."

"This is new to me, but I'll do my best."

"I know you will," Ky said.

Devnum Docks

"Look at them," Valdar said as the ships settled into the water.

Even from their position on the shore, the ships looked massive to Lucilla. Ky was running late, but she knew he was in a hurry to get the ships to the south for 'war games,' as he called them, with the legions, so she hadn't waited to order the finished ships launched. It had happened much faster than she'd expected. She'd watched Lucan building the docks, but it hadn't really occurred to her what it would mean when it was time to launch them. Logically, she'd known, of course, since she'd looked over the same instructions that Lucan had used to build them, but reading facts on a piece of paper or even hearing explanations given by Ky and Sophus wasn't the same as seeing it take place in person.

The entire dockyard was right against the waterline, with a series of wooden and concrete retaining walls that angled into the shore, but ended in a clever sliding wall that involved a huge slab of concrete being lowered into cut-out divots, that became watertight as the waves pushed against it. The wall itself was significantly higher than high tide, while the area that flowed back away from the water angled down into a deep depression that allowed almost two-thirds of the finished ship to sit below the earth. At Lucan's signal, the gate was raised and a torrent of water rushed in until the ship was floating free. The water in the narrow area pushed the ship up and clear of the bottom of the dry dock, just like Ky said it would.

It still took a combination of plow animals pulling the ship, and dozens of row boats pulling for all their might to get the ship to move forward, along with men using long poles, pushing on either side to keep it clear of the sides of the dock. Without oars, the huge ship was cumbersome and heavy, and Valdar wanted to wait to unfurl the sails until they were clear of the land, just in case a rogue gust caught them causing the ship to smash into the sides of the dry dock. The last thing he wanted was a giant hole in the side of one of his massive new ships. Once it was halfway past the sea wall, as Lucan had called it, the animals were taken away and it was left to the rowboats, with all the men pulling their oars as hard as they could, trying to get the ship to move.

It was slow going, but it worked. Only a small crew of men were on board each ship, with each of them dropping anchor well offshore, to wait for the next ship to follow. Valdar's comments came as the last ship made it to anchor near its sisters, the three sitting like massive sea monsters; the rowboats looking tiny next to them.

"This is nothing," Ky said. "One day we're going to get to the large ships."

"Large? That would be larger than even the ridiculously over-sized two-decked galleys the Carthaginians have built as their flagships, and those things are barely seaworthy, not able to sail even partway across the middle sea without swamping. I'll admit, these look a lot more stable than I thought they would just by looking at your plans, but larger? It's hard to fathom."

"It's true. We are a long way from there, but I have some frigate designs I'll give to Lucan one day that have three gun decks plus a hold. Actually, even before that, I told you these were going to be the smaller ships we'd introduce, and after this, we'd talk about some larger cargo vessels."

"I know, but honestly, I thought you were pulling my leg. These can already easily fit five times the amount of cargo my ship could carry, and mine was designed specifically as a trading vessel."

"True, but until now that mostly meant getting rid of all but a few oars. It's still essentially a shallow draft ship with cargo stacked around the single mast. The ships I'm thinking of will be about twice the size of those caravels, although still notably smaller than the frigates I was just mentioning. They can carry three times as much as the caravel, although they sit a lot lower in the water, so all of the guns are on the decks, as opposed to having a row on deck and a standalone gun deck, which means they aren't as defensible."

"Against ships like this, maybe, but even one row of cannons is going to be enough to deal with even a fleet of galleys carrying soldiers and maybe a scorpion."

"Probably. Their weight also means they've got a much deeper draft. So no more sailing up rivers and they're going to be slow. Slow enough that, given bad wind conditions, a galley might keep up with it. If the Carthaginians got enough boats in the water, they could still overwhelm you and take your ship. Sure, you'd do damage, but you'd still go down."

"That's what these are for. In a year, we'll have a small fleet of these, wiping out the Carthaginians. There won't be a vessel of theirs for days in any direction."

"Small fleet might be a stretch. At this rate, we'll get maybe nine built a year, and that's with the Empire footing the bill for a massive amount of labor. Even if we spread them out evenly around the islands and down the coast of the continent, clearing the path for whatever transports we can round up or get built at the smaller ports, you're still talking about enough room between each ship that entire invasion fleets could sail through without anyone noticing. No, we have a long way to go before we rule the waves, as it were," Lucilla said.

She could see Ky give her a look out of the corner of her eye, but ignored it. Sometimes when Sophus would get lost in a subject, going seriously overboard on details, she actually listened. Partly so she could better anticipate Ky's next move, or at least be less in the dark about them, but also for a moment like this, when she could be the one to surprise him for a change.

"Rule the waves," Valdar echoed. "I like that. And yes, I might have been overstating the case a bit, but they won't be just searching the seas blindly, will they? That's what your spies are for, and we could put the smaller scouting vessels to use as well. It's also not like they can just hide in deeper waters. The Carthaginians might have the largest armies anyone has ever seen, but they are shit sailors. If they get those galleys out of sight of the coast, they'll lose half their fleet for us."

"Maybe, but they have enough men and material that they can take those losses, and they just need one invasion fleet to get through to change everything. Especially once the legions are off on the continent."

"I guess that means I'd better do my job."

"I guess it does," Lucilla said, smiling.

"Speaking of how many ships we can produce this year, we've had some requests," Lucan said. "We've had a lot of interest in getting more of these built, and in the two new slips we started on. I've had several ship masters ask when some of our new ships can be purchased by private buyers. Word has trickled out about the cargo capacity of these three, which as you pointed out a minute ago, is smaller than the new designs you want built. If there's a fair amount of demand now, I can't even guess what it will be like when the fifth slip is finished and we start on the first of the cargo ships you want to use to move soldiers and supplies to the mainland."

"It's understandable," Ky said. "I know if I was a shipmaster, I'd want a larger, faster, more seaworthy vessel. You could carry more cargo and sail more direct routes ..."

"Not without the new navigational aids and charts you provided," Valdar added.

"No, although I'm sure descriptions of some of those have already gone out and it won't take long for an enterprising captain to draw up and sell his own charts. Still, for now, we have to put all of our efforts towards the war ..."

"Are most of the interested parties Britannians or merchants who are just settling here?" Lucilla asked, interrupting him.

"A few, but there are very few Britannian captains who need ships like these. Aside from the guys who followed Valdar's lead, most of whom became citizens based on promises of access to their ships after the war, I think, Britannians don't do a lot of long-distance trade. Your sailors tend to stick close to the shore, and are more fishermen than traders."

"That will change, I think," Ky said.

"Probably," Lucan agreed. "But not yet. So no, the vast majority are not Britannians. They're mostly Scandi and a few shipmasters from Asia who sailed down from the northern passage or across the Sea of Serpents, after hearing from the Scandi that there's money to be made."

"I thought as much," Lucilla said. "I think both of you have a lot of work to do. Those ships need to be provisioned and I believe you have both slips to finish and new ships to start."

Both men looked at each other at the abrupt shift in the conversation, but the dismissal was unmistakable. With short bows, they each left to handle their responsibilities.

"I assume there was a point to that," Ky said once they were out of earshot.

"Of course there was," she said, giving him the look that he'd started to recognize as the one she reserved for stupid questions. "Working with Valdar, it's quickly become apparent that we are lacking in skilled shipmasters. There are maybe three Romans in the entire Empire who've sailed anything that wasn't primarily oar-driven and none in either Caledonia or Ériu. There is no one in the Empire who hasn't lived under the thumb of the Carthaginian fleets, who take any ship they could get their boarding ramps on. Those that were allowed to remain on the water are all fishermen. Valdar may be putting the cart before the horse when it comes to us controlling the seas, but his instinct is right. I've listened to you, Sophus, and my father, enough to know that right now we have benefited from fighting on our home territory. We haven't had to worry about supply lines or lines of communication. Our reinforcements, or at least those we've been able to get, have always been on hand. When we finally get to Africa, that's going to be a different story. We will need to control the seas, and to do that, we need skilled sailors."

"And you have a plan to get them, I take it?"

"Yes, I do. Those," she said, pointing to the ships out in the bay.

"I thought we were letting Valdar buy those when this is over."

"We are, and it's what's made him an enthusiastic convert. Valdar has vision. He could see some of our other improvements and extrapolate what that would mean for ships, just based on your descriptions. It's not hard to understand why most of the other Scandi didn't initially follow him. It takes a rare mind to hear small details, look at inventions outside of their area of expertise, and put together a picture of what the future will bring. Most of these men believe what their eyes tell them, and that's it. Now, though, they've seen what Valdar's ships can do. They've been out in their fishing ships and galleys, and seen Valdar's ships with their small collection of new sails cutting past them. They've now seen these new ships. I know you keep saying they aren't that impressive, but to us, when all we've seen are war galleys and fishing vessels, they're massive. The sudden demand to obtain them is real, and shows the difference seeing can bring."

"And you think giving them a chance to buy ships will do it when they passed on it before? I get seeing the ships changes things, but enough to get over their reservations for throwing in with us that made them say no before?"

"Yes, well, partially. There might have to be some variations to what Valdar was offered."

"And that won't piss off Valdar, his competitors getting a better deal than he got?"

"I don't think so. Is there a design that has the better sails and an increased cargo capacity, but is smaller than these ships?"

"I don't know, considering our priorities, that's kind of ..."

"There are several schooner designs that would fit that capacity," Sophus said, interrupting Ky, causing him to make a face.

"Maybe, but as I was trying to say, that kind of goes against our priorities. We have three slips now and two more that will be done maybe next month. I'm not even sure we'll have enough transports with all five working through the summer. Diverting them to build schooners is definitely not what we need."

"Strategically, it is a workable scenario precisely because it is unlikely the necessary transports for the invasion of the continent will be ready in time."

"Did you fry something? That makes no sense."

"It has already been determined that the invasion must happen before the winter, to keep the Carthaginians from mobilizing the bulk of their armies against a potential landing, which they must know is coming. It is also certain that you will not get enough transports built to carry a large invasion force efficiently. These things being true, it means that our forces will be required to use an inefficient mix of transports to cross the channel. For this plan, that is an acceptable trade-off because the chan-

nel is fairly calm and only a short distance, and the use of a large number of small ships to transport soldiers across the distance has already been proven in our future's past, albeit in the reverse. Substituting one or two large corvettes in the process will not add significant inefficiencies into the processes."

"Fine, so it won't mess up our timetable, but why complicate things with smaller designs."

"There are benefits to the schooner design, most notably speed. Their cargo capacity is smaller, but still larger than that of the largest ships currently in use as merchantmen."

"If they are that much faster, wouldn't that help solve some of the problems you just pointed out? That the ocean is huge and it's hard to patrol all of it?" Lucilla asked.

"Maybe, but you're not talking about adding these to our fleets, you're talking about building them for private owners," Ky said.

"It doesn't have to be all one or the other," Lucilla said. "We can still require some service from them, such as helping carry the legions across to the continent, report on enemy ship movement, and so on. Those that want to see some level of service, maybe doing patrol runs for the fleet, we can sell cannons to and train them to use them, much as we're doing with Valdar. Even if they don't, you've already listed numerous raw materials we need from Asia and other far-off regions. Having merchants capable of fast transport would be of benefit to us."

"If we give up one slip to creating the schooners, how many men will that really bring in?"

"That's the other part of it. Valdar's been complaining for weeks that he wasn't sure how we were going to crew his ships, based on the number of men you said he'd need. His ships needed maybe ten or fifteen men, which was one of the reasons the Scandi use them instead of galleys, which require a lot more manpower. He could put together a handful of seasoned men for each ship, but that's it, which means nearly every ship would be crewed by novices."

"That has always been the weakest part of this plan," Sophus said. "While unavoidable with the resources at our disposal, these ships need to commence patrolling as soon as possible. Every record of Carthaginian movements suggests their first attempts to move armies to counter our landings will be done by sea, which makes the current *timetable unfeasible. It is imperative that these ships begin interdicting any Carthaginian fleets attempting to sail up the coast. This will force the armies to march overland to oppose us, which should allow time for our forces to land and prepare defenses."*

"Which is where these ships come in. To get a spot, a captain has to commit a certain number of men to serve aboard our ships until their vessel is ready."

"Why would they agree to put their men in harm's way for the right to purchase a ship? It still seems like a stretch."

"Not if you think about it. These ships are unlike anything they've sailed before. It works equally as a chance for their men to train on these new-style ships. They all know how dangerous the waters here can be, which is why most of them train in the Codanus Sinus which, like the middle sea, is much calmer than Oceanus. For this, however, they would have to have an untrained crew sail these new ships around Britannia, and navigate into their protected seas before everyone, including the captain, is forced to learn by trial and error. I guarantee you that if we offer them a way to learn how to sail these new vessels, with us paying their men while they are unable to earn a living, and a place in line to buy one of the fast new schooners, we'll get sailors. More after the first ship rolls off the docks and other captains can see how fast it is. They'll all know that in a few years' time, the only traders able to make money will be those sailing our ships. Sure, some will try and copy the designs, but that will be a slow and very expensive process. We'll have men and captains lined up for spots to sail with our fleet. It solves all of our problems in one go."

"She is right, Commander. Although my projections of human behavior leave much to be desired, her suggested outcome appears to be the most likely and corrects several problems still existing in our operational doctrine."

"And they say I'm the one with all the new ideas," Ky said, smiling at his wife. "I like it, although I want to be clear that anyone who wants one of our ships must be a Britannic citizen. The men who want to sit on the fence, face none of the challenges or dangers, and simply profit from our war shouldn't get access to any of these new ships. If they want to play, they have to have skin in the game."

"An odd saying, but I get your meaning. Yes, that makes sense."

"Good. This might work out after all," Ky said, looking off towards the launches making their way towards the caravels.

Chapter 11

Emain Macha, Ériu

"How could you let her live," Conchobar bellowed, looking from his elevated throne at Llassar.

"Because having her killed would have meant generations of her people trying to undermine the rule of you and your son. The Empire can't afford to keep legions here indefinitely, and we need as many of your men as possible to join us in taking the fight to the Carthaginians. That only works if we've successfully pacified this island, which again, won't happen if their queen is dead and her killers are ruling over them," Llassar said.

"It also won't happen with her free to try to overthrow me or sitting in my dungeon, which is the same as if she were dead in the eyes of a peasant. At least dead, she couldn't make things worse. If she were to get free, it would be even worse. She'd be out there and would have successfully made us look weak, which would help her convince more people to join her cause."

"Which is why I have another idea. You're going to hate it and probably threaten to throw me in the dungeon with her, but hear me out. I think this will work."

"I promise nothing," Conchobar said, but waved for him to continue.

"She should marry your son."

"**What?!** Have you lost your mind? That woman hates me, took in Fergus, joined the Carthaginians, and had dozens of my villages burned and hundreds of my people killed. Now you think I should make her the mother of my son's heirs? You're right; I should have you thrown in the dungeons with her."

"I know it seems extreme, but it solves all of your problems neatly. Yes, she hates you. And yes, she tried to overthrow your rule, but she *knows* she's beaten. She and Fergus had no children and she has no heirs. She knows she'll never rule in her own right again. A chance for her children to eventually rule will go a long way to easing her hate, and it's not like she would be their only parent."

"So my son would have to remain home like a woman, raising children instead of out earning glory and honor for our house? If not, then she will have much more influence over them and children killing their parents in order to rule is not unheard of, nor unusual. What you're saying is you want to set my son up to be murdered by my grandchildren."

"That might be a possible outcome if they stayed here, but there are ways around that. You are still young and have many years of rule left in you, and your son will have years of rule in him once you are gone. It will be decades before your grandchild will be in a place to rule. I can speak from firsthand experience that, over time, hate can fade. To ensure that, she and your son shouldn't stay here. Send your son to join the legions, working under the Consul. Cormac still needs a lot of seasoning, and the war is changing. He will be in place to watch it change firsthand. When the war is over, he will no longer be a young whelp, wet under the nose. He'll be a seasoned soldier, ready to lead. To understand the ways of war, there is no better man I can think of for him to learn from than the Consul. Hopefully, it will take some of the fire out of his belly and replace it with more brains in his head."

"I can hear you," Cormac said. "And don't I get a say in who I want to marry?"

"No," both Conchobar and Llassar said, simultaneously.

"Like I said, wet under the nose," Llassar said.

"You've been raised on too many tales from the lore masters, who've filled your head with nonsense. You have many responsibilities and who you marry is important."

"You married the woman you loved," Cormac shot back.

"I wasn't King at the time, and it didn't seem likely I would be. And look what happened to your mother."

Llassar had heard conflicting stories about the death of Cormac's mother. To hear the men at court tell it, she had died of a wasting disease that spread across the country while Cormac was a child. Cormac and his father both believed that she died from a curse Fergus paid a witch to put on her. Llassar was as wary of witches as any other man, but having heard Conchobar tell the story, it seemed a little too practiced. He'd always found the king to be a little too calculating, and this was just the sort of thing he would use to help solidify his rule.

"She's a beautiful woman and, in spite of whom she chose to ally herself with, a capable leader. Her kingdom, of all the kingdoms on this island, has been your biggest threat since she took the throne. She's smart and clever, traits that would be good to pass down to your grandchildren."

"Also traits that would lead her to try to overthrow my house."

"True, which is why I don't think she should remain on this island. This option actually eliminates many of the problems created by her very existence. In marrying your son, she is elevated to a place of honor, which will take a lot of fire out of the bellies of her followers. But, she also won't be here to cause problems and she'll be under the eye of thousands of legionnaires and a man sent by the gods, which is a pretty good way to keep her in line. She will, in effect, be a hostage; but in a way that no one who supports her can complain about. She should remain in the Britannian capitol and off this island for several years and any children should be brought back here, to be raised under your guidance and free from her influence. By the time you step down and your son becomes King, hopefully they will be old enough that your guidance will have sunk in, shielding them from their mother's influence."

"This is insane," Cormac said. "You can't agree to this."

"Can't I?" Conchobar said, his head turning from Llassar to his son. "Llassar makes excellent points. This might actually work in our favor. Once your children are born, it will help cement her people to our kingdom. The people of the other kingdoms that stood up to the Carthaginians were left leaderless. They're predisposed to support us over anyone who might have had a hand in the destruction of their homelands. With Medb's people placated, that gives us support from a majority of our new subjects. Better, her kingdom was the second largest next to our own before the Carthaginians arrived. With your union, your children's claim to leadership will be much better than either mine or yours, which strengthens our family and ensures we endure. I have to hand it to you, Llassar, this idea is very clever."

Llassar only dipped his head in acceptance of the compliment.

"We are, of course, not our own people any longer. Do you have any idea what our new Emperor or this Consul of yours will think of the union? Have you run this idea past them?"

"No, although strictly by the rules of the Empire, you are free to govern your kingdom as you see fit, as long as you follow the guidelines passed by the Imperial Senate. As far as I am aware, nothing they have passed would affect internal politics, political marriages, or the like."

"Good, then at least they haven't screwed that up. While we're on the subject, I am not overly pleased with the laws they are passing. I assume you heard about the compromise they worked out over our fishermen killed by your people?"

"I did."

"And what are your thoughts on that?"

"I don't have any thoughts. My people and your people each have an equal say, and I can tell you that my people aren't going to be overly pleased with this compromise either. From the maps I've seen, it gives your fishermen the prime waters. I'd think this would be a victory for you."

"A victory would be someone being held accountable for our dead subjects."

"I have found that when people start declaring blood price as victory, it often turns into an endless loop of revenge killings after revenge killings until people start hating each other on principle and forget why they were ever actually angry in the first place. Better to leave everyone with a poor taste in their mouths and end the cycle."

"Nothing sets your blood on fire, does it you old goat." "Blood spills a lot faster the hotter it gets, I've noticed. Better to leave it cold."

Factorium

"I wish she would say why she wanted me to dissolve copper into the sulfuric acid," Sorantius said, looking at the pages he was just delivered.

The messenger, one of Lucilla's Caledonian guards, just shrugged. Sorantius didn't consider himself particularly bigoted or prejudiced against the northerners. In fact, he had many Caledonians working in his new chemical factories, two of whom were supervisors overseeing the day-to-day work during their shifts. This one, however, he found particularly grating every time he showed up with something new from his mistress. The short, broad-shouldered man, who Sorantius was pretty sure was named Cywing or Cryrig or something like that, had a habit of just staring at him, hovering around while waiting to get the pages back.

He also found these new rules about the instructions infuriating. He understood the security concerns, but he hadn't had anything stolen and didn't see why he should be punished because Hortensius was absent-minded. The tasks he was performing weren't like melting iron or banging out swords on an anvil. Even with the notes and the detailed explanations on these pages, this was incredibly delicate work using very dangerous chemicals that he still only half understood. The smallest error could cause volatile reactions, and he was having to either travel halfway across the complex of factories to the small document storage building that had just been finished or rely on his memory, giving him the choice between taking additional risks or slowing the process down.

He'd already asked that they be provided extra guards who could deliver the documents and wait with them as needed, or at least a guard for his enclosed office allowing him to keep what documents he needed there during the day, and have the guard return them that evening to the storage building. It seemed like a good solution to Sorantius, but so far, no one else agreed. So he was forced to stand here, attempting to memorize instructions and measurements while this man stared at him, as if he wanted Sorantius to make a mistake.

The philosopher was about to give his latest complaint to the man, even though he knew it would fall on deaf ears, when there was a loud boom from inside the factory. Turning, he saw one, then four, and then a dozen men come running out of the building, all coughing and covering their faces. Several men stopped to retch into the dirt once outside and another collapsed mid-run, smashing into the ground. Some were tearing their clothes off and Sorantius could see holes in them and festering wounds on the workers as their skin was exposed.

Shoving the papers at the brute, he said, "Go get your mistress and any guardsmen you can find."

Thankfully, the man didn't argue, grabbing the pages and sprinting off.

"You," he shouted to one of the people running up to see what the sound was. "Get water and soap. Grab as many men as you can. Help scrub down the wounds of anyone with burns, but do not touch the area. Use long brushes. Get them out of those clothes."

He'd spent long hours going over the Consul's notes, and one of the pages had been directions on what to do if some of the acids spilled on a worker. There were more detailed instructions for the medics on how to treat the wounds, but the part he'd committed to memory was how to deal with it immediately, and every note had been clear. Get the acid off their skin as quickly as possible.

Several men went to grab buckets of water while Sorantius ran towards the building to see what was happening and what he could do for his people.

"No," one of the workers said, grabbing him before he could go inside. "It's dangerous."

"Is anyone else inside?" Sorantius asked.

He already knew their answer. There had been maybe a hundred people in the factory at the moment the explosion occurred, and he'd seen less than two dozen come out. There were several rear entrances, and surely some had left that way, but knowing the layout, there should have been more on this side, since the rear of the building was used more for storage while the working areas were closer to the front, allowing a clear separation from some of the more volatile mixtures in areas that had open flames.

"Some," the man said, choking. "I saw men on the ground, but ... it was so hard to breathe."

"What happened?"

"I don't know. Everything seemed normal; when all of a sudden the third vat for preparing the sulfur, the one we just put into production, exploded. The acid spilled out, splashing all over. There was this green smoke the color of moldy fruit. It filled the room so fast. So fast ... There wasn't anything ..." he said, and then stopped to cough so hard Sorantius thought he might pass out for a moment. Thankfully, he managed to get his breath back to continue. "I don't know what happened. No one was even near the vat. I was looking right at it. It all seemed normal. It wasn't until we smelled it that we realized something was wrong."

His eyes were bloodshot and red, his face was flushed, and the man was taking ragged breaths. Sorantius could hear his chest rattle with each inhale.

"You," Sorantius yelled at the closest apparently healthy man he could see. "Send for the physicians. And have someone find the Consul or Lucilla. We're going to need help."

Lucilla looked over the scene in the dying light and was appalled. The injured had all been moved, some to clean facilities here in Factorium, but most by carriage back to Devnum, where they could be taken to the hospital. Not much different than the valetudinariaLucilla had been familiar with, Ky had widened their purpose to be for all Romans and not just veterans, giving the people of the city a centralized place to go for medical care, instead of requiring physicians to visit the home of each sick person, or a sick person being taken to the physician's home.

There had been some pushback from the physicians initially, since it meant they were all operating out of the same place, which meant competition for their patients, and more importantly their patients' money. In the end, Ky had worked out a compromise with them to make sure no one lost any money. Of course, since Ky was still giving them new ways of treating people, which meant more patients they could actually help, they couldn't very well say no. It meant more expense for the Empire, but at least this time that expense was offset by what the physicians had to pay back for using the new tools and medicines Ky was introducing.

Most importantly, it had worked. The physicians were actually making more money, because patients were coming to them instead of the physician needing to travel from house to house, and people were able to get medical help faster. Everyone was benefiting. Or at least, everyone in Devnum.

Seeing the piles of burned clothing, the ground still wet with sickness and blood, it was clear they'd have to do more. She'd already considered the need to put something similar in other towns, but she hadn't thought of the complex of factories as a town, so she hadn't considered the need to have one here. In hindsight, that was foolish. The number of people who worked here, how dangerous their work could be, and how very far they were from Devnum meant they needed physicians here permanently all the more. She didn't doubt that some of the men sent to Devnum for treatment would die on the way if the description of their condition was at all accurate.

"My lady, thank the gods you're here. They said the air had a green fog that fell to the floor and burned anyone it touched. Men were coughing up blood ... it was terrible. I don't know what to do. I can't send my men in there to check if the gas is gone and short of having them arrested by the praetorians, they won't let me go in."

"It's alright," Lucilla said. "What did you do for the injured men? How were they when they left for the hospital?"

"I followed the Consul's instructions. Their clothes were removed and the burned areas were cleaned with water and soap.

He didn't say what to do about coughing up blood, though. I … I didn't know what to do."

"For most chemical burns, that would be the correct treatment, although it is impossible to be positive without analyzing the chemicals released inside the building."

"You did the right thing," Lucilla said. "Just get all your men back from the building."

"You can't …"

"I won't go in. I just need to walk around the perimeter and try to see if I can tell what happened."

Sorantius looked doubtful but obeyed. She knew that, even though she'd been the one giving him most of his instructions, he'd assumed they'd come from Ky. She didn't fault him for it; that was just how people were. She'd dealt with it her entire adult life in politics, and she was the Emperor's daughter, which meant that she was given more leeway than most other women. It hadn't been a surprise to her that healers and philosophers would have the same prejudices.

"We can find out what's happening, right?" she asked softly as she approached the doorway, out of earshot of the workers Sorantius ushered away from the building.

"Most likely," Sophus said. *"When it is clear, send the drone into the building. I will run an analysis of the air and equipment to determine the cause of the toxin."*

She reached into the pouch she secretly carried and pulled out the small plate size object, looking over her shoulder to see if anyone could see what she was doing before holding her hand out flat, the drone resting in her palm. Instantly, it leaped from her hand, light as a hummingbird and darted inside.

Once it was out of sight, she started walking around the circumference of the building, making sure to look at the ground, the walls, and anything else she could think of to make it look like she was doing some type of investigation. Hopefully, she'd have answers soon, and she wanted to have a plausible explanation for how she came up with them.

She'd almost made it to the rear door of the building when Sophus finally spoke.

"The gas seems to have dissipated, most likely through a cross breeze created by the open windows, rear door, and main door."

"Do you know what it was?" she asked.

She knew the word only because Ky had described it to her, and she'd had to write a description of it in one of her informational sheets for Sorantius. It was still a little hard for her to wrap her mind around small parts of matter that you can't see, that makeup the smells and even the air she breathed. She knew about steam and smoke, but she had always thought of those as just existing, and not being comprised of smaller parts she couldn't see. The idea that everything was made up of smaller things was something that had been thought of since the Greeks, but the scale still boggled the mind when she thought of what Ky had tried to teach her.

"I believe so. One of the vats was torn open from what looks like out-gassing. I have detected residues of hydrochloric acid and chlorine in the higher areas along with several other substances. Although I cannot be positive without more data, the highest probable extrapolation from available data suggests that these vats have been used to create multiple chemicals without being properly cleaned between uses, creating a form of chlorine gas."

"How in the hell did they make chlorine gas?" Ky, who had apparently been listening to their conversation, said, breaking in.

"You recently gave Sorantius the formula to create a crude form of sodium hypochlorite for disinfecting and cleaning of medical areas. It is plausible that, hearing it was used for cleaning, it was used to clean a vat that was then used for hydrochloric acid. There are other traces present, however, that would have changed that reaction, which could explain the explosive nature, since chlorine gas on its own would not create the pressure levels necessary to rupture the tank."

"My instructions specifically warned against putting the bleach in contact with any acids. I even included vinegar in the list of things to not put it in contact with."

"It appears they did not listen to that warning, Commander."

"Damn. What about the wounded?"

"Sorantius followed your instructions. The wounds were cleaned with water and soap before the injured left for Devnum."

"At least he did something right," Ky said.

"I know this is bad, but the situation here has been difficult. We have him working on at least a dozen projects, all involving precise and complicated mixtures that he has to travel halfway across the complex to confirm."

"Commander, these types of accidents were common during the industrial revolution and we are introducing advancements from over a hundred-year range in just a few months. Errors such as these are a statistical certainty."

"That doesn't help the injured parties," Ky said.

"No, but it doesn't matter. It's not like we're going to be able to get rid of Sorantius and find someone else to take his place. We'd be starting over and this is the first accident like this. It's no different than when Hortensius blew up the gunpowder building."

"Maybe not. We need to make it clear to him what caused this and make sure it doesn't happen again. We also need to rethink the use of bleach."

"Although an irritant, it is safer than the phenols originally suggested as an antiseptic cleaner due to its possible toxicity and corroding nature on the less protected steel currently in use."

"We still need to think of other options if they're going to be creating chlorine gas."

"What do I do about the factory here and now?" Lucilla asked.

"Give it five more hours and the building should be clear of the gas, although perhaps it's better to shut it down for a few days. It should be safe, but they still need to clean every surface with soap and water once they get back inside. And make sure he knows how this happened and what to do to keep it from happening again."

"I'll take care of it," Lucilla said.

Chapter 12

Coast, Southern Britain

The galleys cut across the water, slamming into the beach hard, driving up onto the sand. As soon as the boats stopped, men in heavy armor began piling over the sides in twos and fours, quickly crowding the entire beach with hundreds of men.

Another group of legionaries sat across from them, crouching and covering their heads, as centurions walked up and down the line, telling this group of men or that group they were dead.

A spectator watching the proceedings would have been very confused by the entire thing. Thankfully for them, and the training legions, there weren't any spectators. The praetorians had cleared people out of the area for more than a mile in all directions, ensuring the training could continue without any spies getting a look at what the Britannians were practicing.

"Move up," Velius yelled as he hit the beach, pushing men gathering in clumps by the boats towards positions forming halfway up the sand. "Boat teams; get them back out in the water. Let's go. Let's go."

Velius fumed. Men moved, but not fast enough. They knew this wasn't real and some were treating it more like a bit of fun than the training it was supposed to be. It was true that, before the Consul, this kind of training didn't happen so the men weren't used to it, but after seeing it used several times successfully, Velius saw the benefit of it. Getting five thousand men to see it too, however, was harder.

The men did finally start forming up, however, and the first galleys were starting to move back into the ocean, clearing the way for the next wave. They would have to pick up the pace if this was going to work for real, but otherwise, things were going according to plan. The legion playing the part of the Carthaginians started releasing small groups of soldiers to charge the Britannian line, but they weren't enough to break through.

Bomilcar had been against this part of the war game, arguing that the Carthaginians would hold their men together until they could form up for a concentrated push. While Velius could see his point, since that was how phalanxes normally fought, when under this kind of barrage, some of the men would break. In his experience, some of the men would run away and some would prematurely attack. For once, the Consul had agreed with him and not the Carthaginian.

Some of the men whacked their attackers a little harder than they should have with their wooden swords and there would be a fair number of bumps and bruises the next day, but as long as the cannon barrage was accurate and could fire continuously, it seemed this plan would work.

The second wave landed and was half unloaded when things went south. Men were still trudging through ankle-deep water, trying to form up with the men already on the beach when two groups of legionnaires carrying long poles to represent the phalanx spears came out of the woods from either side of the lined-up invasion force.

They were a distance away and the cannons could have engaged them, but it would have meant slacking fire on the main body at the tree line, not that it mattered, since he didn't have any way to signal the ships. They were watching through spy glasses, but it was decided to focus the first several waves on just front-line soldiers, and save support units like messengers and signalmen for the last wave. They also only had partial cohorts, and not all the leaders were on the boats in the first wave. One cohort had a senior centurion leading it and only two prefects and a tribune as it made ashore. Worse, he only had one messenger available to pass orders.

"Tell the leftmost cohort to turn and block their advance," he said to the messenger he did have, pointing at the force coming from that direction.

As the man ran off, Velius ran to the cohort on the right, which was also the one with a senior centurion leading it. The man had done well, getting his soldiers lined up and prepared for battle, but he was in over his head and not trained to make decisions on his own, like turning his men to face the threat from the right.

The battle devolved from there, with the left flank collapsing under the pressure, causing the center to roll up before Velius could shift men to shore it up. Finally, he called a halt to the entire exercise. It took time to find the signal team, waiting with the 'opposing forces', so that he could signal the waiting galleys to go back to port. The men who had already landed would march back to their base camp a few miles north of where the exercises were taking place.

By the time he got all of the men situated, the Consul and Bomilcar had shown up riding in with the other legates who were training nearby.

"That was a disaster. I thought the goal was to make this as realistic as possible, but the opposing force broke into three parts for that insane attack. They wouldn't break a force into three small units like that. They went from having a numerical advantage to three outnumbered units. I've never seen a phalanx do that in my entire life. What general would even do that?"

"I would," Bomilcar said. "In fact, I did."

"See, this is what I was talking about," Velius said to Ky. "I thought the goal here was to give our men real battlefield training so they would know what to expect and how to react when the day came. Instead, they're going to be confused, looking for attacks that won't be there, and they'll lose cohesion. The whole exercise was wasted on tactics the enemy would never use because they know it wouldn't work."

"Except, it did," Ky pointed out.

"Only because we weren't expecting it."

"Which is exactly why I did it. Your men were in disarray. You only had a handful of battle standards on the field and it took much longer for them to form up than I've ever seen from a Roman, or

128

Britannian, army. The obvious answer was you didn't front-load officers, opting for fighting men instead. You'd already pushed off ships and started your second wave, so I knew what you were doing and I could see the galleys waiting to come in. It wouldn't have been hard to figure out, even without knowing what I know, but I waited until the second wave landed because a general would want to make sure he knew he was right about the ships standing just offshore before committing. Knowing that, I knew I had a limited amount of time where I would have both numerical superiority and greater cohesion, which has always been the Roman strength. That meant I couldn't wait for you to start your attack. You already had men lined up and the shelling would have made it difficult to hold men in line to cross the beach, so I pulled two-thirds of my army and sent half one way and half the other, reasoning that you couldn't hit them all at the same time, considering there were only three ships in the harbor firing. It was the best solution at the moment, and one our enemies will try if our actual landings are anything like these."

"Which is the point of these exercises," Ky said, trying to cut some of the tension. "I think we can see we need to make some adjustments to our order of deployment."

He didn't point out that those changes were the same ones Bomilcar had been arguing for already, and Velius had been arguing against. At the time, Ky had sided with Velius since it made sense to get as many fighting men on the beach as possible in the first wave, and he himself downplayed the possibility of the Carthaginians taking advantage that early in the battle. The odds were they wouldn't be deployed to meet the Britannians before the second wave even landed and no one on that side of the field would have ever experienced being bombarded by explosive shells. Ky still believed the most likely outcome was that either the Carthaginians would break under fire completely or would be locked in place, both of which would make the move that Bomilcar had performed unlikely.

Of course, the whole point of this exercise was to prepare for the unlikely. There might not have been actual explosions here, but the Carthaginians were on an island with nowhere to run, which would be a pretty good motivator.

"Don't make the mistake of assuming your opponents are idiots," Bomilcar said. "Yes, you've won amazing battles, including the one against me, but it was never guaranteed. The thing that led you to victory in those other battles was superior generalship. Yes, you had some new weapons, and I will grant you that the ones the Consul has brought out now are even more impressive, but even the most advanced weapons can be deployed poorly and lead to a defeat."

"He is correct. There are numerous occasions where a technologically superior army was defeated by an inferior opponent with superior generalship. The British at Kandahar or the Battle of Isandlwana during the Zulu Wars are excellent examples," Sophus said, flashing descriptions of the battles across Ky's vision.

Ky hadn't needed the object lesson, but it reinforced the lesson for him.

"He has a point," Ky said to Velius. "Although it is unlikely, I believe we should take the lessons from this and adjust our plans to keep it from happening. If the most likely scenario occurs and the Carthaginians are fully suppressed by our cannon, then it won't matter. If it doesn't and Bomilcar is right, we will be glad we had the proper force disposition to deal with it."

"I guess," Velius said, sounding almost like a spoiled child, upset that he was proven wrong.

Ky frowned. He'd picked Velius for his role as the prime legate and head of the Britannian legions because of how flexible and reasonable he was. This level of inflexibility whenever Bomilcar was involved was out of character for the man. One of the things that had helped them succeed against the Carthaginians had been how short-sighted and poor the Carthaginian leadership had been, Bomilcar aside, especially in comparison to the Britannic leadership. The last thing they needed was for their top commander to start exhibiting some of the Carthaginian weaknesses.

"Can you gentlemen excuse us," Ky said.

Bomilcar simply bowed his head slightly and rode off towards the men on the beach but several of the other legates and aides gave side glances to Velius. Ky normally didn't believe in calling out men in front of others. He found it bad for morale and discipline, even asking to speak to a soldier alone when it was clear to everyone around what was about to happen. He, however, didn't have a lot of time and needed to nip this feud in the bud, now, before it started making problems that could not be corrected.

"We have a problem," Ky said.

"I agree. I don't know how he convinced you that he's reformed, or changed allegiance, or whatever, but he's going to get my men killed."

"Bomilcar isn't the problem. You are."

"What?"

"Velius, you're a good man. You care about your soldiers and you're willing to do what's necessary to achieve our goals. You have a solid tactical mind and you're loyal. You, however, need to find a way to keep your personal feelings from affecting your professional judgment."

"I'm not ..."

"Bomilcar has done nothing to suggest he's working against our best interest. If you were to stop for even a minute and put your dislike for the man aside, you would see he was right when he said we were too focused on holding the force in front of us here. I know I agreed with you in the planning session, but he showed us both that *we* were wrong. You were on the field so you should see it the best."

"Maybe, but I think he's distracting us from where our focus needs to be. Maybe he isn't doing it on purpose, but he's doing it."

"No, he's not. He's right, though. If the cannons are able to maintain suppression then changing the balance of the early waves won't affect anything. But if they can't, then he's right, and it's the difference between winning and losing. Our army's strength is its cohesion and that fell apart today."

Velius didn't say anything in response. Ky waited a few beats to see if he would, but the man only clamped his mouth shut more firmly.

"You're a good leader, Velius, and I don't want to replace you, but I will."

"Because I won't accept him?"

"No, because of you. I need you to be able to follow orders you may not like or agree with. It's how the chain of command works, and it's breaking apart now. I need to know that you'll hold to my

131

or the Emperor's decisions and not fight against us. If you can't do that, I'll find someone else who will."

"I can follow orders."

"Good. I like you, Velius, and you still have a long way to go in your career. I would hate to have anyone else leading our armies, so get your shit together. Understood?"

"Yes, Consul."

"Good. I have to return to Devnum, again, and then I need to sail out with the Valdar for at least a week. Their first run with the cannon went just as well as this did and if they can't hold their fire on target, being flanked by the Carthaginians will be the least of our worries. While I'm gone, I need you and Bomilcar to get these landings sorted out. The training went well and the actual unloading part of the landings was solid, so I know you two can make this work. Run this scenario a few times if you need to and work out as many problems as you can. Bomilcar's goal is to try and trip you up any way he can so we see the problem spots before they happen. Don't push your head in the sand and refuse to make the adjustments just because you don't trust him."

"I'll try," Velius said.

"Good, because this is the second time you and I have had to have this conversation. There won't be a third. Is that clear?"

"Yes, Consul."

Emain Macha, Ériu

Cormac looked out the window of his room, staring down at the circular building that was the seat of Ulaid government. The night air was cool and crisp, helping clear his head, which was still spinning from the large amount of mead he'd drunk at the wedding feast.

Wedding feast. It still felt odd to say that, even to himself. A month ago, being married seemed like something far off in his future. He'd been out on the battlefield, ready to prove himself like his father had. Although it could have been better in places, Cormac felt he'd done well. He'd even gotten one or two kind words out of Llassar, which was a feat since all that old goat seemed to know how to do was point out his flaws. True, he'd made some mistakes, but he'd learned from them and thought he'd have more chances to continue learning.

Out of nowhere, Llassar and his father had ambushed him, telling him he was going to be married, to Queen Medb of all people, and that it was going to happen quickly. And it had happened. Which explained the drinking.

He was sure the people at the feast had thought it was because of his dislike of Medb or maybe because everyone knew his father had picked his bride and ordered him to marry her. The real reason, and one he'd probably admit to no one, even under torture, was that he was scared. He'd never considered marriage, especially not to someone like Medb, and he wasn't prepared for it. Worse, there was tonight. The wedding night was a big deal. Stewards would come in the morning and claim the furs and bed sheets to prove the marriage was consummated.

It was pointless, really. Medb had been married previously, so there would be no blood stains for the priests to examine, but tradition was tradition. Cormac was no stranger to women. He was rich and he was a prince, so women had thrown themselves at him ever since he came of age. This was different. Most of those women he knew he'd never have to see again or if he did he wouldn't have to care what they thought of him. He'd had his fun and moved on.

This was a new challenge. For one, Medb was ten years his senior. She was experienced and a warrior, unlike the farmers' daughters and clingers on he'd previously bedded. Yes, Medb was still beautiful in her own way, but also frightening. She wouldn't be like the farmers' daughters, afraid and shy, which in turn scared Cormac.

"So here we are," her voice came behind him.

Most of her things were in the rooms she'd been staying in as his father's 'guest' and she'd gone to retrieve some changes of clothes and the like. For such a large, powerful woman, she moved quietly, like Llassar. It was unsettling. He turned to find her in a simple tunic, slippers on her feet. A change from the regal way she normally dressed, adorned with jewelry and accessories. Even during their wedding, she'd been dressed as fine as any queen, which she'd been until recently, so that at least made sense.

Her hair was down from the tight coils she normally wore it in, hanging over her shoulders in a wavy cascade. She looked even more beautiful like this, dressed simply. It was like he was seeing her for the first time. She was still startling, in a way. Taller than him, her arms sculpted in sharp lines showing just how powerful she was, although not as bulky as the picture he'd had in his mind.

"Uhh, yeah," he said, not moving from his place by the window.

"You're not afraid of me, are you?" she asked, seeing right through him.

"No. I'm just … this happened very fast. I'm still adjusting to it."

"Yes, it did. I honestly didn't see this coming," she said, moving to sit on edge of the bed in the center of the room, on the side closest to him. "It was smart of him. He's managed to keep me from being a threat to his rule of my kingdom in a way that wouldn't cause my people to rise up against him. It's much cleverer than I've ever given him credit for being."

"It wasn't his idea. Llassar was the one who suggested it."

"Really?" she said, cocking her head slightly. "How interesting."

"I would have thought this would make you angry. Losing your kingdom and being forced to marry me. You seem to be taking it well. A lot better than I would have."

"My other choice was to let your father take my head, and then kill a lot of my people when they rose up in revenge. I decided I liked the idea of being married a lot more than being dead. Besides, you aren't that bad of a bargain. You led the armies that defeated my people and were smart enough to send that advisor of yours, Llassar you said his name was, to defeat Fergus, and you're quite handsome, actually. More than Fergus was, anyways. He was all muscle and no brain. I'm glad you managed to get rid of him before I actually had to marry him. I can't even imagine what a disaster that would have been."

"Handsome?" Cormac said.

He hadn't actually planned on saying anything. He'd wanted to play it cool, not letting her know how the compliment had felt to him. He wasn't an idiot and knew she didn't actually care for him and was probably still maneuvering by flattering him and feeding his ego. And yet, it did feel good to hear it, and the words escaped him on their own.

"Absolutely. Strong, well-muscled without being obscene, and full of youth. I could have done a lot worse."

"You don't need to try to flatter me," he said, getting ahold of himself.

"Sure I do. I'm your wife. Making you happy is now my duty," she said, although the sarcasm was thick enough in her voice that they both knew she didn't actually mean that. "That isn't why I said it though. I know you're suspicious of me. If I had to guess, you were probably forced into this by your father. I know how I would have felt in your shoes, being told I had to marry some old hag."

She was so blunt and matter-of-fact about everything, it was a little disconcerting to Cormac, who was used to people always choosing their words so carefully.

"You aren't an old hag," Cormac said.

"Now who's flattering who?"

"I mean ... I'm not ..."

"It's alright," she said, and then patted the bed next to her. "Come sit down. I promise I won't bite."

Cormac hesitated for a moment and then did as she asked, although leaving a distance between them so she had to twist her body to look at him.

"Look, I know this is awkward. I feel it too. You're trapped by your family and I'm trapped by my obligation to my people ... and my own life, if I'm being honest. Neither of us has any reason to trust the other, let alone feel any sort of affection for one another, which only makes things harder. Does that sound about right?"

"Yeah."

135

"Since we're stuck, we should figure out how to make this work. Your father can order us to marry each other, but he can't tell us how to deal with each other once we're married. I don't know if we'll ever like each other, let alone love each other, but we can at least not be miserable."

"I can work with that," Cormac said.

Chapter 13

Factorium

"I'm looking at this thing, and I've gone over every part you had me make, but I'm still not sure what this is actually going to do or how it's going to completely change the way we work," Hortensius said, looking at the plans Ky handed him. "Some of it makes sense, but I'm not sure how this is going to generate the kind of force your instructions and documents indicate."

"Like I said, there is a lot of theory here that's going to be fairly far out there for you, but the basic principle is simple. We hold steam under high pressure and use this flap here to release small portions of it into this chamber," Ky said, pointing at sections of the plans. "It pushes the piston up and then releases it to lower it. We use that generated motion to turn this crankshaft here. From that point on, it's really just like the water wheel and you'll see some of the improvements I added to the water wheels we've been using when they are implemented here as well."

"What about this spinning thing here? I don't see how that regulates the force being generated."

"The centrifugal governor," Ky said. "As the speed increases, the central spindle of the governor rotates at a faster rate, and the kinetic energy of the balls increase. Once it passes this point, it causes this part of the valve to constrict, decreasing the amount of steam released and lowering the pressure on the pistons, which in turn decreases the speed. That causes these balls to lower, which then opens the valve back up to its full position. An issue with steam power is that the energy isn't released evenly, causing an alternating increase and decrease in power, almost like a wave if you were to draw a diagram of it. This oscillating nature of it causes vibrations to build, which just intensify the longer the crankshaft and other parts further down the line extend how far the power is being sent. If there's enough distance, the waves actually get out of sync and you have alternating vibrations that can literally shake this equipment apart, or at least damage it to the point of catastrophic failure. It's actually something I considered adding onto the improved water wheel design when we first started updating things, but for it to work well it really requires more precise machining, which we couldn't do until now."

"Ohh. I mean, yeah, I have noticed some vibrating along the crankshaft of the water wheel, but it never seemed bad enough to cause a problem. It was just something we dealt with. I never gave much thought into what was causing it."

"That's because until recently, you were using it mostly for grinding and the speeds were very low."

"So the main thing I'm seeing is that this just frees our factories up from having to be located next to a water source. This is going to be useful, but I'm not sure how it's going to revolutionize our industry."

"A couple of ways. The main way is there is a limit to the amount of power applied by water power, which limits what we're able to do with it. With this, we can press and cut steel with machines, allowing us to make more precise parts out of strong material. It eliminates the need for hand forging most products, which means the production of parts will be radically faster and the parts will be exactly the same every time. It will also allow us to press steel through large, powerful rollers, making our steel a uniform thickness, again allowing for precision. These machines can also be operated by one or two people, instead of dozens of men to forge items the old way and with significantly less training. That's just in steel production. We're also going to be setting up a factory here for Quirnius and a steam engine for that factory as well. Where he now needs a building full of women slowly weaving cloth, we're going to put in machines that will be able to do what dozens of workers spinning and weaving would be needed to do.

It's going to allow mines to be drained much more easily, allowing for deeper mines and greater access to materials."

"Ohh, I hadn't realized. So we're going to have a major increase in productivity?"

"Among other things. New weapons and better tools are helpful in this fight, but manpower has always been our biggest weakness against the Carthaginians. We need more and more men for the legions, Valdar needs to crew larger ships, and we need more farmers and miners out getting the resources our growing Empire needs. Everyone is fighting over a limited man pool. The only way we're going to defeat the Carthaginians is to be able to match them in production, and we can't do that through brute force like they do. Efficiency, lowering the skill level needed for tasks, and increasing individual productivity are the keys to out-producing them."

"I have been having trouble filling the new factories and forges, so you're right about that. I guess now all I have to do is build it."

"Yes. It's going to be a lot of work, and precision is the key. The parts you've made look good and you've got the precision down. There are a few ways we can improve the process and get the error rate down, but it's close enough to work."

"I'm more worried about these chains and belts for splitting the power. Does it really have enough for all of these? And isn't this too complex?"

"Yes, it has enough power, and no, it's not too complex. It does mean you'll have to train men to maintain this equipment and watch over it, but the higher tolerances and greater precision will allow it to work smoother. Some of the notes about using oils for maintaining the parts will also help reduce wear. You'll have breakdowns, but once you get used to it, it won't seem so daunting."

"I hope so. Well, it looks like I have a lot of work to do, including refitting some of these buildings to make room for all of this equipment and machining."

"Yes. Let's start with the steel mill for now, since we're going to need what it produces quickly. But yes, it's a lot of work, especially once we include the textile mill. Get ready my friend, we're about to enter a whole new world."

Southern Britannia

"Damn it," Velius hissed, barely containing the curse from becoming a yell.

He wanted to throw his helmet to the ground and stomp, venting his frustration. They had just finished their third war game since the Consul had left, and each one had gone disastrously. With each attempted landing they made changes to their tactics, and with each one, Bomilcar had outwitted him. It was getting frustrating, and not just because of the continuing blows to Velius's ego. It was almost the end of spring and they would need to actually make their invasion by mid-summer if they were going to have time to turn around and make separate landings on the continent before winter set in.

"You left your left flank too weak. You're compensating," Bomilcar said, riding up and climbing off his horse.

"You only know about that because you know what forces we have and can read our markings. And because you guessed that was what I was going to do after you hit me from the right last time. I still say this isn't an accurate test of what your friends are going to do when we hit them for real. They won't even know we're coming, let alone have this kind of inside knowledge."

"They know more than you think. I knew exactly what legions I faced, your force disposition, and which sections were the weakest when we faced off against each other. The empire had good spies here at one point, at least enough to know about your military units, leaders, formations, and even the types of tactics each leader preferred."

"You mean Caesius," Velius said, almost as a curse.

"Apparently, although I didn't know where the information was coming from at the time, only that it was accurate enough that

Zaracas would have captured the Emperor's daughter, if not for the timely intervention of the Consul."

"And how do you feel about that?"

"Which part, her almost being captured or the intervention?"

"Either," Velius said, studying Bomilcar closely.

"I don't feel anything about it. I was doing my duty at the time, and would have accepted anything that gave the people I served an upper hand."

"And you don't see the problem with that?"

"I understand that, at the time of the Consul's arrival, the Emperor was very sick. Let me ask you, would you have served Caesius if the Emperor had died and his son was elevated to the throne? Knowing what you know now, does that reflect on you morally?"

"That's not the same. You knew the kind of people you served, while I had no idea what Caesius was up to."

"How would the Caledonians react to the idea that the Romans were peaceful and didn't do anything," Bomilcar said, and then held up a hand to stop Velius's reply. "I'm not trying to start an argument, I am just pointing out that who is evil and who is not is a matter of perspective. If a bear kills someone, it may very well seem evil to that person's family, but the bear would see it as protecting its territory. Thankfully, for us, perspective can change. The Consul and my former emperor's actions showed me who they really were and gave me a strong motive for switching sides. I have given the Consul, Ramirus, and anyone else I was directed to talk to every piece of information I know about my former countrymen. I am actively trying to make this landing a success. If it is we will almost certainly kill many of those same former countrymen, some of whom very well might have served under me at some point. I've come to terms with that and accepted that this is still the right thing to do. Can you understand that?"

"I can, but I have trouble believing it. I can't imagine any scenario that would lead me to serve your former masters."

"I couldn't either until my entire family and most of my friends were executed simply to make a point and inspire fear in their other commanders. It seems unlikely, but if the Consul did that to your family, I assume you'd at the very least stop leading his armies."

"I suppose."

"You're a good general, Velius. You're methodical and patient. You care about your men and try to do the best by them. But, are you willing to do what it takes to secure victory? I deeply appreciate those qualities in a commander, and am happy to serve under you as an advisor."

"I hear a but at the end of that sentence," Velius said, interrupting the general.

"But, you have a fixation problem. You are stuck on the fact that I used to serve the people we now fight and refuse to see past that, no matter the evidence you're provided. Caution and suspicion can be good things for people in our profession, but too much is counterproductive."

"Strange, the Consul said something very similar to me, and I'm now wondering what put those ideas in his head."

"No one did. They're your largest flaw and they've been on display since I was brought into the first planning meeting. The Consul is a smart man, and can figure it out for himself. Or, are you suggesting the Consul is so easily manipulated? You've known him for longer than I have and have been closer to him. Should this be something I'm concerned about?"

"No."

"Then if you're hearing this from separate commanders, consider that there might be some truth to it. Moreover, it gets to what I wanted to bring up. You exhibit these same qualities in field command. In a defensive campaign, they are exactly the right instinct, but they are limiting you when you're on the offense. Pulling back to the edge of the beach, moving men to defend a blow, holding in place, is exactly the wrong thing to do. You need to crush the phalanxes, not let them beat against your shields until they are exhausted and run to hide back in their fortified port."

"So what's your suggestion then, attack? We're outnumbered, especially in these early waves."

"I know, and yes, that is exactly my suggestion. If, upon seeing a real attack moving in and it consisted of a majority of the forces brought against you, you should have shifted your men and attacked the flanking attempt."

"We don't have enough men to encircle them. How could I possibly defeat a larger force that's coming at me?"

"Not every battle has to be another Cannae," Bomilcar said. "If the shelling is effective, then as you attack their flanking maneuver, your flank will still be secured between that of the ocean to your one side and the shelling to the other. The odds were greater against you when you held my forces with a very thin line, and the odds here are not nearly as bad. You'll also be receiving reinforcements as the additional waves come in. You have to see the battlefield in its entirety and not get fixated on the force in front of you."

Velius wanted to snap back. This Carthaginian, of all people, had no place telling him anything. Except, he wasn't wrong. Velius knew it. He was fixated on the force in front of him. After each disaster, Bomilcar had said something similar, but Velius had dug his heels in, refusing to listen because of his distrust of the man. Part of him wanted to keep doing things his way and ignore the Carthaginian, but he also remembered what the Consul had said.

"What would you do in my place?" he finally asked.

North Sea

"This would have been easier in the channel or the sea between the islands. The waves here are making aiming the cannons very hard with the ship rolling up and down," Valdar said.

"If we end up landing in Iberia you're going to face some of the same conditions, so better to train here," Ky said. "Besides, if you can hit your targets with the ships moving this much, you can hit them that much better when the ships are barely rolling."

"Are you sure? It seems like this is as much anticipation for the gun captains as anything else. If they get used to this, they may overshoot and put the shots into the water instead of the enemy."

"You'll need to do both, but it will be less challenging going from rough seas to a calmer sea than the reverse."

"We've been in the North Sea for two days and they seem no closer to hitting the barrels than when we first started. We're going to have to return to port by tomorrow to get more gunpowder at this rate."

Valdar wasn't being hyperbolic. The barrels that floated out from the ships as targets had either ended up sinking on their own or floating out into the distance. Hundreds of cannonballs had been fired so far, and every one of them was now sitting at the bottom of the ocean, none getting within a hundred meters of their target. He knew the men were getting discouraged, but there was no way around this stage of training. This would be the hardest part, since no one on the ship had any experience with this. As new ships were finished, they could mix the gun crews from this ship into the newer vessels, giving the men with the best training positions as gun captains.

Eventually, the cycle would take care of itself, with new men training with experienced gun crews, learning the craft and eventually passing that knowledge down to the next set of men. Unfortunately, that process had to start somewhere. Worse, Ky couldn't help them. He could see exactly where the ball was going to go thanks to Sophus's projections, but he didn't have the feel for the guns that people without computers in their heads would need. He could give them the calculations Sophus was making to achieve the same feats, but they were never going to be able to do that level of precision math and still make well-timed shots.

"Then that's what we're going to have to do. Right now training is the most important thing we can do. This takes a lot of practice and all of your people are starting from the beginning. We're not even at the worst part yet. Right now, we're at anchor, so the biggest difficulty is firing while the ships move up and down. Wait until we start firing while moving, giving you two axes to worry about."

"It seems impossible. I know you did it, but … I've heard the stories about you, and so that's different. We're just mortal men."

Ky didn't want to ask what stories he'd heard. He'd already realized he could never squash all the rumors that he was sent by the gods and whatever else their prophecy said, even though he'd tried his best. Now, he could only ignore it and pretend he didn't hear it.

"It's not impossible, I can promise you that. Where I'm from, fleets of these ships would sail, firing away at each other, and hitting their targets. It's just new, and so it takes a lot of practice to get the skills needed."

"Do we even have enough gunpowder to get there?"

"Hopefully. Our production numbers are going up every day and I'm working on some additional ways to get more. If we need to use up every bit in the Empire though, it's worth it. Your ships are the most important thing in the Empire."

"I would have thought that would be the legions."

"The legions are important, don't get me wrong, but we live on islands. Our first line of defense is the ocean and your ships. What's more, with these, we will be able to control the seas, or at least we will when we get enough ships. Being able to stop all ship-bound trade and troop movement will give us a serious advantage. If they have to march their armies across Africa, up Palestine, and across Europe, it will be a lot harder for them to replace losses, greatly reducing the number of men the legions will have to face. It will also make it easier for those tribes thinking about abandoning the Carthaginians to leave them and ally with us. So yes, your ships are the most important part of our strategy. But only once you're able to actually hit things with the cannons. Which means more training."

As if to accentuate his point, the cannons on the deck below them roared to life, spitting long tongues of fire and billows of smoke out of the small port holes cut into the side of the gun deck. After a moment, water spouted up in twos and threes, some in front of the barrel and some far behind the barrel. The shots were a little closer this time, but still far enough away from the target that if it had been another ship, they would have missed entirely.

"A lot more training," Ky repeated.

Chapter 14

Devnum Docks

"Join the Praetorians, they said," Mettius Volusa Carantus griped, as water poured off his helmet. "See the Empire, they said. The only part of the Empire I've seen is this stinking city. You can't farm in the fields in weather like this, meaning I could have stayed inside where it was warm and dry. Well, at least dry."

"If you'd stayed working for Servius Gratius, you would have been complaining about that. At least we don't have to listen to him huffing air through that fat head of his anymore."

"But we'd be dry," Mettius said, although more to just whine than anything else.

He'd learned quickly in training that complaining was one of the best ways to pass time as a soldier. Admittedly, he hadn't stayed a soldier long, or at least not a legionnaire, but the same method worked well for a Praetorian. Desiderius wasn't wrong though, he was glad he didn't have to listen to Gratius and his yelling any longer. It was strange to think that a year ago he and Desiderius had been slaves, working in Gratius' fields, barely fed, living a life with no future. Then the Sword had come and changed everything. He freed them and told them they were vital in the fight to save the Empire.

Gratius had tried to convince them to stay, offering wages of half what the factories were paying, not that Mettius wanted that any more than he wanted to stay in the fields. His father had done manual labor as a slave his whole life, the brutal end of which Mettius had been forced to watch. Injured and without the hand that he'd lost in the accident with the plow horse, Gratius had thrown him out to starve, which he hadn't been far from before he was thrown out. Mettius had found chances to visit him in the poor house, taken in by the Daughters of Spes, who did their best to help the poor and sick in the city. Every visit he'd looked closer and closer to death's door, until the time a daughter pulled him aside to tell him that his father had succumbed to the wasting disease that had swept through the poor house.

No, Mettius had vowed to not end up like his father, giving his physical health over to make someone else rich. He'd heard that the legions were taking in freed slaves. He and Desiderius left the day they were told of their freedom, with only the clothes they were wearing, to join the legion. It had been an experience, but he'd also had better clothes and more food than he'd had in his entire life. True, the Battle of Venonis had been terrifying, pushing with his shield against what seemed like the entire world trying to break through, but he'd survived. And then came the chance to move to the Praetorians.

Himself, a child born to slaves who were themselves children of slaves, was now a monitor, second in command of dío Contubernium, éna Maniple, twenty-third Praetorian Centuria, guarding the Devnum dockyards. Of course, one day he might make it to decanus, in charge of the contubernium, and he'd be the one sending men out into the rainy night while he 'took care of something.'

"Let's go check on Voconius and Mattavius and make sure they haven't slipped off to some place dry, leaving their post unguarded," Mettius said.

He'd hesitated putting those two together, but the south side of the docks was usually the quietest and in this rain he wanted his best men watching the north side. The morning patrols had reported unusual activity on that side of the dockyard, and Mettius didn't want anything happening on his watch.

He'd wished he had more than the ten men in his contubernium to patrol on a night like this, or nine rather, with their commander staying inside the guard hut where he could stay dry. It could be worse, Mettius contented himself. After the Battle of Venonis, the guard had been changed to the new unit structure as a test for the legions, which meant increasing the contubernium from eight men to ten. On a night like this, two more men was a lot, considering how large the dockyard was.

Mettius could only imagine what having a full maniple and its five contubernium would have meant for patrolling the dockyards instead of just the one. Fifty men would have made this a lot easier to cover. Unfortunately, the Praetorian Guard was still stretched thin, with only two cohorts assigned to cover all of the Roman province, which was not enough. He was just contemplating being promoted to optio in charge of a full maniple when movement caught his eye.

At first, he thought it was an animal or maybe a trick of light from the shadows being thrown off by the lantern he carried.

"What?" Desiderius said when Mettius pulled his horse up, leaning forward and staring into the night.

"I thought I saw something," he said, still trying to make out shapes in the inky darkness. "Ride around that way and cut back towards the berm."

Desiderius gave a nod and pulled his sword as he rode away, following instructions. Mettius didn't look to see where he went, trusting Desiderius to understand what he wanted as he cut in the other direction. He could almost make out Desiderius coming back towards him when he saw it. The form of a man hurtling over the berm.

"He went over," Mettius yelled, sliding off his horse and throwing himself over the berm after the figure, holding the lantern high as he slid down the sandy slope, trying to keep the light from going out.

He could see the person running south, away from him as he landed and pulled his sword. The man must be desperate, because here on the beach, he had nowhere to go. Maybe he panicked and hoped they hadn't seen him clearly, thinking that going over the berm would hide him. It hadn't worked, and he was now caught between Mettius and Desiderius, who was running towards them, with the ocean to one side and a steep sandy climb to the other. The man halted as he saw Desiderius, allowing Mettius time to get close enough to see him clearly.

He was dressed in a worker's trousers and tunic, and had the look of someone who spent a lot of time in the sun, but Mettius was certain this man didn't work at the docks. Besides the fact that work halted in the evening when the light dropped too much, Mettius had seen a lot of dock hands over the last several months, and this man had the wrong look for one of those. If he had to guess, he worked as a farmer or something similar. To an outside observer, dockworkers and farmers might have the exact same look of manual labor, but Mettius had worked in the ground all of his life. He could see the difference.

"Halt," Mettius said, holding his sword up. "What are you doing here?"

The man looked at Mettius and then Desiderius on his other side, at their swords, and then over Mettius's shoulder and towards the berm. Mettius could see the man contemplating how to get away and if he could make it over the sand and back into the night before they skewered him through.

"I ... got lost," he said, stumbling over his words. "It was dark, and I thought you were brigands."

"This close to Devnum, wearing legionary armor and liveried horses? Where were you lost from? Where is your farm? Or do you work on one of the larger estates?"

"I'm from Clo ... what farm?"

Nothing the man said sounded true. The question startled him, and he'd almost answered, proving Mettius's guess, before clumsily trying to cover it up.

"I think you should come with us."

"That's not necessary. I'm sorry for the trouble, but if you'll just let me go, I'll ..."

"You can either come with us or I can put this gladius through your chest," Desiderius said. "Which do you prefer?"

The man threw one last panicked glance at the sea berm before Mettius watched the fight go out of him, his shoulders and head dropping.

Devnum

"I'm sorry to bring you out this late, but I thought you'd want to see this," Ramirus said as Lucilla came through the door, her clothes rumpled and disheveled looking from hastily being thrown on, pulling off a soaked cloak that she had thrown over herself as protection from the rain.

"They said you caught someone?" Lucilla asked waving off his apologies.

"Yes. The Praetorians patrolling the dry docks found a man near them that shouldn't have been there."

"In this weather?" she asked.

Ramirus worked out of the palace complex, so Lucilla had only had to step outside briefly to cross between buildings, and her feet and sandals were soaked and muddy from that short journey.

"That is what made the guards suspicious in the first place, and he was in the dark without a lantern or torch. He then ran from them, but didn't make it far before they caught him."

"Do we know who he is?"

"Not yet. We've just started the questioning, but I didn't want to wait until we finished to let you know what was happening. One of the guardsmen grew up as a field slave before the Consul freed him and says he is pretty sure the man is a farmer or works on one of the large estates."

Lucilla gave a sigh and Ramirus nodded. She'd been pushing hard for Ramirus to catch and deal with the last of the insurgents, but so far they had only been able to identify small pockets, and knew they were missing a lot, including Decius Sestius Gorgonius. They'd captured and executed his son, but the current leader of the insurrectionists was still in hiding. Ramirus had gotten close to him a few times, but the man moved constantly, making it hard to pin him down. What they did know was that most of Decius's support came from the large landholders outside of the city. Men who'd lost the most when the slaves were freed and were benefiting the least from the new technology and materials the Consul had introduced.

Ramirus had already proven several treasonous and had their land and property seized by the Empire, but they were certain there were several they had missed.

"Do we know who he worked for? What he was doing out there?"

"Not yet, but it's still early. The interrogation has just begun. By the morning, we'll know everything he does."

"Which means next to nothing, if he's anything like the others we've caught."

"We'll know what he was doing out there," Ramirus countered.

"We know what he was doing out there. He was either trying to gather information on our ships to send back to Carthage or trying to destroy or damage some of the ships under construction, or maybe both. It's why we have the guard patrolling the docks in the first place. What it isn't doing is getting us any closer to the people planning these attacks and coordinating everything. We still have no clue who took those documents from Hortensius's factory, and yet you and Faenius have been investigating for more than a month. I know you are stretched thin with operations here and on the continent, in preparation for our next campaign, and I know Faenius is still short on men, but we need results."

"We are trying, my lady," Ramirus said, looking decidedly nervous.

Lucilla rarely lost her temper. She believed in giving her people time to do their jobs and she tried not to expect the impossible from them, or at least not hold their feet to the fire when they fell short of the impossible. Her patience, however, had worn thin.

Ramirus had promised he would track down the insurrectionists when they killed a senator, when they made the first attempt on her life, when they burned a warehouse of military supplies, and when they'd made the second attempt on her life. Faenius had sworn his men could keep facilities vital to the Empire's war effort safe. Both had failed at their promises. She was lucky she'd survived the first two assassination attempts, and doubted she'd survive a third. More importantly, she didn't know if the Empire and everything she'd fought for would survive if the insurrectionists managed to get the designs of these new technologies to the Carthaginians or killed someone important to their plan.

So far, they'd been focused on her, but Hortensius and Sorantius were both incredibly vital to the future of the Empire. They hadn't figured it out yet and she already had guards watching the manufacturer, but someday the rebels would realize they could do just as much harm killing Hortensius as they could by killing her, and he was not nearly as protected.

No, the time for patience was at an end.

"Not hard enough. I don't care what you have to do, but you and Faenius need to put an end to their operations now, before they can cause any more harm. You have worked for my father your entire life and you know how much you mean to both of us, but if you can't do the job, I will find someone else who can. This isn't an idle threat. Stop them or step down."

"I ..." Ramirus started to say, and stopped.

She had clearly rattled him, which was good. That was exactly what she had been trying to do. She'd tried patience and gentle pressure, and that hadn't worked, which left only blunt force.

"I can try to set a trap for them," he said, his mind clearly racing as he tried to think of something he could do.

"We've tried that, haven't we? I seem to remember multiple attempts at trapping their people and we got, what, two low-level members who knew no one and a courier who wasn't even part of the movement?"

"We were playing it safe with the bait, I think. Maybe what we put up wasn't worth the risk of them using anyone notable? Perhaps, if we used something more tempting, they would feel the need to use someone more senior. Someone connected to them who could tell us where to find the leaders."

"That sounds like a lot of maybes," Lucilla said. "So what, exactly, is your plan for bait?"

"We could plant new documents. They are clearly trying to find information on some of our new technology to send back to

Carthage, so we set something up that they will want to get their hands on."

"That's ..." Lucilla started to comment, and paused. "That should be fine. Go ahead and do it, but I hope you get some results."

"We will," Ramirus said, bowing and hurrying out, either to continue the interrogation or start setting his plans in motion.

"Lucilla, it is unlikely that the people behind the thefts and attempts on your life will be fooled by making documents suddenly accessible, especially after so many new security procedures have been put in place to protect what documents we have."

Lucilla stepped outside and followed an outcropping around the side of the building to stay dry, gesturing for her guards to give her some space.

Turning her head so they couldn't see her mouth, she said, "I know. Ramirus is very good at organizing information sources and gathering information, but counter-espionage is not his strong suit. The Carthaginians never gave the practice much thought, I think, preferring to rely on brute force for every solution. If I had to guess, I'd say my brother was behind this. But, that means Ramirus doesn't have the experience to deal with this like he does in collecting information. He's panicking, trying to throw everything he can at the wall, to see what sticks."

She looked around again to make sure the sound of the rain was covering her voice. None of her guards seemed to flinch and the palace guards were mostly in doorways, trying to remain dry. She was already getting wet, even though she was partially protected by the outcropping, and tried to look contemplative, like she was thinking the problem through. She knew her guards had probably figured out she 'talked to herself' sometimes and had gotten used to her weird behavior. It was more the palace servants and guards she was hiding from than her own people.

"If you do not expect his plan to work, then why would you not stop him and direct him to different methodologies that will work?"

"Because the insurrectionists are going to be looking for a response. If they don't know already, they'll figure out soon that we have their man. I want them to see Ramirus's trap for what it is. I have found that once people find what they're looking for, they tend to stop looking any further."

"You have your own plan to catch the perpetrators?"
"Yes. Yes I do."

Factorium

"Consul, you have amazing timing," Hortensius said, meeting Ky at the entrance to the main steel factory.

It wasn't, in fact, amazing timing. Lucilla and he had been in near constant communication for the last week, mostly discussing her insane plan to catch the insurrectionists, but also with intermittent updates on the new ships starting construction, the chemical works, and upgrades to the hospital, now that real disinfectants were becoming available, and on Hortensius's assembly of the steam engine. On Valdar's latest resupply run, Ky stayed behind instead of continuing to monitor the progress of that training.

It had been a productive few weeks, and Valdar had it in hand now. The gunners were still not hitting their targets as consistently as Ky wanted, but they were now at least hitting the target part of the time, which was a significant step up from where they'd been when they first launched the ships and started training. He knew this process was going to take time, but they were running short on it. The assault on the Isle of Mann, or Insula Manavia as the Romans called it, had to happen in the next several weeks if they were going to make their new timetable.

Unfortunately, he'd have to leave it in Valdar's hands to see that the gunners could handle their part of the job; just as he'd left the training for the amphibious landings to Velius and Bomilcar, who hopefully hadn't killed each other yet. The pace of military operations may have slowed down, but the scope had increased significantly, which meant that technological progress had to follow suit. And the first step to that was getting the steam engine online.

"I got word that the steam engine should be done," Ky said.

"I bet you did," Hortensius said, all but winking in response. "Still, I just fitted the last parts on today, which means your timing is still amazing, even with your spy."

"Good. I'd hoped that would be the case. Getting this working is going to open up a wide range of new products that we're going to need by the end of winter, or hopefully before winter's end, if you can pull off some miracles."

"I'll do what I can. Let me show you what I've managed to accomplish."

Hortensius lead Ky through the factory to a room he'd started building as soon as Ky had explained the purpose and function of the steam engine. Ky also noticed that much of the additional machinery needed in the ceiling of the factory was already going into place as well. Crankshafts, belts, and branching machinery to allow the one engine to work multiple machines and allow that work to stop for some lines but continue for others was beginning to fill the rafters in a dizzying display. Ky had been unsure if these would all work when writing out the instructions, but Sophus had promised him that this equipment was in use for hundreds of years on his earth and all of it was well tested.

The steam engine itself was massive with a giant, cylindrical boiler taking up a large part of the room, as well as a large furnace. Its smokestack stretched up and through the ceiling.

"Impressive."

"Isn't it," Hortensius said, standing back and placing his fists on his hips. "I can't wait until I can get more of these made and installed in some of our other factories. Just looking over that last batch of documents you gave us is giving me all kinds of ideas."

"I'll bet! Although, you know the next version you make will be much smaller. This design has to be large because, as steam engines go, it's fairly inefficient. We didn't have much choice with this one, since the power we had limited how precise we could be and the strength of the material we could operate with. With this, we can build the tools to make metal stronger and thinner, cut precision parts that are identical every time, and grind the steel to make a better-finished product. That's just here. Once we get the second version running in the steel plant, we'll be able to increase our output and make an even better steel."

"That was one of the documents I was thinking about," Hortensius said.

It made sense. Before Ky's arrival, Hortensius was primarily in the metal-making business and only got into the manufacturing because he couldn't sell enough of the raw product to others. He'd shown amazing talent at producing the weapons and equipment the Empire needed, but his heart was in the iron itself.

"Alright, let's fire her up," Ky said.

Chapter 15

Devnum

"We can't get to the gunpowder," one of the men said.

Decius frowned. Caesius's messages had been getting more and more frantic, demanding they get him samples of the explosive powder they'd been hearing about and instructions on how to make it. They had yet to get a man inside Hortensius's factories, but they'd gotten into the social circles of the workers, at least enough to hear the men gossip and talk about their day.

The problem was, most of the workers didn't know the details of how things were made, and those that did tended to get nervous when his people started asking more specific questions. This wasn't about troops marching out of town or what a specific mine was producing. The information they were looking for was very technical and not something that came up in basic conversations, especially with people they only knew from the tavern.

They knew the gunpowder contained sulfur, burned wood, and something derived from rotting urine. The last part was still confusing. It wasn't hard to know that they were collecting it, since for months Hortensius's men had been digging up barns and latrines, taking away the soil and putting in new soil. Questions about that, at least, made sense, but the only answer they were getting was there was something in the soil after urine soaked into it that was extracted and used in the production of gunpowder.

That wasn't enough detail for them to send to Caesius, who would almost certainly ask what, and more importantly how, they were taking whatever substance out of the soil. For that, Decius still didn't have an answer. He also didn't know what amounts of those three things were needed in the mixture to make gunpowder.

He'd been hoping it was in the scrolls they'd managed to steal, but none of the ones they took had anything to do with gunpowder, or cannon, or any of the new things Hortensius was now working on. Mostly they were about metalworking, new farming techniques, and the arcuballista, which they'd already managed to send back to Carthage. The metalworking might end up being useful, but it was clear they were pushing for something militarily useful that could be exploited quickly.

"Why not?"

"It's too well guarded. Anything not currently in use is constantly guarded by Praetorians, not just paid men like some of the factory buildings. Anything that's not in one of the storage areas is either taken straight to the ships or the legions, where we can't get to it. Worse, all of their storage locations are well outside of the Devnum and Factorium, apart from any other buildings, making it incredibly difficult to sneak up to them. To get in one, we'd have to kill the guards, which would require most of the men we have left."

"I thought you were looking to get someone inside the praetorians, who could get us access to those buildings."

"We've tried. I don't know how, but the praetorians seemed to figure them out every time. Two more tried and were just rejected, but three others were held for questioning and broke under torture. We've lost two cells because of it, which is a problem since we're running so short on men."

"If we used enough force, could we take one of the warehouses?"

"I don't know. They are better armed and armored than our people, and I know they have a signal fire set up away from the building that they will set off in the event of an emergency. They had some kind of issue at one of the buildings a few weeks ago and we saw the guards light it. Men on horseback showed up about ten minutes later."

"Ten minutes would be enough time to roll a couple of barrels out though, right?"

"Yes. We'd lose men though. Our recruiting is still very slow. I'm not sure we can afford those kinds of losses."

"We also can't afford to not get Caesius what he asked for. Unless you see another opportunity, this is all we have."

"There is that new document storage building not far from the Imperial Palace. It's a lot less guarded than the document storage building in Factorium or the one we heard about inside the palace complex. That might mean it has less important documents, but those could still be valuable. He was happy with the last set we sent him, right?"

"Yes, but I don't trust this information," Decius said. "Word of that new storage building came out only a few days after we took the scrolls from Hortensius's office, and the building itself doesn't make sense. You said it was in a fairly congested area with a lot of buildings nearby that would give cover to anyone trying to break it. That's almost exactly the opposite of what they did for the building they put up in Factorium. Our people have watched Hortensius and a few others making long trips from their factories to the document building. I can't imagine that's very convenient, but they put this one in a crowded area. Also, what's over here that would need its own storage building? The new building for the physicians, hospital I think they called it, is halfway across the city. It's so close to the palace complex, why not just store them there?"

"Maybe their storage areas in the palace were full?" the other man offered weakly.

Decius snorted in derision, "I can't imagine they're short on room. You saw it yourself when they were repairing it after the Battle of Liberation. That doesn't seem likely. Plus, they would have the palace guards and the praetorians to guard them. No, this feels like a trap."

"So you want us to throw nearly all of our manpower into raiding one of the gunpowder storage buildings? That's a big risk, Decius."

"I know, but Caesius's last message said his benefactors are thinking of sending their own people here to handle our network. I think that might be why his messages are getting more urgent. We're trying to put Caesius back in his rightful place. According to Eborius, at least before he was murdered by our new Consul, Caesius was forced to work with the Carthaginians because he had no other choice, but he always planned to double-cross them the moment he was in power, and take back what Rome lost. Yes, this was made harder when Londinium fell and he was forced to flee to Africa, but not impossible. However, if he is forced to let the Carthaginians come here and direct our people, instead of us, it will be harder to take things back when it is time. That is why we have to show some kind of progress. We need the Carthaginian's networks to pass messages, we need their money, and we need their muscle. We don't, however, need them. Especially not here."

He looked around at the handful of men, the very last of his inner circle still alive, to make sure he had their attention.

"So yes. We use what we have to take some of their gunpowder from them. With that, Caesius can reestablish himself with the Carthaginians, defeat the Consul, and take back our home. For the glory of Rome!"

"For the glory of Rome!" the men repeated.

Factorium

"Right, release the pressure value," Ky said, his simple tunic covered in dirt, soot, and rendered whale fat that was the closest thing to oil that the Britannians were able to make.

The furnace had been burning most of the morning and the pressure was up in the furnace, but so far they hadn't really let it go. They'd spent the better part of the last two days bringing the pressure up slowly, making sure the boiler itself would hold together without bursting. Ky was already pretty certain it would, with his enhanced vision and Sophus's ability to analyze the material strength, rivet points, and any other place where the large cylinder might rupture.

His ability, however, was one that no one on the planet would be able to match for several thousand years and he wanted to get Hortensius and the handful of other workers who were training along with him used to doing things the smart way. People had a bad habit of taking shortcuts if they thought they could, and this was one place where that would be a fatal mistake. Along with his plans, Sophus had several first-hand reports of early steam engines rupturing, going off like a bomb, one that added boiling hot liquid to the metal shrapnel.

They needed the time, anyway. Workmen had been clambering all over the factory, putting the finishing touches on all the parts needed to work the machine and getting the metal lathe hooked up to one of the branches, allowing it to apply the much larger force to cutting metal, which in turn meant the ability to work with some of the newest steel Hortensius was producing and much thicker metal. While that would all be useful, he'd mostly picked it because it was the most readily available piece of equipment he could prepare for real mechanization. Once this was ready and working, Hortensius would have a chance to see the steam engine in actual use and not just test runs.

"I will never get over how loud this is," Hortensius shouted from next to Ky.

Ky hadn't actually considered the noise level. To him, the engine wasn't particularly noisy, at least not compared to a booster lighting off on the back of his fighter rocket. Of course, before now the loudest things in this time were the clanging of hammers and slamming of wood. He'd never really thought about the difference in sounds between post and pre-industrialization, and people's reaction to them, until they turned the engine on the first time.

Half the factory had crowded by the door, trying to figure out what all the racket was about.

"You'll get used to it soon enough," Ky said, getting an odd look from Hortensius, who clearly didn't believe him.

Ky gave the machine a final once over, to make sure it was working, and left the 'engine room', as Hortensius had started calling it, much to Ky's amusement, and went back into the factory proper. There were still going to be boiler men in there, keeping the fire going so the pressure would stay up, and Ky made a mental note to come up with some kind of ear protection for them. He didn't want to be the reason certain classes of men started going deaf.

The noise level dropped notably once they were out in the factory proper. He could still hear the engine through the open doorway, but the walls mostly blocked the noise and the factory was larger, giving the sound waves less area to bounce off.

Ky's eyes followed along the ceiling and catwalks as they walked towards the section of the factory that held the lathe, and the two additional lathes currently under construction. The crankshaft was spinning at a decent speed and all of the belts and parts seemed to be working well, from his vantage point, which was very good, again using his enhanced vision.

"It looks like we're good. Turn it on," Ky said to the worker, as he stepped up next to the machine.

The man reached out and threw a mechanical lever on the lathe, which started the headstock spinning at speeds far greater than it had been able to do using water power alone. Ky had spent some time modifying this device, especially its dial for locking in measurements. It would need correction over time, but one lathe with good precision could create another, and this time without his supervision. With this, they could make the milling machine, borer, and metal stamp, and then things would really start moving.

"It's going so fast," Hortensius said.

"Yep. With that kind of power, we lock in a specific size and can cut down anything you need, and it will be exactly the same every time. This is the future, my friend."

"I can't wait."

"Speaking of that, I have something new for you," Ky said, putting an arm around the manufacturer and leading him to his office. "I know you already have plans for the next couple of machines you need to make, but I'll be leaving in a few days and probably won't be back to Devnum or here until after we retake Insula Manavia, and I don't want to slow you down on our next big project.

"Which is?" Hortensius said, leaning over the table where Ky was lining up pages.

"More of the same, actually," Ky said.

"Another cannon?" Hortensius said. "This is steel, but you said we were working with bronze because if it failed it would be safer."

"I did, and it is, but this has a new feature that is not possible with bronze. Look here. One of the new tools you're going to be making is a borer capable of not only cutting a hole into a solid cast cannon, allowing us to make variable, and exact, thicknesses, but it will also be able to cut this helix-shaped grove down the length of the barrel. The cannon will require a new kind of projectile called a shell, and the grove will cause the shell to spin in flight, allowing it to fly much straighter and further."

"Like an arrow," Hortensius said, not as a question, but as a statement.

"Exactly. It will also be easier to both fill these shells with gunpowder and create a new kind of impact fuse that will allow it to explode when it hits something, as opposed to the cut fuse that we've been working on, that only allows timed explosions."

"So you can make sure you damage your target without it going off early and have it do more damage, since the explosion is right on top of where it hits."

"Exactly. I know I promised a big step and this is another cannon, but this one feature alone is going to be the key to our victory."

"Between the borer, the plans for the milling machine you showed me, the stamp press, and the metal roller, I have a lot of big steps already. You don't have to worry about me. I'm just excited to get started."

"Excellent. Then I'll leave you to it. I have to rush back to Devnum. Valdar should be back and I have some last-minute updates for him, then off we sail for battle and glory."

"I'll stick to my forges, thank you," Hortensius said with a smile.

Outside Devnum

Mettius stood by the door of the gunpowder shed, bored. He understood the rule of rotating units across duties in their assigned areas. They were still assigned to Devnum and the surrounding area, meaning they were still familiar with the people and the city, which helped keep them from becoming confused, but new duty posts kept things from becoming too routine. Theoretically, that kept the mistakes down. Yes, it also meant they were doing slightly different jobs, but the jobs weren't so different that it meant they were starting over each time.

There was very little difference between riding patrols along the docks and standing next to a large building. Look for people who shouldn't be there and keep them out. Simple enough.

The biggest problem was that at least riding a post meant slowly changing scenery. Here, he could see the same stretch of road, the same dozen bushes, and the same four trees. There wasn't much to hide behind, so it wasn't like anyone was going to sneak up on them. True, it was pitch black out there, but they had a fair number of lanterns around the building and his men made regular sweeps around the perimeter of the storage building, far enough out that it was unlikely someone could just sneak up on them. If someone did manage to sneak up on them, they were all wearing armor and armed with arcuballista and gladius, and he always had a man on horseback, which would make them fast and deadly. It was hard to imagine a force large enough to get past them.

"This is so dull," Desiderius said, echoing his thoughts from the right side of the large doors.

"A few more hours and Nepos's contubernium will be here to relieve us."

"You'd think after catching the saboteur they would have given us the week off like the heroes we are."

"You don't know he's a saboteur. He could have just been a spy."

"I'm just saying, we should have gotten a reward."

"The honor for our centuria is reward enough," Mettius said, getting a head-tilted look from Desiderius. "At least that's what the optio said when I mentioned giving us a week's pass for our good work."

"I swear, that guy shouldn't be leading a chorus in song, let alone men in battle."

"He's not so bad. He came out of the Seventh Legion and they said he handled himself well. He's just bought into all of that 'Praetorians forward' stuff the tribune was going on about."

"I don't … Did you see that?" Desiderius asked, staring out into the dark.

"Let's go be heroes again," Mettius said, lifting a lantern high and heading out with his sword pulled.

He had to leave his shield behind, since he couldn't carry all three, but he still had his armor on, in case it really was something. Most likely it was an animal of some kind. This far out from town they got the odd fox or rabbit coming to look for food. It seemed unlikely it was another spy. When they'd first joined up, the men who worked for Ramirus, sometimes with a detachment of Praetorians, were regularly digging up spies and saboteurs, arresting men in the middle of the night. But that activity had fallen off months ago. Mettius assumed they must be running out of men, but maybe they were just getting better at not getting caught.

Of course, the guy they caught by the docks had not been that stealthy. Still, the odds were against them finding two people in such a short period of time. It didn't matter. The farmer had been dressed in simple clothes and wasn't armed, so it was doubtful that anyone out there would be able to hurt them.

Moving forward slowly, Mettius heard a noise this time. Rustling from his right in the tall grass. After a moment, he heard more, but from Desiderius's left.

"Who goes there," Mettius said, holding his light high.

Desiderius lifted his lantern in turn, peering into the night. For a moment nothing happened. And then as if some unheard signal had been given, the tall grass in front of them exploded with men jumping to their feet and charging.

None of the men were armored, but they were armed. From what Mettius could see, their weapons were old and of poor quality. An assortment of axes, old swords, and sharpened poles being used as makeshift spears.

Mettius dropped the lantern and stepped back, closing with Desiderius so they could protect each other and yelled, "Intruders! Intruders!"

If the rest of his contubernium could not hear the commotion that the men running towards them were making, they would almost certainly hear his yells. The area around the gunpowder building was quiet and had been all night, so there was no way they could miss this commotion.

He didn't have time to think about that, though, as the men set upon them.

Their attack was clumsy, making up for skill with enthusiasm and numbers. Mettius was far from the best fighter in the guard or the legions, but he'd trained hard and taken it seriously, but most of that was fighting as part of a wall, with men protecting his sides. He had Desiderius, but that wasn't going to be enough. There were almost two dozen men coming towards them, more than Mettius's entire contubernium, even if they all had been there.

He didn't have time to think about that, though, as the first sword shot toward him. Mettius brought his sword in an inward sweep as his training optio had shown him, forcing the enemy's weapon away from his body, past his side. True, it took his sword out of position too, but that was to plan. Normally, he would have struck forward with his shield, smashing it into the man's face. Without that, he improvised bringing his left foot up and smashing it into the man's stomach, causing him to double over. As the man fell, Mettius brought his sword swinging back, parrying the new attacker's sword past the other side of Mettius's body, which left his weapon in place to stab forward, skewering the man in the throat.

The first blow hit him as he pulled his sword free, an old pitchfork smashing into his armor, one of the prongs breaking off as the weapon skidded along the metal plates. Mettius repaid the stab with one of his own, which found no armor stopping its forward progress. A man also lay at Desiderius feet, dead. For a moment, Mettius thought they might make it through this. He heard shouts from his comrades, behind him, coming to join the fray, and then the first of the attackers' weapons found its mark. A makeshift spear stabbed out, catching Desiderius high in the chest.

Mettius was stunned. He'd seen soldiers die in battle and his friends drop dead from overwork in the fields, but Desiderius was his best friend. They'd been together since both were barely able to work unsupervised, Desiderius purchased from a merchant and sold after his parents died in the mines. They had gained their freedom together, joined the legions together, and moved to the Praetorian Guard together.

His friend didn't go down without a fight! His sword stabbed out, killing the man that had killed him, the pair dropping, each skewered by the other's weapon. Mettius didn't have time to grieve as he parried another stab and slashed up on the return stroke, a deep red streak appearing across the faces of the newest attackers. From his peripheral vision, he saw two of his men at his side, both standing over fallen bodies, joining the attack.

Mettius pressed forward, his anger ragging, ready to avenge his friend, when the sword with his name on it found its spot. At first, Mettius wasn't sure what happened. It was strange, he didn't feel pain, just his sword dropping as his legs suddenly stopped working, a warm feeling in his throat and the taste of copper on his tongue.

He landed next to Desiderius, looking straight into his fallen friend's open, lifeless eyes. He'd miss the guard, Mettius thought as his vision darkened and the ground turned cold.

A foot stomped near him. Mettius thought maybe they stepped on him. Something heavy fell on him. He knew he was dying. He felt sad. He felt angry. Mostly, he felt acceptance. He'd given his life for something that mattered and not for a fat land owner, growing crops he'd never eat. Fighting for the Empire was worth his sacrifice. It was a good death. He just wished Desiderius hadn't had to die, too.

He was going to miss his friend.

Chapter 16

Devnum

"This is a terrible idea," Ky said for the thirtieth time.

"Mmm-hmmm," Lucilla mumbled quietly.

Surrounded by a half dozen people on the raised platform, a crowd of citizens spread out in front of her, she couldn't exactly reply, which gave Ky the chance to make his feelings known without her shutting him down.

They'd argued for two days, which was how long it took her to put her insane plan into action. He'd argued against it, Ramirus had argued against it, and even her father had tried to talk her out of it, but she wouldn't budge. She would have been furious, regardless, by the death of an entire Roman squad of legionnaires and the theft of gunpowder, especially after her recent warnings to Ramirus, but she was taking this personally. This was the same squad that had recently captured an insurgent and she'd made a point to visit them and congratulate them on their good work. The fact that she'd met these men, shaken their hands, and looked them in the eye meant these weren't just names, they were her people.

Ky understood that, but he also understood that in war you couldn't let your emotions override your senses. Soldiers died. Often your friends died, but you still needed to do your duty. He actually wasn't that worried about the stolen gunpowder. Even if they managed to get it shipped from Britannia, across the continent and all the way to Africa, without fouling it or otherwise ruining the gunpowder with something like salt water, it was extremely unlikely they'd be able to take that mixture and work out its exact components. In a world without microscopes or spectrographs, it was going to be difficult to reverse engineer the explosive enough to not only know what went into it, but the exact ratio of those components or the methods needed to combine them. Nor were they likely to work out the physics behind the weapons to take advantage of gunpowder even if they did.

What it did confirm, at least for Ky, was that they hadn't managed to learn the secrets of gunpowder from more traditional sources, like turning someone who worked on it or getting copies of the instructions he'd given to Hortensius to make it. It also suggested that their precautions on guarding the documents with that information were working.

This was by far the largest move made by the insurrectionists since the actual insurrection. Twenty-one of the thieves had fallen in the battle with the guards defending the storage building, which according to Ramirus, would be a huge part of the remaining manpower the insurrectionists had. The sudden shift of targets from stealing documents and destroying storage buildings to all-out assaults was notable, and spoke to their desperation.

Besides, the first thing the insurgents would have done after getting their hands on the gunpowder would be to get it off the island and on its way to the Carthaginian capital. Even if her plan worked, they weren't stopping anything, and yet she was willing to risk her life, which would have massive consequences for the Empire, and him personally. He knew she knew it and he knew that she didn't care.

"We could have at least used someone else. Your nanites do not make you invulnerable. You got lucky last time. You could have at least let me do it. I'm not sure there's anything they could do that my system couldn't repair."

"Shut up," Lucilla said.

She'd been trying to stop herself, but he kept nattering in her ear. She'd heard him out, but she wasn't changing her mind. He needed to know that. These men, they fought and died for her. Well, maybe that was an overstatement. They served her father, but she was his daughter and felt every obligation he carried. After her time with the Caledonians and guardsmen, she felt a connection to the soldiers. They were her people. Ky kept saying not to take it personally, but she was, and she wasn't planning on stopping just because he thought she should.

"My lady?" Faenius said beside her, looking a little startled.

"I'm sorry. It's ... the noise from the crowd. I just have a bit of a headache."

"We don't have to do this, my lady. I still think this is too much of a risk for you. You're too exposed."

Ky should be happy he wasn't the only one arguing against her plan. She was practically the only one who thought this was a good idea. Her guards, Faenius, Ky, even her father, they all thought it was a mistake. She didn't care. She'd managed to at least get her father to back down. The rest of them, they worked for her, so they didn't get a say.

"We've been through this," she said, both to Faenius and Ky. "No other bait is going to work and we need to put a stop to them before anyone else dies. You just make sure you're ready for their attack."

"My lady," Faenius started to say, but she cut him off.

"That wasn't a suggestion."

Faenius sighed but bowed and climbed down from the platform. The crowds were starting to gather and the sun was just reaching its apex, which is when she'd told the praeco to announce her public address. Showtime, she thought.

"It is a dark day for the Empire," she said, starting her speech.

Ky stopped pestering her as she began her speech. This might all be a ruse, but word had already spread about the annihilation of an entire contubernium and the possible theft of military supplies, and tensions were high. Most of the citizens of Devnum, not counting the new arrivals since the formation of the Empire, had lost friends and family during the insurrection, which had damaged huge sections of the city. People were scared and needed to be reassured.

That was one of the main points Lucilla had used in her arguments. The people needed to see her, or her father. They needed to hear that the Empire was taking these deaths seriously and that there was no threat to the safety of the Empire as a whole. Ky couldn't help but think if someone did manage to attack her, it would do the exact opposite, but she wasn't swayed by that argument.

He had to give it to her, she was very good at these speeches. Much better than he'd ever be. He'd already heard pieces of it when she'd been practicing the night before, but he was still impressed by how much presence she had when she kicked her performance into high gear.

Unfortunately, Ky couldn't pay that much attention to it. His attention was on the crowd and the windows overlooking the large plaza in front of the palace complex. He was in one of those windows, behind where the stage had been strategically set up, so he could see everything. It meant he had a small blind side at the back, but that was the least likely place for an assassin to try and strike, considering all of the legionaries and praetorians lining the front and back of the stage.

"Anything?" Ky asked Sophus.

"No Commander, although it will be impossible to tell if an assassin is in the crowd until they begin their attack. The only member of the insurrectionists we have a description of is their leader, who is unlikely to be used in a direct action."

"I know. Just keep your eyes peeled. I want to know the moment something happens."

"I do not have eyes, Commander."

Ky rolled his eyes. Sophus was sentient, but he was very bad at understanding colloquialisms. He didn't, however, feel the need to get into an extended conversation with the AI over that at the moment. He knew Sophus was watching the situation from the drone he'd borrowed back from Lucilla, which was at the moment under Sophus's direct control high above the crowd where it was unlikely to be spotted. Ky could have watched the feed himself, but he couldn't truly split his focus like Sophus could, so he continued to scan the crowd using his enhanced vision instead.

The AI was assisting him, constantly highlighting potential threats. The whole time Ky watched over the sights of a crossbow, ready to fire the moment an assassin appeared. With Sophus's help and his enhanced reflexes, he was confident he could hit anyone headed for Lucilla before they got into range to actually hurt her. Which was one of her other reasons for arguing this plan wasn't as dangerous as it seemed. He appreciated her faith in him, but ...

"Commander," Sophus's voice rang out, almost sounding panicked. Almost.

A box appeared over a figure in the back of the crowd, in a direct line with Lucilla below. Ky zoomed in on him just in time to see the arcuballista spring up to his shoulder, his finger pressing on the trigger.

Ky saw the calculation Sophus was doing and the targeting profile and was glad that he and the AI were so in sync. Ky pressed the trigger on his crossbow and dropped the weapon, reaching for a second loaded weapon on a table next to him as he watched the take from the drone's feed, which was following the flight of the arrow as it raced towards Lucilla.

Lucilla didn't know what was happening. One moment she was in the middle of her speech, looking out across the crowd, and then there were screams. She looked towards the back, where people looked to be panicking, just in time to see a man pointing an arcuballista directly at her.

The whole scene felt like it was playing out in slow motion. She saw the man fire and the arrow snap out of the weapon, hurtling toward her. She started to duck, although she knew there was no way she'd move more than a hairs width before the arrow hit her, when the unthinkable happened.

An arrow appeared from above and behind her, smashing into the head of the arrow flying towards her, driving it into the ground, barely missing a woman who was starting to run with the other people in the crowd. Lucilla was shocked but didn't have time to think about it as another arrow shot out of the building behind her, catching the assassin in the shoulder as he turned to run away.

The man stumbled and was just getting up when Ky appeared, sailing out of the window he'd been in, crossing half the plaza, and landing a short distance from the man. The crowd froze at the sight of him and his inhuman feat, as did the assassin, who fell back on his butt, staring wide-eyed at Ky, who now loomed over him.

For a moment, Lucilla thought Ky was going to kill him. She couldn't see his face, but she could see his body language and knew what it looked like when Ky was furious. Instead, he reached down and lifted the man by his neck using only one arm, the man's feet swinging as he came off the ground. Praetorians came on the run and Ky practically thrust the man into one of them before turning and stalking back to the stage, a serious look on his face.

"You can't still be mad at me," Lucilla said to Ky hours later, as they waited outside of one of Ramirus's interrogation cells.

"I can be. I told you this was dangerous. Do you know how close you came to dying today?" Ky asked, his words curt and short.

"But I didn't," Lucilla countered.

"Lucilla ..."

"Ky, it was worth it. We got him and no one was hurt, well, no one other than the assassin. I knew you could protect me, and you did."

"We got lucky. I appreciate your faith in me, but the number of variables for a shot like that is astronomical. Sophus is good, but it's not infallible."

"I've seen some of the things Sophus and you have done together. I had faith in you."

"He is correct, Lucilla. There was a fraction of a second available to run those calculations and the smallest change in air currents or humidity could have altered the projection enough to cause our projectile to miss. This was, as Ky likes to say, a fortunate happenstance."

"Luck," Ky corrected. "Yes. It worked out, and I'm happy it did. Hopefully, this guy knows something and we can take care of this insurrectionist problem once and for all, but you can't take chances like that. I almost lost you once, I won't do it again."

"You're right," she said. "I'm not sorry I did it and I do think the fact that it worked proves it was the right decision, but I am sorry for making you worry. You've put your life on the line multiple times for us, I think it's only fair I'm allowed to do the same."

Ky sighed, "I'm not winning this argument, am I?"

"No, but I think it's cute you keep trying."

Ky just shook his head. He couldn't stay mad at her. He would be damned if he ever let something like this happen again, but he couldn't fault her for her bravery or determination to get the job done.

"You realize your little display today is going to make it a lot harder next time you try to tell someone you weren't sent by the gods."

"I doubt most people could even see what happened to the arrows," Ky said.

"No, but they could see you jump clear across the plaza. That was beyond the ability of anyone who's ever lived. Only the Sword could do something like that."

"You know ..."

"Yes, I know, but most of our subjects don't have the same kind of relationship you and I have, or Sophus talking in their ear."

"Damn it. I was just starting to get people to quit it with all the Sword stuff."

"They only quit it around you, my love. Most of the people have never stopped believing you were sent to save us. That's a side effect of, you know, constantly saving everyone."

"Not everyone," Ky said.

"No, not everyone. But most of us."

Their conversation was interrupted when the door opened and Ramirus came walking out, wiping his hands on a piece of cloth.

"That went faster than expected. Apparently, he's convinced he's angered the gods, swears he believed the people who told him you were a false avatar, and he just ... gave up everything."

"See," Lucilla said, nudging Ky with her elbow. "I told you that little display was going to convince people."

"Since I was specifically ordered not to be there," Ramirus said, giving Lucilla a look. "I assume you're talking about the Consul jumping clear across the city."

"It wasn't that far," Ky said defensively.

"Nearly all the way across the palace plaza."

"Impressive," Ramirus said, actually sounding anything but impressed. "It worked on him. He's convinced he was following false prophets and is desperate to keep from angering Jupiter."

Of course, Ramirus wouldn't be impressed. He probably had reports of everything Ky had ever done that was beyond the normal range of human ability. Not that he wanted the attention, but Ky oddly found himself wishing Ramirus showed just a little bit of astonishment, instead of complete apathy.

"He isn't going to get away with trying to kill Lucilla," Ky said.

"We shouldn't execute him, though," Lucilla added hastily. "I know that's been the standing policy, but I think we need to use this. Use him to convince some of the others they are wrong. I'm not suggesting we set him free, but I think he could be a valuable piece of propaganda."

"Maybe," Ky said begrudgingly. "For right now, though, the big question is does he know anything or is this another errand boy."

"He got his orders directly from Decius himself, although it seems Decius has some kind of inner circle that was also there."

"Excellent. So we know where they are and can round them up."

"It was a meeting place. Apparently, they have several and rotate to keep from being in one place consistently. He also couldn't give us the names of most of the inner circle, since he doesn't know but one or two."

"Fine, we round up the one or two and get them to talk," Ky said.

"We don't know which meeting place they'll be at," Ramirus said. "We can raid them, but we might just get lower-level people."

"Then let's ..." Ky started to say, before being interrupted by Lucilla.

"I assume you have a suggestion," Lucilla said.

"I do. We put men on the houses we know about, follow anyone leaving them and if they go to a new meeting place, put people on those. Once we have as many of the insurrectionists identified and located as possible, we take them all."

"That is going to require some pretty complicated coordination," Ky said. "What if we lose them or tip them off?"

"We'll find them again. Some might get away, but we're going to take everywhere they've used for refuge and all of their resources we can get our hands on, and we'll know the names of more of Decius's associates. But we won't lose them. My trap may not have worked well, but this ... this I know how to do. Following people, gathering information, this is what my people do. Have some faith, Consul."

"Fine. If I ..."

"No," Lucilla said.

"No?"

"No. You have things to do, or did you forget? Valdar's ships are loading right now to join the transports and legions. You've pointed out, several times, how tight the timeline is for operations before winter sets in. We can handle this, Ramirus and I. We can watch over the operation, just as well as you can."

Lucilla stressed the 'we' and 'watch over' in that sentence, making hard eye contact with Ky, hoping he'd get what she was saying. After a beat, he nodded, understanding. He still had the drone, but he'd been planning on returning it to her before he left, since she still needed it to let Sophus examine the progress of work so it could make recommendations. Similarly, Sophus could control the drone through her comm unit just as well as Ky could, and tell her what was happening.

"Fine. You're right. You two have this. Just be careful. This is our moment to put all of these distractions behind us for good."

"We'll do our duty, Consul," Ramirus said.

"So this is the capital of your Empire," Medb said, looking out the window onto the city as the sun slowly set, coloring everything in an orangish light.

"I guess, although I don't know if I'd say it was my Empire. We've only just joined them," Cormac said.

"You commanded their armies in the field though, right? When you crushed the Carthaginians?" She said, turning from the window to look at her husband who was sitting on their bed.

It had been a whirlwind several weeks. His father had been good to his word and married them two days after announcing it was happening, and then promptly stuck them on a ship bound for Devnum. He understood the reasoning behind his father's actions, and he'd even agreed with them when his father initially told him about his concerns, along with the need for him to be the one to marry her. After spending time with her, though, Cormac was no longer sure.

He'd been worried about having to deal with her even before the wedding. She was older than him, had been a queen in her own right, and a seasoned warrior. Cormac talked a lot, but he could at least be honest with himself. His father was the hero, winning the right to rule the kingdom and then defending it against what seemed like the world crashing down on them. He'd negotiated a strong position in the new Empire and already was seeing their people begin to rebuild.

Cormac had done little. Until Llassar showed up, he'd been kept in Emain Macha, for his protection. He'd never seen battle, never led anyone. When he did get the chance, he'd screwed it up. He could still remember Llassar looking at him on those battlements like he was something unpleasant the older man had stepped on. He hadn't been wrong, either. A lot of his soldiers had died in that assault. At the time, Cormac had thought it valiant. Worth the sacrifices to show their enemy who was really in charge.

But they'd bypassed two other fortifications after that on their way to Medb's capitol, isolating them without losing a man. Both of those forts had given up once Medb surrendered. They could have done the same for that first fort, he wouldn't have lost any men, and they would still have taken the city in the end. His father had left him with Llassar to learn, and he had. He'd learned how much he didn't know.

"No. I watched while Llassar and the Roman, uhh, Britannian, I guess, legates led the men. My one time in combat was ... less than spectacular."

It had been difficult, ever since. He'd taken to berating himself in the quiet moments, starting to doubt his own abilities.

"Only because you didn't get the support that you needed. Your father might have left you with that old goat to learn, but what you got was someone keeping you from learning."

"Llassar's not that bad. He involved me in councils of war and explained why they were making this decision or that."

"But he never actually gave you a chance to make your own decisions. I know you like him, and I'm sure he's a fine person, one on one, but as a teacher, I've seen his type all my life. When my father died, his advisors, men my father left to teach me how to rule, tried instead to take my throne from me. I'm a woman, they declared, and not fit to lead. Trust me, I know the type. Men who use the hand of friendship to hold you back."

"We took your throne too," Cormac pointed out.

"Yes. Yes, you did, but that was my fault. I'm not sure I'd ever say this to people like Llassar or your father, but here with just you, I'll admit it. I made a mistake. I saw the Carthaginians and how they'd handled some of the other kingdoms. I knew I'd be crushed if I didn't join them, so I decided to try to make the best of the situation. I thought maybe I could get a good place for my people when the dust settled. In my defense, how was I supposed to know the Romans would form this alliance, develop staggering new weapons, and clear both islands of the Carthaginians in less than a year?"

"You're a rare person, Medb. I'm not sure if I could forgive the people who deposed me, if I was in your place."

"I'm a survivor," she said, moving from the window, to sit next to him. "Besides, it hasn't been so bad. When Fergus fell, I thought I was next, but here we are. We get along well and we have a real chance to make something for ourselves in this new Empire, probably more than your father does, away from the real power. Seeing everything happening in this city, especially the tour of those factories outside of town and those massive ships in the harbor, my loss was a foregone conclusion. I think, maybe, this is where I was destined to be. I love my people and I won't lie, I liked being queen, but we would have been a small backwater in this new world."

He smiled at her. It was strange. Instead of being difficult, challenging, and looking down at him, she'd been supportive. They'd talked like this every night. She never talked down to him and always treated him like an equal. That might have been expected with most married couples, but they were not most married couples. She was an impressive person, and she treated him as if he was just as important. It was … exciting, really.

"Maybe, although it's hard to see how that destiny will play out. I mean, they already made it clear I wasn't to leave the ships during the battle coming up. I haven't even gotten to see any of the training yet."

"Give it time," she said, putting her hand in his and intertwining their fingers. "They're not going to give you anything' you're going to have to take it. Just bide your time. When the moment comes, stand up and take what's yours."

"How will I know when it's time?"

"You'll know. You'll see something, something the others will have missed, and you'll step in and show your quality. They'll have to give you a place of power after that."

"You think so?"

"I do. We have to be ready, though. They've made it clear they don't plan on giving you the place you deserve, so when the time comes you're going to have to demand it. And when you do, we'll make sure they can't push either of us out again. We're going to be unstoppable, you and me."

Her eyes were like fire, and Cormac felt himself get swept up into them.

Chapter 17

Insula Manavia

Velius wiped the ocean spray off his face and looked at Bomilcar, who stood slightly ahead of him, staring off the front of the galley, resisting the urge to frown. They'd gone back and forth for weeks, but in the end, Velius had to give in. Every trial run they did showed the same thing. They needed to be in the first wave. There were just too many variables and during the first few waves, their position was going to be precarious. He'd tried to convince Bomilcar to stay back with the later waves, but the general had insisted that he needed to be there too.

Velius had to give in to that too. Bomilcar had shown that he just thought differently than the rest of the Britannians, which meant the people defending the island would, too. It also meant Bomilcar was the most likely one to recognize their tactics as soon as they happened, which meant with him the Britannians would be able to react almost as soon as the Carthaginians made a move, instead of having to wait to see how things played out.

Velius knew his annoyance was childish and beneath him, but he couldn't help it. Thankfully, he was about to have a good distraction from his internal battle.

The beach was coming up in a rush, although he felt it was slower now than it had been in training. The galleys were much slower than Valdar's new ships, which he'd had a chance to ride on after the fleet picked up the legions and sailed back north for the attack. Velius was no sailor and weeks ago he hadn't even considered there would be faster ships than the large galleys the Romans and

Carthaginians used. After experiencing the new ships, however, it felt like they were crawling.

"Prepare to disembark," Velius yelled back at the men, his command echoed by tribunes and optios.

A signalman put up flags that rose high up the mast, passing the word to the other galleys in the first wave. He didn't really need to shout the orders. They'd gone over this again and again. Everyone knew their jobs and where they needed to be. He just felt, as the man nominally in charge of this landing, that he should do something.

He braced, holding onto the railing, knowing what was coming next as the bottom of the boat slammed into the wet sand of the beach, slowing the ship until they were just a few paces from dry sand.

"Over," Velius yelled, vaulting over the side, the sound of dozens and then hundreds of feet slamming into the water resulting in the sand reverberating up and down the small section of beach.

He ran forward, grunting with the effort of moving his legs and armor through the water as the sand sucked at his boots. They were almost on dry sand, and Velius couldn't see anything in the tree line in front of him.

The Consul, however, must have seen something, because the noise of men grunting and equipment clanking was suddenly dwarfed by a steady series of booms coming from behind him. Velius wasn't sure he'd ever get used to that sound. It was like thunder, but coming from the ground instead of the sky. It was unnatural and chilling.

What followed next was even more fantastical. Clumps of sand and dirt sprayed high into the air as the cannon balls began to land, the dirt showering back almost as far as the boats. If that wasn't astonishing enough, a few of the shells exploded in midair, the metal balls turning into balls of fire, just as they passed the tops of the trees.

Velius had yet to see those in action, but the Consul had warned him about them, and he'd in turn passed that warning down to his officers and men, once they were underway. Normally, that kind of information wasn't something you'd pass to the average legionnaire, but this was so far outside of their experience he didn't want any of them panicking.

Velius still looked left and right at the men around him, checking for signs that the sudden display might disrupt the men forming up in the assembly area. Several men slowed to gawk open-mouthed and one or two even stopped, at least until an officer prodded them forward with an open hand or the bottom of a boot.

"Move into line. Get your asses moving," Velius yelled at the men closest to him, pushing and shoving them to get them moving again.

Looking back, he could see their training had paid off as the last stragglers were making it out of the water and onto the sand. They had bested the Consul's original timetable for the boats to unload by a solid two minutes. That included men freezing when the cannon fire started. Unfortunately, that was the one part they couldn't simulate. Short of burning through their limited supplies of gunpowder, there was no way to simulate the visage of the underworld that the men behind those trees must be experiencing at this moment.

"Signal the boats to pull out and the next wave to start their approach," he said to the signalman who finally caught up to him.

He could see the oars from the galleys already pushing against the water, pushing against the tide, propelling the boats ever so slowly back toward the sea. The captains knew their business and probably would have done their job without his prodding, but a good commander didn't assume anything.

"This is going too smoothly," Velius said to Bomilcar, who finally joined him with the rest of the command team behind the thin line of legionnaires holding in front of them.

The general had stopped close to the shore, staring at the tree line through one of the improved field glasses they'd been issued only a few days ago. They were impressive, better than even the original ones the Consul had given him, that he'd found almost magical at the time, but Velius wasn't sure what the general was looking at. Fire had broken out among the trees and the entire edge of the beach was covered in flames and smoke. It was impossible to see what the enemy was up to.

"It's about to get a lot less smooth," the general said, collapsing the spyglass and putting it in the protective pouch at his waist.

"Why?" Velius asked, looking back at the exploding tree line.

"They're going to hit us from the left. Probably before the next boats make landfall. We've only got a few minutes before they break the tree line."

Velius looked where Bomilcar was pointing, and frowned. He didn't see anything that would indicate an imminent attack.

"I don't see anything."

"Look at the animals running out onto the sand and then down the tree line at the birds flying west, away from us. Something is moving through the trees away from the area under shelling and a little further back, but I think they're just circling around to keep from being caught in the line of fire. Otherwise, they'd already be on us."

"The animals are running from the shelling," Velius said.

"They're running from the shelling and something else. The animals on the right flank are running in all directions, except they aren't coming onto the beach. They can see our people and hear the commotion we're making, even with the shelling. Animals don't generally run toward more predators. Something is moving in that direction, disturbing the wildlife, and it's already started them turning toward us. We don't have time to argue this. You can either believe me or not, but if you're going to do something, it has to be done now."

Velius stared at him hard for several seconds, the sounds of crashing cannonballs and the occasional explosion drowning it out as he focused on the Carthaginian. He was right. He could either ignore his warning or trust that the Consul was right and the man really was trying to help them.

"Velius," Bomilcar said, prodding him.

"Damn it," he cursed and then turned to one of the signalmen next to him. "Signal all cohorts except the Eighth. Stand to the left! Eight cohorts will hold forward, remaining will angle off to the left towards the surf. Prepare for imminent contact."

Velius paused a moment, considering, before adding, "All additional landed units are to reinforce the eighth cohort under the direct command of Bomilcar."

Turning to the general, Velius said. "Just in case this is a feint, you'll get all the reinforcements. If you see us wavering and think there isn't a second attack coming from the right or straight ahead, reinforce us using the men that land with the second wave as you see fit. Do not abandon the forward line."

Bomilcar made hard eye contact and gave a slight nod, "I'll take care of it. Once they're on the beach, it's unlikely they'll try and flank us further. They'll want to keep the phalanx compact."

"I hope so," Velius said and ran to join the men flowing out of line and to the left of eight cohorts, which was thinning and expanding to try and cover all of the empty space created by their companion's departure.

"Runners," Velius yelled, looking around for someone to help him pass orders.

Because of the lack of signalmen who'd landed and the need to continue communicating with the boats waiting for their turn to land, he'd had to leave the one he had with Bomilcar, who'd have to deal with getting all of the men ashore on his own.

"Who's the highest officer on shore and not in the Eighth?" Velius asked the messenger who ran up.

"Sagarius." "Tell Sagarius to stretch the line. Pull it to three deep and go out as far as he can until he runs out of beach or men. Have the command staff from the other cohorts spread evenly down the line. Don't worry about unit makeup at the moment. Just get the line solid and then hold. He also needs to pull at least fifty men and send them back to me as a reserve."

The messenger nodded and ran off to find the prefect, one of the few high-ranking officers who'd been in the first wave. Velius followed behind him, occasionally yelling a command here or there to the men forming up, although it was more to feel like he was doing something and so the men knew he was with them. They did themselves proud, every man moving with purpose, quickly getting into the extremely thin ranks.

It was a good thing too, because the line was still adjusting when the Carthaginians burst from the tree line well down to the left of their original position, exactly where Bomilcar said they would. It was a smart maneuver, trying to flank him, but they'd gone too far. Now that his line extended into the surf, they weren't getting around him. They'd given themselves more sand to trudge through than they really needed to, although perhaps they just wanted to get further away from the explosions.

Velius was pretty sure the cannon fire was affecting them, as their formation was shaky and still came in far down his left. In a position like his, where his line cut sharply in one direction to avoid being flanked, the weakest point was the corner created where they connected with the line still facing forward. A smart commander would hit there, since the men right at the corner lost the benefit of the shield wall, and would be able to be attacked on multiple sides. Attacking halfway down the line extending back and to the left didn't gain them anything, other than distance from the explosions.

Of course, they outnumbered his men and were compacted, where his line was only three men deep. It wouldn't take much for them to create a hole and roll up his whole force.

"Fire," Velius yelled, the command rippling down in both directions as it was relayed by the officers.

The men in the second and third rows had already pulled up their arcuballistas when they saw the approaching Carthaginians and, as a group, released a volley that cut hard into their formation, causing it to break slightly as it marched forward, another sign they were shaken. It gave Velius a thought.

"Second rank, shields up. Third rank, reload," Velius yelled. "Hold fire."

As close as they were and as thin as Velius's line was, the smart thing to do would have been to have all of the men sling their arcuballista and get ready for contact, since where the wall was hit would feel the pressure of that initial contact, and they'd need the third rank to push back and replace men from the first and second rows as they fell. With how thin his line was, he couldn't go with the smart thing.

Velius watched as the Carthaginians continued to close the distance. It was a startling sight. He hadn't been this close to the front rank since his early days as a legionary. He didn't have entire cohorts between himself and the enemy now, and it was terrifying, seeing the rows of spears that could almost reach him once the lines clashed.

"Fire," Velius yelled as the Carthaginians passed an imaginary line he'd put down, just a dozen steps or so from their front line.

Arrows rippled out from the third line past the shoulders of their comrades, tearing into the Carthaginians. At this distance, the arcuballista still had almost all of their punch and the arrows tore through shields and men. Their line didn't break, but it was uneven from all of the gaps created by the fallen men, and those that were left were shaken from the sudden punch of the arrows.

They didn't stop, however. The phalanxes had momentum, the rear rows pushing forward, forcing the men in front of them to keep moving no matter the carnage they were receiving at the front. It was one of the things that gave the formation its power and allowed them to overpower their enemies. It was also the thing that made them so inflexible, and had allowed the Romans to beat them many times, since their men were able to adjust more quickly or even stop as the situation called for it.

The Carthaginians slammed into his men, who held fast, their shields up, gladius already punching forward, trying to catch a spearman. Men fell here and there, but not as many as the enemy needed to be able to punch through the line. Between the large Roman shields and the uneven contact from the disturbed Carthaginian line, the attack was too light and didn't have the power to push through the thinner Britannian line.

Velius looked past the Carthaginians to the empty beach behind them. There were no other units coming out of the trees. He guessed that the Carthaginians had put all of their men together for a solid blow into the Britannians, as opposed to staggering smaller groups, to give them options once they made contact. He didn't know that for a fact, of course, but Velius was pretty sure that was right. The cannons were still firing and he was confident the Consul wouldn't continue burning through gunpowder if it wasn't necessary, which meant there were still men opposite the Britannian's front line.

"Order to Sagarius," Velius called over the sounds of shouts, pain, and clashing weapons. "Swing the left end of the line up, pivoting against the point of contact. Wrap our line around the Carthaginian formation."

He didn't know Sagarius well, but the reports he'd gotten on the man were good, and he trusted him to pull off the maneuver without breaking their own line. It was a gamble. If Velius was wrong, a second Carthaginian force could now easily loop around his men and scrape off the thin Britannian line, like so much butter.

At first, it looked like they would hold, but the thin line was straining as men started to fall. Velius began plugging weakening spots with the small reserve he'd pulled aside, but those men began to dwindle fast. Sagarius was moving his men, but it was slow, since they had to keep solid contact as the line swung around. If they moved too fast, gaps would start to form at the points where the men were in contact with the Carthaginians, which would be as good as if they hadn't extended their line at all, since the phalanxes could push the exposed flanks caused by the gaps, wiping out his line.

Worse, the Carthaginians knew they couldn't just run away. The Britannians had done a good job of sinking any boat that might be used to get them off the island to escape, they could see more Britannian ships landing, and they'd experienced the damage Britannian shelling could do. They were fighting as hard as any Carthaginian phalanx he'd seen. In the end, they'd still lose. At this point, it was a certainty. All that was left to decide was how many men Velius would lose in the process. Something he could ill afford.

Unfortunately, the more Velius watched the more apparent it became that he would run out of his reserves before Sagarius finished his partial encirclement of the Carthaginians. As he sent in the last of his reserves, another weak point opened up right at the edge of the line, just where he'd feared the line would break. Two, then three, then a fourth man fell. The men in the second and third lines began filling in the gaps, but they were soon down to a single line, which wouldn't hold.

"Follow me," Velius yelled at the few messengers, the single signalman, and an aide that had made it to shore and stood with him behind the lines.

Velius grabbed a dropped shield as he ran and pulled his sword. He could see the men following him realizing what he was about to do, take their weapons in hand, fear in their eyes. Velius didn't pity them. He'd always made it clear that his men were soldiers first, from the highest commander to the lowest cook. If they were in his legion, they were expected to train, know how to fight, and be capable of going into battle as the situation needed.

The sand churned under his boots as he charged in, leaning slightly forward, fighting against the difficult ground. He was glad he didn't hesitate, as two men at the exact corner of the line fell under a barrage of stabs from swords and spears. Without a line behind them, it opened up the exact point he'd been worried about. He and the few men with him slammed into the Carthaginians just as they tried to exploit the opening. They'd been so focused on killing the men in front of them and then getting their comrades rallied for the breakthrough that they hadn't seen Velius coming, or expected the sudden attack.

Velius slapped a spear out of the way and slammed the shield into the shorter Carthaginian leading the breakthrough, sending the man sailing back into the soldiers behind him, causing several to fall in the confusion. His legionary days came back to him in a rush as his sword flashed out, catching a man in the side, his blood spilling out on the sand as Velius pulled his weapon back, ready to strike again.

The sand was hard to get a good foothold on. It wasn't even particularly sand anymore. It was now a reddish, muddy mixture of sand, blood, and bile, slippery and squelching against his boots. The aide pushed in next to him, just in time for a Carthaginian spear to slash in, catching him just below the jaw. The man dropped, but Velius knew he couldn't worry about the man, now. If he was destined to live, then he would. If not, he'd die. Velius had to focus on the men trying to kill him.

He pushed his shield up, ducking his head slightly, forcing the spear tip meant for him to bounce off the metal edging of the borrowed shield. His arm flashed out again and he felt the familiar feeling of flesh trying, and failing, to resist a stabbing weapon. He didn't know if it was the man who tried to kill him, but someone fell. One of his messengers slotted in next to him, his expression terrified, but pressing hard against the shield.

Battles against phalanxes were as much massive shoving matches as actual combat with swords. You had to lean into the shield, trying to push them back as they did the same to you. While it was a contest of strength and skill, the biggest deciding factor for either force was endurance, if matched one on one.

His gladius stabbed out again and again, sometimes killing the enemy and sometimes sliding off shields or armor, and then the messenger fell. The other men he'd brought were on his left, which meant that was the last man he'd brought with him. He tried to edge to the right, hoping he could hold the spot, but there wasn't much hope. He looked over and made eye contact with the Carthaginian in front of that hole, and knew the man recognized the opportunity. He pulled back, trying to get his spear angled to catch Velius, when suddenly a shield came in, out of nowhere.

The Carthaginian had been as focused on him as Velius had been on the Carthaginian, and neither had seen it coming. The Carthaginian who'd just seen his chance to kill a Roman and break through the line fell, the gladius being pulled out of his chest coated in red.

Hands pulled at Velius from behind. He recognized the signal, men trying to switch out with him, and resisted at first, until more hands joined in and a man pushed in next to him, adding his weight to Velius's shield, his hands trying for the straps so they could switch out. Velius gave it to him and backed up, which is when he realized there were more men running at them. Several dozen, including Gordianus, his second in command, were moving up from the boats that looked to have just landed.

Velius backed up further, as reinforcements poured in. Stepping back, he could see the battlefield again. Sagarius had pressed in and already the Carthaginian phalanx was crumbling. The danger had passed.

"You have no idea how good your timing is," Velius said to Gordianus, slapping the man on the shoulder.

"Thank you, General, but it's not all my doing. The men had already started for their assigned positions. I just gave them a small push."

"I see," Velius said, looking back to the shoreline, where he thought he could make out the Carthaginian stalking back up from the boats to the line Velius had left him in charge of.

Velius also noticed the cannon fire had slackened off, which hopefully meant the Carthaginian force had run or been destroyed, and not that Valdar was running out of gunpowder.

"Sagarius has them half encircled. Finish it and either kill them or take them prisoner. I'm going back to the main line and see where we're at. I think we might have pushed them back."

"Don't curse us, Legate," Gordianus said with a smile.

Velius shook his head, slapped the man on the back, and went to see where they stood. He knew the actual end result was never in doubt, but it looked like they were going to do it without losing too many men, which was always the real goal.

They might have just pulled this off after all.

Chapter 18

Devnum

"Did any of you actually see this happen, or is it just gossip?" Decius asked, causing the other men to look back and forth at each other.

"No. We agreed that it was best if we only had one man in the crowd, just in case Ramirus was watching the crowd or they detained everyone for questioning afterward, but the story we're hearing has been very consistent. He flew clear across the court-yard. It's unclear if he had wings or was simply gliding like a leaf on the wind, but everyone was clear that he crossed the entire plaza from a window behind the platform set up for the Emperor's daughter to give her speech."

"One of my son's neighbors was there, and said he fired a bolt from an arcuballista, shooting our man's arrow out of the air. She said it landed right in front of her, almost hitting a man. One arrow had impaled the other."

"Wings. Shooting arrows out of the sky," Decius said, sounding dismissive. "All we're doing is building his myth, which will make it harder to turn the people around when the time comes. You all know how bad people's detailed memory of events is. Most of these stories didn't start until days after it happened. If he really did sprout wings, we would have heard it that day. It's all fairytales. It also isn't what's important. What we need to find out is what happened to our man. None of your gossip says anything about that."

"Everyone started running when he fired and the Consul made his ... display. The plaza was also well-guarded, and they cleared the area quickly. The only witness I've been able to find said that he saw the Consul standing over our man, but not what happened after that."

"I heard his body was rushed out by the Praetorians after he was killed by the Consul."

"Why would they rush a body out?" Decius asked. "If he was alive and they wanted to get him to physicians to keep him alive to be questioned, or they just wanted to make sure we didn't kill him before they questioned him, that I'd understand. But rushing out a body? No. If that happened, then he's still alive, which means we're going to need to change everything. He could expose us."

"We don't know if he was alive, though. And it's been days since he was taken. If he was alive, why have they not come for us? Ramirus's torturers are good enough to get the locations he knew about out of him by now. No, if he was taken alive, they would already have us."

"That's a good point. We're still going to make some changes, just in case. First, we ... did you hear that?" Decius said, cocking his head to the side as he tried to figure out what the half-heard sound was.

He started to stand up when the door to the villa they were using for tonight's meeting was smashed open, flying back on broken hinges and slamming against the opposite wall. Following through the broken door were almost a dozen Praetorians, moving fast in spite of their heavy segmented armor. Decius turned to run the other way, out the back door of the villa, when more armored men came through that entryway. His colleagues tried to push their way past the Praetorians and were promptly thrown to the floor, swords at their throats and rope going around their hands and legs.

"You can't ..." Decius started to say, protesting their treatment, when he saw movement from his periphery.

He'd only just turned his head when he recognized the handle of the gladius just before it smashed into the side of his head.

Insula Manavia

Holding a cloth over his mouth, Velius watched the large ships sail into the docks. He was looking forward to leaving this place. At the meeting the Consul had called, he'd been told that he would be leaving the death and destruction his army had wreaked on the Carthaginians soon. Valdar's ships had done a good job of sparing the docks, which would make getting prisoners and legionnaires off the island and bringing in teams to begin repairing the damage go much faster, but they had not done the same for the rest of the city, where the Carthaginians had holed up behind their walls. Velius had offered terms for surrender, but their commander had scoffed at it, forcing Velius's hand.

He wasn't surprised. Word had started to filter in from the continent through Ramirus's spies, that the Carthaginians had begun executing anyone who surrendered, from the commanding generals all the way to the lowest soldiers, *and their families.* It was brutal, but it insured most of them fought to the last man. In the long run, Velius was sure that policy would hurt them more than ensure victory in battle. As the Britannians expanded their reach, and the blanket of protection they could offer, the oppressive policies of the Carthaginians would make it much easier for newly taken villages to switch their allegiance, joining the Britannians instead of fighting against them.

Of course, that didn't do anything to help the poor bastards who'd huddled behind the walls of the small town set up by the Carthaginians as a supply depot. Valdar's ships had nearly leveled most of the city, showing the real power of the cannon. The explosive shells were the worst. The damage they did to bodies was horrifying. But until he saw them in action, Velius had not realized how dangerous they could be to cities built mostly out of wood.

Most of the city had burned to the ground, the men defending it and everyone who'd been unable to get out burning with it. The few that survived the horrific shelling and fires made it to the docks, where they huddled until the fires died down enough for the Britannian legions to close their encirclement, which had taken the better part of two days. The survivors left huddling on the docks were so weakened by hunger and exhaustion that they barely put up any fight.

He'd already seen them in action a little bit, but this was the first time Velius had seen the Consul's new gunpowder weapons in their full glory and knew a radical shift was about to take place in the way wars were fought. With enough cannons, shield walls and phalanxes were going to be a thing of the past. His legions as they were now could stand up to thousands of spearmen slamming into them, pushing back with their large shields. But he knew that they too would crumble under cannon fire.

It was unlikely the Carthaginians would be able to duplicate their weapons for some time, at least not without getting their hands on either the Consul's plans or someone like Hortensius, who knew how the weapons were created. What was likely was that the Carthaginian armies would change the way they fought to adapt to the Britannians' new weapons. Velius's mind already worked through what some of those changes might be, but he knew he would end up surprised anyway. Either way, war was going to change.

"Those are a welcome sight," Bomilcar said, coming to stand next to him, indicating the ships slowly pulling into the docks.

"Yes. I know the men are looking forward to getting off this cursed island."

"It's not cursed. At least not for us."

"Maybe not, but this entire end smells like death and burning meat. I'm not sure how much longer I can stomach it."

"It is jarring. The Consul wasn't kidding about the effects of his explosive shells."

"I was just thinking the same thing," Velius said.

The two men fell silent, watching officers corralling men, getting them prepared to begin boarding the ships to be shuttled back to Britannia.

After several minutes of silence, Velius finally said, "I owe you an apology."

"It's fine," Bomilcar said, not looking at him.

"No, it's not," Velius said, turning to address the general directly. "I've been hostile to you since the day the Consul decided to grant you an amnesty and bring you into the councils of war. I believe my reasons were good, but I should have listened to the Consul when he told me to get my head on straight and watched the work you were doing getting us prepared without the skewed lens I was using to see through. You were right about the response we'd face here. If you hadn't persisted and forced me to put in at least some of your precautions, we would not have been able to respond to that flank attack in time. Hell, even partially prepared, we were very close to being caught unawares if it wasn't for your keen eye giving us time to adjust the plan. You saved a lot of men's lives."

"Thank you," Bomilcar said, not changing his stoic attitude.

"Damn it, man. I'm trying to apologize here. You were right and I should have listened to you."

"And I accept your apology."

"Were you always this difficult?" Velius asked, turning back to the ships, a bit annoyed that he'd come halfway and the general refused to meet him there.

"If you asked the people serving under me, yes; but that was about discipline, and maintaining the chain of command. This is different. You aren't the only one who looks at me like I am something unpleasant they stepped in, and I understand. I did lead men intent on destroying you. I'm sure that, if our positions were reversed, I'd harbor the same kind of resentment against you. You should, perhaps, consider for a moment what it's like for someone like me, leaving everything and everyone I've known to serve people who might always hate me. I'm not unique in this situation. You have hundreds of soldiers who've agreed to become Britannian citizens, just as I have, fighting for you instead of against you. I'm certain they've faced some of the same prejudices

I have, although maybe not to the same degree. I say that because, while I am fine with the place I have in this, you should consider the message you send them when you rail against me and my allegiances in front of the men. You are, perhaps, creating something of a self-fulfilling prophecy, as these men learn the forgiveness they were promised never comes to fruition."

"That's a good point, and I will try to keep it in mind, but I think you might be trying to change the subject from the point I was trying to make."

Bomilcar sighed, turned to the legate, and finally said, "Because I have no answers for you. I appreciate the apology and I will continue to try to help the Empire in any way I can, but I will never be one of you. Even the Consul, who treats me as equally as anyone I've met here, still sees me as something else. Other. It's the price I must pay to make up for my previous allegiances, and I do it willingly, but I will not do it blindly."

"I hadn't considered that," Velius said. "Maybe one day that will change."

"Maybe."

Factorium

"My lady, it's good to see you well," Sorantius said, coming out of his factory to meet her.

She disliked going inside his buildings, where the very air made her eyes feel like they were on fire. Even outside, the smell persisted. She knew Ky had ordered more improvements to the building to help with worker safety, but she couldn't imagine being around this place regularly.

"Thank you. How are your people doing since the accident?"

"It's hard to say. The physicians tell me some should recover, but most of the men who were inside the building and close to the tank that ruptured don't seem to be getting any better. The Consul has checked on them, I know, but I got the feeling he knows their case is hopeless. He did say it was unlikely any more will die immediately, so that's something."

"I see," she said. "I've prayed to the gods that they recover, and will burn offerings for them."

"I'm sure they appreciate it," he said.

It was such a change after dealing with Hortensius, who was always so enthusiastic, and then coming to Sorantius, who was so muted and stand-offish by nature. She'd worked with him enough now, and seen him with others, to know that this wasn't personal. He was like this with everyone. But it was still jarring on the days she had to work with both men.

She knew it was a sign of his focus, which was intense, and what made him so good at what he did. If the side effect was a blunt and slightly disagreeable personality, she'd live with it.

"Well," she said, getting to the point of her visit. "I have some additional notes from the Consul for you. We discussed these in-depth when I saw him, so I should be able to answer any questions you might have."

With Sorantius, she was back to the fiction that she'd memorized the answer to practically any question he might ask. While it had been a security risk, she was happy Hortensius had worked out her and Ky's ability to communicate, because it allowed her to be more straightforward with him and not have to hedge everything within the umbrella of their cover story.

This was another area where Sorantius's focus and lack of social skills were welcome. He rarely questioned any of the explanations she gave for how she knew the answers he needed. All he was interested in was any information that would make his work easier or more efficient.

"The new bleach, I think the Consul called it, is getting rave reviews from the textile and paper manufacturers, both of whom are saying it's notably increased their productivity and made their products more reliable."

"Good. Good," Sorantius said, not really even hearing her.

She waited, but he said nothing else, his focus on reading the pages she'd handed him.

"That one is for a new adhesive. There are multiple uses, but one of the main things the Consul wants to use it for is to bind pages together into something he calls a book, where the pages are held between a hard outer shell, and stay together as you flip back and forth, so they're always in the same order and don't get mixed around."

"That's interesting. It does get difficult shuffling between stacks of these pages, looking for one specific item."

"You aren't the first to say so. He has already talked to some men and is working on setting up a process of organizing the pages by subject. He also has them producing a front page that will list where in the book you can find specific topics. It's really quite clever."

"Some of the other uses of this adhesive are interesting as well; but the book thing? Yes, I think that will make my life a lot easier. Although not as much as letting me keep these documents on-site like I used to."

"We've gone over that," she said, as they ended up on his favorite subject of debate. "For now, we have to be careful with our security. Eventually, we'll be able to relax things and will be able to have copies of these here, but not while we're at war."

Ky actually had said they could probably do it once they got advanced enough. The gap between the Britannians and the Carthaginians was already growing, and they would eventually get to a point where, without the intermediate steps, the information would be all but useless, since it required a knowledge base they wouldn't have. Arcuballista they could recreate right away. The same with some of the steel making changes and even the gunpowder, if they learned the right proportions of the components.

Something like the steam engine, however, was a culmination of dozens of advancements, all of which were needed to make the machine work.

"Yes, yes. Security," he said, flipping pages.

"The adhesive is going to be helpful, but it isn't the most important thing I've brought you. This is called mercuric fulminate, and requires *strict* adherence to all of the safety warnings, *plus* a new, separate building for production. This product is *extremely* dangerous, much more so than even the chemicals which caused the recent accident. It combusts and explodes very easily, so even a slight mishandling can cause the rest of it to go off, meaning a mistake could destroy an entire factory if we aren't careful. Shock, friction, or even too much heat will cause it to explode. The Consul reiterated that there can be no avoiding or simplifying these safety measures. They are critical."

"I see," he said, reading. "What I don't see is why you would need something this volatile. If you were to fire this out of one of those weapons Hortensius has been testing, it would explode before it ever left the thing."

"As I understand it, its main use will be in very small amounts, used to set off gunpowder or something else. It won't be used by itself."

She'd had a similar question while writing this and Sophus had given her a much fuller explanation, but she thought it best for now if she kept it close to the chest. Sophus had explained the future of their military, based around something it called a rifle, and this was, apparently, a key component to making that work. She didn't really understand all of it, but the use of a primer, which would be made using this chemical, wasn't hard to figure out.

"From the tests I've seen, gunpowder is easily set off using an open flame. I watched the test firing of Hortensius's new cannon yesterday because we were also testing these new sulfur-tipped sticks, umm, matches the Consul called them, and it worked well. I'm not sure why a percussion-based explosive would be needed for that."

"This is more in preparation for some additional advances the Consul plans on introducing in the coming months. You know how he works. First he has to get all of the parts in production, and then he shows us how they go together."

"I see. Well, if the Consul commands it, then we will make it."

"Just make sure you follow the safety precautions he included. I can't emphasize enough how important they are."

"I will do my best, my lady," Sorantius said.

She knew it annoyed him when people repeated themselves, since he'd once mentioned it was a way for people to show they didn't think you were listening or might not be smart enough to understand their point, but she had done it mostly for herself.

Sophus had described some fairly horrific accidents involving these explosives that ended in disaster.

She'd already lost enough of her people to accidents. Since she couldn't stand over each worker's shoulder to ensure they were being careful, she had to settle for pestering their supervisor instead.

Chapter 19

Devnum

"The princess came back from Factorium today," Medb said as she readied their room for the evening.

"I don't believe the Romans, or I guess Britannians, call the Emperor's daughter a princess," Cormac said, watching her work.

He was still surprised at how quickly he'd found appreciation for his new wife. Any thoughts of her being too muscular or mannish had left his head after their first night together. Now, watching her work, he could already feel his heartbeat quickening. She was quite the woman.

He just wished he wasn't so tired from watching worthless old men argue pointlessly all day. Llassar, under the Consul's direction, had decided the best way Cormac could prepare for his future was to sit in on the Imperial Senate, listening to those fools, instead of out with the legions, leading men into battle.

Wounded legionnaires had begun pouring into Devnum for several days, bound for the Imperial Hospital. Word of the conflict had come with them. None of the men had been in a condition to be interviewed personally, but from what Cormac could gather, the victory had been stunning and the Carthaginian port had been left a smoking ruin.

"Well, she apparently rushed back, from what I hear. I also heard that the Consul was sailing in tonight as well. I guess that explains the rush," Medb said, giving him a suggestive eyebrow wave.

"I'm sure that has something to do with it, but I overheard in the forum today that the Emperor has called for a new council of war in the morning. I understand the legates are all returning tonight as well, along with several others. I'm not sure what they are discussing, but whatever it is, it's going to be big."

"They didn't inform you about it directly? I thought all attendees would have gotten a message telling them when and where to be."

"I haven't been invited," he said, his teeth grinding. "Llassar has, I know, but I guess they still don't feel I have enough experience to contribute to something like this."

"And how do they want you to get this experience? Your father sent you here to learn how to lead. I know you like Llassar, but he isn't one of us. Everyone here, even Llassar, has their own agendas. I think you might want to ask yourself why they'd want to make sure the future heir of one-third of the Empire remains inexperienced?"

"I don't know," he said. "I mean, I understand what you're saying, but it doesn't seem right. They have been working with me, having me watch how the government is really being run. I know it's not everything, but it's not nothing."

"Cormac, you're a great man, but you have to stop looking at everyone as if they're your friends. Of course it's nothing. Not only have they kept you out of any of the real meetings, the ones about the progress of the war, but I heard a rumor that the attack on the princ... the Emperor's daughter was a trap. We don't know, because you weren't in the room where these decisions were made. Was Llassar, who isn't even on his country's list of successors, in the meeting? Hell, if anything, you should be on the same footing as Llassar. He's his chieftain's or whatever's representative to the Empire, just as you are your father's representative."

"Except, my father told me to come here and learn from Llassar."

"And he's falling down on that job. You need to show that you can take the initiative and handle your own advancement. Decisiveness is the key to good leadership. I know this is getting old from me, telling you to make them include you; but I don't want to see you pushed to the side. The more I've come to know you, the more I realize everything that's happened, happened for a reason. Yes, I tried to rule and failed, but I think that was what the gods meant for me, because it was my path to you. I see in you the future of all of the people of Ériu. It's why I refuse to let others convince you that you aren't worthy of your place or are somehow subservient to them."

Cormac listened as the passion in her voice ramped up. He wasn't sure he agreed about the whole 'ordained by the gods' part, but he had to admit it felt good to hear those words. His father had always been hard, even before he became king. Good was never good enough. To his father, anything short of perfection was a failure, and he was quick to point out that failure.

"I appreciate your support, but right now, I don't really have the ability to force them to do anything. We're not in my father's kingdom, and he gave Llassar specific instructions to take charge of me. How do I force their hands when I have no leverage?"

"By being smarter than them," she said, coming over and sitting astride him, her legs going around the back of the chair. "Go around Llassar. Find your moment when someone like the Consul is there, and make it clear to him that you're here as your father's proxy and demand your place at the table. Don't be a child, hiding behind Llassar's apron, be the man I know you to be. Don't ask for your place. Demand it. Be like Moccus, his tusks set to gore his enemies; be not like a sheep, waiting to be slaughtered."

Her face was inches from his and he felt himself getting lost in her eyes. There was a fire and a passion there the likes of which he'd never seen before from anyone else, and it was directed entirely at him. His voice caught in his throat, so he just nodded, his head almost bumping into hers.

She smiled at him with that wolfish smile, the one where he wasn't sure if she was happy with him or planning on eating him. As she kissed him, he knew he'd be happy with either one.

Ky had arrived early in the audience chamber, sitting on his small stool next to the Emperor's high-backed chair which sat at the end of the table. It was unusual to have councils of war in the large

audience chamber meant to hear proclamations and greet digni-
taries, but this was the only room large enough for the number of
people needed at this meeting.

Britannia had reached a turning point, and what they decided
today would either be the first step to ending the war, or open
the door for Carthage to destroy their fledgling Empire and salt
the ground left behind. Ky had brought a lot of advancements
that gave the small Empire a fighting chance, but Carthage still
hadn't brought its full weight to bear against them. Ky had seen
Ramirus's reports. If they were even only half right, Carthage had
a massive manpower pool that made the armies the Britannians
had faced so far look minuscule. So far, they'd kept the Carthaginians off balance, but if they made the wrong move, allowed the
Carthaginians to regain some equilibrium, they would be able to
land armies so large that no amount of technology would be able
to counter them.

He and Sophus had spent the trip back from Insula Manavia
working on the problem and had some options, but Sophus's databases and processing ability only went so far. One of the reasons
ships in his former Empire hadn't been made fully AI run was
that no tactical computer, no matter how advanced, could make
the intuitive leaps that a human could. War, both on a tactical
and strategic level, was more than just cold analysis. There was
a feel to it, a sense that someone with enough experience could
recognize and use. In every simulated war game he'd seen, an
experienced commander had been able to beat his AI counterpart
by predicting the AI's moves and making moves that, on the face
of it, defied logic.

The men he'd gathered for this council had been fighting in this
world's conditions for years, some of them their entire lives. They
would be able to see things that both he and Sophus would miss
if the decision was left to the two of them alone.

He was just preparing to start the meeting when a commotion
near the end of the room drew his attention. It wasn't until he got
up to the small group that he saw it was Llassar arguing with the
son of the Ulaid king, who'd come over to observe and learn from
the Britannians, in order to gain some experience. Ky had been
unsure of the plan, but Llassar had endorsed it, which was good

enough for Ky. Llassar had already shown multiple times that his judgment could be trusted.

"... supposed to be here. We don't have time for lessons today. I promise I'll bring you up to speed when we're done and we can discuss it, but this council is important, and we don't need the distraction," Llassar said.

"Hearing about what is decided won't teach me anything," the prince said, clearly agitated but still under control. "From what I've heard, this is the largest meeting of this type that has ever occurred in any of our nations. I have this one chance to actually see it, and you want me to sit aside and wait for your summary. That isn't what my father sent me here for."

"Cormac," Llassar said, his legendarily cool facade fading a bit. "We don't have time for this. You need to go back to your rooms. I promise we'll have this conversation when it's over."

"I can't ..." Cormac said, before he was interrupted by Ky clearing his throat loudly.

Ky could see they were going in circles, and this was becoming a distraction from starting the meeting. Llassar had dug in his heels and wasn't listening to Cormac, and Cormac had the self-assurance only possessed by the young, and clearly thought any opinion but his was wrong on the face of it.

"Is there a problem?"

"My apologizes, Consul," Llassar said, giving Cormac a look. "The prince wasn't invited to this council but apparently heard it was happening and decided to attend of his own volition. I was just requesting that he return to his rooms until after the council was finished. I'll get him out of your way."

Llassar reached over and took a hold of the prince's arm, apparently intending to lead him out, but the prince wrenched free of his hold and instead rapidly approached Ky.

"Consul, we haven't met yet, but I'm Cormac Cond Logas, son of the rightful king of the Ulaid, Conchobar mac Nessa. I was sent here to observe your government and act as my father's direct representative. I demand to be allowed to stay and take part in the council, just as Llassar, as his chieftain's direct representative, is allowed to stay and speak for his people."

"Cormac," Llassar said, finally losing his temper. "You're not in any place to demand …"

"Llassar," Ky said, putting his hand on his friend's shoulder. "I appreciate your assistance and I apologize. Not inviting the prince here, as his father's representative, was my oversight. I'm sure the prince understands the importance of this meeting and will listen intently and refrain from interrupting or causing any distractions if he stays. Isn't that right, Cormac Cond Logas?"

"Yes, Consul," Cormac said, grinning, although whether from besting Llassar or just being allowed to stay, Ky couldn't tell.

Llassar, for his part, took the overruling well, simply giving a slight bow of his head and saying, "As you wish, Consul."

"Now, that that's settled," Ky said, raising his voice so it was audible to everyone in the room as he returned to his seat. "It looks like we're all here, so let's get started."

All eyes turned to Ky as he stood at his place next to the Emperor and across from his wife.

"We are at a turning point. We've done well for ourselves and gained a moment's breathing room, but the Carthaginians are far from beaten. I know that may seem obvious, but I've already overheard talk that, thanks to our new weapons, our victory is all but assured. I want you all to understand that, as the person who understands the capabilities of these weapons best, that is far from true. We are still vulnerable and a misstep can still end with our destruction. All of you have a part in commanding our armies and contributing to our final success in this war, but only if you all take this seriously. Is that understood?"

All of the faces around the table nodded slightly when they realized Ky wasn't going to continue until they agreed.

"Good. Now, I have the beginnings of a plan, but I wanted to lay out the issues and get your input on my thoughts. We all know our next step is to establish a foothold on the continent. Even with the new ships in Valdar's fleet or under construction, we cannot hope to both land and supply an army in Africa from the Britannic Isles. The distances are just too far and the odds we'd face when landing are too great, even with our technological advantages. That means we need to set up a base, or preferably bases, to stage an invasion of Africa, preferably close to Carthage itself, since the challenges of fighting in North Africa make landing and marching along the coast equally as challenging. Most of the landing points closer to Carthage, however, are well into the Middle Sea, which also presents challenges. Sicilia is close, but without control of Italy, we'd be in constant danger of being overrun, considering Carthage's hold on the peninsula. Sardinia and Corsica also present problems, as does an overland route to take Italy, which would stretch our supply lines and require a crossing over the Alps."

"I'm not sure I'm clear how a foothold on the continent gets us any closer to our goal than marching straight across the continent to our homeland or sailing through to Sardinia would get us. We have the same problems of distance and supplying our men, which will require a lot larger force if we are to protect those supply lines," the Emperor said.

Ky had actually discussed a little of this with the Emperor and Lucilla already, so he knew the Emperor was more addressing concerns that the other men at the table would almost surely have, but might be hesitant to vocally express.

"Are you thinking of using the continent, say southern Gaul, Italy, or Hispania, or were you thinking of using some of Sardinia, Corsica, or some of the smaller islands?" Velius asked, building off the Emperor's point.

"Both, actually," Ky said. "We've already established that we have to keep pressure on the Carthaginians to keep them from uniting their forces for a decisive blow against us, but to operate off of just islands in the Middle Sea we'd also need an extended amount of time to build our fleet enough to control the sea, the coast up to Britannia, and then run supplies and men along that route to somewhere like Sardinia. However, the islands ultimately make a better base to launch attacks against Carthage than somewhere like Hispania or Italy. With our new ship designs and cannon, we will eventually have complete control of the Middle Sea, making any island base we establish much safer than a base on the continent itself."

"So we put pressure on the continent to keep them off balance and then, once our fleets are strong enough, we take Sardinia or one of the other islands and begin preparing for the invasion of Carthage itself?" Bomilcar asked.

"Yes," Ky said.

"Doesn't that stretch us very thin?" Ursinus asked. "We don't have enough men to operate on the continent and prepare for an invasion, which means we'd have to pull all of our men off the continent once we secure Sardinia, or wherever, and begin preparing for landings in Africa, which just puts us right back to where we are now, with extended seaborne supply lines."

"Yes. As always, the greatest limiting factor we have is manpower, and it's one we have to solve to make this work, because I am not suggesting we abandon any gains we make on the continent; at least, not while the war is going on."

"Perhaps you should just explain your full plan, then, now that we all understand the challenges," Llassar said.

Ky could always count on the Caledonian to cut through the niceties and get right to the point.

"This will happen in several stages. Stage one: we attack the continent, with an eye on multiple goals. One: to keep pressure on the Carthaginians. Two: to control enough territory to allow for a land-based corridor between our side of the continent and the Middle Sea. The most likely option is along the neck of Hispania on one side of the mountains there or the other, although a long stretch across Gaul might be an option as well. There are several ports on the Middle Sea side that would work as a staging point for later stages, so our goal would be to at least control a corridor from the channel to whichever port we make our goal. Three, we need to build local allies. A lot of them."

"The tribes on the continent control a lot less land than even we did when we joined the empire," Llassar said. "Bringing those people into the Empire would mean adding a lot of voices with an equal say into our current structure, who bring comparatively small populations and resources as their contribution. I'm not sure my people would be happy with that dilution of our power in the Empire."

"Ours either," Cormac added quickly.

"I know, and we've actually discussed this before, although at the time both of you were on Ériu. I am not proposing we bring any of these people into the Empire, but instead set up an extended alliance, the details of which we will have to work out, that will give them some trading and technological benefits in return for their supplying us with resources and manpower. The problem of arming these people with some of our more advanced weaponry has been brought up as well, and that also remains a concern, but one we will have to deal with as the war goes on. We will give them some of our weapons, but probably none of the ones using gunpowder, which allows us to maintain a secure advantage."

Ky looked to Llassar, to see if this addressed his concerns, which the Caledonian acknowledged they did with a tilting of his head.

"So where are you thinking of making our initial landings on the continent?" Velius asked. "The Carthaginians have had ties with Hispania for a long time, back before we were even pushed out of Italy. It might be our best location for establishing a corridor of control that gives us a land bridge between our side of the continent and the Middle Sea, but it also seems unlikely that we'll find much in the way of allies there."

"That's true, which is why I'm proposing two landings," Ky said, which elicited negative expressions from several of the faces along the table. "I know that will stretch our manpower thin, even with the new units in training, and is the main problem I wanted to bring to this council. My recommendation is that the bulk of our forces land on Hispania, where we set up a coastal base from which we can push out to the opposite coast, using the mountains separating it from Gaul as partial protection, where we establish another base on the shores of the Middle Sea. The goal of this force will be strictly military, since I agree it is unlikely many of the people still living in Hispania would be easily swayed to our side. Before those landings, however, I am proposing a landing along the Germanic coast, preferably north of Gaul, although not quite as far as the sea between the Scandi and Germania."

"Why not?" Valdar asked. "My people may not have wanted to join your alliance, but they are predisposed to supporting you, and you would have an easily protected path back to Britannia. Why not circle around into the Sea of Serpents and land on the northern side of Germania."

"Because the main goal of this landing would be to pull forces that would otherwise be used against our troops in the later landings in Hispania. If we land too far north into Germania, either the Carthaginians will pull men from closer to Asia, or wait to see what we do, either of which leaves their full forces in Hispania and Gaul available to go after the second landings. We need to pick a spot for the first series of landings that puts us close enough to pull forces out of Hispania itself, that has tribes likely to support our cause, and if need be, is close enough to Hispania to offer support to those units, should something go wrong."

"How about Belgae?" Lucilla said. "The distance between Britannia and the tip of Belgae is the shortest, which would be the natural point for us to invade if we were simply attacking the continent, which should be enough to convince the Carthaginians that it's our primary and only landing. It will pull forces from Germania and Gaul, but it's still close enough to Hispania to pull some forces from there, and if we make enough noise, maybe even from their forces closer to Asia."

Ky was impressed. One of the downsides of her picking up more and more of the work creating instructions for Sorantius and Hortensius was that it left less time for the two of them to talk. When they did, they avoided everything but the most pressing official business, so that they would at least have a little personal time. All of that meant that Ky had only discussed the fact that there were two landings but not actually where he thought the northern landing should be. He and Sophus had actually come to a similar conclusion as she had, and with similar reasoning, but he'd wanted to put it out to the table without influencing them with his own thoughts.

"I concur," Bomilcar said, beating Ky to agreeing. "That region has the added benefit of having the least Carthaginian presence of any of the choices along the western coastline and is the most likely place for us to find allies. The fact that the majority of the Germanic refugees have either come from or have traveled through that region is evidence of that."

"If we do go there, we need to look at restructuring the legions to put the bulk of men who've joined from that region in the group that lands there," Velius said. "Seeing their countrymen or even family members among our military will make an impact and might even convince more of them to immigrate to Britannia. I know we're planning on using their warriors as auxiliary forces, but having worked in the field with that kind of arrangement already, I think we will only see limited usefulness out of it."

When Cormac frowned and tensed up at the comment, Velius added, "I mean no office, Cormac. Your men fought well and were brave; but as we've adapted the legions, our units have become more integrated and specialized. This makes it much harder to integrate those kinds of forces with ours. Having seen some of the plans for the cannon, and the new training requirements the Consul has enacted for the legions that will receive the first of these new weapons, suggests that the problem will only get worse, not better. While I'm certain there will be uses for allies fighting alongside us, and this is something we'll absolutely need, I think we need to be careful before planning to incorporate local allies into our forces."

"Have we given much thought to how to best incorporate local allies not trained in our methods or with our weapons?" the Emperor asked.

He and Sophus had given a lot of thought to the problem of integrating local auxiliaries and how that would work with their current training program. They had based their training around the concept of rifled firearms against armies armed with spears, swords, and bows, which was great for their own forces, but didn't work well for auxiliaries. Ancient and Napoleonic forms of warfare just did not mesh. Maybe if they had men who'd trained to fight in phalanxes, they could use that same organization and training to turn them into riflemen, but Germanic warriors tended to fight as single warriors.

Without a lot of time to train, any new allies would be limited to being scouts and skirmishers. That actually was workable since Sophus's databases also produced examples of native auxiliaries performing just those types of roles in his original history, but there was a catch. Those examples in Sophus's records had still been armed with firearms. If they took any allies and just threw them against the Carthaginians as they were now, they wouldn't have the manpower to do much damage to the Carthaginian phalanxes, which would make their sacrifices pointless.

The obvious answer was to arm them. Even if they didn't operate with the precision of the Britannian units, they'd still be able to do damage, firing and falling back, harassing the Carthaginians. If they armed enough of these men, even if they weren't operating with the Britannians, they could cause havoc within the Carthaginian forces. Hit-and-run tactics with firearms would make them much more deadly and cause fewer casualties each time.

While this would work, the obvious problem with this had already been pointed out. Eventually, some of those allies might not remain allies. Armed with Britannian firearms, they could pose a serious threat. There was also the danger of Carthaginians getting their hands on these weapons. It was unlikely they would be able to reverse engineer gunpowder and firearms, much less the new technologies necessary for producing them in any sort of quantity. What was possible was allies losing any of the weapons given to them or actually selling them to the Carthaginians or some enterprising group taking weapons intended to be used against the Carthaginians and turning around and selling those same weapons to their enemies, either for just profit or to curry favor, especially if they thought the Carthaginians would ultimately come out on top as the victors.

"Yes," Ky said. "It does present a problem. While we need manpower, I think it's obvious we can't just put those allies in our existing formations as they are, and considering the spread-out nature of the tribes, we don't have the time or manpower to train each one up to our standards. We also have the issue of just giving them the same weapons we're producing for ourselves, since they could use them against us or sell them to the Carthaginians. What we need is a way, with minimal training, to equip these allies so they can operate on their own or as skirmishers, but not end up creating future problems for us."

When Ky paused the Emperor said, "From that, I assume you have a solution in mind."

"Yes. I know I've talked to some of you already about the new weapons we are just about ready to start producing. For those who haven't heard, we will shortly begin issuing a smaller version of the cannon, about the size and length of a small spear, that can be used by individual legionnaires. Once the first rifle prototypes come out of Hortensius's factories, we will hold demonstrations, but you need to know that the ranges of these weapons are significant, multiple times further than Carthaginian archers can shoot arrows, or even the distance capability of their siege weapons. There is, however, an intermediate design of this type of weapon that we are skipping over. While still able to cause a large amount of damage, this simpler version has a significantly lower range and fires more slowly. If armed with these, any new allies would be much more dangerous to the Carthaginians, while still unable to counter our weapons, if they should turn against us or sell them to the Carthaginians."

"Given the numbers, I think we're talking about, I'm not sure I have enough facilities to arm our men and auxiliaries. At least not without expanding significantly," Hortensius said.

"That would be true if they needed the same facilities, but they don't. Most of what we've been working towards, all of the new equipment and processes, has been geared towards producing rifles. These alternate weapons, which I guess we can call muskets, although that's not exactly what they would have been called in my homeland, are produced more like the original run of cannon. Once we get into it, I think you'll find it won't add that much to your production schedule. Yes, our output will be limited at first, but the more we get into our allies' hands, the better."

"Are we planning on giving these weapons away?" Lurio, the imperial treasurer, asked. "Even with the new taxes and higher efficiency of much of our industries, the imperial finances are already strained. I assume even if these weapons are easier for us to make, it will be difficult for anyone without Hortensius's facilities to replicate. If we could sell these to them, it would go a long way to easing that strain."

"For now, we are giving them away," Ky said.

He was aware of how dangerously tight the Empire's finances were. Lurio had been warning Lucilla for months that they were pushing too fast, what with all of the building and supplies, new workforces, and more, needed to grow the legions. So far, taxes and contributions from their partners in the Empire had helped keep them from falling behind, but if they were to incorporate more territory into the Empire, they would have to find a new way to pay for the continually growing costs, especially if they were going to be pouring resources into people who didn't, at least directly, financially contribute.

"You understand ..." Lurio started before Ky, who could sense the beginning of the lecture that had started to feel very familiar by now, interrupted.

"I do, and eventually we will. When we finally beat the Carthaginians, we will have introduced a new problem that will have consequences. Introducing these weapons to our new allies, ones that we will not have any direct influence over once our shared enemy is gone, will upset any balance of power that may result in the areas the Carthaginians currently occupy. While this is a problem for the future, and one we cannot allow to control our decisions today while our very existence is on the line, it *is* one we need to be aware of. Anyone we arm with these weapons will have a distinct advantage over anyone we haven't given these weapons to. We will discuss this more when the time comes, but I think we can at least have some control over that and help our strained treasury at the same time. Most of the people we will be giving these weapons to will not be able to produce their own gunpowder. There will also be those who will want these weapons for themselves, to defend against some of the tribes we're currently arming, opening up the possibility of a market for these less advanced weapons. Like I said, this is really a conversation for the future, but I have given it thought."

"Hopefully our treasury holds on until we defeat the Carthaginians," Lurio said, more to himself than anyone else.

Ky resisted the urge to roll his eyes. He agreed with the man, whose abilities he had a lot of respect for, but whose interpersonal skills could use some work.

"I trust, with your already proven abilities, you will find a way for us to continue until that time," Ky said, before turning back to the Emperor. "As with everything, this will all take time, which is the one thing we don't have. Initially, we will be relegated to our current tactics and weapons, at least for some of our forces, since I do not believe we will have enough of any of the needed weapons ready if we're going to make our landings before winter sets in."

"So all of this focus on new weapons and training is pointless then?" the Emperor asked.

"No. The new rifles are going to be important and will be a deciding factor, but only for one of the two forces. Looking over Ramirus's reports, the bulk of the Carthaginian forces in this area are gathering in southern Gaul. They have, in fact, pulled most of their forces out of Iberia already, first to build up the last army they sent against us and to start building the new force they are gathering to re-invade our islands. They have other forces gathering in Africa, Italy, and Anatolia, but those groups are far enough away that by the time they get to us, the tactical landscape will be played out. With the way we're landing, we should arm the southern force with all of the new rifles and cannons, as well as those legions that have already begun training in the newer tactics to exploit them.

"But the northern force is landing first," Velius said. "Since they're going to be the first to engage, wouldn't they need the newer weapons sooner? We could always arm the southern force with the next batches of rifles and cannons produced."

"That is the dilemma. Once the southern force lands, the Carthaginian army in Gaul will either have to double back and go for our southern force, which is much closer to putting their homeland in jeopardy and our most obvious path into Africa, or continue north. There is no real way of predicting which way the Carthaginians will go, which means we have to be prepared for either eventuality. I think that, if we were to break our forces apart evenly between armies and split the weapons across them evenly, both would be vulnerable. Instead, what I think we should do is to have one force much larger than the other, but armed with only a small number of the new weapons. They will be sticking mostly with the more traditional tactics we've used so far, although that force will also be assigned some of the first runs of the cannons. These cannons won't have the range or power of the newer ones. Meanwhile, the second force will be smaller, but will get the bulk of the new weapons. Partly this is because only two legions have begun the basic training of how to fight with rifles, instead of the more traditional way, but also because the rifles themselves are a significant 'force multiplier,' if used properly."

"I assume you'll be going with the smaller legion, since they'll be using less familiar weapons?" Velius asked.

The legate had most likely worked out that his legion would be one of the two in the southern force, since it had been the first to start training in the new methods of maneuver and formations to take advantage of the rifle.

"No. We still have several months of training time for you to get acquainted with the new weapons, and I will make sure you start getting the rifles the moment they roll off the production line, to give your men as much training time as possible with them. While it's true the northern force will be using more traditional tactics, they are also going to be more vulnerable in spite of that army's larger size. It's going to have to maneuver, hopefully avoiding direct contact as long as possible, and we will have to find the right ground to fight on that limits what will certainly be the enemy's size advantage. The best chance to be able to do that is if I'm there, given my advantage of seeing troop movements at a distance. You'll be leading the southern force."

"I see."

"We have some advantages. We'll both need to stay in contact with the shoreline if possible. Our ships will patrol the waters near prearranged locations, and will be able to carry messages to and from the two forces, at least giving us the advantage of some coordination. Once the production of rifles is started in earnest, I will be traveling south with Valdar to check the southern coastline all the way down to the Middle Sea. Our goal is to maintain control of the entire coastline, so we have supply and communication lines with Britannia throughout. You will need to maintain a defensible position near the coast to work as a supply depot, and then push along the mountains from there as you see fit. I know that sounds counterintuitive to what I was saying about the northern force needing to stay mobile; but you'll find that with these new weapons, the defender will have a significant advantage, especially if the ground is chosen well for your defensive works. Don't worry; I will go over specifics of how to best take advantage of your weapons before you sail for the continent."

Velius ducked his head in a nod, his face set. Ky had faith in the legate who'd already led a successful campaign on his own without any of Ky's advantages to help him. Properly armed, Velius's army would be able to take on all but the largest forces, and even against a truly massive army, the enemy would have to be willing to take unrecoverable damage to best him.

"I think we have a plan, then," the Emperor said, rising. "After the harvests, Ky will land a force on the northern coast of the continent and, once he signals that the enemy has taken the bait, Velius will land a second army in Hispania, with both armies working to gain a secure corridor to the Middle Sea in preparation to setting up forward bases to invade the Carthaginian heartland. While we wait for the harvests, Hortensius and the other, I think the term Ky used the other day was, industrialists will work to produce as many of these new weapons as possible. Now you must all go and put this into action. Offerings to Fortuna and Jupiter will be burned in preparation for your undertaking."

"May the gods go with us," Lucilla said.

Chapter 20

As soon as the council of war had ended, training had begun in earnest. By week's end, the legions had been divided into the northern and southern armies, each with a unique focus. The southern force focused on the new formations, doing unusual drills for marching and quickly aligning in smaller, three-man rows at the sound of a trumpet call. They learned odd commands like kneeling in ranks, which made a little sense once the Consul had them train with arcuballista, which apparently would be used in similar ways to the new rifles.

The northern force, on the other hand, trained in marching and deploying with cannons, keeping clear of where they might fire until the last moment. They had also taken to firing the cannons around the men from time to time, apparently to acclimatize them to the sound of gunfire.

Llassar was still unsure where he was going to be during all of this. The prince was going to be attached to one of the armies, where Llassar could continue with his education while still being able to help lead the men in combat. If he had his pick, Llassar would prefer to go with the northern force. He appreciated the deadliness of the cannons after seeing them in action and had no doubt the Consul's rifles would be just as impressive, but he'd already had to adapt to the Roman, or at least Britannian, way of fighting which was vastly different from what he'd grown up learning.

Besides, he hadn't been involved in the training Velius and his legion had been undergoing over the past few months. He'd had to remain in the capital with Cormac, ensuring the man was focused and learning how this new government was supposed to be run.Their world was changing, and the old ways and their leaders had to adapt with them. It would be up to people like Lucilla and Cormac to lead them into whatever form this new empire evolved into.

As if his thought manifested his existence, Llassar saw the prince striding toward him, determination etched upon his brow. While it was a change from the way the young man had been avoiding him, spending far too many hours in his rooms than where he needed to be, there was something in the prince's expression that bothered Llassar.

Cormac stood before Llassar, hands defiantly clasped behind his back as if mirroring Llassar's stoic pose. Llassar studied him, his gaze unwavering.

"Cormac, I thought you were spending the day with the Emperor observing the public audiences."

Cormac's voice was tinged with frustration. "I was. We've been going all morning, and they've taken a short break, but I don't think I'm going back when they reconvene."

"Why not?"

"Because this is pointless. Farmers upset about legions damaging their fields during training exercises, merchants angry about tariffs or accusing the Empire of favoritism, it's all so hollow. These matters could be handled by bureaucrats. A true ruler needs to make decisions, lead his people, not adjudicate petty complaints."

"Normally, they do go to bureaucrats. The Emperor and the Consul believe there's some benefit to the people having direct access to their leaders. It also allows the Emperor to keep in touch with the Empire's realities. It's how most things are handled in Caledonia. Don't you think a leader should be accessible to his people and understand their desires?"

Cormac's eyes flashed with impatience. "He should understand what they want, I guess, but these people are only worried about their little problems, not the fate of the kingdom as a whole. If it's really important, the leader can always talk to those bureaucrats and find out the people's concerns."

Llassar arched an eyebrow. "Is it possible those bureaucrats might have their own thoughts and agendas? Is it wise to know your people solely through the eyes of another man?"

"Fine, I guess not," Cormac conceded, "but I didn't come looking for you to get into more rhetorical debates."

"Then why were you looking for me?"

Cormac's voice took on a determined tone. "I know my father wants me to learn from you and observe how the government runs, but I need to do more than just watch and listen to meetings. I need to be out there, making a difference."

Llassar's expression remained unchanged. "You'll have plenty of time to make a difference when your father steps down. But the only way you'll succeed is by understanding how to do it right."

"You didn't learn by listening to others talk, nor did my father. You both fought your way into power. You learned to lead by doing. I'm done being treated like a child, hiding behind others while they make the real decisions. My father assigned me to be my people's proxy here. As equal members of the Empire, we deserve equal say. You were at that council of war. YOU had a seat at the table while the Romans had nearly a dozen. My people deserve representation beyond my mere attendance and expected silence. I demand my rightful place."

Llassar frowned, his gaze still fixed on Cormac. He had spent much time with the prince, who had many flaws, but this tirade felt off.

"What, exactly, did you have in mind?"

"I'm not doing any good watching the senate or the Emperor arguing about this or that. The real fight for our future is happening with the legions, about to cross over to the continent. I demand to go with them."

Llassar contemplated his response. "You understand this will become far more dangerous. There's a chance none of the men who take part in the invasion will return. Neither Talogren's son nor the Emperor's daughter is going with the legions, and the Emperor's daughter is married to the man leading the northern army. Do you think it's wise to put the sole heir of your people in harm's way?"

Cormac's voice grew defiant. "Don't give me that. If the legions fall, there'll be nothing stopping the Carthaginians from reclaiming our islands and putting us all under the sword. It's just as dangerous here as it is out there with the legions. I'm not asking to

220

be on the front lines, but I could learn from traveling with either Velius or the Consul, watching them lead armies in the field."

"You've watched armies in the field already. Now is the time for you to learn other things."

"No. There won't be another chance to witness a war like this, and I won't shrink from my part in it. I'm not a sheep in the field. I refuse to stand idly by while others fight for me."

Llassar frowned again, his suspicions growing as he realized exactly who the Cormac sounded like. Llassar had heard the princes new wife speak of sheep in fields on multiple occasions, referencing something out of their mythology.

"I will write your father about it," Llassar said, opting to stall while he considered his options. "There's still time before the legions sail, and I'm sure your request will sit better with your father if you can demonstrate your proficiency in governing."

"Fine. I'll go back and continue to listen, but you need to take me seriously. I want to be a part of this invasion."

"Believe me, Cormac. I am taking this very seriously."

The prince eyed the older man for a moment before storming off. Llassar was left to ponder the situation. When the prince had started spending extra time in his quarters, he'd initially assumed Cormac was simply enjoying the pleasures of a new marriage. Medb was, after all, beautiful in her own right. But now he wondered if there was more to it.

Conchobar had warned him that Medb was cunning and that Llassar should be cautious around her. Although he'd tried to keep an eye on her as she toured Devnum or spoke to various groups of women, his focus had been on Cormac. As the couple appeared to be getting along well, Llassar had thought their union was working out.

Perhaps he hadn't taken the king's warning seriously enough, after all.

Factorium

"Let's see it," Ky said as Hortensius lead him excitedly into the factory.

Ky had made multiple trips to the rapidly growing industrial center over the last week, going over every detail of new rifle construction. Because of the groundwork Ky and Lucilla had had Hortensius lay over the last several months, all of the tools needed to construct the rifles were more or less in place, which meant they only needed to construct the first prototypes of each piece of the weapon and make sure everything fit together well.

There were some obvious places where they could speed up the process, such as the manufacturing of the body of the weapon itself. Hortensius had set up a separate building to deal with carpentry back when he'd first started working on the arcuballista, which also had a solid wooden body. Ky hadn't given it much thought at the time, since they'd been able to keep up with the construction quotas quite well and the quality had been good enough, but with the machining factory now under steam power, it turned out that making the bodies of the rifles themselves was actually the slowest part of the process.

A lot of the process was still being done by hand, including the parts turned using water power that were still guided by eye and cutting to blanks, instead of having a machine that could lock in precise measurements and cut the exact part every time. He'd already had Sophus put together plans for a more sophisticated wood processing facility, that could be used for more than quickly producing the rifle blanks, but that would ultimately call for a second steam engine to be built.

It was all doable, but it would take time, which they didn't have. Ky's decision to equip the northern force with older cannon had been made for this very reason. There simply wasn't enough time to arm a full legion, let alone multiple legions, with the new rifles and artillery.Velius might be getting two legions, but only one of them would be armed with the newer weapons and cannon. The other would essentially be a replacement force to pick up the weapons of their fallen comrades, at least until manufacturing could catch up.

It was also why Ky had held off the landings until the last possible moment. He hoped the delay would give Hortensius the time he needed to produce enough weapons.

Hortensius led him to his office, where a finished rifle sat on the table. Sophus' images had failed to capture the impressive length of the weapon, which would be almost as long as he was tall once the bayonet was slotted in place.

"She's a beauty," Hortensius said, lifting it up gingerly.

Ky's eyes roamed over the assembled weapon, taking in every detail with quiet admiration.

He had seen and measured the individual components, refining the machines that produced them with minute adjustments. Seeing it all together, however, was something else. Hortensius had outdone himself. There were a few places the weapon could use some refinement, but even as it was, it rivaled anything built by craftsmen in the nineteenth century.

'The new, narrow borer Hortensius built has done especially well,' Ky thought as he looked down the barrel, letting Sophus examine the rifling. Maybe the experience he gained building the larger borer for the cannon has paid off. If this was the case, then the rifles only improve over time.

"You've truly outdone yourself," Ky praised, his voice carrying a hint of awe. "There's room for refinement, of course, but this weapon is ready for the field as it stands."

"Thank you, Consul. What surprises me most is how easy this is to produce, once we got everything in place. It's a complicated weapon, but compared to how we would forge weapons and armor just a year ago, this took a lot less time and manpower, thanks to the machines. I am still amazed by how simple some of these machines make the process. Not only is it surprisingly fast to set up the machines and cut, bore, or mold a part compared to the time and effort required to slowly beat metal into shape by hand, but the training has become so much more simple. I can train a man in a few days to operate one of these machines, as opposed to a lifetime of apprenticeships and training to get a worker capable of making usable equipment."

"I told you, when we first started working on improving your foundries, that we would make every part of the manufacturing process easier and more efficient. It's the only way we are ever going to produce enough military supplies to compete with the Carthaginians."

"Well, it's a good thing too, because this is extremely time-consuming to make, considering you need hundreds of these for every one of those," Hortensius said, holding up a small paper tube about the length of one of his fingers, although significantly thinner than the man's sausage like digits.

Ky sat the rifle down and reached over to take the paper cartridge from him. As he held it up, slowly rotating it, Sophus put up a display showing the size of the round compared to the rifle muzzle he'd just been examining.

"You used the wooden blanks to roll them to the right size before tying them off?"

"Yes. That was actually pretty clever. I can't imagine how hard this would have been without them. We also finished the first of the small measuring tools you described to quickly measure the right amount of gunpowder and then easily pour it into the tied-off paper tube. Even with those, it's a slow process. If everything is set up right at a station, it still takes almost two minutes for a worker to construct one cartridge. To get the numbers you've indicated, it's going to take a fairly large workforce. Probably larger than what I need to run the factory producing the weapons to fire them."

"Yes. Unfortunately, the amount of changes needed for a version of the weapon where we can more easily automate the cartridges is significant. For the last year, I've been hitting you with one new technology after another, and since the winter, those changes have been even more significant. What we need now is time for your people to settle in and work with the same technology for a while, instead of constantly learning something new. Machine-driven efficiency is good, but it can't reach its full potential if the workers are constantly having to learn this or that new piece of technology."

"So, this is it for new toys for a while, huh?" Hortensius said.

"No. We'll still introduce new things here or there, but they will be smaller changes and at a slower pace."

"You're the Consul. If you say it's so, we'll follow."

"I still want your participation. You've made some interesting additions and corrections of your own once we got these things off the page and into production. Did you have any questions or concerns? I'm going to be sailing out with Valdar in a few days, and we really need these new production lines to get up to full speed as quickly as possible."

Hortensius furrowed his brow in thought. "A few concerns. The demand for paper is already high, and using it for these cartridges is going to put a strain on that. I can already see that being a bottleneck in cartridge production."

"I'll check on them next. With the introduction of the new bleaching and pulping chemicals, they are increasing production speeds, but I agree, it's going to be an issue. We'll look at expanding their facilities so they can bring on more workers."

"Which we're also running short of."

Ky sighed, acknowledging the reality. "Yes, I know. We'll do what we can to get you people."

Manpower remained their largest bottleneck, across all industries and the legions themselves. Every factory, mine, and mill owner asked for more workers, and the legions had still not reached the recruitment numbers they needed. Even with the addition of the Ulaid and the influx of immigrants, there just weren't enough people for any single part of the war effort, let alone for it as a whole. If things went well in Germania, he hoped it would increase immigration of people to Britannia, looking for safety, work, or both.

"I did have a question about the bullet. I'm confused both by the name, since this looks nothing like jewelry, and the design. While it's much faster to produce since it's lead and doesn't have to go through the entire process of becoming steel, it's still much slower than making balls of lead like you have us making for the grape shells or even the larger cannonballs."

"Round ball molds are easy to clean and reuse, and it is easy to make new molds as the old ones wear down. This design, with its ridges, pointed top and slightly concave bottom makes the molds both harder to clear and use again and becomes misshapen much faster. From every description of how the rifles operate, I don't see why a ball wouldn't work as well, and it would be much easier to manufacture. The same problem exists with these shells. That, at least the name I understand, since some are going to have the interior cavity for gunpowder, but we have that with round shells now, and they work well."

"I can see from a manufacturing standpoint balls would be a better choice, but for these weapons, it won't, although not always for the same reason. The main reason for the design of the bullet goes hand in hand with the softer metal. When the gunpowder explodes, the pressure pushes the bullet forward, like with the cannon you're already familiar with, but it also distorts the end of the bullet, because of the concaved end. It expands the rear edges of the bullet until it locks into these rifle grooves, which causes it to spin."

"Yes, you mentioned that when we were starting work on the new cannon, and doing the rifling on those, but we hadn't gotten as far as making any of the shells yet. I'm not sure what I expected, but this shape almost certainly wasn't it."

"I know it's very different, but it's for a reason. Not only does it get a rapid spin from the rifling, but the cone shape also helps it fight against air resistance. The two together is what gives this weapon the kind of range it has."

"The air dynamic that you told me about."

"Aerodynamics. Yes."

Hortensius pondered, then connected the dots. "Then these other rifles you gave me plans for, without the rifling and using the small round projectile, won't have the same capabilities."

"These other weapons are something my people would call a musket. Rifles get their name from the grooves cut into the barrel, which we called rifling, and yes, the muskets are a significant step back. The main difference between the two is accuracy and range. There's also a difference in stopping power, but inside each weapon's range, the stopping power is enough that the difference won't matter. Our allies will get these muskets. They'll be a significant step ahead of armies still using swords and bows, but will still leave them outmatched by our legions if they either turn on us or sell the weapons to the Carthaginians."

"I see. I guess that answers my questions."

"Good. What about the primer caps? Have you had any problems with those?"

Hortensius shook his head. "No, but we're going to have to build a second stamp press for them or cut back our production of rifles. Between parts for rifles and these muskets, we're already pressed to keep up with the assembly processes. Especially since we need significantly more of these copper pieces if Sorantius's demands for deliveries are correct."

"They are," Ky confirmed. "We're going to need a lot of these bullet cartridges and a lot of these primers. Sorantius has already started to work on what he's going to put in them, but we're going to have to be very careful with them every step of the way since the entire point is for them to explode when enough force is applied."

"For now, we'll split the time on the one stamp press we have between each of the weapons and the primer casings, until we get more presses built. I think we're going to have to expand again, to make room for all of this, which means going into another building and having to build another steam engine, in addition to the one you promised the woodworkers and weavers. We're starting to get stretched thin. We might be able to bring on people to assemble the bullet cartridges fast, since it doesn't require a lot of training, but I only have a handful of men able to assemble the precision equipment."

"I know. I think this will always be our problem. Do the best you can, both in getting the supplies we need and the people trained so you can expand. Thankfully, it'll be winter soon, and that should slow down the pace of operations to help you catch up. If things go well by the beginning of winter we'll start seeing a larger influx of refugees from northern Germania who will be looking for work."

"Until then, we'll do our best, Consul," Hortensius said.

Devnum

Ky stood on the bustling Devnum docks, watching Valdar's ships being loaded, men running up and down the gangplanks. In a way, it felt oddly comforting and normal. It reminded him a bit of his squadron in the hanger bay, preparing the ships for a patrol. True, the occasional seagull call changed the soundtrack of the moment slightly, but it still had the same feel.

"Consul, do you have a moment?" Bomilcar said, suddenly appearing next to him.

Surprised, Ky turned towards the Carthaginian. "I thought you left with Velius this morning."

Bomilcar shook his head. "I asked to stay behind. There are some things I wanted to speak to you about when you returned from Factorium."

"You have good timing. Valdar has been pretty impatient, and started loading even before I returned. We should be leaving in the next hour or so."

"Lucilla told me where I would be able to find you. I've been here at the docks since shortly after breakfast."

"This sounds important."

"It depends on what your answer is to my proposal. Since the council meeting, I've been thinking about our objectives, and how I can contribute to them."

Ky eyed him curiously. "With Velius and the southern force?"

Ky had half expected this request. He'd been surprised by a note he'd received from Velius shortly after the council of war requesting that Bomilcar travel with the southern force as his second in command. During the assault on Insula Manavia, it was all he could do to keep Velius from putting the Carthaginian general in chains, so the request had been especially surprising.

Still, Bomilcar had participated in most of the training for the legion that was going to be assigned rifles first, so it made sense. Ky had already approved the request, since Velius was going to be out on his own and Bomilcar's excellent tactical sense would help ensure their success.

"No. I'd like to travel to Germania, but not with the northern force either. I have contacts among several of the tribes currently under Carthaginian rule. While it wouldn't be a stretch to say they hate Carthage, I actually got on with them fairly well. They understood we all had our duties to perform, and I did what I could to help them. I arranged for several food shipments during a bad harvest; and for their young men to at least stay in the region, instead of being shipped off to Persia or somewhere else far away. At the time, it had been a purely strategic move, since support in that region had always been weak and I considered a little inconvenience on our part was a small price to pay for strengthening allegiances. My view wasn't popular, but at the time the emperor and his advisors were focused on pacifying the newly conquered Persian territories, so they let me do as I liked. I heard that the person who replaced me in that area changed many of my policies when I was reassigned to begin the preparations for deployment here."

Ky's brow furrowed, concern etched on his face. "And you think they'll remember you and agree to listen to you. You know it could end badly, right?"

Bomilcar nodded. "I'm aware. Hopefully, they'll give me a chance to defend myself before things go too far, but either way, I think it's worth the risk. If I'm to redeem my former allegiances, I must do it all the way. Only making amends when there's no personal risk doesn't count, does it?"

"Maybe not. You know there will also be ... concern here if you leave?"

"I know. That's why I'm asking your permission," Bomilcar replied, his eyes never leaving Ky's.

Ky hesitated a moment, considering. It was time to see if what he'd told Velius had been true or not. Either he believed in Bomilcar's change of allegiance, or he didn't.

Finally, Ky said, "Alright, then I'll take the heat here. Lucilla will help you with Ramirus, and he'll smuggle you onto the continent."

Bomilcar straightened, gratitude in his eyes. "Thank you for having faith in me."

Chapter 21

"You're sure we've got them all?" Lucilla asked, perched on the edge of her father's seat in the Imperial box, gazing down at the colosseum floor.

The sandy stage for the glory of chariot races and the fierce athleticism of wrestling matches, had been transformed into a gruesome display. A wooden platform loomed, its sole purpose to hold the headsman's block and a ghastly urn designed to catch the severed remains.

"All the ones he and the rest of the men we picked up could tell us about," Ramirus said. "He was definitely in charge of what was left of your brother's supporters here, but I won't discount the possibility that the Carthaginians have their own people here as well, separate from the insurgents."

"Which is to say, just because we finally caught Decius doesn't mean we can loosen up on any of our security arrangements."

"That would be my suggestion."

"How many in total?"

"Sixty-three, so far, and counting. We're still integrating several of the second and third-tier targets we acquired. Decius swears most of those men didn't have the names of anyone outside of their cell, but since he didn't keep records, we're just going off his word for it."

"What about the men who carried out the raid on the gunpowder storage? Did we get them?"

"Yes. We've rounded up everyone who survived. Several were still healing from wounds they got in the fight, and several others did not survive the interrogation, but we're bringing the ones who can walk out with Decius."

"Good," she said, rising from her father's seat and stepping forward to the edge of the box.

As the men were marched onto the arena floor and up onto the platform, their gazes met hers, and she could not help but feel the weight of what was about to happen.

"Like the men who stood on this same ground after trying to overthrow the Empire, you have all been found guilty of treason and your lives are forfeit," she said, the words echoing off the colosseum walls. "You have given support to the people who have tried to destroy us and to kill every man and woman in the Empire. For your crimes, your lives are forfeit, while your families, or at least those who knew nothing of your treason and took no part, will be spared, your property is forfeit. With your deaths, we finally put the darkest part of our recent history behind us and leave it to the gods to judge you."

"You will never be your brother," Decius's said with a snarl.

"No, I won't," she said coldly, giving a nod to the executioner.

Whatever retort Decius had prepared was lost as he was yanked to his knees, his head placed on the block and tied in place. The once-proud man now trembled like a leaf caught in a storm, his bravado gone, as the sword descended, severing his head from his body.

Lucilla didn't look away. These people had tried to kill her three times. They would have too if it wasn't for the tiny machines Ky had put in her body. She felt a cold satisfaction at seeing the men behind the deaths of her soldiers finally meeting their fate, but this wasn't about vengeance. She had sworn to herself that every punishment meted out would be fair and impartial. She only hoped that this would put an end to this chapter of their history.

Off the Coast of Hispania

"Well done," Ky praised, his enhanced vision capturing the same image Valdar observed through the spyglass pressed against his eye.

Beneath them, the guns roared to life once more, a thick veil of smoke spewing from the side of the ship. The vessel carved an elegant arc through the water, encircling the barrels they'd deployed for target practice. As they watched, water spouts erupted in a tight formation around one barrel before it shattered into a storm of splinters.

"For a while, I doubted we'd ever reach the point where we could hit anything, even stationary targets," Valdar admitted, a wry smile playing on his lips. "But you were right. With enough practice, we improved. You made it look so effortless that first time; I think everyone assumed they'd share the same success."

Ky chuckled. "The same could be said for sailing your ships. I'm sure plenty of landlubbers imagine they could master the skill the first time they set foot on deck. But everything requires time and practice."

"Well, we're not quite as proficient as you yet, but that grouping isn't half bad. Especially considering our speed. I suspect we'd still struggle in rough seas, but give me time, and I might even excel there, too."

"I admire your confidence," Ky replied. "You won't get much target practice on tours like this, since you'll need most of the powder for sinking Carthaginians. But we must ensure your ships rotate through regular training stints when possible."

"I will. We'll also need to start training the men who've signed on to crew the four new ships, as they'll likely be ready by the time the legions require transport to the continent."

Ky nodded. "I spoke with Lucan before we left, and he agreed. We must maintain these patrols but rotate one of your three ships back for training until then. I understand it'll make your job out here more challenging, but that issue will resolve itself as we increase our fleet. That won't happen if we lack trained crews."

Valdar furrowed his brow, concern etched on his face. "Are you sure? Even with fishermen and friendly merchants, it's difficult to patrol such vast waters with our limited fleet. We're bound to miss some Carthaginians."

"I know, and we'll have to accept that. They're keeping most of their ships in the southern part of Hispania for now and relying on land routes for supplies. So, even if we manage to sink every vessel we find, it won't significantly impact their response to our operations. They send the majority of their shipments across the Middle Sea and then overland. We won't truly cut them off until we control the Middle Sea, but that requires more ships and a base for those ships. Once we achieve that, they'll have to march around Persia to reinforce their forces on the continent. Until then, it doesn't really matter."

As Valdar opened his mouth to respond, a voice called down from the loft above the center mast, interrupting him.

"Sail!"

"I swear, that might be the best improvement you made," Valdar mused as they strode to the opposite side of the ship, eyes following the lookout's outstretched arm.

Ky understood his sentiment. In their older vessels, lookouts precariously perched at the prow, scanning the horizon with un-aided eyes. On a clear day, the open sea offered expansive views, yet the horizon remained a steadfast barrier. Now, with the crow's nest and spyglass in hand, they could identify ships kilometers away.

"I see it. It's got our new triangular sails," Valdar observed, squinting through his spyglass.

"It's one of yours. The Skinbladnir, I believe," Ky confirmed.

Valdar lowered the spyglass, a wry expression on his face. "I wish you could bottle your gift and infuse it into this," he said, brandishing the glass. "These are incredible, but I can barely discern the sails' shape. I bet you could tell me how many men are on that ship."

"Only at the front. The back half remains obscured by the horizon. Give me a few minutes, though..."

Valdar merely shook his head and waved over his first mate. "Signal up."

234

Ky acknowledged the crow's nest's usefulness but felt they underestimated the introduction of signal flags. Previously, ships had to sail dangerously close to communicate, risking boarding by hostile vessels. Signal flags and spyglasses now enabled communication at far greater distances.

While training, the ship's signalmen developed a communication system and procedures for encountering other ships, allowing swift identification and coordination.

As the Skinbladnir drew nearer, the signalman commenced communication with a flurry of flags.

"They've sighted a small group of Carthaginian ships," Ky revealed, not waiting for the signalmen to translate the message.

"How many?" Valdar asked.

"They don't say. South by southeast. A few hours sail."

"Signal back. How many ships and were they spotted," Valdar instructed the signalman.

Flags flew up and down the pulleys to the crow's nest, as Ky observed the Skinbladnir as it angled to meet them, facilitating communication.

"Eight ships," Ky announced. "They don't think they were spotted."

Valdar nodded, eyes scanning the sails and rigging as he calculated in his head.

"Seventy degrees," Ky said, anticipating his thoughts.

Valdar shot Ky a glance but didn't question his knowledge of wind direction or required sailing angle.

"Sailing Master," he bellowed to a man beside the main mast, "hoist the foresail and mainsail and trim for a close reach."

As orders echoed and sailors scurried up the rigging, Valdar turned to the quarterdeck and bellowed, "Helmsman, make your course south by southeast, at seventy degrees."

The helmsman consulted the large mounted compass Ky had designed for the new ships and the wind gauge, turning the ship wheel and altering their course.

"Signal the fleet to follow, south by southeast, at seventy degrees. Prepare for contact. Then signal our thanks to the Skinbladnir."

The signalman rummaged through his stack of flags, hoisting them to the mast.

Valdar approached the quarterdeck, pausing near the hatch to the gun deck and the helmsman. Ky observed him glancing toward the foredeck, understanding the sailor's thoughts. In the past, the captain would stand near the bow, directing combat and observing the enemy—a viable strategy when ships were mere wooden platforms for soldiers. Now, however, lookouts would spot enemy ships from a distance, communicating their findings with hand signals. It was more effective for the captain to be close to where he needed to issue commands. Combat was no longer up close and personal, unless they aimed to capture an enemy ship. It was a change that would take time for the old sailor to adapt to this new way of fighting.

"Boatswain, clear the deck and run out the guns," Valdar yelled to a third man before turning to Ky, his voice softer. "Now we'll see if our training pays off."

The training had them sailing in a tight line, and Ky watched as the three ships gracefully maneuvered in a coordinated circle toward their new direction. Ky's knowledge of sailing ships was limited to historical documents provided by Sophus, but he was well-versed in piloting fighters. Despite radical differences, he marveled at the shared fundamentals between these wooden vessels and their modern counterparts.

Giant capital ships, armed with missile bays, particle beam cannons, and high-intensity lasers, would travel in similar formations, exchanging broadsides with opposing vessels. Though it had been ages since anyone but the empire could build such formidable spaceships, the tactics remained the same. Ky hadn't considered those massive training battles since crossing into this reality, but the sight of the three ships gliding in tight formation brought back vivid memories.

The speeds, however, were incomparable. These ships were swift for their time, especially in favorable winds, easily outmaneuvering anything Carthaginian. But compared to vessels traversing at fractions of light speed, they seemed to crawl towards their destination.

Hours passed as the small fleet sailed southeast, angling toward Hispania. It wasn't challenging to deduce the Carthaginians' location. Lacking sextants and compasses, navigating beyond the sight of land was perilous, particularly for galleys on the Atlantic. Carthaginian fleets invariably clung to the coast.

Despite this knowledge, the possibility of overshooting the enemy fleet remained, as they traveled south while the Carthaginians moved north. The vast ocean and the horizon's limitations made locating the enemy difficult. Ky longed for his drone, which, while not perfect, could extend their visibility. However, Lucilla needed Sophus's help to oversee the weapons' construction, which meant she needed the drone. They'd have to manage when Ky took the drone for their invasion, so a little inconvenience now would grant Lucilla more time to arm the legions.

Thankfully, Valdar's expertise rendered the drone unnecessary this time. He possessed an uncanny sense for where the wind might lead the ships. Yes, he consulted the compass and navigational aids, but also observed the sky, birds, and waves, making subtle adjustments to his course. Ky refrained from intervening. While he held knowledge and experience foreign to these people, it didn't negate their own expertise. Valdar's life revolved around the sea, understanding it as intimately as a farmer knew his land. Ky couldn't contribute anything to improve the search.

"Sail!" cried the lookout from the crow's nest.

"Ease off the sheets and brail up the topsails," Valdar commanded. "Signal the fleet. Fire as we pass. Captains may select targets."

Ky had provided extensive guidance on deploying guns and models for ship warfare, such as boarding actions, broadsides, and crossing the T, a maneuver every admiral in the age of sail attempted that enabled their ships to fire straight down the enemy line without taking return fire. But he'd also entrusted much of the tactical decision-making to Valdar. Most examples and strategies Ky and Sophus recommended were based on two equally armed fleets clashing. Few records existed of a cannon-armed, sail-based fleet engaging galleys with spearmen and archers, save for a nineteenth-century war between Britain and China, and even those weren't an accurate comparison. Those vessels weren't precisely galleys, and they still possessed cannons, albeit inferior ones with shorter range and reduced accuracy.

Ky had left it to Valdar to devise the best strategy until the Carthaginians adapted their weaponry. Valdar settled on a variation of the broadside. Aware that some Carthaginian galleys boasted catapults, he approached from well beyond their range, which informed most of the gunnery training.

Ky had observed all this during target practice, but hadn't heard about captains selecting their own targets until now.

"Are you sure everyone isn't going to end up pounding away at the same handful of ships?" he inquired.

"No. They're watching ahead for the position of the ships in the line, keeping in mind the reload time. At our speed and distance, we'll pass these ships rather quickly."

The galleys reacted to the incoming threat. Clearly not warships, they attempted to scatter in different directions instead of facing the attack. They were no match for Valdar's nimble fleet, however, as the caravels bore down on the eight sluggish galleys, now even slower as panic set in.

Survivors from the previous Carthaginian fleet must have returned home, recounting tales of Britannian prowess. And that had been with a single cannon on Valdar's old flagship. These new ships, with their multitude of sails, must have appeared colossal, looming over the smaller galleys.

Then, the first cannons roared to life.

Devnum

"Ready to go?" Velius's voice cut through the noisy docks, startling the commander who was lost in thought.

"Velius! I thought your men were still in the field training."

"They are," Velius responded. "I left them in Gordanius' care. I heard you were sailing out today and wanted to see you off."

Bomilcar smiled, grateful for Velius's company. Their relationship had changed dramatically from the days when Velius questioned his every move, suspicious of Bomilcar's loyalty.

"As soon as the Scandi captain finishes loading his ship. Apparently, there's quite the demand for the excess arcuballista now that the Consul has approved selling the extra stock," Bomilcar said.

"Just imagine what the demand for the lower quality rifles, muskets, or whatever will be. These will be outdated almost by the time they get into their new owners' hands," Velius replied.

"The Consul won't allow those to be sold, except for use by our allies. At least not for a long while," Bomilcar explained.

"You know they won't stay in the hands of the people we sell them to. Some will be sold, some will be lost in battle, and some will be stolen. It's going to happen," Velius said.

"It will be a while before they can produce their own gunpowder," Bomilcar said. "Even without needing the primer cap thing Hortensius demonstrated for us, they will still go through a good amount of gunpowder, and stealing or buying extra gunpowder from people we sell it to isn't going to be enough."

"It will eventually balance out. The secret of making gunpowder won't stay secret for long. While we have had to set up massive operations to get it made in quantity, there will be people out there who will figure out how to get it done. I've found it generally best to assume that nothing remains secret or exclusive," Velius said.

"Maybe. Either way, the market for these weapons is going to be short-lived," Bomilcar said, his thoughts turning to the future.

"Probably, although I can imagine a secondary market will begin to appear between the original buyers and new people further out from us in Asia wanting to buy them. These will travel faster than the harder-to-get muskets," Velius said, impressed by Bomilcar's knowledge.

"You know a lot about trading for a general," Velius said.

"Not trading so much as reconnaissance. Knowing what kind of weapons you might face and how people might arm themselves is critical, especially if the people you serve are bent on conquering the whole world," Bomilcar replied.

Velius nodded, impressed by Bomilcar's unique perspective. Unlike other Britannians, Bomilcar had experiences and knowledge that allowed him to see things in a different light. But in the end, it was all theoretical. The reality was that there were people who wanted to buy the arcuballista, and the Britannians needed raw materials. So, they would sell whatever people were willing to buy.

"I guess. Are they taking you into the Sea of Serpents?" Velius asked, using the Scandi name for the sea that separated the continent from the Scandi homeland.

"Yes. They'll drop me as we pass through the mouth of the sea. According to Ramirus, several of the tribes I know have migrated there, trying to get as far north as they can, away from Carthaginian interference, while still being in their homeland. It will also be easier to deal with them if there aren't a lot of Carthaginians around. There may not be enough Carthaginians on the northern coast to face off against our legions, but there's more than enough to put one old man in shackles," Bomilcar explained, his voice tinged with uncertainty.

"Are you sure they aren't going to remember you simply as a leader for the people who've oppressed them, and kill you on sight?" Velius asked, worried for his friend.

"I'm not, but it's still worth trying. I'm already on a second chance for my life, and I figure I might as well try and make good use of it. If I die, at least I die doing something useful for once. Who knows, maybe they'll give me a chance to speak before they execute me," Bomilcar said, his voice heavy with the weight of his past mistakes.

"I hope they give you more time than that," Velius said, his hand outstretched to his friend as they saw the Scandi captain waving for his passenger. "Good luck and may the gods watch over you, my friend.

"Thank you," Bomilcar said, grasping Velius's arm.

Chapter 22

Carthage

"How many this time?" the emperor asked, glaring down as the messenger bowed, his forehead nearly touching the cold marble floor.

"Eight, Your Magnificence. The ill-fated vessels were not far from shore when disaster struck. One desperate soul managed to cling to life, swimming ashore to deliver this dire news."

"And the enemy?"

"Three ships, Great One. The survivor was disoriented, yet he spoke of massive vessels adorned with a dozen or more sails, looming like giants on the open sea. He claimed they dwarfed our own galleys, both in height and length, yet maintained a similar width." The messenger trembled as he recounted the survivor's tale.

A skeptical murmur rippled through the emperor's advisors.

One, a portly man with a neatly trimmed beard, scoffed, "Such monstrosities could never stay afloat. Even the skilled northerners, with all of their knowledge of the sea, sail ships comparable in size to our galleys. If larger vessels were possible, those greedy merchants would have seized the opportunity long ago."

The emperor's gaze drifted to another figure, who stood halfway up the dais. "In previous encounters, have we seen anything like these behemoths?"

"No, Excellency," the man replied, his voice firm. "The enemy has used traditional Scandi ships, albeit armed with the devastating smoke weapons we've heard tell of."

The emperor's brow furrowed. "And did this lone survivor report any sign of these fearsome smoke weapons?"

The messenger nodded, his voice shaking. "Indeed, your Excellence. He spoke of evenly spaced holes lining the sides of the ship, emitting plumes of smoke just before boulders tore through our vessels. He also described a metal ball, which exploded into fiery shards, felling men like ripe stalks of wheat."

A note of disbelief entered the emperor's voice. "Hallucinations, you say?"

"Frantic, your Excellency. He was utterly terrified and on the brink of death when he washed ashore. However, he remained certain about the smoke weapons and the fiery explosion. He even speaks of it in his sleep."

The emperor's eyes narrowed. "Why have you come here, then? Why not bring this man to me for questioning?"

The messenger swallowed hard. "The healers fear he is too weak to survive the journey, Your Magnificence. The commander decided it would be better to ensure his eventual report, or to allow someone to interview him, rather than risk his life in transit. He asked me to beg your forgiveness for his presumption."

The emperor's frown deepened as he considered the words, then turned to his spymaster. "Send your best agent to interview this man. We must learn all we can about these mysterious ships." He then addressed the messenger once more. "Where did this disastrous battle occur?"

"Off the northern coast of Hispania, Your Magnificence, just east of the point where the coastline bends southward."

The emperor's face darkened as he turned to one of the gathered generals. "They draw ever nearer. Do they plan some sort of assault?"

The general's eyes shifted uneasily, as if he were grappling with some unspoken burden. "They may well have designs on Hispania, Your Magnificence, for it was the final prize they lost before we banished them to their rocky island. They would surely need it as a stepping stone to our shores. Yet, even with their recent ... fortunate encounters, a full-scale invasion appears improbable. Their numbers, even with the combined might of their fellow barbarians, would fall short. It is more likely they seek to safeguard their maritime trade and thwart our own efforts at landing troops."

"But is an invasion still within the realm of possibility?" The emperor's voice trembled, betraying a hint of vulnerability.

The general hesitated, weighing his words carefully. "It is unlikely, but not impossible, Excellency."

The emperor's thoughts turned to the vast fleet they were amassing, and he couldn't help but wonder. "Considering their formidable smoke weapons, would our invasion force stand a chance?"

The room fell silent as the men exchanged wary glances, each hesitant to voice the grim truth. But the emperor would not be denied. "Speak!" he commanded.

Reluctantly, the general complied. "No, Your Excellency. Their ships outmaneuver our galleys with ease, sinking them at will. The perilous voyage, coupled with the enemy's superior firepower, would render any coastal assault a doomed endeavor."

The emperor's eyes narrowed, but he seemed to accept the general's candor, at least for the moment. "And how many vessels do we believe they possess?"

"We cannot say for certain, but their numbers are limited. Only a fraction of our ships have ever encountered a Roman vessel, and these engagements were far from their island stronghold."

"What of the Roman? We offered him sanctuary in exchange for intelligence. Where is he now?"

"He departed a few days ago to consult with one of his contacts," the general replied cautiously.

"You allowed him to leave unescorted?" The emperor's nostrils flared, his anger barely contained.

"No, Great One. Two of the Brothers accompanied him."

"I see," the emperor acknowledged with a curt nod.

The Brothers of Mot, a fanatical death cult, were instantly recognizable by their skeletal face paint and black attire. They revered the god of death and were among the first to proclaim Emperor Hanno as Mot's earthly incarnation, a title passed down through generations to the present ruler. While the emperor's divine status was widely accepted throughout the empire, the Brothers took their devotion to an extreme. They would not hesitate to kill in his name and viewed death in his service as the ultimate ascension. The Brothers' unwavering loyalty made them the emperor's most trusted spies, their presence a source of terror for all.

The emperor's voice hardened. "And what, pray tell, is your grand strategy for dealing with these elusive ships? Surely you have something more inventive than merely sacrificing fleet after fleet?"

"Indeed, Your Excellency. They have proven themselves to be formidable adversaries, deftly remaining beyond our reach during each encounter. It appears they lack the manpower to withstand a boarding assault. Since we cannot outpace them, nor can we withstand their devastating smoke weapon, we must strip them of their ability to flee. We are devising a stratagem to lure them into a trap, where we shall encircle and board their vessels. With fortune on our side, we may even capture one or more of their ships and seize their advanced weaponry for further examination. If not, we shall consign them to the ocean's depths."

The emperor's patience was wearing thin. "See to it that you succeed. I grow weary of your constant failures."

"Yes, Excellency," the general replied, bowing deeply before retreating from the dais, beckoning the messenger to follow.

Once they had safely departed the emperor's throne room, the general turned to the messenger, his voice a hushed whisper. "Tell me everything you know about these enigmatic ships."

Devnum

"To what do I owe the greeting?" Ky asked as he descended the gangplank, his boots thumping on the wooden dock.

"Hortensius sent word that our first shipments of rifles were ready. I came up to make sure we got enough ammunition and gunpowder to get training started in earnest," Velius said.

"Training's going well then?"

"It is. We've finally mastered deploying from marching columns into firing lines while maintaining unit cohesion. I'm eager to put rifles in the men's hands so they can grow accustomed to them before facing real combat. The demonstration Hortensius provided was enlightening, but there's a world of difference between hearing cannons roar and feeling the blast of a rifle in your own hand. My only regret is that our training couldn't be conducted closer, as I waste precious time traveling between here and the legions."

Ky nodded in understanding. "The prisoner camps have claimed much of the surrounding land, and the city requires the remaining fields for crops. A wider expanse was necessary for maneuvering practice. But why the frequent trips?"

"I saw Bomilcar off a few weeks ago."

"Ah, He got off alright then?"

"Yes, although it will be several days before he lands, given the circuitous route he's taken. His arrival should go unnoticed. Do you think he'll persuade the local tribes to ally with us?"

Ky shrugged. "It's hard to say. Bomilcar knows them better than we do."

"Is it safe?"

"Nothing is safe in a battle to the death against an empire vastly larger than ours. But Bomilcar is crafty and experienced; if anyone can survive, it's him."

"How did the hunting go?" Velius asked, indicating the ships.

"Quite well. We sank two small fleets, one of eight ships and another of ten. Valdar has done an exceptional job preparing his modest fleet. I can't wait for the day when we have a formidable fleet capable of truly pressuring the Carthaginians. While establishing a foothold on the continent is vital, we'll be overwhelmed unless we can disrupt their ability to quickly deploy forces and maintain control. Sending ships into the middle sea and forcing them to march around will be our first step in crippling them."

Velius shared Ky's enthusiasm. "I look forward to having those ships with us when we land. Their performance at Insula Manavia was impressive, and if they've improved as you say, they'll ensure any landings and coastal supply bases have sufficient firepower to deter even the mightiest Carthaginian army."

"True, they would. Unfortunately, I have bad news for you on that. You'll receive the entire fleet, but they'll remain only long enough to unload troops. Save for one ship, the rest will then depart."

Velius sighed. "I knew I wouldn't keep all of them, but I'd hoped for two or three. One ship can only cover a limited area while we construct fortifications. And if it must resupply, we'll be left vulnerable during its journey to and fro."

Ky empathized but stood firm. "We have little choice. The fleet must maintain pressure on the Carthaginians. Transporting men along the coast is still faster than overland travel. Your presence will strain their supply lines, and if you secure a passage to the middle sea, you'll effectively cut off that region from the rest of their forces. We need our fleet on the water. However, we won't leave you defenseless. Other ships will bring supplies, so your lone vessel won't need to return for resupply."

"I suppose that's something."

"Consider yourself fortunate. I'm moving the bulk of our forces across in galleys and what Scandi ships we can pay. The distance is short, but it's going to take dozens of trips to get everyone across."

Velius managed a weak smile. "I'll try not to complain too much about my good fortune."

"Good," Ky said, clapping Velius on the back. "Are you returning to your command soon?"

"Yes, I leave tomorrow morning with the weapons for my legion."

"Has Hortensius mentioned how many rifles you'll have by the time you ship out?"

"Perhaps five thousand; insufficient for both legions. We'll have to distribute them evenly, which limits the number of men we can field effectively. We've modified our deployment strategy to accommodate the remaining soldiers armed with shields and swords. I've only tested it with one cohort, but it shows promise."

246

Ky furrowed his brow, uncertainty creeping into his voice. "And?"

"I plan to deploy lines four deep instead of three. We'll maintain the three firing lines, but I'll add a front line of shieldmen. I realize it deviates from your original instructions, but with only half a legion wielding the new weapons, we risk being overrun by a sizable force. Until we have enough rifles, I want to use the unarmed soldiers as a protective force. They'll kneel, allowing the ranks behind them to fire. This added protection will also help against arrows if the enemy comes within range. The firing ranks will stand, so they can still shoot over the shield wall."

Ky furrowed his brow, attempting to visualize the formation. It wasn't the strategy he and Sophus had devised, but it held potential. He wanted his commanders to think critically about such challenges. With the vast differences in technology, no historical battle could guide their strategies for the upcoming conflict. He and Sophus had chosen the best options available, but neither had considered blending old and new tactics like this.

Intrigued, Ky said, "I'd like to see this for myself. I must speak with Hortensius and Valdar first, but I'll follow you afterward to observe your men in action."

Velius nodded. "I'll have them prepared, then. Until then, Consul."

"Until then," Ky echoed, clasping Velius's forearm in the Roman style of a handshake.

Ky strolled leisurely toward the palace, relishing the calm that had settled over him during the past three days. Hortensius had been busy at Factorium, and Ky had seized the opportunity to spend precious time with Lucilla. Though it had only been a few months since they were last together, their duties had kept them apart, making the time feel far longer. He understood the necessity of their separation but couldn't help feeling the pang of longing when apart from her.

While there was much to be done, Ky found solace in his brief respite. He checked in on the hospital and the diligent physicians working tirelessly to develop the rudimentary antibiotics that Sorantius had begun. Under Lucilla's watchful eye, they had made significant progress, but the road ahead was arduous. Introducing penicillin was only the beginning; they also had to develop safe methods for taking blood samples, create simple syringes, and devise an alternative growth medium for the medicine. Historical records indicated that corn extract was the primary medium due to its abundance of complex carbohydrates, but they had to make do with wheat, which proved challenging. If not processed precisely, it easily transformed into yeast, unsuitable for cultivating penicillin. Ky hoped to eventually acquire seed corn from the Americas or soybean from China for an easier medium, but for now, they had to work with what was at hand.

Through trial and error, the team had managed to develop a process for drying the penicillin and mixing it with calcium fats. The result was a semi-shelf stable penicillin tablet, but production quantities were frustratingly small. The silver lining, however, was that the advancements made in penicillin production would eventually be applicable to food preservation and canning, making it easier to supply food during winter, to ships at sea, and to armies on the march. In time, these processes would save countless lives, as important as the development of penicillin itself.

Scaling up production remained their most significant hurdle. The current processes yielded less than a thousand units, a meager amount considering the lower potency of this early medication. This quantity was barely enough to treat one patient for a single day. With synthetic versions of the medication far out of reach, their only option was to ramp up production massively to create sufficient quantities of the life-saving drug.

Sophus had some recommendations, but it required yet another expansion of the facilities in Factorium, and the need for even more manpower, which was the one thing the Empire could simply not get enough of.

Ky's wandering train of thought snapped back into place as he found Hortensius and Valdar waiting for him. He wished Lucilla could have been there with him, but her father's illness had placed her in the role of his stand-in, leaving her to face the Roman senate and petitioners. He empathized with her frenetic schedule, which seemed even more daunting than his own.

"Thank you both for meeting me here, especially you, Hortensius. I know you're swamped with preparing rifles and ammunition for Velius's legion," Ky said.

"My foremen have it under control. It's nice to be somewhere quiet for once," Hortensius replied.

Ky marveled at Hortensius's definition of quiet, considering the bustling and ever-growing capital of Devnum. Then Valdar, ever the pragmatist, cut straight to the chase.

"What can we do for you, Consul?"

Valdar had his hands full as well. With new ships launching soon and a smaller schooner being sold to Yrsa, a prominent Scandi merchant, Valdar's schedule was packed. He would be overseeing the fleet that carried Velius to Hispania while training Yrsa's crew on the new sail plan.

Ky took a deep breath before revealing his request. "We need to obtain specific plants that grow in far-off Asia, beyond Carthaginian control. They resemble dandelions but with subtle differences. We need the seeds they produce after their flowers close up. Valdar, I know you have contacts with Asian merchants who travel to these remote regions. We'll provide you with details on where to find these plants and how to identify them. It's crucial we obtain the correct plants, and if we do, we'll pay the same amount we would for gold or silver, by weight."

"Why would you pay so much for what you just called a weed?" Valdar inquired, a hint of skepticism in his voice.

"Because we can extract a vital substance from them. The problem is, this will all take time. I should have asked someone to start looking for these plants last winter, but with armies bearing down on us and the need to start production on things like gunpowder, it just ... slipped through."

Hortensius, ever the inquisitive one, asked, "What are they used to make?"

"Individually, nothing. But when combined, they create a new plant called a Russian Dandelion. The roots from these plants can be turned into a sticky substance that, when processed with other chemicals, will make a bouncy material called rubber, which has a wide array of uses. However, it will take a long time to produce even after we get the flowers."

"So this is something like gunpowder," Hortensius mused. "We grind the roots up and mix them together to form something new, right? Does that mean you want to grow them here? I assume you know they'll grow in our climate, but doesn't that mean waiting an entire year for the plants to grow? And wouldn't you have to use a large part of that crop to grow even more plants?"

"Yes, the end result comes from drying and grinding the roots, but no, I don't want to mix them together. Each plant alone doesn't have the properties I need. If they are bred together, they'll create a new plant with the properties I seek."

Ky and Sophus had extensively discussed their options for rubber. Their new ships would be able to travel to the Americas, where they could obtain useful items like potatoes or corn, but rubber posed a more significant challenge. They couldn't simply transplant rubber trees as they could with corn and potatoes, as rubber trees required a tropical climate to grow. Defeating Carthage and establishing trading posts near the Gulf of Guinea might help, but that wouldn't happen anytime soon and would present its own set of problems. Trade with Southeast Asia was also an option, but it remained out of reach for the time being.

The European answer to tropical-based rubber trees lay in the Russian dandelion, a plant developed during a nineteenth-century global conflict as a substitute for rubber by one of the warring nations. However, it wasn't a naturally occurring plant during the Roman era; it was a hybridization of two other plants with much lower concentrations of latex, the base material that could be transformed into rubber.

Though they lacked the time for an extended, decade-long breeding program to create this plant, Sophus believed he could hasten the process. He thought he could use the nanites in Ky's blood to genetically modify the two seeds together, creating their own Russian dandelion. He'd already demonstrated that he could modify Ky's nanites for use in another organism, but this was a significant leap, and Ky remained skeptical. For one, the nanites relied partially on the heat produced by the human body, and there was no way to extract the nanites using their current technological capabilities.

Sophus's proposed solution involved placing the seeds in a nutrient bath of water and boiled-down simple sugars. They would keep the mixture warm, albeit cooler than the human body, as the dandelion seeds would begin to break down at around ninety degrees Fahrenheit. Ky would then introduce his nanite-laden blood into the concoction. It was hoped that the nanites would survive long enough to start converting the seeds, editing and splicing their DNA together. The nanites wouldn't self-replicate in the mixture, so Ky would have to periodically add more blood as the previous round of nanites expired. Even if it worked, questions remained about the amount of blood Ky would have to sacrifice to alter the seeds and the subsequent impact on his health.

Long term, Ky wasn't worried about his health, as his body would continuously produce new nanites as long as he lived. However, even with his advanced biology, Ky needed his blood and could only generate so much at a time. Considering his numerous responsibilities and the constant demands on his time and attention, the process would greatly weaken Ky, affecting every other project.

If the first batch grew successfully, they would start producing seeds for the new strain of plants, which meant the process would only be needed once.

"And yes, they will grow here," Ky continued. "You're also right that we don't have time to wait an entire year for a new crop. I'm going to give you a design for a new kind of greenhouse that uses the new glass we're making for its sides and roof, allowing light in and retaining heat. I think once some of the farmers see this, we'll see these buildings popping up elsewhere, as they'll enable us to grow some seasonal plants year-round, helping with our food supplies in winter. While we wait for Valdar to obtain our plants, I want to start building the greenhouses, so we can begin planting as soon as possible."

"You understand these regions are far from where we operate. Even my contacts don't venture out this far. We'll likely have to go through two or even three middlemen to obtain them," Valdar cautioned.

"I know, which is why I'm willing to pay so much for them. We don't need this to be a long-term arrangement. I just need a large enough batch of each."

"I'll see what I can do," Valdar promised.

Chapter 23

Legion Training Camp

"Consul, you made it," Velius greeted, riding up to Ky and his small party.

"I said I would. I'm excited to see what you've done here," Ky replied.

"I have my command up on that small hill, which offers a splendid view of the training field, especially for you. Let the centurion lead you up there while I get the men set for a demonstration," Velius instructed, gesturing to the aide sitting on horseback beside him.

Ky and his group trailed the centurion as Velius cantered away enthusiastically. The legate was correct, the modest incline provided an ideal vantage point for observing the bustling activity below. Ky watched as the men scattered throughout the vast open field began responding to commands, assembling in orderly marching columns. One of the legate's other aides galloped briskly towards the fortified camp in the distance, returning ten minutes later, accompanied by teams of horses hauling three cannons and a group of unarmored legionnaires sprinting behind them.

It wasn't until Ky saw the artillerymen that he realized the lines of rifle wielding legionnaires still donned their armor. It was peculiar to see men clad in segmented armor while brandishing long rifles with their bayonets already affixed; a bizarre fusion of two eras coexisting in the present. He had grown so accustomed to the sight of men in traditional Roman armor that the incongruity hadn't struck him until he saw the unarmored artillerymen, who appeared more in line with his expectations for men wielding such weaponry.

Ky and Sophus had extensively debated the subject of the legionnaires' armor. If they confronted adversaries equipped with similar arms, it wouldn't be a concern, as the armor couldn't stop a proper rifle round, and shedding it would facilitate marching and fighting for the soldiers. However, for the time being, they would engage men still wielding swords and spears, against which the armor would undoubtedly offer protection. Sophus had contended that they should adhere to his historical files, arguing that the enemy was unlikely to engage in melee combat and, given the numerical disadvantage, the armor would be of little help in keeping the legion alive even if they did. Abandoning armor production would also free up foundries to manufacture more necessary weapons.

Though Ky believed the AI was likely correct on both counts, he considered the psychological aspect of the armor. The legionnaires were already grappling with numerous changes in their combat tactics, and their armor provided a sense of familiarity. Ky wasn't concerned about the weight of the armor during marches, as these men had been marching in such gear for quite some time. Furthermore, there remained a possibility that they would find themselves in hand-to-hand combat, which was why Velius had incorporated shieldmen in the front rank. Ultimately, Ky conceded that they would have to abandon the armor at some point, but for now, he thought, this could work. He'd left the decision up to Velius, who'd clearly chose to continue using the armor for the time being.

It took nearly thirty minutes, but at last, Velius came riding back up the hill to rejoin them. Ky had to admit, the presentation was nothing short of spectacular.

The two columns marched forward, two abreast, until the piercing sound of a bugle call resonated through the air. With remarkable precision, the clusters spread out into battle lines four men deep. As promised, the first line comprised shieldmen armed with gladii, while the rear three ranks bore long rifles resting on their shoulders, resembling the spears of a phalanx as they advanced.

The line appeared considerably thinner than those that would have been employed before. Rather than tight cohort-sized units, they were more dispersed, with each century functioning as an independent unit and a slight gap between them—save for three spots where the break was more substantial. Additionally, there were three centuries positioned slightly behind the rest, evenly distributed along the line, seemingly serving as a reserve force.

Ky observed as the men halted, and the front shield line dropped to their knees, allowing space for the rows behind them to fire. The reason for the three larger gaps quickly became apparent when horse teams rode up and executed a tight arc, stopping when the cannons were roughly aimed in the direction of the imaginary enemy. As soon as the horses ceased movement, the artillerymen unlimbered the guns, leaving the wheeled caisson containing the guns' ammunition and shells still attached to the horses. In under a minute, the men had rolled the guns forward into the gaps in the line.

A bugle call reverberated, and the front-rank rifles descended in a somewhat uneven line, discharging their weapons. The shots were not perfectly synchronized, as there were a few intervals between this or that century, but within a five-second window, the entire front rifle line had fired and then knelt as the second rank's rifles lowered.

As the second rifle rank unleashed their fire, the cannons boomed, their thunderous roars nearly drowning out the sounds of the second line firing, followed by the third rifle rank's discharge. Just as the first rifle line sprang back up, a bugle sounded, halting their fire. The entire sequence had taken perhaps thirty seconds, and it was evident that it could almost instantly recommence. For sustained fire, that was rather impressive, slower than the three rounds a minute rate indicated in Sophus's records from their history, but noteworthy nonetheless.

"You chose to go with a lighter sustained fire over heavier volleys from the centuries as a whole?" Ky asked.

"Yes, I discussed it with Bomilcar before he left, and we've conducted trials with both patterns. Surprisingly, having the entire line reload and reset proved to be slower on a rounds-per-minute basis. We concluded that continuous fire would be more effective in repelling or slowing a charge than concentrated volley fire, which might be more advantageous against an enemy employing the same strategy and both sides experiencing the same lag time. Furthermore, to make that work, we'd have to abandon the front shield wall since it necessitates the front rank to kneel."

"You understand this type of formation won't endure for long. Once we have enough guns, the benefits of having additional men firing will outweigh the minimal protection offered by the shield wall. The ability to rapidly eliminate more of the enemy from a distance will be more valuable."

"Yes," Velius said, nodding thoughtfully. "That much became evident early on. However, the shield wall does provide some extra protection for now, and the alternative would be to have them waiting behind the lines to pick up fallen weapons. Once we have sufficient rifles, the transition will be simple enough for the men to learn, so there isn't really a downside."

"I see," Ky replied, his tone neutral.

In truth, he thought Velius was likely correct. The tactics they were employing now didn't deviate significantly from those they would use once they had enough guns. The legate wasn't wrong there.

The artillerymen swiftly limbered up their cannons and moved them aside as the cavalry thundered through the gaps left in the cannons' wake. The timing was impeccable, but a brief window of vulnerability emerged, as the rifles had to cease firing once the cavalry charged through and suddenly obstructed their aim.

"That seems like a risky maneuver," Ky observed.

"This is only to be executed once their line starts to crumble, but they are still not close enough to exploit the gaps in our formation. We would initiate this if we noticed their cohesion deteriorating to the point where it was unlikely they could reassemble their ranks before our cavalry could strike. We have distinct signals for all left or all right flank attacks, where they maneuver around either side, or a split flank attack where they emerge on both sides. There are more nuanced commands, such as flank and drive for the center or slicing along their formation's edges, allowing our guns to continue firing, for instance."

"You've really done good work taking the tactics I gave you and adapting them to suit our needs."

"Thank you, Consul. However, much of the credit must go to Bomilcar. The moment he witnessed the first rifles being test-fired and the devastation they caused, he was brimming with ideas on how to make that work for us."

"Good. I'm glad to see you two have started working better together."

"It's more accurate to say that I've learned to work better with him. He has always been professional, and all I can do is extend my apologies to you for my stubbornness."

"You're forgiven. We all make mistakes, and you were genuinely doing what you believed was best. Though, you should probably apologize to him as well."

"I already have."

"Good, good. Well, I must say I'm thoroughly impressed with what I see here. Let's go watch some of your men's target practice and determine if they can actually hit their mark from these intricate formations you've devised," Ky suggested, a hint of playful challenge in his voice.

Devnum

"Llassar, it's a pleasure to see you," Medb greeted with feigned warmth as she opened the door to the quarters she shared with Cormac. "Please come in."

"We need to have a conversation about Cormac," Llassar said firmly.

"Why? Has something happened?" She asked, her face a mask of false concern.

"You can drop the act," Llassar said. "I'm not a naive young man you can lead around by his nose like some kind of prize bull."

"You assume it's his nose I'm leading him by," Medb retorted, the sing-song voice she'd been using gone. "What do you want?"

"I want you to stop meddling in Cormac's affairs. I know you're behind all of the demands he's been making, and I can only imagine what else you've been filling his head with."

"I'm simply trying to adjust to this new life you've thrown me into. You could have left me to help my people, but instead, you marry me off and bring me to this place. I know I don't have the power to get my life back, so all I can do is make the best of what I have now. You told me to be his wife, so that's what I'm trying to do."

"You're also planting ideas in his head, pushing him to request a command for himself. I can only guess you're trying to get him killed off to free yourself of him."

"If you're concerned about him being frustrated by not getting an opportunity to prove his worth, that's your issue, not mine. I'm not implanting any notions. His father was a warrior who claimed his throne; do you believe he requires me to persuade him to take a more active role in his life? He's a headstrong, young man. I'm simply supporting him, because he's right. If I were in his position, I'd demand the same."

"You aren't going to rule through him," Llassar declared.

"No. I'll rule alongside him, and for that to happen, he must be alive, mustn't he? Are you accusing me of attempting to control his throne through him or wishing him dead to escape this marriage? It can't be both."

"I'm accusing you of trying to influence him. I'm trying to teach him how to be a leader, and I can't do that with you whispering in his ear. If you keep interfering, his father will find out and he will have your head. You aren't going to control him for your own purposes, and the sooner you realize that the better your chances of survival will be."

"I'm not trying to do anything but be a wife."

"You've been warned, Medb. Stop now," Llassar cautioned..

As he turned to leave her quarters, he could feel Medb's eyes boring into him. Her message was clear. She had no intention of stopping. Llassar knew Cormac was smitten with his new bride, so having his father kill her would only make matters worse. That option would be reserved as a last resort, in case she went too far. Until then, he'd have to find another way to address this.

"You have to keep cleaning the surfaces with this antiseptic every time a patient is released," Ky said, annoyed to be having the same conversation for what felt like the hundredth time. "Doing it once doesn't make it completely clean for all time."

"Then what's the point?" the physician countered, clearly irritated. "IIf these small demons can be put here at any time, what's the point?"

"They're not …" Ky started to say and stopped, working hard to keep in his sigh. "They can come in on anything. Other patients, you, tools you might not have sterilized well enough, which can include the bedding. It can grow on its own if a wound starts to fester, or even come in on insects. We can't keep it all away, but the more we *do* keep away the better chance the patient has of recovering. I'm tired of having this conversation. We have these new rules in place for a reason. The physicians who follow them have nearly half the number of dead patients as you do, and it's because you refuse to change the way you do things."

"Or it's because they put a curse on me to drive away my business."

"They didn't …" Ky started, when Lucilla's voice rang out in his head, drowning out whatever he was thinking to say.

"Ky, come to my father's chambers now. He's … something's wrong."

Her voice was full of terror.

"Just do it. I'll send people to check on you, and if you keep this up, you will be barred from working on patients inside the Empire."

Before the physician could answer, Ky turned and stormed out, breaking into a run as soon as he exited the cramped hospital. For him, it was closer to a jog, but he didn't want to leave his guards behind. They already looked concerned at his sudden dash toward the palace and he didn't want to cause them, or any other onlookers, to worry that something terrible was happening.

"Lucilla, what's happening?" he asked as he ran, but she didn't answer. "Lucilla."

"Her comm unit is still active, Commander, and I am picking up other people's voices very near her."

"Do you know what's happening?"

"It is unclear. She is talking to a physician, but I was not monitoring her unit until she contacted you. She has asked that I allow her privacy unless there is something urgent, you are trying to contact her, or one of a selection of keywords is said that might pertain to work she would need me for."

"I see."

Sophus had recently asked questions during one of Lucilla and Ky's more ... intimate moments, which had upset his wife greatly. Ky hadn't known she'd talked to the AI about it directly, but it didn't surprise him. Ky had no embarrassment about Sophus's interaction, but he'd lived with the AI in his head most of his adult life and was comfortable with that, for Sophus, there was no emotional reaction, good or bad, from overhearing their activities. Lucilla had a habit of humanizing it, which maybe caused her to see Sophus as closer to human, as far as thoughts and emotions went.

It wasn't a long run, even keeping his sprint at more or less a standard human level, and a few minutes later Ky vaulted up the stairs, three at a time, arriving at the Emperor's quarters, Lucilla rushing to him as he burst through the doors.

"Ky, he's ... something's wrong."

"I'll look at him," Ky said, shooing away the servant who was mopping the Emperor's brow.

The Emperor looked bad. Ky knew he'd been fighting some kind of illness recently and had to ask Lucilla to sit in on his duties multiple times over the last month, but all evidence had pointed to some kind of virus, based on the Emperor's symptoms. Ky's nanites regularly destroyed various viruses that attacked the respiratory and digestive systems, which was a testament to how many existed around them all the time. Seeing the Emperor now, however, Ky realized he and Sophus's diagnosis had been wrong.

He was visibly sweating in spite of the cool fall breeze coming through the window and his skin had a distinct yellowish tint to it.

"Jaundice is a sign of kidney failure, especially when coupled with his other recent symptoms."

"How is he having kidney failure?" Ky sub-vocalized. "The medical patch we applied should have fixed any damage to the kidneys while its nanites were still active, even genetic ones. There hasn't been enough time for environmental factors to do this much damage after it was repaired or for something like cancer to grow."

"Without access to a full medical bay, it is impossible to tell. It is possible that some small portion of the poison he was given wasn't completely removed. Given its low dosage, or unintended alteration by the nanites, it could have remained in his system, slowly causing damage to his kidneys over time. That would explain his fevers, difficulty breathing, sleeplessness, and nausea prior to this incident. All are common early symptoms of kidney failure which, if left untreated, could fail rapidly once they reached a tipping point. Especially if the poison was still in effect."

"How did the nanites miss some of the poison?"

"While the medkit is a powerful tool, the nanites are not tuned to a specific person's genetics and would almost certainly not carry the base programming to identify an obscure ancient toxin. They isolated and removed anything that fits a broad profile, but if there were mutations or slight variations, some of the toxins could have remained. They also can only repair to a broad human template, but again, are unable to fix more specific problems that might not match that template. They are meant for emergencies. Any person treated with a medkit is advised to seek more directed medical assistance as soon as possible for that reason."

"I thought you were monitoring the nanites," Ky said.

"I was, but there was a limit to what I could do besides monitor their functions, and a limit to the types of information fed to me from the nanites because it is assumed to be unaided by AI control. They aren't fitted with the necessary transmitters, which means there is limited access to the nanites beyond the informational data streams that are in place."

"What about ..." Lucilla started to say out loud, and then stopped as her eyes darted to their guards and servants gathered near the doorway of the room.

Sophus had included her in the conversation it was having with Ky, but she realized, almost too late that no one else was, which would have made anything else she might have said concerning.

"Leave us. All of you," Ky said, adding the last part when his and the Emperor's guards didn't move to follow the servants out.

"It's alright. Please give us some time to sit with my father," Lucilla said to her father's guards, who still looked hesitant.

Ky appreciated their sense of duty. They'd seen Ky with the Emperor innumerable times, and he was now the Emperor's son-in-law, and still, they were hesitant to leave their liege's side. Lucilla's request, apparently, was enough to prod them to step outside, although Ky was fairly certain they wouldn't have moved far from the doorway.

"Can't you give him some of the small machines you put in me? They were able to heal my stab wound which, according to Sophus, should have been fatal."

"I'm sorry, but no, Lucilla. If this is kidney failure, which the symptoms strongly indicate, even the introduction of altered nanites would not be enough to repair them. Ky's nanites, which are grown with his genetic structure hard-wired into their core memory, would be able to heal his, but the ones passed to you are altered, with much of that core memory blocked, to allow them to repair you without causing damage by confusing your biological systems with his. While it is true your wounds would have been fatal, none of it was damage that your body couldn't repair on its own if you were able to survive the blood loss. The nanites can speed up the repairs your body would already be able to do and minimize scarring, but they cannot replace your organs. Or in this case, your father's."

"But it could still help. Please, all you have to do is kiss him, right, and you'll transfer the machines to him. They might be able to help."

"Again, I'm sorry, Lucilla, but that isn't possible. I cannot hold modifications of two subjects simultaneously, and any modifications would transmit to the nanites in your system. If we waited a few weeks for the

nanites in your system to degrade and flush out, I could generate a new profile for your father, but I don't believe we have the time for that."

"But you have to help him," Lucilla said.

"I'm not kissing Ky," the Emperor, who had woken, said.

"Father," Lucilla said, circling around Ky and dropping to his side. "How are you?"

"Like I could go win fame and glory in the arena," he said, with a weak chuckle that devolved into coughs.

"We have to help him," Lucilla said, a tear breaking free and rolling down her cheek.

"I know. There are some things I can try, but ..."

"It's not likely to work," the Emperor said, finishing the statement Ky didn't want to say.

"No, Princeps. I'm sorry. I thought the medkit would heal you completely, but I was wrong. It healed enough, but either there was poison left in your body or damage that was unhealed, and all it did was hide the symptoms for a while. If this is what it looks like, the technology doesn't exist to heal it."

"Then build it, damn you!" Lucilla yelled.

"I can't," Ky said as gently as he could. "I'm so sorry. If I could, you have to know I would. There's nothing I wouldn't do to try and help your father, but it's just not possible."

Her anger faded and she collapsed in his arms, crying.

"How long?" the Emperor asked.

"I don't know. I can treat many of the symptoms. There are herbs and simple medicines that can act as ACE inhibitors, which should lower your blood pressure and reduce your kidney's workload. Some diet changes, diuretics, and natural supplements. None of these are cures. Even if all of these work, six months, maybe a little more or less, until the organs give out completely. If none of the treatments work ... less."

"Well then, I think there are some things you need to do, Lucilla," the Emperor said.

"Me?" she questioned, looking at her father and then at Ky. "But Ky needs to ..."

"Do nothing. You heard him. Do you think Ky would hold back if he knew a way to heal me?"

"I can still think of something," Ky said. "Just give me some time."

"I know you'll do your best, but if you don't succeed we don't have a lot of time," the Emperor said, his voice trailing off into coughs. "Lucilla, I am an old man. I would like to stay and be with you longer, maybe even see a grandchild, if the gods are kind, but we do not have the luxury of wishing. Please don't cry. I should have been dead last year. I would have been without Ky. I made my peace with death then. Instead, I got more time. I lived to see our people escape the thumb of the Carthaginians and actually take our land back. I got to see a mighty new Empire rise up that will keep our people safe well after I'm gone. And I got to see you find someone you love. You've always been too serious."

"But I don't want to lose you," she said, burying her head into his shoulder.

"I know, but this is a part of life and was always going to happen. Now, enough of this. You have a duty, young lady, and you must do it. The Empire needs their Empress."

"What?!" Lucilla said, sitting up bolt upright.

"You heard me. Who else would it be? Not your brother, that's for sure. He is my greatest regret, but he chose his own greed and ambition over his people. And it can't be Ky. Sorry, my boy, but as great of an asset as you have been and as much as you have given to us, you are still an outsider here. It also continues our line and makes your child, when you have it, more secure in their throne."

"I'm happy it isn't me. You and Lucilla have always been more cut out for politics than I have."

"But I can't rule. There has never been a woman Emperor."

"No, but there's nothing saying there can't be one, and you have more support than anyone else. Our people are behind you and the Caledonians love you like one of their own. You might have issues with the Ulaid, although they've been known to support queens ruling them, so they might be more flexible on the subject than any of us. You've led the legions, or part of them, into battle. Everyone knows you are as big of a part of our amazing new technologies as Ky is. You've spent time in the hospitals, and worked with the new immigrants and the merchants. There isn't a part of our society that you haven't been the face of. If there was ever a woman the people would accept, it's you. Moreover, you already know what to do. I might not have been able to guess this was how it was going to end up, but you've trained for this your entire life."

"I'll do you proud, Father."

"I know you will, and I'm not dead yet. Even if Ky does find a way to heal me, I think it's still best if I pass my reign to you. If he finds a cure, I will be able to continue helping you, offering advice as I can, but if not, I still have several months and I will not go out screaming to the gods about my fate. When I go, I want to know my legacy is secure."

"It will be," Lucilla said, reaching over and tightly grabbing his hand.

Chapter 24

"Is this the last shipment?" Ky asked watching four large wagons packed with crates stamped with the recently adopted Britannic seal.

"Almost. We still have another shipment of ammunition and one last cannon and then we'll be ready to go, although Valdar says it will only take three or four days on the outside, depending on the winds. Since your diversion needs a full week at the least to pull off any of their armies, we're going to be sitting on our thumbs for almost that long just waiting. Hortensius has taken the extra time as a challenge and thinks he can get at least one more cart load of rifles to us before we set sail. He's already beaten his target, but the man is nothing if not ambitious."

"I know. I can't believe how fast he's moved. We didn't get as many of the muskets as I wanted, but at least I feel less bad about taking a hundred of your rifles with us."

"Now he just needs to keep this pace up so we can arm the rest of the legions. So, are you sailing today?"

"Yes. Ursinus marched the men over to Londinium and the eastern ports days ago, so the men have the least amount of time to sail. Even splitting our troops across multiple docks, the number of smaller ships we have to load up means half of the men will be sitting on board ships for almost a full day before the fleet gets underway."

"Are they going to be able to get some rest before they start marching?"

"A few hours at most," Ky said. "The last word Ramirus got was that there's one small force in the area already, dealing with some unrest, and we have to start our swing south to threaten the larger Carthaginian forces in that direction."

"Good luck," Velius said, looking past Ky's shoulder. "Hopefully I'll see you when our forces rejoin each other on the coast of the Middle Sea."

"I look forward to it," Ky said, clasping arms with the legate and turning to see what had grabbed his attention.

The what was Lucilla, making her way down the docks with her guards in tow. She was taking her time to get to him, since she had to stop every few feet to greet this or that soldier, sailor, or just random citizen calling her name. Ky knew, in a vague sense, how popular she was with the people of the empire, but it still surprised him to see it in effect when they were out in public. People reached out to touch the hem of her stola, held their hands out for her to brush her fingers over theirs, or shoved small children in her direction for her to touch. It was touching, although it made getting from point A to point B very slow for her at times.

Finally, she made it to him, inside the small bubble of space created by his guards, and now reinforced by hers. They didn't have to bother. As she embraced Ky, the people gave them room, almost purposefully looking away to give the two of them privacy in the midst of the throng. Yet another sign of respect for their beloved Lucilla.

"I'm going to miss you," she said, wrapping her arms tightly around him. "Every time we get a few days in the same city, time seems to fly by, and then it drags interminably once you leave again."

"At least we can still talk to each other, which is more than the other men separated from their wives and families right now."

"You say that every time. It doesn't make me miss you any less. Just tell me you love me, you'll miss me, and you'll think of me every moment you're gone."

"I love you, I'll miss you, and I'll think of you every moment I'm gone," Ky repeated.

"See how much better things go if you just do what I tell you to," she said, smiling up at him.

"It's funny how that works," Ky said, matching her grin. "I'm glad you came to see me off, though. I don't know how long I'll be gone."

"Not long. Father wants my coronation to happen within the month, and you're going to have to be back for that."

"That might not be possible. It depends on where the field operations are at the time."

"The first snow should be falling by then, and the Carthaginians will have to pull back south if they want to keep their men supplied. Even if they cut you off from the coast, you can be supplied from the Sea of Serpents, but with us controlling the waters, they have to send food and supplies the long way."

"Or take it from villages in the area that've put aside food for the winter."

"If they're dumb enough to do that, they're doing us a favor. All we have to do is feed those people to bring them to our side, and thanks to how much you were able to increase the harvests this year with the new plows, fertilizers, and that stuff that cut down on bug infestations, we have enough surpluses going into the winter to do just that."

"True, but that means even more work for me to do."

"You have competent subordinates. Ursinus, Auspex, and Llassar all know what they're doing. They can manage for some time even without your powers. I want you back here when the time comes."

"I'll do my best," Ky said.

"I know you will. I also came down here to give you this," she said, slipping the drone out of her stola and putting it in an empty pouch at his waist.

"I know this is going to make some of the work with Hortensius a lot harder. I'm sorry about that."

"We'll manage. You've gone over everything new he's doing, aside from that new impact fuse design you wrote up yesterday, so most of what needs to be done is the refining processes, which I don't think will require Sophus's need to visualize."

"I might need this for a while. I do have a new project I want to start Hortensius and Sorantius on in the spring, but I don't want to distract them from getting as many rifles, muskets, and cannons produced as possible. We'll need all of our legions and as many of our allies as possible armed with the new weapons as soon as the snows melt, because the Carthaginians will spend the winter building up their forces, and they'll be throwing them all at us as soon as they can."

"I know. I worry about that."

"Don't. They're going to be the ones worried once they face firearms for the first time. Even with a huge push from them, we'll be able to control the pace of battle since they're not going to know how to deal with our new weapons for quite a while."

"I hope you're right. So what is this new technology that makes up for not having your drone in the field?"

"It's hard to explain, but I think you're going to be impressed when you see the first of our people high up in the sky, separate from any building."

"You're going to teach our people to fly?" she said, pulling back in surprise.

"In a manner of speaking. Don't worry; it will make sense when I show you what I have planned. Until then, you'll just have to use your imagination."

"So you're just going to say something like that and then leave?" she said, faux angry.

"Yep," Ky said, bending down to lightly kiss her on the tip of her nose.

He turned to leave, almost laughing, when she grabbed him hard, spun him back around, and pulled him in for a hard kiss. Shouts, cheers, and several almost indecent suggestions rose up from the men walking around the docks.

Carthage

"What do you mean 'wiped out'," Caesius said to the bedraggled man.

"Just that, my lord. Your father's men captured everyone from Decius down to our newest recruits. The few of us that were away from home when the raids happened ran, but I've heard that most of the others got caught before they could get off the island. They knew my name, my family, and where I lived. Everything. I barely made it off myself and the captain who brought me can't ever go back. We pushed off from the docks just as the praetorians got there. It was sheer luck that the warships they've had sailing around the island were away when we ran for it."

"I thought he had his men working in cells that didn't know about each other, so they couldn't be captured. How did this happen? What happened to Decius?"

"I don't know. I had already been sent to come here with the latest dispatches and information when it happened. I heard a rumor that he'd been captured, but I don't know."

"What about this gunpowder he managed to steal? What happened to it?"

"I don't know, my lord. I think they were still trying to find a way to get it off the island without the praetorians finding out, but they didn't tell me things like that. For all I know, it's still wherever they hid it."

"So we have no one left? At all?"

"I don't think so."

"Fine …" Caesius, no longer seemed to notice the messenger. "Go."

The man looked perplexed, but bowed and left, leaving Caesius to his thinking, which had turned very dark. Daily, the emperor complained that he wasn't holding up his side of their deal. He wanted the secrets of the smoke guns and of the black grains that were apparently at the heart of them, and he expected Caesius to get it for him. When he'd received the last message that they had pulled off a daring raid and stolen a dozen barrels of the stuff, Caesius had been excited, reporting that he'd have samples shortly. And then nothing. Days and then weeks stretched on, with no word.

Each day Caesius didn't deliver the prize the emperor became more and more impatient. After a month, impatience turned into anger. Caesius had found reasons to be out of town, excuses about messages from his contacts and information on the shipment, but those excuses had started to wear thin. After two months, the emperor had assigned him his watchdogs. Terrifying men in all black, except for their skull masks. Only their eyes were uncovered, enough to know they were always watching him.

So far, they were at least not following him into every room, but that wouldn't last long either. Caesius could feel the moment coming when the emperor, or his functionaries, would order the death disciples to stick closer to him. He was running out of time.

"Go to the docks. Procure a ship for yourself, a passenger, and some servants. Tell them it's a sickly brother that you want to take to Greece to see one of their healers. Pay them to be ready to leave at a moment's notice. I have a few things I must clear up here, and then I will join you. There will probably not be time for a warning and it's likely we'll have to be ready in a hurry," Caesius said, putting a stack of coins in the man's hand.

"Where are we going? Greece?"

"For now, that's all you need to know. We'll deal with our real destination when we're safely on the water. This is important. Talk to no one about what you're doing. Go. Now."

The man bowed and hurried out, while Caesius began to pace. This wasn't going to be easy. He needed to secure assets. He wouldn't have an empire supporting him anymore, and wherever he landed would just be a stop on a journey. He had to get somewhere that wasn't controlled by either the Romans or the Carthaginians, which didn't leave a lot of options. Even some of the far northern reaches, like the Scandi, were off limits, since the word was they had begun trading heavily with his father's Empire.

He'd also need to find a way to get his guard dogs off his scent. He had no problem killing them, but he had no guards of his own and only a few servants he trusted. Men who'd escaped his homeland after the Carthaginians lost it and had come searching for him. None of them was a match for the Brothers, or whatever the skull-masked men called themselves.

It was going to be tricky, and he didn't have a lot of time to figure it out.

Belgica

"Consul, the men need a break," Ursinus said, riding up to Ky's small group.

"I know," Ky said, not looking at the junior legate. "We'll be able to rest in a few hours. They're still almost all a few hours march behind us. There's a good ford ahead where we can cross this river. It's isolated and narrow. If they cross and keep in tight pursuit, we can pick them off one at a time, but I'm assuming their commander will figure that out, which means he'll hold his men on the other side until his entire force has made it there, which will easily take until nightfall. If he holds, we'll break to camp early, giving the men a longer rest tonight."

"Is the other side clear?" Ursinus asked.

It was a fair question. Multiple times they'd tried to find a place where the ground gave them some advantage to fight or a way to take on isolated parts of the Carthaginian army, and every time those plans had fallen apart when a large band of Germanic or Gaelic warriors appeared, forcing the Britannians to continue marching. They'd been marching for four days with hardly any breaks, and the men were starting to feel the strain.

Ky had known this was going to be difficult, but he'd hoped they'd be able to find the right ground to keep his small army from being swamped by the massive number of men chasing them. Classic Roman tactics, arcuballista, and a hundred rifles plus a few cannons were powerful force multipliers, but it still wasn't enough for the numbers they faced.

Ky had brought almost twenty thousand men with him to what was known, at least in his timeline, as Belgium. It wasn't enough. When they'd first started out, there had been almost sixty thousand Carthaginians after them, which was more than the last estimate Ramirus had given him, but still, a number they had dealt with successfully before when they were on the right ground. Ky had hoped that they would find a good position once they got out of the lowlands and into the more broken ground where they could more easily limit the front line, but so far they'd nearly been flanked every time.

The Britannians had done well for themselves, marching fast and constantly threading the needle between large warrior bands that might have slowed them down enough to allow the Carthaginians to catch up to them. When the thread was thousands of soldiers in heavy armor, that wasn't an easy feat, and the men recognized this. Good spirits helped, but only to a point; and the nearly non-stop pace had pushed the Britannians to that point.

Worse, each of those bands of warriors had joined the main body of Carthaginians after missing the Britannians, steadily growing their size until now there were well over a hundred thousand men chasing them, which included warriors from dozens of tribes by this point. That actually made it worse than the number of men they faced.

One of Ky's main goals was to get those tribes to switch allegiances and ally themselves with the Britannians, since taking away manpower from the Carthaginians while increasing their own was the only real way they would win this war. Based on Ramirus's reports and Sophus's analysis of what it was seeing through the drone, it seemed like every tribe in an almost hundred-mile radius had sent every able-bodied man to join the Carthaginian army.

That was bad. The Carthaginians had pulled together all of the security forces they had in northwest Europe to chase the Britannians down. This also meant there weren't soldiers forcing those tribes to send all of their men to fight the invaders. That suggested more support for the Carthaginians than Ky had predicted they'd face, at least based on what the refugees who'd escaped to Britannia had told them. Even if they did manage to defeat the army chasing them, if they didn't start to build an effective power base here Ky's entire plan was going to fall apart.

"*Commander, there are indications of a large movement of men from east of the intended crossing point,*" Sophus said, interrupting Ky's train of thought.

Because he only had the one drone, Ky had been forced to use it to both observe where they were going and the forces chasing them, meaning that, even with its height, it had to zip back and forth constantly, since it was impossible for it to see both at the same time. Ky's attention on it had waned as Sophus had been moving it back to a position beyond the ford they would be crossing shortly.

Sure enough, a couple of miles beyond the ford he could make out maybe a hundred and fifty men in rough furs all carrying weapons, moving slowly but steadily towards where they were crossing. A hundred and fifty wasn't a lot, but it could cause problems if they hit them as they were crossing and they probably weren't seeing everyone. The Germanic tribes they'd seen before had come in very close, usually spread out over a mile or more. There might be hundreds more warriors beyond the range of the drone's cameras, and they wouldn't know about them until they were actually crossing the ford, since the drone was already operating at its max range.

"We have a problem," Ky said to Ursinus. "Germanic warriors are moving toward the other side of the ford."

"Damn it. So I guess we aren't stopping."

"It's worse than that. We're at a bad angle. If we try to follow the river southeast, we're going to hit a point where it connects to another, larger river. We'll be trapped with nowhere to maneuver, and the Carthaginians will be able to push their full weight into us. If we go northwest, we're going to hit some very marshy ground that will both slow us down and make it very hard for us to fight. It's why this ford was so good for us, because there are not a lot of other options for crossing without making a wide detour."

"So, we cross and push through the tribesmen?" Ursinus asked.

"Yes, but we have to hurry or they'll hit us mid-cross. Send a messenger to Vibius to pick up the pace. Run them if he has to, but we need to get across that ford in the next hour. Once across he's to push forward half a mille passus and then form up for action. The other three legions will come up behind him for support. I want

274

your men on the right and Marcus' on the left. Auspex will bring up the rear, crossing and then reversing to guard the crossing from the Carthaginians, just in case their lead elements get to us before we are able to get on the move again."

Marcus Sextus Thurinus had been the senior tribune in the legions, just beating Gordianus, Velius's second in command, by a year. They'd picked up enough recruits to reform the second legion after it was dissolved following the insurrection and Marcus had been promoted to lead it. He'd actually been next in line when Ursinus had been jumped from optio all the way to legate, but he'd taken the news well and earned some credit in Ky's eyes at the time. He actually had more experience than Ursinus, but he was still a little too stuck in the old ways of doing things, which was a habit that they'd have to break by next year when his men got issued their rifles.

"This is going to slow us down and even if they don't catch up to us we aren't going to be able to give the men extra rest unless the Carthaginians are unbelievably slow crossing the river."

"I know, but it can't be helped. I don't know for sure yet, but there are probably enough warriors up ahead that we can't just ignore them. Get us across as fast as you can."

"Yes, Consul."

The next two hours seemed to drag by. The men held good order, but the narrowness of the ford meant a slight pile-up while they tried to get all twenty thousand across. Some things broke in their favor, however.

Although there were more tribesmen than Ky originally thought there would be, with the total number closer to two hundred, they exhibited some odd behavior. After their lead scouts cleared the tree line enough to see the crossing Britannians, instead of having their men charge in while they were vulnerable, the Germanic warriors pulled back, holding almost half a mile away from where Vibius was finally getting his front lines set up. It didn't make any sense to Ky. They might not have fought Romans with their tall shields and tight formations but they, or at least their fathers, would have fought against Carthaginian phalanxes enough to know that it was better to hit formations like this before they got set rather than waiting until they were ready.

And yet that was exactly what the Germanic tribesmen were doing, even as Ursinus and then Marcus crossed, extending the Britannian lines. Now, instead of hitting them when only twice their number was across, the two hundred tribesmen were facing a line of fifteen thousand mostly seasoned soldiers.

"We should just start marching forward. They'll either scatter or be crushed under our boots," Marcus said as the four legates gathered with Ky to discuss the situation.

"This smells like a trap," Auspex said.

"So? There can't be that many more of them out there, even if they are trying to lure us in. We can push over them and keep going," Marcus said.

"Almost half of the army now chasing us is made up of local warriors," Ky pointed out. "It's hard to tell, but it seems like they have been pulling these people in from across the continent, maybe to make up for the lack of trained units they could get here before winter. Our sources this far inland have not been great, so it's hard to tell. My original plan assumed they would have some local support, but not the level we're seeing. You might be right, but we just don't know. Besides, most of the war bands we've faced in the past haven't used these kinds of tactics, which makes me pause. We're missing something, and that worries me."

"This is good ground," Auspex said. "The ford narrows down the front they can advance on more than any of the places we've considered so far for a stand-up fight. The ground is also terrible for them. It's wet, muddy, and rocky. Not only won't they be able to get an entire phalanx in line as they cross the ford, but they'll have to do it on terrible ground. We can put a single cohort there and block the entire thing."

"The ground will be just as bad for our men. Our line will struggle to hold together with such poor footing," Ursinus said.

"We don't need to. We put one cohort here, at the ford. The ground lifts up from here, giving us an opportunity. We put our hundred riflemen and four cannon here, at the high point before it starts to even off, and we can even fit in two, maybe three centuries of men armed with arcuballista in addition to the cohort at the ford who are also carrying them. The rifles and cannons can keep them under fire all the way to the opposite tree line. Shortly before they get to the ford, they'll also come under fire from our arcuballista, which will make crossing even harder. What forces do make it across will have difficulty holding their formations. If they bring up archers, we can shift cannon or rifle fire at them, which should keep that in check. There isn't even enough room here for one legion to operate, let alone all four, which means the remaining three legions can hold their positions facing whatever they have planned for us from the other direction. As positions go, this seems very solid to me."

"I agree," Ky said. "I am hard-pressed to believe that they have another army larger than the one chasing us in front of us, which makes them the greater danger. The ford and lay of the land will take away most of their advantages. Bring up the riflemen and cannons and get them in position. Hold our baggage train and supplies in between the two forces and get the rest of your legion in position. You three, hold your legions where they are and be prepared for contact from the northeast. Make sure your men stay focused on what is in front of them, regardless of what they're hearing from behind them. I don't want all the firing to distract them from their duty."

The four legates saluted and went about their business. Ky had a similar plan already in mind once this new group of warriors stopped when they should have attacked, but he was glad to hear Auspex voice his version of it. Soon all of the legions would be armed with rifles and cannons, and it was important they stopped thinking like men leading armies made up of spearmen and heavy infantry. Fighting with rifles required thinking of things like fields of fire, chokepoints, and distances of contact. True, they didn't have to worry about the enemy's distance of contact or counter-battery fire, but the mindset was still what was important. It surprised him that Auspex was the one to present the plan. His legion had had the least amount of time to train in the new tactics. It required serious lateral thinking and was worth considering Auspex for future advancement.

Ky moved the drone to watch the Carthaginians. The huge horde was moving slowly, but steadily, which gave the Britannians plenty of time to get into place. Finally, they reached the river bank and Ky could see the moment the Carthaginian general realized the problem the ford presented to him, as he pulled his huge army to a stop. They held there for a moment, maybe trying to figure out what the Britannians were up to, just waiting on the other side.

On the face of it, it was probably pretty obvious, what with the legionnaires and their large shields lined up across the mouth of the ford that limited the length of the front line. What must have been confusing was that they were spread out on the opposing slope instead of packed tight against the river to better refute the phalanxes, as would be the tactic of the day.

He had probably heard about the arcuballista's impressive stopping power and maybe he was judging if he could push his men forward enough to counter that threat. It certainly wasn't a concern for the casualties they'd encounter, since the Carthaginians had never shown any concern about that before. Finally, the man made up his mind and trumpets sounded on the opposite shore, sending the large force lurching forward again.

"Hold your fire," Ky commanded.

The Carthaginians hadn't encountered gunfire before and Ky was fairly certain they would turn and run once it started. The goal here wasn't to just escape this army, it was to destroy it, or at least a good part of it, so it wouldn't do to fire early. Ky wanted their forces to be halfway across the large river, with the forces behind pushing to try to get in on the battle, which would make it difficult for the bulk of them to run when the firing started.

"Wait," Ky said, watching the first Carthaginians begin across the ford.

"Wait ... open fire!"

The command echoed out over the field. The cannons closest to Ky's position boomed with thick clouds of smoke drifting up from them, followed by the rippling crackle of the rifles, tearing into the middle ranks waiting to march into the ford. Birds from the tree line jumped into the air at the sound of the sudden, unexpected thunder. Arcuballista strings snapped as the legionnaires closer to the shore took aim at the men now in the ford trying to run across and engage the Britannians.

Confusion erupted on the opposing shore as what must have seemed like the end of the world began. Men by the dozen were smashed or flung into the air by cannon balls smashing into them.

An invisible scythe slashed through their midst as hundreds of men suddenly dropped, dead or screaming. At this range and with the Carthaginians packed so tightly, more than half the bullets punched through one man and into another. It was pure slaughter.

Then something Ky didn't expect happened. Instead of the lines thinning out as men began to run rearward, the Carthaginians began to push tighter against the river, to the point that men started to get pushed into the water. Ky repositioned the drone to the rear of the Carthaginian line and saw something amazing.

The front of the Carthaginian force had been their phalanxes with local auxiliaries bringing up the rear, as was their standard deployment. What was different this time was that those local auxiliaries in the rear had suddenly and ferociously attacked the Carthaginians in front of them, hacking and slashing their way into the ranks.

The Carthaginians reeled, men in the rear trying to push to the river while the men by the river tried to push to the rear, both trying to escape annihilation, with the men in the center being crushed to death by the weight of their own comrades.

It was a slaughter.

"Adjust your fire low, targeting only those forces by the river-bank," Ky ordered, not wanting the rounds being pumped into the Carthaginians to hit their unexpected new allies.

Now they just had to wait for sixty thousand or so men to die.

Chapter 25

Off the Coast of Hispania

"Captain, enemy sails," the sailor holding a spyglass called.

Yrsa pulled out his own spyglass. The sails of two Carthaginian galleys danced in the distance, turning hard toward the mainland. Yrsa watched the single galley sails, calculating their angle to the mainland and distances, trying to work out where they were headed. Southern Gaul, perhaps?

They had seen the Britannian fleet and were running, which meant they weren't a threat. He could have easily caught them if he wanted. The small ship he'd been sold in exchange for his swearing allegiance was the fastest ship Yrsa had seen in his twenty years of sailing. Any of the Valdar's lumbering ships could have caught the galleys, and Yrsa had had to pull in his sails to keep from outpacing them. He could have scooped up the Carthaginians at will if he wanted.

"Signal from Valdar's ship," the lookout announced, pulling out the Britannian 'book' of flag descriptions. "They want us to break away from the fleet and pursue. We are to sink them before they get to port and can spread the word about the fleet."

Yrsa sighed. He'd hoped Valdar would just let them go. It wasn't like the Carthaginians weren't going to figure out what they were doing once the several thousand men in their little fleet hit the shore. He'd been warned that he might be required to do this. They'd loaded supplies for the soldiers onto his boat but none of the actual soldiers, expecting his swifter vessel to act as security for the rest of the fleet.

"Fine. Signal our confirmation," he commanded, before turning to his sailors, half of whom were waiting around for commands. "Trim the mainsail and loose the jib. Helmsman, make your course northwest."

Even the commands Yrsa gave felt foreign to him, like trying on someone else's coat. He wasn't quite sold on the idea of entrusting the wheel to a crewman when he felt he could manage it himself. Yes, the new ship's sails and rigging were complex, but he still wanted to keep his destiny under his control.

For now, he yielded to Valdar's ways, still learning the ropes of this new vessel. His ship broke away from the fleet, slicing through the water like a finely honed blade. The galleys' decision to sail with the wind had sealed their fate.

A galley's only advantage in this new age of sail was that it could travel directly against the wind in a way that his ships could not. If they'd been smart, they'd have tried to swing around the fleet and then sail directly into the wind, which would take them to several of Carthage's Hispania ports. This way, it wouldn't take them long to close the distance.

"Prepare the cannons and clear for battle," Yrsa called, adrenaline coursing through his veins like wildfire.

He relished the moments before combat. He'd never been a pirate himself, but he'd considered it. He loved that moment before the screams and blood, with its intoxicating mix of excitement and fear. Many Scandi merchants avoided conflict, but Yrsa's warrior spirit burned like an eternal flame.

"Take us between them," he commanded the helmsman, his grip on the railing strong and steady. "They've lined themselves up nicely. Prepare for raking fire as we pass."

"Sail," a lookout shouted. "Multiple sails. South, east, and north."

Yrsa cursed inwardly, realizing he'd been too focused on his prey. He swung his spyglass from vessel to vessel, a sinking feeling in his gut.

"They're starting to turn," the helmsman noted, pointing toward the ships they'd been chasing.

"It's a trap," Yrsa muttered, feeling the sting of his own carelessness.

"Hard-a-lee," he barked, directing the helmsman to turn the wheel sharply left, steering the ship away from the coastline and toward the open sea. "Haul in the jib, and trim the foresail. We're turning sharp into the wind. Gunners, fire as she bears, whichever ship you can reach."

As the ship swung hard left, the guns on its right side fired in a staccato rhythm, each crew lighting off their weapon in time with the turning schooner. The starboard ship narrowly escaped, the turning giving gunners little time to aim. The other ship, however, suffered a brutal fate. Multiple cannonballs tore through it, creating a deadly storm of splintered wood that pierced oarsmen and painted the deck with blood. More cannonballs punched through the deck and into the ocean, sending geysers of water skyward. The remaining blood-soaked oarsmen dove off the ship as it tilted for its final descent to the ocean floor.

Yrsa admired his gunners' accuracy, but they were far from out of danger. Eight sails had appeared so far, veering towards them from seemingly every direction, including one between them and the open ocean to the west. Yrsa marveled at the Carthaginians' coordination, despite their reputation as terrible sailors.

Not that it mattered. They'd managed it and now Yrsa scanned the horizon, assessing each sail. They were undoubtedly trying to get close enough to board or at least get within arrow range. They couldn't chase him down, so their only hope was to surround his ship and overwhelm it. And they were very close to succeeding. Unfortunately for them, the trap closed unevenly, with some ships coming in faster than others.

"Forty degrees starboard into the wind and hold fast," Yrsa called out. "Loose and trim the jib."

The ship turned partially back, its wake forming a serpentine pattern as it curved again. It would be a close call, but there was still some distance between the ships. They would come under fire, but it wouldn't last long.

As the distances closed, Yrsa focused on the two ships he needed to navigate between, timing the pass just right to avoid the possibility of them throwing lines for boarding. His ship was impressive, but a galley could hold many men. If they intended to take his ship intact, they would be able to fill his decks with more soldiers than he had crew.

Sure enough, Yrsa noticed the prows of both galleys sporting long boarding planks with massive spikes intended to pierce the deck of a ship, holding it fast for boarding.

"Prepare to fire. Ready the buckets," Yrsa commanded, tension lacing his voice. "Helmsman, three degrees port."

They began to veer away from the closer of the two ships, which angled menacingly toward them, attempting to corner Yrsa's vessel. The situation was dire; if Yrsa turned hard, the other ship would be perfectly positioned to spike his schooner. Arrows started to rain down, and although most missed due to their forward momentum, the cries of hit crew members pierced the air.

"Haul that cannon to the prow," Yrsa barked. "Move, damn you."

His crew struggled with the weight of the gun, sweat dripping from their brows. In frustration, Yrsa cursed and shoved two men aside, his massive frame bulging as he popped the cannon off the rails that held it in place. The sailors, though strong, couldn't compare to their colossal captain. The cannon rocked dangerously before settling.

"Wheel it up to the prow. Now!"

"Captain, if we fire the gun, there won't be a gun block to stop its recoil. It will jump halfway across the ship," one crew member warned.

"Then let it jump. Or do you feel like dying today?" Yrsa snapped, but he knew the man had a point. "Watch yourselves and watch out for this gun, but keep to your weapons."

Yrsa knew the risks. If he lost some men, so be it. He had to do something about the encroaching ship, and this was his only option.

"Aim on the down heave. Take your target. You get *only* one shot at this."

The man at the rear of the gun appeared nervous as he readied the primer and pull cord. He stood to the side, but it was impossible to predict where the gun would jump without being secured to the deck. Despite the danger, he held his position. If the man survived, Yrsa would consider promoting him.

The ship dipped and lifted, surging against the waves as the enemy ship played hide-and-seek with the horizon. On the third downward heave, as the enemy vessel came into view, Yrsa roared, "Fire."

Smoke erupted from the end of the cannon and the gun shot backward, missing the cannoneer by inches. He flinched back as the hot gasses still spewing from the end of the cannon singed his whiskers.

A sailor further back, near the mast, wasn't so lucky as he was turned into a long red streak across the deck when the sailing metal tube smashed over him. The cannon finally came to rest near the rear of the ship, thankfully not continuing on into the ocean.

Despite its smaller size, the cannonball wrought destruction as it shattered the hooked plank and careened across the crowded enemy deck, tearing a dozen men to shreds. Unlike Yrsa's cannon, which spared his ship's mast, the Carthaginian vessel wasn't so fortunate. The blood-slick cannonball tore through the towering wooden mast before ricocheting off the stern to roll chaotically across the deck.

Yrsa watched as the Carthaginian sail swayed and collapsed to the starboard side, crushing more oarsmen beneath its weight before crashing onto the deck and sliding into the ocean.

"Fire as she bears!" Yrsa roared to his gunners as they sailed past the foundering ship, unleashing a devastating full broadside.

The galley trembled and nearly disintegrated under the on-slaught of the schooner's barrage, with multiple holes punched near the waterline. Yrsa's port side gunners fired at the other galley as it came into view. It had turned to try and ram his ship, making it a difficult target for his gunners, sparing it from the same grisly fate as its sister ship. However, the rounds that did strike slowed its oarsmen, preventing it from reaching the schooner before it escaped the trap.

"Now let's get moving and show these bastards what this ship can really do," Yrsa declared, his fierce bearded face breaking into a triumphant grin.

The crew's energy surged in response, screaming a war cry as the schooner loped into the ocean, once again predator instead of prey.

Belgica

The aftermath of the battle stretched on for days as Britannians moved the mounds of bodies into huge mass graves. Ky'd been surprised after their first significant conflict, learning that it had been Roman practice to bury enemy dead in mass graves when time allowed. He was grateful for it, though.

Thankfully, they hadn't needed to bury all sixty thousand Carthaginians. About half the army, consisting of actual Carthaginians and some auxiliaries from southern regions who'd been under Carthaginian rule long enough to become true believers, were slaughtered. Even those who tried to surrender. The survivors were mostly Gauls or Germans, forced into Carthaginian service before Londinium's fall.

None were loyal to the Carthaginians, particularly since it was evident their home villages would either rebel or be soon liberated. Too many had perished before the slaughter ceased, but once everything settled, Ky's new allies swelled to nearly fifty thousand. They were from across the continent, even deep within Asia, but all recognized a genuine opportunity to end Carthaginian tyranny.

This was the real weakness of the Carthaginian system of conquering people and forcing them to fight for their overlords. Their conscripted soldiers were only loyal as long as they thought their families and villages were still under threat. As soon as a chance to break free was offered, their armies fell apart. Ky just had to hope this would be a problem with future Carthaginian armies. If they could only rely on their own people, there was no way the Carthaginians could maintain their massive empire, and they'd collapse all on their own.

"Any word from the scouts?" Ky asked Ursinus as the legate entered his tent.

"Not yet, but this would have been most of the Carthaginian forces within a hundred mille passus of us. If the forces near Hispania have started marching towards us, our scouts won't even be in the area they could have marched to for several more days. The locals have sent out riders to every village this side of the Pyrenees Mountains. We'll know about them before they get close."

"Assuming those villages switch to our side. The closer they are to Carthage or Italy, the more they'll still fear Carthaginian reprisals. We need to be on the lookout for bad intel."

"Fortunately, I found someone to help us sort through that," Ursinus said, grinning.

"Really?" Ky asked, uncertain where this was headed.

"Absolutely. Come in, General," Ursinus said, raising the tent flap for Bomilcar to join them inside.

"Bomilcar," Ky said, standing quickly and grasping the Carthaginian's arm in greeting. "I knew you had to be behind our sudden good fortune. The chieftains we've talked to all kept mentioning a Carthaginian turncoat, but none seemed to know your name."

"I felt it best to keep a low profile among people I didn't know personally. At least until I was safely with the legions again. I knew the man who was in charge of this army, and if he heard any of the tribesmen mention my name, he would have figured out this was a trap. Sorry I couldn't let you know it was coming before we made our move."

"I was just happy you did. We were in a tight place."

"You would have won either way. The way you blocked off the ford, you would have ripped apart the Carthaginian army before they ever pushed through."

"I don't know. Most of our gunpowder went south with Velius. I don't think we could have maintained the firepower to completely defeat this army. It would have pulled back and come at us again."

"Maybe. Still, you did some real damage. From what I've gathered, there's only a force in southern Hispania and one out in Greece left on the continent. They haven't even moved their Persian armies yet. Wiping out this army means we've essentially cleared Germania, with the exception of a few small detachments. They'll have armies in the field come spring, but we should have a good long winter to consolidate our forces and work with our new allies."

"Speaking of, how's that going?"

"Good. I told them about some of the new weapons we're willing to give them. They were skeptical at first, but seeing your men in action, they haven't stopped asking when they can get their hands on some of the thunder weapons, as they keep calling them."

"They understand what we're giving them isn't exactly the same as what we used here, right?"

"Not really. I tried to explain it, but it's all magic to them at this point. I actually brought several of the tribal leaders from the larger tribes. I've mostly been dealing with them, and they've been working with the smaller groups to put this together. We're going to have to think of something more long-term soon, to keep these men from dominating our relationships, but for now, they're who we need to talk to."

"Lucilla has some thoughts on how to handle that problem. For now, we'll work with them. Bring them in."

Bomilcar lifted the tent flap and waved in five men. They were a motley group, one dressed in the Carthaginian style and the other four in a collection of furs and leathers. All wore massive beards that seemed to be the style in Germania.

"Givellan of the Vandili, Aliverko of the Anglii, Trasuinda of the Istvaeones, Uegitus from the Alamanni confederation, and Bernia of the Anarti. These men represent the largest tribes or groups of tribes that agreed to come together and help us against the Carthaginians. I promised to show them wondrous weapons they could use to win their freedom in return. After your display, they're very interested in getting their hands on them."

"Do you speak all of their languages?"

"No, Consul. Aliverko speaks Phoenician. Givellan and Trasuinda speak Aliverko's native language, Givellan also speaks Uegitus's language, who in turn also speaks Bernia's language. It has been ... challenging to communicate."

"I see. So the closest shared language is the one from the Anglii, then. Could you ask him to speak to me for a bit in his native language? The specifics don't matter; he just needs to use a wide range of words."

"I will ask," Bomilcar said and relayed the message.

So far, Sophus had constructed databanks for Ulaid, native Latin, several Caledonian languages, multiple Scandi languages, and Phoenician. In this time period, most groups, excluding superpowers like the Romans or Carthaginians, seldom ventured beyond a small region, resulting in languages developing in isolated pockets. This made translations across multiple communities challenging. Eventually, they would all start learning the most common trade language, but that would take time.

Worse, with the exception of some tribal collections, they would no longer be dealing with single rulers like they had with the Caledonii and Ulaid. Instead, they would have to negotiate with hundreds of tribes individually, complicating the process of building a larger alliance.

The chieftains appeared perplexed but continued their conversation for several minutes, allowing Sophus to build a database of sounds, structures, and words that would be continually updated as the language was spoken.

"Primer created, Commander. Accuracy should be eighty percent, which is the previously specified threshold."

"Can you understand me?" Ky said, the harsh-sounding language bearing a strong resemblance to parts of the Earth Standard language he'd spoken in his time.

"You ... speak our language?" the man asked, surprised.

"Learning languages quickly is a skill I possess. I will improve as we continue to converse."

"Amazing," Givellan remarked.

"I do not know the tongues these two men speak. Please translate my words for them. In time, I'm sure we will find a language we can all converse in, but for now, this will have to suffice."

The process was bound to be slow, as Givellan relayed Ky's words to Uegitus, who in turn repeated them to Bernia. Sophus began constructing separate databases for each of their languages, but for the moment, Ky only communicated in the language of the Anglii to keep things simple.

"I want to thank you for your assistance. I know you have all suffered under Carthaginian rule. We have recently liberated our islands from their grip and have come here to help free your people as well. I must be honest; we didn't come to aid you specifically. Our goal is to push through to their homeland and end them as a threat forever. To accomplish this, we need help. We need people to fight alongside us, supplies and raw materials to build our weapons, and workers on our islands to help work our forges. In return, we offer weapons like the ones you saw us use, tools, and a market for your goods."

"With your thunder weapons, why do you need us? From what I witnessed, you could annihilate every death worshiper single-handedly," Aliverko said.

"I wish that were true. They are powerful, but they do not render us invincible. If the Carthaginians bring enough soldiers, they can overwhelm us. That's why we fled for so long, searching for the right battleground to counter their manpower advantage."

"And you'll provide us with these weapons?" Givellan inquired.

"If you fight with us, yes, along with training on how to use them if you agree to join our cause."

"How will you prevent favoritism in distributing these weapons among us? What's to stop our neighbors from turning these weapons against us once this conflict is over?" Aliverko asked.

"A valid concern. I understand that these weapons have the potential to shift power dynamics in a region, so it's reasonable to be apprehensive. These weapons are more akin to bows than swords in that a bow is useless without arrows. Similarly, these weapons require ammunition, and unlike arrows, not everyone can manufacture them. If one of your neighbors begins to misuse the weapons we provide now or might sell later, we will cease supplying the ammunition, rendering the weapons virtually ineffective."

"So you intend to become an overlord, just like the Carthaginians," Trasuinda stated, more as a declaration than a question. "You may exert control over us by deciding to whom you sell weapons, but you still plan to dictate how and where we live."

"I won't deny that we have our own motives, and we will utilize the tools at our disposal to achieve them. Our primary goal is peace, where each of us can live as we desire. If, once the Carthaginians are vanquished, someone tries to disrupt the balance and incite war again, then yes, we will endeavor to stop them. I would prefer to resolve matters diplomatically, but we will also wield the power that comes from being the sole supplier of these weapons. I contend that this isn't equivalent to being an overlord or mirroring the Carthaginians. We all act based on our own interests. I assume you aren't here purely out of benevolence. So yes, I concede that we have an agenda, but we don't seek to dominate you. We merely search for allies and offer an opportunity to liberate yourselves from the Carthaginians permanently."

A long moment stretched between the men, each looking at the other, gauging their responses.

"So, what will this alliance entail?" Aliverko finally said.

That was precisely what Ky had been waiting for. The chieftains were intrigued. Granted, they would remain skeptical, but each one desired the weapons the Britannians offered, and none could afford to let their neighbors accept the deal and arm themselves while they abstained.

Now, all he had to do was work out the specifics.

Hispania

"The Pyrenees were crossed a couple of days ago," the scout reported, barely clinging to his saddle. "An army of ten to fifteen thousand strong, with a significant cavalry presence. I was able to see their scouts with the spyglass, and they've adopted our stirrups."

The adoption of their stirrup technology wasn't surprising to Velius. In fact, he was astonished it took the Carthaginians this long to mimic some of the Consul's innovations. Despite several enhancements made to the stirrups since their first use, the core principle remained unchanged, and it would make their mounted units a lot more difficult to manage.

Shaking off the thought, Velius focused on the weary messenger. Covered in dust and sweat, the man appeared utterly drained. The crispness of the approaching winter air underscored the exertion he must have endured to reach their lines.

"Thank you. We've prepared a tent with food. Eat and rest for now. You'll likely have another assignment soon."

Too exhausted to show relief, the man nonetheless saluted with a fist against his chest before steering his horse towards the developing encampment.

"The Consul didn't withdraw the southern Gaul army after all, or we missed something," Velius observed.

"We knew that was a possibility. I think he got some to take the bait. The reports indicate fewer troops than expected for that reason. The first scout estimated around ten thousand, while this one reported ten to fifteen thousand. Even if it's fifteen, it's still half the number there should have been," Aelius said.

"True, but it's still equal to, if not greater than, the number of men we brought with us. We didn't anticipate the second army crossing the mouth of the middle sea and marching north to confront us. Worse still, they've moved slowly enough to coordinate, meaning they'll attack us simultaneously from two directions."

"We could position the legions opposite each other," Aelius suggested.

"No, they'll outnumber us, and even if we anchor one line at the beach, the other would be dangerously exposed. The Consul took almost all of the mounted units with him."

"So, do we line up with our backs to the beach? They're approaching from the north and south. Whichever way we face, we'll leave a flank vulnerable."

"No. I have a plan, but it will require time to prepare, which is in short supply. Let's get to work."

As dawn broke over the Iberian shoreline, the Britannians found themselves watching the fires flickering on the mountainsides before them throughout the night go out. These fires marked the encampments of thousands of enemy soldiers. Situated just off the beach, at the base of the small mountains that adorned the western coast of Hispania, the Britannians had a clear view of the force they would soon confront. Velius took solace in the resilience of his men, even though they knew the adversaries surrounding those fires wouldn't be long now.

For three relentless days, they had toiled until their scouts reported the imminent arrival of the Carthaginian armies. As Velius had anticipated, the enemy forces had coordinated their approach expertly, converging on the Britannians almost simultaneously.

Velius had prepared as best he could. His troops formed a three-sided rectangle with their backs to the beach. Two rows of soldiers stood at the ready—the outer row comprised of his legion, armed with the latest rifles, while a few paces behind, the inner row consisting of Aelius's legion, wielding swords and shields. The rectangle's corners held six cannons, three on each side. Hastily dug trenches and sharpened logs served as makeshift defenses, intended to slow down the enemy's mounted and infantry units.

As the sun gradually burned away the morning haze, the distant sounds of tens of thousands of men echoed through the trees. Finally, a trumpet blared.

"Ready," Velius commanded, and his men rose to shoulder their weapons. "Hold your fire until they pass the marked lines."

Large rocks had been strategically placed at specific distances from the Britannian lines, offering a visual indicator of when to fire. Velius remained uncertain of the enemy's reaction once the guns roared—whether they would charge or flee in terror. He opted for a middle-ground strategy, holding fire to ensure continuous volleys should the enemy retreat or provide cover should they advance.

The Carthaginians emerged from the tree line in what seemed like an unending tide. Velius could sense his men's anxiety, as some instinctively retreated a step from the advancing onslaught.

"Hold!" he repeated firmly.

The enemy's spears, initially raised in a marching stance, were lowered in unison, transforming their formation into a formidable, bristling hedgehog. Sunlight glinted off the spear tips as they advanced from all directions, encircling the Britannians in a vast arc of steel and determination.

"Take aim," Velius roared, his eyes fixed on the approaching enemy soldiers nearing the stones. "First rank. **Fire!**"

A cacophony of thunder erupted as the kneeling rank fired their rifles, covering them with a dense curtain of smoke. An unseen, colossal hand seemed to sweep away the first few ranks of Carthaginians, their bodies crumpling to the ground. The Carthaginian ranks hesitated, bewilderment etched on the faces of the front row. No arrows or visible projectiles had been launched—only the sudden appearance of their comrades collapsing, some dead, others writhing in agony with gaping wounds.

Then the cannons bellowed, leaving a gory trail that sliced through the enemy lines, culminating in a fiery explosion that sent limbs soaring skyward. The Carthaginians further back, spared from the cannon's devastation, pressed forward as they had been trained.

"Second rank. **Fire!**"

Another deafening blast resonated as another fifteen hundred rifles discharged. The bewildered Carthaginians, who had faltered moments before, now tumbled lifelessly atop their fallen brethren, the relentless pressure from their rear ranks forcing them forward.

The Carthaginian frontline's hesitation transformed into a refusal to move forward. Witnessing two, three, even four rows of comrades fall like severed marionettes, the soldiers balked as fear gripped them.

"Third rank. **Fire!**" Velius commanded, his voice resolute.

That proved to be the breaking point. Confusion, which had given way to indecision, now turned to terror as an inexplicable force decimated their numbers. The front ranks of Carthaginians discarded their spears and turned to flee, only to collide with the advancing mass of soldiers behind them, ignorant of the carnage that awaited them.

As the Carthaginian advance stalled, their front ranks struggling against the rear, the Britannians continued their deadly barrage. Thousands of casualties soon multiplied into five and then nearly ten thousand before the Carthaginian army realized the terrible reality of what was happening, its mass turning to retreat. A macabre tapestry of corpses blanketed the beach and coastal fields. The two Carthaginian armies, once confident of victory, now scrambled into the trees and up the mountainsides, desperate to escape the relentless onslaught.

And still, the ruthless tide of death pressed onward.

Chapter 26

Carthage

Caesius strode across the bustling dock, his eyes darting from the laborers unloading crates from the wagon to the captain of the small galley. His impatience was palpable, as he all but put his boot to the backs of the workers, urging them to move more quickly.

The captain, a weathered seafarer with a wary eye, watched the crates pile up on the dock with growing concern.

"I told you what I was bringing," Caesius snapped, his voice laced with a hint of menace.

"You said you were bringing some personal effects and supplies," the captain retorted, his voice rising in frustration. "This is an entire ship's worth of cargo!"

"These are supplies," he growled, his hand resting on the hilt of his sword. "I'm paying you handsomely and I'll need every bit of this when we get to our destination. You can either take us and get paid, or I can have my men kill you and we can take your boat."

The four large men standing behind Caesius shifted threateningly, their hands resting on the hilts of their own weapons. It was clear that they were not afraid to use them if necessary.

For Caesius, this voyage was a matter of life and death. It had taken every contact and favor he had to arrange his escape so quickly. Twice, since he had sent his servant to begin arranging the escape route, the emperor had called him to an audience where his lackeys had chastised him for not bringing them samples of the Romans' new weapons or intelligence about what was happening on the British Isles. Caesius had made many promises that he would provide what the emperor wanted, but he now knew that was never going to happen.

His ring of informants was gone, that much was clear. Only one man had escaped the island after the last set of raids by the praetorians, and he reported the total collapse of the ring of loyalists and the disgruntled followers they had put together since the failed insurrection. With that, Caesius had lost anything he had to offer the Carthaginians, who were actively looking for scapegoats to feed to their bloodthirsty emperor.

The final straw had come that morning when word trickled in that the Romans had not only crushed a huge army in Germania but had convinced dozens of tribes to join the fight against Carthage. Caesius had been lucky that his man had been at the docks, working on preparations for their escape, when the wounded and dying man, after a mad dash across the continent, had landed there.

The man's weakened state led to an unforeseen delay in bringing him before the emperor, affording Caesius a fleeting opportunity to stay a step ahead. The survivor's sudden arrival signaled that Caesius could delay no longer. There was no time for Caesius to execute his meticulously crafted plan to evade the ever-present, watchful eyes of the emperor's guard dogs, who had been relentlessly stalking him for months. Caesius had been utterly convinced that this most recent failure would be the tipping point that sent him spiraling towards the cold embrace of the executioner's block, compelling him to rely on desperate improvisation.

Once Caesius had dispatched his accomplice, to hasten the captain in readying the vessel, he dealt with the two death-masked guards tailing him. Their deadliness had been astonishing; half of the hired ruffians Caesius had recruited to safeguard his passage to Asia had perished. Yet, they had fulfilled their purpose. Their deaths mattered little to him. There were always more brutes for hire. Time, or the absence thereof, was the true enemy that gnawed at him, which explained Caesius's impatience with the sluggish pace of the men loading the ship.

"We'll be prepared to set sail within the hour, my lord," the captain assured him, a note of trepidation coloring his words.

"Twenty minutes, no more!" Caesius snapped. "After that, we depart, whether you're ready or not."

"I can't ..."

"My lord," Caesius's servant interjected, his finger urgently pointing at something further down the docks.

A force of two dozen guards, spearheaded by six of the menacing death-masked men, marched steadily toward them. Panic seized Caesius. How had they been discovered so swiftly? He had been meticulous in his dealings, only using intermediaries and avoiding these remote, seldom-used docks himself.

"Go. Delay them," Caesius barked at his remaining guards.

His men exchanged nervous glances, eyeing the advancing guards, and took flight. Their desperate sprint led them directly into the path of another dozen guards approaching from the opposite direction, who showed no mercy as they cut them down without hesitation.

"Move. Cast off. Get me away from here," Caesius pleaded with the ship's captain, his voice trembling with terror.

"No. Not me. I didn't know," the captain stammered, his words aimed more toward the encroaching guards than Caesius as he dropped to his knees in a prostrate display of submission.

"Caesius Germanicus, by order of the emperor, you are under arrest," the guard captain announced, as they reached their quarry.

A pitiful whimper, unbidden, escaped Caesius's throat as they seized him.

Hispania

"The wall must be angled thirty degrees in this direction and extend seamlessly into the water," Velius instructed, gesturing toward a section of the beach. "Check the architect's notes about sinking the pillar far enough into the ground. If they bring in ships armed with siege weapons, we need these to hold up to sustained fire."

It had taken almost a month to clear the multitude of bodies that littered the beach and extended up the mountainside. While they hadn't exterminated every last Carthaginian, the defeat had been absolute. Velius had sacrificed only thirty men in the exchange, marking this as potentially one of the most uneven victories in history. He was under no illusion, however, that this triumph would go unchallenged. The groundbreaking rifles had taken the enemy by surprise, instilling terror and confusion. Regrettably, that shock would probably only serve them once.

The next time, the Carthaginians would be ready for them. Had they maintained their formation and advanced, accepting the mounting casualties, they would have eventually breached the Britannian lines. The bayonets, devised by the Consul to function as spears, when required, were ingenious, but they were no match for heavily armored soldiers. If the Carthaginians had reached them, the outcome would have been disastrous.

Velius understood the Carthaginians' callous disregard for the lives of their soldiers. Conscripted men, driven by the chilling knowledge that failure would result in their families' demise, were willing to be sacrificed in battle. The Consul had dubbed them "cannon fodder," an apt term that seemed fitting given the devastating effects the cannons had on the Carthaginian ranks.

Thankfully, the approaching winter provided a respite for preparations. Their strategic landing site was nestled within the embrace of towering mountains, which afforded natural protection. This characteristic was common on this side of Hispania, yet in proximity to the Pyrenees' main trench, the mountains formed a horseshoe-like barrier around the coastal region. Snow had already begun to fall and would soon have the passes through the mountains completely closed off. Once the thaw arrived, the Britannians would march out, carving a corridor to the Middle Sea. They would require a solid base of supply behind them, which meant fortifications were needed.

"This is very impressive," Valdar said, from behind him, indicating the rows of ditches being dug for the long front wall of the fort.

Velius grinned, turning to clasp forearms with the ship captain. "It will be," he said. "All set for your return to Britannia?"

"We are. We're leaving the Concordia with you; in case the Carthaginians get any ideas about sailing around these mountains over the winter. You should be safe through the winter."

"Good. Come spring, we'll be able to take whatever they throw at us, especially if Hortensius can keep sending us shipments of rifles and gunpowder, along with the other supplies you'll be bringing us. With two rifle-armed legions, I'll be able to take on all of Carthage at once."

Valdar raised an eyebrow.

Velius chuckled. "Alright, that might be a little much, but we'll be formidable."

Valdar nodded, glancing towards the docks. "Well, good luck. We have to get going. Yrsa is ready to start tearing ships apart with his bare hands if we don't release him from service soon."

"It's not just him. I know being stuck on land isn't your idea of a good time."

"It really isn't. Strong winds and calm seas, my friend."

"Thanks," Velius said, gripping the captain's forearm again before he turned and started back towards the docks and his escape to the sea.

As he watched Valdar disappear from view, Velius couldn't help but feel a surge of confidence. They might just make it through this yet.

Devnum

Ky had never seen such a massive throng of people, packing every inch of the main thoroughfare leading from the palace. Even the nearby rooftops were filled with spectators, in some cases practically hanging off the sides of the buildings. It was a once-in-a-lifetime moment for most of the people out in the crowds, as the first power transfer was taking place for the Britannic Empire. The fact that a woman was the one being elevated, especially while her older sibling still lived, added to the day of firsts.

But it was Lucilla's almost universal popularity that set her apart from previous Roman Emperors. Unlike most Emperors who were not common public figures when they took power, Lucilla had been involved in nearly every aspect of Britannic life. Even the first Emperor, Pinarius Germanicus, Lucilla's ancestor, had been a military commander, more known by his legions than by the average citizen. Moreover, she had grown a large part of her legend even before having access to Sophus. Ky couldn't imagine a more deserving person for adulation.

"Fellow citizens of Britannia," Senator Taenaris said, holding up his hands for quiet. "I come before you with grave news. As many of you know, our beloved Emperor, Titus Flavius Germanicus, has fallen ill. In his wisdom, instead of gripping the reins of power until the moment of his death, he has decided to pass leadership of our Empire to his daughter, Flavia Lucilla Germanicus."

Taenaris had to stop as the crowd shouted their love and admiration for the Emperor. Germanicus, who sat on a litter next to Lucilla, covered tightly in a blanket, waved weakly to his people. When he'd returned from Germania, Ky had been shocked at how rapidly the Emperor's condition had deteriorated. Ky had hoped Lucilla would have more time after the coronation to spend with her father, not only to help with the political transition, but because he knew how much she loved him. Now, they'd have to spend more time dealing with matters of politics than saying goodbye properly. The thought made Ky sad.

"The Emperor's firstborn son, Caesius Titus Germanicus, attempted to take control of the Empire ... by force. His insurrection led to the deaths of thousands of your fellow countrymen, and will be a black mark on this Empire for generations to come. By royal decree, his name is stricken from the Empire and all claims of the traitor Caesius are deemed null and void, leaving the Emperor with his only child, Flavia Lucilla Germanicus, to take up the mantle of leadership. You all know Lucilla. Many of you have benefited from her works, as she has spearheaded the transition of our people into the great Britannic Empire. She is a young woman of great intelligence and courage. She has been trained from birth to rule, and she is ready to take her father's place."

He had to stop again as the crowd cheered for Lucilla, shouting her name and various pledges of love and affirmation. Lucilla, for her part, looked embarrassed as the cheers washed over them.

"The Imperial Senate agrees with the Emperor's choice and hereby proclaims that Flavia Lucilla Germanicus, daughter of Titus Flavius Germanicus, shall be named Empress of Rome, to rule with wisdom and justice, upholding the great traditions of our Empire. Under her rule, we will defeat the Carthaginian scourge once and for all and enter into a new era of prosperity and peace. Long live the Empress, Augusta Germanicus, Mother of Britannia! Long live the Empire!"

Shouts of 'long live Lucilla', 'Augusta Germanicus', and 'long live the Empire' seemed to come from everywhere as Ky grabbed her hand and raised her arm high in the air.

The crowd went wild.

To be continued ...

About the author

Travis writes science fiction, fantasy, and thriller novels (and the occasional coming-of-age story), with the hope of transporting and enthralling readers. Publishing novels since 2015, Travis's passion is creating worlds and characters that live and breathe, and experiencing the joy of those stories with his readers.

When not writing, Travis enjoys connecting with readers and other writers, managing the popular Complete Marvel Reading Order website, where he works on his other passion for comics and graphic novels, and spending time with his family.

If you have enjoyed this book, please consider taking a moment to rate or review it wherever you found your copy, as it helps new readers find my works and ensures I can continue writing book into the future.

Find out more at:
amazon.com/TravisStarnes/e/B072YBDC3S/
Or visit
https://tstarnes.com

Signup to get free previews and notifications of upcoming books at
http://tstarnes.com/preview-notification-newsletter/

Also by

Volume 1
The Sword of Jupiter
The Trumpets of Mars
The Sands of Saturn
The Depths of Neptune
The Fires of Vulcan
The Triumph of Venus
Volume 2
The Wings of Mercury
The Plains of Pluto

Shattered Lands Series

In the Shadow of Lions
An Ending of Oaths

False Start Series

Second Down

The Veilguard Saga

Threads of Destiny

Stand Alone

Going Home